THE MARKER

BOOK ONE IN THE BRIDGE SERIES

ANN HOWES

THE MARKER

by Ann Howes

Cover Design:

Taylor Sullivan at
https://www.facebook.com/ImaginationUnCOVERED/.

Editing: Gillian Holmes
https://reedsy.com/gillian-holmes

Thank you for selecting this book out of all the choices you have and for considering taking the time to read it.
I hope you enjoy.

You can find me on Facebook at
https://www.facebook.com/AuthorAnnHowes/

or visit my website at

www.authorannhowes.wordpress.com

and sign up for my newsletter regarding new releases.

To my children:

Without your encouragement, your great ideas and opinions on plot points this would have been much harder than it was. Thank you for being you and for keeping it real. I love you to the moon, the stars and the purple castles in the sky.

1

THE PAST REVISITED

~

I should've known not to make eye contact.

Especially as the last thing I need right now is to be recognized by anyone from my past. Normally, it wouldn't be a problem, but today it is, and I did.

"Shelley De Luca?"

Perhaps I can blame my distraction on the stabbing fluorescent lights as I struggle to focus my swollen, bruised eye on cheap concealers at the drugstore. Still, it doesn't prevent me from looking up at the sound of my name, being said in *that* voice.

"Shelley?" she calls again, louder. "Is that really you?"

Since in general I'm not a rude person, I suck it up and turn to face her.

"It *is* you," Cherry Meloni yells, pushing a squeaky cart loaded with toilet paper and Diet Coke.

"Golly gee, what a coincidence. I haven't seen you in forever."

Golly gee?

Who the hell says that?

"Since junior year, I think," Cherry continues. "When you and me and Joey Cadora broke into the school's snack shop the night before...oh." Her head jerks forward as her gaze settles on my eye.

That's the moment I remember my sunglasses are on *top* of my head, and not hiding my face like I intended.

Sigh.

"Yowzer!" she says, pointing a long, unpainted fingernail in the general area of my face. "What happened to that?"

"Um...hi Cherry," I mumble and hope if I ignore her question, she'll catch a clue. "It's been a while."

On second thoughts, it's doubtful. If memory serves, Cherry and clues never seemed to occupy the same area code. Then her gaze drops to the concealer in my hand before popping right back up.

"Joey give you that?"

"What?"

Joey, among currently not being a part of my life, is many things (not all of them good) and did many things (not all of them legal) but he never beat the crap out of me.

"No," I smirk. "Why would you think that?"

"Ha!" she barks and I swear relief registers in her expression as her shoulders relax. "For a second I thought you were the one who shot him. You know...like payback?"

Payback?

Shot him?

Dean, my ex, must have done more damage to my head than I thought because clearly I'm missing something.

"Oh, my golly gosh." She claps her hands together and bounces on her toes. The sound moves through my head like a whip cracking. "I'm kidding. Didn't really think it was you."

Okay, wait.

"Did you say someone shot Joey?" I ask.

"You didn't know?" Her eyes widen and then she blinks. "He's dead. Can't believe you didn't know. I mean, wouldn't you be, like, the first to know?"

My mouth drops open but no words come out.

"Got hit in the back of the head. Apparently, they made such a mess of his face, they had to identify him by his fingerprints. Pity, because he had such a pretty face."

My synapses start reconnecting.

"Guessing there won't be an open casket..."

"Stop." I raise my hands, palms up, then press my fingers to my temples. "Please, Cherry, just stop." I pull in a breath, count to three, let it out slowly. "Is this one of those bullshit moves like you pulled back in high school?"

"Uh...?"

"Like when you put rotten fish guts from your dad's store into people's shoes?"

"Oh shit." Cherry takes a step back, looks down and maneuvers her cart so it's between us. "I did that to you?"

I stare at her, stunned. What is wrong with this woman?

"I don't remember doing that to you," she goes on, shaking her head, causing her gold hoop earrings to jiggle. "No...in fact..."

"Cherry!"

"What?"

"Joey?"

"Oh yeah...I'm not lying, Shelley, I swear on my firstborn. Someone shot him."

I close my eyes. This can't be. No. I just talked to him on the phone a few days ago. "Any idea who did it?" My voice comes out a little shaky.

"Well, you know, the usual rumors, of course."

"And that means what, exactly?"

"Uh...he's always messed with the wrong people, Shelley. You of all people should know that." Leaning forward she whispers, "The Cadoras aren't the only family in this town you don't mess with."

She has that right.

At least, that's how I remember it, but I've been gone from the Bay Area a long time. Things could've changed.

"I remember you and Joey had a thing back in high school," she continues, "but God, if I had my choice of brothers it would've been Gianni. If he so much as looked at me, I'd go all wobbly and wet my panties."

Ewww.

Cherry's wet panties aside, I am unprepared to hear his name. It rumbles through me like an earthquake, the resulting tremor leaves my own legs a little wobbly.

"You and every other girl in town," I mumble as soon as I catch my breath.

"Lordy, he was hot. I wonder what he looks like now...probably fat and bald..."

"Do you know when the funeral is?" I jump in, mostly to shut her up, but also thinking to wrap this up and get the hell away from her.

"It's today! At three, up at Angel of Mercy. You know, where the rest of them are buried."

Holy crap. A quick glance at my phone tells me it's after one already.

"You're going?" Cherry asks, shifting from foot to foot.

"Of course, aren't you?"

Cherry shakes her head, her eyes wide again. I don't allow myself to wonder why.

"Well, if I'm going to make it," I say, "I'd better move."

I glance at the concealer in my hand and determine it'll have to do. Damned if I'm going to say *nice to see you again* to her, so I say, "Tell your dad hi from me, will you?" instead. He, at least, was one member of her family I liked. My parents often shopped at his store for fresh seafood back in the day and he always gave them a deal.

Before it all went to shit.

I head towards the registers, dodging another customer juggling two toddlers on a leash coming down the aisle.

"We should get together sometime," Cherry calls after me as I round the corner. I toss her a wave over my shoulder.

How messed up is my life that after ten years of not seeing or speaking to Joey, we reconnect and he goes and gets himself killed? Who would dare? Don't they realize who they're screwing with?

I nibble on what is left of my thumbnail, waiting as a stooped old lady with a too-large wig counts out change and hands it, coin by coin, to the sales clerk.

Once my credit card's swiped and the concealer shoved into my hoodie pocket, I tackle the two blocks back to my apartment, all uphill. After which I ignore the dubious and more often than not broken-down elevator, trudging up four floors to my tiny corner studio.

I can't complain, really, since it's all I can afford and Marshall, the building manager, took a liking to me because I'm the same age as his daughter. And for the same reason, he also took pity on me and gave me a deal while I build my clientele at the salon. I don't care what his reason is, I'm just happy he has one.

The second-hand black leather couch that takes up half the space in my so-called living room is cool against my back while I recover my breath.

"Dammit to hell, Joey," I call to his ghost, my voice seemingly lost in my tiny abode. "What did Cherry mean you messed with the wrong people?"

Naturally, he doesn't answer so I drop my head into my hands and allow the tears to come. Tears of shock, more tears of guilt and finally, tears of lost explanations and opportunities.

"Pull it together, De Luca," I admonish myself, yanking the last tissue from a box of Kleenex that was full yesterday. "You've got a funeral to go to."

So I do.

Though I can't say I'm excited to see Gianni again, or maybe I'm just lying to myself. Somehow, I've managed to keep his face and anything else to do with him suppressed from my memory. Haven't even thought of him in a very long time. Cherry's mention of his name resurrected him like a sleepy spirit, who, now awake, won't cross over to the other side. Here to haunt and torment, and occasionally freak me the shit out.

But it would be wrong not to go. Perhaps Cherry is right. Maybe he is fat and bald with a witch of a wife and a hundred kids in tow.

One can hope.

Or maybe not, as there's this little thing moving around my belly that feels an awful lot like jealousy.

But, on the plus side, there'll be people I've not seen in a while.

Los Angeles isn't that far from the Bay Area, but it may as well have been the moon, since I haven't kept in touch. My mother made sure of that.

I push myself off the couch and park my nose a few inches away from the bathroom mirror. I manage to cover the bruising, but no amount of concealer can do anything about the swelling that multiple rounds of icing couldn't reduce.

I could always wear my sunglasses. The same kick-ass pair of D&Gs I scored from a second-hand store in Beverly Hills that I should've been hiding behind earlier. No one would think it strange. It's a funeral, after all.

My only black dress is appropriate enough: simple, with a low V-neck that reveals a little too much of my minuscule cleavage. I scrounge around my jewelry box—I have two vices: good wine and a life-long addiction to silver jewelry—until my hand settles on something I haven't touched since...well, since then. A heart-shaped chunk of amber Joey gave me the day before my dad died. Then he dumped me the day after.

I never wore it, but couldn't get rid of it. Somehow it seems right for the moment, and when my fingers wrap around the cool amber, a wisp of air kisses the back of my neck. Like a soft breath, or an affirmation. My skin erupts into goosebumps.

Weird.

Almost like he's giving approval.

GETTING out of the city is difficult and due to traffic being its usual awful self, I arrive at the church ten minutes late. The inside is softly lit, the Virgin Mary stained-glass window bathes the mourners in soft, colorful hues.

Only one seat next to a hulk remains, so I squeeze myself into it. The hulk wipes away tears with a blue handkerchief that hides most of his face. It's only when I lay eyes on his Karl Malden nose that I recognize him. Despite the overwhelming sadness in the church, a wave of joy and tenderness sweeps over me.

He's changed in the ten years since I last saw him. Bigger, balder, but by the looks of things, his suit fits better. Billy "the Barrel" Niccaterra has come up in the world. He was once my father's best friend.

I touch his hand and lift my sunglasses. "Fancy meeting you here," I whisper.

His face beams like he's lit up with an internal light bulb, and a wide, toothy smile spreads across his face.

"Good to see you, kiddo." We grin and through some force of their own, our hands find each other, before we turn our attention back to the ceremony.

Joey's closed casket is at the front of the church, next to the altar, and covered in a mixed display of white lilies and red roses, their perfume mingling with the bouquets of gardenias attached to the end of each pew.

Next to it, a giant color photograph of him smiling with a San Francisco Giants cap on, takes center stage. Not one of him as the teenager I was more familiar with, but one of him as a man. The man I never got to know again.

I take in a huge breath in an effort to keep my tears in check, hold it for as long as I can before releasing it.

Such a waste.

Billy's hand holds mine until the service is over. He was a big part of our lives, but the last time I saw him was at another funeral. My dad's, when I was seventeen.

People stand, waiting out of respect for the last two immediate family members to pass and exit first. Mama Cadora holds her silver-gray head high as she leads the way.

Directly behind her is *him*.

Gianni-fucking-Cadora.

Joey's older brother and now head of the family.

My heart seizes.

A warm flush, starting at my toes, rushes up my body, prickling my skin. When it reaches my head, I'm pretty sure I'm glowing.

Not fat, and definitely not bald. From what I can see, no little witch traipsing behind him either.

He's matured, and done it well. A testament to the good genes and bone structure all the Cadora men are blessed with.

The lines in his brow are slightly deeper, but he's even more beautiful than I remember. The years adding an edge, a hardness that translates into dangerous.

A small scar cuts through a dark eyebrow that pulls attention to those thickly lashed, crystal-clear blue eyes. Right now, those eyes are stuck on me.

My heart restarts with such an intensity I'm convinced everyone in church can hear it pounding. They drop to the low V-neck of my dress before claiming my gaze again. Only now they're narrow and look decidedly pissed off.

Is my cleavage *that* obvious?

I resist the impulse to clutch at my necklace. As he gets closer it becomes increasingly clear he's not happy to see me. The muscles working in that stubborn jaw a dead giveaway. Only when he can no longer hold my gaze without turning his head, does he break eye contact.

I try not to think about what that look means, because no matter what our history may be, it's ancient.

Billy's hand tightens around mine while we wait quietly for the last mourners to pass. All too soon it's our turn to pay our condolences to Mama Cadora and Gianni, who stand just outside the church doors.

Billy senses my reluctance and nudges me forward while I resist the urge to chomp on my nails.

"I'm sorry, Mama." I lean forward to embrace her tiny form and accept her hug and kiss on the cheek. A sad smile crinkles the corners of her eyes, the exact color of her son's.

"Thank you for coming, Shelley. It's good to see you again, even under these circumstances. Despite what happened, I remember you loved him too."

I nod, because it's easier than speaking over the lump forming in my throat. Mama Cadora squeezes my fingers before she turns to Billy. He lifts her hand to his lips. Billy is nothing if not gallant.

This, however, leaves me with no alternative other than to face Gianni. With my heart still hammering, I take the small step closer and raise my eyes to meet his. They're hard and glittery and scary as crap.

One thing my parents taught me though, was *look 'em in the eye*.

In case they shoot you.

Yah.

Easier said. Though I don't think Gianni will shoot me, at least not in front of his mother...still.

All I have to do is get through this, then I can be on my way having done my duty like a good little mafia daughter representing my family. Or what's left of it.

"Gianni," I say, not knowing if I'm supposed to hug him.

Despite his seemingly relaxed posture, he emits such a powerful energy that I'm sure if I touch him, he'd crackle like a downed power line after a storm, both thrilling and deadly.

Not willing to risk the power surge, or the electrocution, I keep my distance.

He makes no move towards me either, but studies me for a long moment, before he speaks in a low, measured voice. "Hello, Shelley."

I'd forgotten what that voice did to me. Smooth and deep, like whisky and chocolate. Intoxicating and addicting.

"Been a while. Nice of you to come."

"Of course." I swallow, not trusting the way he says it. "Why wouldn't I?"

He offers no immediate answer, instead continuing to study me, eyes narrowing and probing past my sunglasses.

I feel it in my belly. Something deep and disturbing that unsettles my equilibrium. I'm about to sway from that all-consuming intensity when he says finally, "Perhaps that's something we need to clarify."

My head jerks a little as I try to make sense of his comment. What on earth would there be to clarify? I'm here to pay my respects.

However, Billy saves me by stepping in and breaking the tension. He hugs Gianni, doing that power patting thing that macho men always seem to do before grasping his face between two giant paws.

"I loved that little bastard." His voice cracks and he takes a second, his throat working, before he continues. "May he find some peace."

Gianni's face is grim and it's not lost on me that he does some swallowing of his own. Despite his aloofness, I know their history. The two brothers had their issues, particularly with each other. And sometimes those issues involved me.

When they separate, Billy blows his nose, shoves his handkerchief in his pocket, and slides an arm around my shoulders. He cuts a glance at Gianni and Mama Cadora. "Excuse us for a moment. I want to reacquaint myself with my favorite girl."

Gianni lifts his chin in acknowledgment, then shifts his gaze to me, resuming that flat, suspicious look the Cadoras seem to have trademarked.

Billy catches the change in expression directed at me. I know because he gives me a gentle, reassuring squeeze and guides me forward, down the wide, red-brick church stairs to the parking lot.

A spot on the back of my head tingles but I refuse to look back. That sensation grows with each step, until we reach a quiet area underneath the canopy of gnarled cypress trees, away from everyone. Billy pulls me into an embrace, lifting me off my feet and holding me for a long time.

"Billy...can't breathe," I wheeze into his chest.

He chuckles and lowers me to the ground. "Don't want to kill you, just missed you, kiddo." With those long arms attached to my shoulders, he studies me. "I lose one little bastard but I have you back. Look at you. All grown up and gorgeous." His face scrunches up, then he pulls me back into his arms and kisses me on top of my head. Something he used to do when I was younger. "How is your mother?" he asks when he lets me go. "She good?"

"Haven't talked to her lately, but she's still in LA. I'm back in San Francisco."

"What? How long you been back?"

"About three months."

"And you didn't call?"

"I wanted to be settled. You know, find a job and a place to live. Things kinda...got a little intense after that."

"Yeah." His face gets hard and I figure he's referring to the edges of my bruise visible under my sunglasses.

"But I'm here now."

"We need to talk about how intense things are."

"Billy, please." I put a hand on his forearm. "I'm sure there's plenty of time for that, but not today?"

He wrinkles his nose and sniffs. A sign I remember from my teens when he didn't like something but was willing to concede.

"Please?"

He lets the air out in a long, slow breath. "Okay, I'll let it go for now. I'm too damn happy you're here, don't want to spoil that."

"Thank you," I whisper.

"Later." He catches my eyes.

"Okay."

"But what's with all the tension between you and Gianni?"

"I don't know." I swallow. "I haven't seen him since Mom and I left. Maybe he doesn't like my dress."

Billy snorts and cocks his head.

"Or maybe he just likes holding a grudge," I continue. "He never liked me. Treated me like an annoying little twerp and only tolerated me because I was with Joey."

He clears his throat. "Whatever. We'll deal with that later too. So much to talk about. Looks like I need to feed you, fatten you up."

I let out a little giggle. "That sounds so good. I think I missed your lasagna almost more than I missed you."

With his craggy, round face, Billy's not handsome but when he smiles, he lights up and those dark, cinnamon-colored eyes with coppery flecks sparkle.

"Hmm," he grunts and lifts his head, focusing on something over my head. "Speaking of Gianni...we have incoming."

The sound of approaching footsteps crunching over gravel coincides with the beginning of an itch at the base of my spine.

"Shelley," Gianni says to my back.

I squeeze my eyes shut.

"A word please." It isn't a request, and not wanting to appear rude I angle my body so my back isn't entirely to him.

"All right."

"In private."

Crud.

I twirl a stray strand of hair around my fingers. Billy looks at me. I shrug. Suppose he can't do much to me in public except set my blood on fire.

"You sure?" he asks softly so only I can hear. "I can stay."

"Yep. I'm a big girl. I can handle him."

"I'll be there if you need me." He points with his chin to the steps of the church and I watch as he lumbers over to a small group of mourners standing at the foot of the red-brick stairs chatting with Mama Cadora. The limp from a bullet he took to his upper thigh years ago still pronounced.

I pull in a deep breath and count to three before sliding my eyes to Gianni's—they haven't softened at all.

"I'm gonna ask you this once and you better fucking tell me the truth. What are you doing here?"

Keeping my voice as even as I can despite my pulse fluttering like an injured bird in my neck I answer. "I came to pay my respects, Gianni. I didn't realize I'd be so unwelcome, but don't worry, I'm not staying. I'll be gone in a few minutes."

"You sure that's all it is? Paying your respects."

"What else would it be?"

"You here to spit on his grave?"

"What?" My hand flies to my throat. Joey cheated and then dumped me, but that is not grave-spitting-worthy.

"So help me, woman, you do anything to hurt my mother..."

"Are you crazy? Why would I do that? I love your mother and I would never do anything to hurt her. Besides, I'm not even going to the burial, let alone spitting on his grave."

Like earlier, those eyes drill into me, but then he shakes that handsome head and turns away so his back is to me for just a moment.

"Fuck me," he mutters so softly I have to strain to hear it, and probably wouldn't have if the soft breeze carrying his voice wasn't blowing my way. "I'm fucked."

This seems like a strange reaction, one I don't understand at all. Some sort of apology? And just when I think he's satisfied with my answer, he turns back and takes a step closer, blocking the early November sun. Before I realize what his intentions are, in one quick movement, he snatches the sunglasses off my face.

Shit, dang it.

Strong, warm fingers wrap themselves around my jaw.

"Who did that to you?" His voice is rough and clipped. Nothing like the whisky or smooth chocolate I detected earlier.

He angles my face for a better look. He's close enough I can smell him.

Delicious, some kind of spice layered with soap, clean and all male. If that isn't intoxicating enough, the man oozes sex and pheromones, sending my hormones into a tizzy.

All those feelings I buried under complicated layers of teenage anxiety years ago bubble up and resurface, as the specter of his face did earlier in my apartment. Fortunately, before my ovaries begin to vibrate and explode, I find the strength to shove his hand away.

"Butt out, Gianni!" I say, with a little more spice than I intended. "You don't get to manhandle me. If you'll excuse me, I've got people to see."

I attempt to walk away, but a hard grip on my upper arm stops me abruptly, then steadies me when I stumble on my heels.

"Jeez. What the hell?" Great, now I'll have more bruises to hide.

"I don't care who you've got to see, you don't walk away from me," he growls. "I'm not done with you, Shelley."

"I'm not a teenager anymore and I'm not part of your little family. You can't boss me around."

His face gets closer until it's within inches of mine. I find myself echoing his words from a few seconds ago. *Fuck me*, because *I* am fucked as I have the craziest impulse to kiss him. All I have to do is lean in and touch my lips to his.

Good Lord, the man scares me—not in the way you'd think a badass alpha jerk would, but in what he does to my body because I *want* to lean in. It takes all my strength not to.

"You've been gone a long time. Maybe forgotten how things work around here."

"I've forgotten nothing."

"Really? From where I stand it looks like you don't remember a fucking thing."

"I'm not afraid of you," I murmur.

"When were you ever afraid of me, Shelley?" Something other than anger flickers in his eyes, but it's gone before I have a chance to read it. Leaves me wondering if I imagined it. "It's what I always liked about you," he adds, almost as an afterthought.

I blink. Either I'm having some kind of delayed reaction to Dean punching me, or I misheard him. But I don't have time to think about it anyway, before he demands, "Who's the asshole that hit you?"

"Stop it."

"Shelley..."

"I said *stop*."

His grip tightens.

"Ow!" I jerk my arm, but his grip is relentless. "What's your problem?"

God.

I'm *so* done with controlling men, but somehow, I keep attracting them.

"You're my problem. You've always been my problem." He pulls me closer, getting in my face.

"You're hurting me, dammit. You men are all the fucking same."

That does it.

Because this time it's him who blinks and the pressure on my arm is gone so fast it makes me stumble again. He takes a small step back as I regain my balance. And then another, still holding my eyes. His are steely, but no longer cold.

He shoves his hands into his suit pants pockets and looks away, while I rub my arm and glare at him. By the way he's working his jaw, I can tell he's fighting. What, I couldn't begin to guess.

The weird thing is, I kind of like I'm having this effect on him. Payback for all those years he unwittingly tortured me.

"Who're you protecting?" His voice is softer, but by no means gentler.

I shake my head. No way in hell I'm telling him. My life is complicated enough without adding him to the mix.

"Well, shit," he says in that drawn out, sarcastic way he laid on me all those years back. "Stubborn as ever. Unfortunately, I don't have time to explore this further right now, but I will find out. You can count on it."

He closes the distance between us, leaning forward until his lips are close to my ear. "In the meantime"—his warm breath fans across my neck—"you tell that piece of shit he touches you again, he'll have to deal with me."

Goosebumps pop up all over and a shiver I can't suppress runs through me.

Too bad he notices, and it only takes a beat before the corner of his mouth curls up. Those sexy-as-sin eyes drop and focus on my swollen bottom lip, then to my nipples. The traitors have perked into noticeable peaks. When he catches my eyes again, his are dark and full of...satisfaction?

"You get me, De Luca?"

I swallow and stare back.

"Say the words, Shelley."

"I get you, Gianni," I whisper.

His lips quirk, then he turns on his heel and walks away with long, easy strides back towards the crowd gathering around the red-brick stairs.

Hoo...boy.

Did I get him?

Clear as church bells.

But that wasn't all I got. Along with my nipples poking through my dress, I tingle in places that are immoral at a funeral. My fingers shake so badly, it takes a few attempts before I manage to secure the strand of hair that's escaped its pins back behind my ear.

No getting away from it, even when he's scary as crap, the bastard still does it to me.

2

DELIGHTFUL AS YOUR ASS IS

~

It isn't until he's back at the church that I realize the handsome jerk has my sunglasses. They may be second-hand, but they're vintage and considering I love them, I want them back.

Facing him again, however, isn't an option. Well, technically it is, but not one I want to handle.

A blast of wind brushes over my body, swirling around my legs and lifting my skirt, reminding me how inappropriately I'm dressed for cool weather. The cypress canopy offers little protection and I rub my fingers up and down my arms. They brush against the other bruises Dean gave me.

What the hell's wrong with me, that I kept my mouth shut?

A couple minutes pass as I wait for my heart to slow. When it reaches a somewhat normal beat, I aim myself towards Billy and the small crowd of mourners he's talking to.

Mama Cadora's about to step into the waiting black limo when she sees me and motions me over.

"Shelley." She squeezes my hands. "Come back to the Sea

Cliff house for a small celebration…it's been so long. Don't let my son's behavior keep you away. I want to hear about you and your mother."

"Wish I could, Mama, but I need to get back to the city." Guilt makes my eye twitch, but there is no way I'm exposing myself to questions about my face *or* screwed-up love life.

"There'll be food," she goes on, eyeing me like I'm a starving refugee. "Looks like you don't eat enough, makes me want to feed you." Her eyes are sweet, and the tiny upturn of her lip, sweeter, considering I can't imagine what she's going through. Joey's death is one of many in a long line of family members.

Despite her petite frame, an underlying strength, her secret weapon, shines through. Anyone caught underestimating Isabella Cadora would be making a big mistake. I often thought she was the real power in the family, keeping her sons from killing each other, and everyone else together.

"I've always been kind of skinny, like my dad," I mumble.

"Ah yes, Jimmy. You have his eyes. That same golden brown, but yours are softer. Papa always said they reminded him of a good cognac." Her voice breaks on *cognac* and she stops, closing her eyes. After a few seconds she continues, "Another time?"

A lump forms in my throat, but I smile and nod.

"Don't be a stranger. I'm so glad you're back." Her gaze shifts to the swelling around my eye and lingers. "Take care of yourself, pretty girl. You know where to find me if you need anything."

Again, I nod. This time acknowledging her unspoken message, then kiss her cheek, helping her into the limo, and waiting as she slides across the black leather seat.

I close the door, bending at the waist to wave through the tinted window and step back when my butt slams into a wall.

Large, warm hands clamp around my hips and I squeal like a piglet.

"Jesus, De Luca," Gianni grunts. "Careful."

My pelvis thrusts forward, as far as his grip will allow and away from what I realize is his crotch. This causes me to wobble (again) in my four-inch heels. "What are you doing?"

"You backed into me." Somehow his hands are still on me, holding me in position, my back to his front. "You gonna fall or should I let you go?"

"Let me go," I quip over my shoulder. "You're too damn close." And his hands are too damn hot, burning through the fabric of my dress.

That scarred eyebrow shoots up, but those hands stay where they are. "This is my fault?"

"Of course, it's your fault. You snuck up on me."

That crackling energy I felt earlier is back as he releases me and steps away, folding his arms across his broad, undoubtedly hard chest. And leaving a cold spot on my hips .

"Why would I do that?" The words are said low and frosty enough to give a polar bear the chills.

I have no answer and stare, capturing my bottom lip between my teeth.

"Hmm. Get this straight, De Luca, delightful as your ass is, I wouldn't sneak up on it. If I wanted my hands on your ass, I'd make my intentions known beforehand."

"Oh."

Delightful?

Under normal circumstance that might be considered flirting. But then this is Gianni. He doesn't flirt, at least not with me.

"Um...okay. I may have overreacted...a little."

"Think so?"

"Didn't mean to imply you were groping." Honestly, though, I kind of wish he would. I'm still tingling from earlier.

"Right."

"Guess I'm just a little edgy."

"Hmm."

Okay.

Why isn't he getting in the limo, and where the hell is Billy?

"Don't let me stop you," I say, waving a hand and stepping away from the car door.

"You're not."

"I'm not?"

In order to keep my eyes off him I do a sweep of the parking lot, and find Billy standing by the stairs, chatting with a tiny man in a suit way too big for him. When I slide my eyes back to Gianni, he hasn't moved and his eyes are still on me. What's he waiting for?

"Why are you staring at me?"

He shrugs. "Not much else to look at while I wait."

Ah. Wait for what though, or rather whom? The absent, witchy wife?

Shit. Not thinking about that. So I steer the conversation into safer territory.

"I know Joey was shot, but can you tell me what happened?"

"Wasn't random. Thinking it's a hit," he says softly.

"When?" I ask.

"Five days ago."

Five days. I do the math in my head and clutch the chunk of amber around my neck seeking a connection to him. Damn tears are threatening again, and I blink to chase them away. "I talked to him a couple days before that, and he said he was having issues. Something to do with a business deal."

Gianni's head cocks to the side.

"What?" Those eyes are suddenly hard as he pins me down.

"What do you mean, what?"

"You were seeing each other again?" It's the way he says it, a little sharp, and if it wasn't Gianni, I would suspect a hint of jealousy but I shrug that off because it *is* Gianni

Sigh.

"We ran into each other a couple of months ago." I lift a shoulder, not sure what his deal is. "When I first got back and we sorta stayed in touch."

He stills. "*Ran* into each other?"

"It's not impossible."

"Hmm."

Hmm?

"Why does that surprise you, Gianni? We were close once."

"Doesn't, I guess," he says after a long moment, like he couldn't care less, then checks his watch. A rather handsome affair with a gold face set in platinum that I'm sure cost more than I make in a year's tips.

Great.

I'm being dismissed. What else is new?

"Um," I mumble as my stomach plummets thinking this might be the last time I see him again. "Before you go, I'd like my sunglasses back."

Now it's his turn to blink but voices behind him catch his attention and he glances over his shoulder.

His gaze is pinpointed on a woman standing at the entrance of the church, and something about how his eyes stay on her makes my stomach drop even further.

"Do you have any idea how much those cost?" She's not exactly yelling, but loud enough to make heads turn.

Gianni shuts his eyes then releases a long sigh. She's gorgeous, of course, with a dark bob and ample cleavage jutting out of a white silky blouse. If I had to guess, I'd go with double Ds.

"Look at this," she says, shoving a shoe in the man's face. He yanks his head back and takes a step away from a broken stiletto heel dangling from a slip of leather. "I need to talk to your boss, *right now.*"

"Christ," Gianni mutters under his breath and drops his head to look at his own shoes.

"*Please* keep your voice down." The man spreads his arms, herding her away from the entrance. "Everyone can hear you," he parries, preventing her from re-entering like a dog blocking a disobedient sheep. "This is a house of worship. Show some respect. Wait here while I call my boss," he says, backing her up a little more.

"Don't care if the whole damn Bay Area hears me," the woman says. "Your carpet broke my shoe and you're paying for it."

As if sensing the stairs behind her, she swivels to navigate, and spots me watching her. But as her glare shifts to Gianni, her eyes widen and she slows. Then that glare changes to something that looks like a smile, or perhaps a grimace as she reaches into her designer purse.

The witchy wife?

Joy.

I glance at Gianni's hands situated low on his hips.

No ring.

Girlfriend, maybe?

"I suppose accidents happen," the woman continues. "Here's my card. Have your boss call me, but you do need to deal with that carpet!"

Catching me still staring, she wrinkles her nose, rips the heel off and shoves it into her purse. Then like a model on a runway, she squares her shoulders, marches on one stiletto heel and one tippy toe in our direction, saunters past me with that fake smile still in place and stops next to him.

Yep.

Girlfriend.

"Hi." I dig deep and find whatever sunshine is left within my voice, squashing the desire to stick my tongue out at her.

"Hello," she responds in a tone that's a notch above acrimonious before turning on the syrup. "Gianni, honey"—she slips her hand around his forearm—"we really should be going."

Without waiting to be introduced she opens the limo door, climbs in and takes a seat opposite Mama Cadora, who's watching me. I give her a small smile and a shrug. She gives me a small knowing one of her own.

When I look back at Gianni, he's looking down at my cleavage. Or rather at the amber heart slightly above. Next to Miss Double D mine must be sadly disappointing.

It does, however, give me a moment to take in how gorgeous the jerk is—even with a scowl on his face—and imprint him in my brain. All that long, dark, wavy hair brushed back from his face, except for a lock that falls across his forehead. Stupid, but I catch myself fantasizing about twirling it around my finger.

"Meant what I said," he says.

"About what?"

A hand moves to my face, the back of his fingers so close to my bruise, I feel the heat radiating off them. It's strangely intimate and I stop breathing, anticipating his touch. But after a moment they drop, leaving a void. Making me realize how much I want him to touch me. How disappointing it is that he didn't. He clears his throat and moves past me to slide in next to his mother, and not *her*.

Interesting.

Mama Cadora takes his hand and pulls it to her lap. That tugs at my belly and makes me happy they still have each other.

"Later, De Luca," he says capturing my eyes before pulling the door closed.

Later. Not goodbye.

It comes across as a promise, though I'm not sure it's meant as one. I release the breath I'm holding as they take their place behind the black hearse carrying Joey's body, clutching my arms against the biting autumn chill.

Billy approaches and bumps my shoulder with his. "You all right?"

"Dandy. Who's that woman?" I ask him.

"Gina De Angelo."

Gina and Gianni. How fucking cute.

Barf.

"Charming couple."

Billy snorts. "What was all that about?"

I shrug. "Dunno. Gianni being Gianni, I guess." I give him a weak smile and ask, "Are you going to the burial?"

"Need to be there, loved that little asshole. Catch you later?"

"Hope so. Now that I found you, you think you're going to be done with me so soon?"

Hooking an arm around my neck, he pulls me into his warmth. "I'll never be done with you, kiddo. We've a lot to talk about."

Indeed, we do.

After exchanging phone numbers, he leaves me with a kiss on my head and as I climb into my Mini, my last phone call with Joey comes to mind.

You sound stressed, what's going on, Joey?

Kicking off my shoes and tossing them onto the seat next to me, I slip on the pair of flats I keep in my car. I never got the knack of driving in heels.

Ah...just a business thing that's not going so well.

The heater takes a minute to kick in and while I'm waiting, I scroll through the playlist on my iPhone for a song and select one by Rob Thomas.

Jesus, Shell, I fucked up.

With the gear engaged, I pull out of the parking lot singing to "Little Wonders" flowing through the speakers.

Nobody got me like you did. Gotta tell you something, babe.

Across the street, the rolling lawn set on a high hill is dotted with gravestones facing the Pacific Ocean. The kind only wealthy people can afford and I'm glad Joey gets that view.

Tell me now.

Can't. Something I gotta do face to face.

I stop at the light and see, at the top of the hill, Gianni stepping out of the parked limo with his hand extended.

Let's go to dinner.

Not a good time, Joey. I'm seeing someone, he gets a little...possessive.

Know that.

As Gianni helps his mother out of the car, the color changes from red to green and a car behind me honks when I take too long to move. I push through, second-guessing my decision to go to the burial. Since I'm in the lane that'll take me to the freeway back to the city, I'm too late and continue on.

What are you saying? How would you know that?

My town, remember. Know everything happening here.

Rob Thomas is done and Train's next with "Save me, San Francisco."

I can relate. Inexplicably, I was drawn back to San Fran. Perhaps for closure, but also for a much-needed change of scenery after yet another bad relationship. Of all the good men in the world, I always seem to pick the beating or the cheating ones. And now, having seen Gianni again, I'm the one who might need saving. The mind might forget, but the heart remembers. And boy, if the way my body reacts to his touch or his breath across my skin is any indication, mine sure remembered.

I may have been Joey's girlfriend, but it had always secretly been Gianni.

And the jerk didn't even know it.

As I merge into a lane, the last thing Joey said to me echoes in my brain.

Shit went down between us, Shelley, but I still love you. That never changed.

Then why did you dump me, Joey?

That's what we gotta talk about.

Though I didn't cry during the ceremony, my eyes blur now, which isn't so great when you're trying to navigate city traffic and pedestrians during rush hour.

How did he know I was dating? I never told him. San Francisco's not that small and in ten years my circle of friends has diminished significantly, so no one I know now knew Joey, or who I was when I lived here.

Parking is as bad as always, but I find a spot in Pacific Heights, a block away from my building. Since I don't see any flashy orange cars belonging to an unwelcome, flashy ex-boyfriend, I climb out of mine, pulling my cardigan close against the wind.

A sliver of the bay, visible in the fading light between the buildings, shows choppy water with little white crests dotting the surface. Today, the constantly changing color is appropriately gray.

Inside my apartment, with my new industrial deadbolt engaged, I hit the shower and wash the concealer from my face.

The heat from the water intensifies the throbbing in my eye and since I'm drained, both physically and emotionally, I figure I may as well self-medicate with wine.

After pouring a glass, I plop on the couch, curl into my throw cushions and turn to a rerun of *The Walking Dead*. At some point, I fall asleep. Something wakes me but, due to the sounds of gunshots coming from my TV, it doesn't immediately register that it's someone pounding on my door.

"Shelley! Open up."

But then it does.

The unwelcome asshole who damaged me. Dean. My heart thumps like a frightened rabbit and I scramble to my hallway closet, pulling out the softball bat I stashed. The one I bought from a second-hand store in case the door didn't hold.

"You're in there, baby, open the door."

"Fuck off, Dean." I muster as much strength in my voice as I'm able, while I ready 911 on my phone. "Go away or I'm calling the cops." Only need to press the green button for it to happen.

"Don't do that, baby. I brought flowers...swear I just want to talk."

"There's nothing to say. Go away."

"Didn't mean to hurt you. I had too much to drink and you... you make me crazy...can't stand it when men look at you."

"That's bullshit, Dean. You called me a slut because I smiled at a waiter."

The door moves and I hear him sigh on the other side. "I know. Blame the vodka. Had too much while I was waiting for you and I lost my temper." He actually sounds contrite but I'm not falling for it.

Blame the vodka? Is he kidding?

Learned my lesson the hard way and I wonder how the hell I ever found him attractive. The charming dimple in his cheek and that athletic ass aside.

"Okay, well, I left something in your apartment. Just want to get it, then I'll go."

"You think I'm stupid?"

"Baby, of course not."

"No way I'm opening the door. There's nothing of yours here." Sweat trickles down the back of my neck. The moment his hand connected with my eye flashes through my brain and I suck in air through my nose, adjust my grip again, testing the bat's weight. It feels solid but not too heavy, the grooves I've carved in the handle for extra traction dig into my palms.

"Shelley...let me make it up to you." That voice, soft and very close, like he's leaning against the door, makes the hair on my arms stand. "Just give me one more chance. That's all I'm asking."

"It's over." Shouldn't have begun.

"Don't *say* that." The door shudders as something connects with it. I'm guessing his boot. How hard would it be to kick it open? Sweat beads on my forehead, I wipe it with my sleeve, doing a quick inventory of any other weapons I have. Only my spare set of shears in the bathroom and since I sharpened them recently, they could do plenty of damage if need be.

"Not giving up on you...need you back."

"HEY!" Another loud, deeper voice coming from further down the hallway overrides Dean's.

My shoulders sag

"What's going on?"

Thank God. Marshall.

"None of your fucking business, old man," Dean answers. "Butt out."

"Asshole, it *is* my business. You don't live here so you better not be bothering my tenants."

My legs flounder and I lean against the wall, using it for support as relief rushes over me like water over a fall.

"Fuck you, old man."

"Get the hell outta my building before I knock you sideways." Marshall's voice is commanding and strong, testimony to a long stint in the military. A moment of silence passes and I tense, waiting for Dean's response.

"Whatever!" he finally spits out. "We're not done, Shelley. We *will* talk at some point and I *will* be back."

"You got thirty seconds before I call the cops." By his tone, I can hear Marshall's losing patience. "I suggest you leave now!"

"Keep your cool, man, wouldn't want you to stroke yourself out." Dean taps on my door and says, "I'll catch you later, baby."

While I peek through the peephole until he disappears from my vision, I swallow my revulsion, knowing he will be back. Men like him *always* come back.

"He's gone, Shelley. Open up and talk to me, will you?"

I scrunch my face for a second before I unlock and open the door a fraction. Marshall stands with his feet apart, bulky arms at his side, one brandishing a tire iron, black eyes wide and irritated.

No wonder Dean gave in.

My attempt to smile fails, because my lips don't quite make it. Maybe if I stand behind the door, he won't notice my eye. No need to piss him off even more.

"Jesus, Shelley."

Dammit.

"He do that to you?"

I nod. Reaction from the adrenaline leaving my system makes my body tremble and teeth chatter, and though I'm sweating, I'm ice cold.

"You okay? Want me to call someone for you?"

"No, Marshall." I shake my head. "I got it."

He eyes me like he doesn't believe me and I don't blame him. I'm not sure I have got it.

"Next time, I won't hesitate. Gonna call the police and have his ass thrown in jail. Not one to get all in your business, but I'm surprised you haven't already. Smart girl like you."

"Understood." I swallow and bite my lip to stop my teeth from making noise.

"Sure?" he asks, raising his brows and waiting for me to acknowledge him. "You know where I am if you need me."

"Marshall?" I call as he turns, stopping him mid spin. He looks over his shoulder. "Could you take the flowers? I don't want to touch them."

"Sure thing," he replies, picking up the vase of long-stemmed red roses Dean left. "Got some booze? Take a slug and try to rest."

After turning and checking the deadbolt I collapse into a ball on my couch, clutching a cushion to my stomach.

Why didn't I make the 911 call?

Stupid question really. A lifetime of mistrust pounded into me as a child is why, and I recall what my father once said. *Our problems, our solutions.*

Sleep seems impossible, so I refill my glass with wine and nurse my eye with a bag of ice. One thing's for sure, I'm never letting Dean get the drop on me again. In order to do that, I'm going to need much more than a softball bat and my shears to protect myself.

Good thing I know exactly who to call.

3

ORANGE FERRARIS

~

B*eep...beep...beep.*

Holy fizz pops!

I sit up with a jerk and launch myself off the couch, adrenaline mainlining through my veins. It takes a second before I realize the ceiling's veiled with swirling white smoke, pluming from my oven.

My brownies!

I forgot to set the timer after I put them in the oven.

Snatching oven gloves off the counter, I pull the pan out, dump it in the sink and hit the faucet. What promised to be double chocolate fudge, is now a black mess of burnt-to-a-crisp charcoal. As the brownies morph into sludge, the metal pan hisses and pops in protest.

"Gah!" I yell, as I flip it the double bird with emphasis.

However, I have more important things to deal with. Like breathing. The smoky air makes me cough and if I don't open a window soon, I might just die. Wouldn't that be ironic?

Since the row of double-hung windows are above my bed, I

climb up and open them as wide as possible and suck in a lungful, staring down at the late afternoon traffic.

No orange Ferraris.

Yay.

Beep...beep.

Heh.

Even at five seven, using a wooden spatula and standing on my tippy toes, I'm still a tad short and keep missing the reset button.

Hmm. I could smash it to hell with my softball bat, or if I owned a gun, I could shoot the thing. Not sure Marshall would appreciate the hole in the ceiling though. Which leaves me with the only option left. I'll have to use my step-stool and with my clumsy tendencies, that could be a death sentence in itself. Fortunately, that's when somebody bangs on my door.

"Shelley?"

Oh, thank God, it's Billy.

Maybe *he's* got a gun.

The smoke's thinning but not enough to stop a coughing fit as I fling the door open and stumble into the hallway.

"What the hell?" Billy staggers back, then grins. "You burning dinner?"

"Noop," I mutter, when I stop coughing long enough to speak. "Just the brownies I was planning for dessert."

"Forgot how accident-prone you are," he chuckles.

"Glad you find me amusing." I point the spatula at the smoke alarm. "Can you kill that thing?"

"Yep, give me that," he orders, covering his nose with his gray San Francisco Giants sweatshirt and holding out a hand.

Happily, I relinquish control of the spoon. A moment later he shoves the end into the reset button and we have instant silence.

Expecting it to start up again, I glare at it.

Any second now.

Hmm.

"How do you do that?" My ears ring and I can barely hear myself speak.

He smirks and waves the spatula under the alarm, circulating the air beneath.

Of course. It wouldn't dare mess with him.

"We on fire?" he asks.

I shake my head, but check my oven to verify.

"You wanna head out of here and get dinner elsewhere?" Billy cocks an eyebrow. "Before we die from smoke inhalation?"

"You buying?"

"You bet."

"Done...give me a second to grab my purse and my sunglasses..." Shit. Gianni still has them.

HALF AN HOUR LATER, Billy guides me to a little Italian bistro with terraced vineyards painted on the walls. White candles, dripping wax, serve as centerpieces on tables draped with red-checkered cloths. Not the plastic kind.

Though early in the evening, the little restaurant is filled with people in business suits and other work attire. A skinny, middle-aged waitress with badly dyed red hair who sounds like she lives on cigarettes and smells like spearmint leads us to a table by the window. Perhaps I should give her my card and offer to fix that hair for her.

As we take our seats, her eyes dart between Billy and my bruise.

"Quit looking at me like that, Maureen," he grumbles. "I'm not the one responsible."

"Mm huh." She smacks her gum and flips open her little black order book. "What can I getchou?"

"How about a bottle of Zinfandel while we figure things out?"

"You betcha." She snaps her book shut and spinning on her heel saunters away to deliver our order to the bar. Moments later she returns with our wine and plonks the bottle down in front of Billy. Hard enough to make the table shudder. "Enjoy."

When she's out of earshot, our eyes meet and we burst out laughing.

"Think she likes you," I say and aim the bottle at the glasses, filling them halfway.

"Kiss my ass," he mutters, lips twitching.

I giggle even louder and push a glass across the table for him. "Here's to having you back, Uncle Billy."

"Cheers, kiddo. Stick around for a bit, will you?"

We touch rims, and I sit back to gaze at him, unable to keep the smile off my face. He never had kids of his own and he used to slip me cash when I had to have the latest pair of hot new jeans or boots, and got me out of a jam or two.

"Remember when I snuck out my window and went with Darren McGee to that college party?"

"You mean when I came and got you 'cause the asshole left you there amongst a bunch of drunk and horny freshmen without a ride?"

"Yep."

"Never told me why he bailed on you, but then again, maybe I don't wanna know."

"Yeah, well...I was too embarrassed to tell you. I wouldn't let him steal third base. So...he got mad and kicked me out of his car, then drove off with Gloria 'big boobs' Tortino." I hated the slut, as she had a knack for constantly popping up in my relationships, but that night she actually did me a favor.

"Thought it might be something like that. Gave him a lesson in how to treat women but I don't believe it stuck."

"I think you gave him more than that. He'd bragged all summer about going to Paris for a modeling gig. I heard he missed his shot because his face was so messed up."

Billy lets out a little huff. "That wasn't me. That honor belongs to Gianni and Joey."

I'm about to stuff bread into my mouth, but stop halfway. "What do they have to do with it?"

"When they heard what the prick did, those two, who never got along mind you, decided to do something about it. Joey gave him the black eye, Gianni cracked his rib."

"Gianni?" As much as I want to believe it, I can't afford to let my heart take any satisfaction. "You must be remembering it wrong. Gianni would never waste his time defending me."

"Kiddo, a man with any kind of honor doesn't allow women to be disrespected the way that prick disrespected you."

Ah!

Honor.

How disappointing.

"I always assumed it was you."

"Oh, I supervised, made sure they didn't do too much damage. Only enough to teach a lesson."

"I never knew."

"Didn't want you to know."

Smile lines radiate from the corners of his soft, cinnamon eyes. "Shithead never saw it coming."

"Oh my God, I actually feel sorry for Darren McGee now."

"Don't. The bastard earned what he got. Last I heard, he's in prison for sexual assault. Perhaps we weren't tough enough."

"You kept tabs on him?"

"Have to with fuckwads like that."

I let that simmer for a moment, then realize I *have* been away a long time.

"I think my parents were the only people *not* afraid of you. Mom almost lost her curlers when you taught me to drive when I was fourteen and threatened to shoot Daddy with his Glock for letting you."

"Gave me hell too," he chuckles. "She's the reason I have two assholes."

"Yep, Mom can be fierce. What she wants, she usually gets." I take a sip of wine, savor it, then sit back in my chair releasing a sad sigh. "Talk to me about Dad."

"Aah...your pop." Billy swallows as his shoulders slump a little. "Smartest man I ever knew. Could hide money like nobody. Without him, Papa couldn't have done business like he did. The feds never had nothing."

"Why didn't you stay in touch, you know...after he was shot?" I twirl my wine glass by the stem, straightening it quickly when I almost spill some.

"I tried," he says and clears his throat. "Lisa...your mom wouldn't let me. Said she wanted a clean break, no contact at all...fresh start for both of you away from our world."

"I felt like I lost you too." My throat's thick and it hurts to swallow. "Mom won't talk about you or Dad or anything to do with what happened that day." I use my napkin to catch a tear. "I've always had this hole I couldn't fill. Guess it's why I'm back here in San Fran, looking for some sort of closure."

"I'm sorry, honey," he says softly. He reaches for my hand and squeezes. "Know it was painful, but Lisa was protecting you."

"I wanted to remember him, and it was like she was trying *not* to."

"Lisa happy now?"

"I guess so. She's remarried and he's a decent guy. Treats her well."

"What about you? He treat you well?"

"He's fine. I sympathize, because no one will take Dad's place, but he's tried to fill the gap."

"Wish it'd been different." He lets go of my hand and breaks off a small piece of bread and dips it into a bowl of olive oil and balsamic vinegar. "Glad you're back because I missed that beautiful face and maybe now would be a good time to tell me who damaged it."

"Yeah!" I suck air through my teeth then chew on my thumbnail. "I've got a problem."

Billy snorts and rubs his thighs. I brace myself to tell him the PG version and figure I may as well just blurt it out. "So, I met this guy."

"Uh huh."

"And he pursued me, was really persistent actually, until I said yes."

"How long?"

"How long he pursued me? Does it matter?"

"Just trying to get a picture on this prick"

"Ah...about a month I guess."

"Mm hmm. And then?"

"Well, things were good at first and after about three weeks of dating he became super possessive. Don't know if it's because I hadn't slept with him yet or what, but one night I smiled at a waiter when he brought our drinks and he lost his shit. Called me a cock-tease and a slut then hit me."

"In front of everyone?" His brows are raised.

"No. We were at a bar after work. It was busy and he had my arm twisted behind my back. Almost broke it forcing me outside into an alley. Then...um..." I clear my throat and take a deep breath. "He...kissed me really hard...*brutally* hard and the next thing I knew his hand was coming towards my face and I was on the ground. He left me there."

"Fucking hell, kiddo."

"Yeah. It kind of sucked."

"How did you get home?"

"Uber."

"When did this happen?"

"Monday."

"Do you love him?"

"At first I thought I could. Now he disgusts me."

"What's his name?"

"Let's just call him the ex, considering I don't want another Darren McGee situation."

"Honey, a man like that doesn't deserve consideration from you."

"I know, Billy. I hear you. I just..."

"Not going to hurt him, I don't do that no more."

I know he's saying that for my benefit, to take what guilt I might feel for any retribution, but I can't tell him. Just like I couldn't tell Gianni.

"I own a bakery now," he continues. "Tell me this...is he still bothering you?"

I shrug, and choose not to tell him Dean pounded on my door last night.

"How can I help?"

"Thinking I need something small and clean, something that will fit in my purse."

"Do you still know how to use one?"

"Puh-lease." I arch a brow. "You're the one who taught me how to shoot."

"Still a sequoia tree in Woodside with a bunch of lead in it. Often wonder if we killed it."

"We sure killed that poster of Osama bin Laden."

"Good face for a target," he agrees. "Okay, but we're gonna practice some. I wanna make sure you're not rusty."

Grateful and relieved that part's over, I summon a smile and refill our glasses with wine. "You said you own a bakery?"

His face lights up. "Yep, called the Flour Barrel. My nephew, Carmine, runs it. I fronted the money and earn a portion of the profits." Billy grins and rubs his girth. "He does a good job, as you can tell."

I shake my head, picturing Billy in an apron.

Our food arrives and he checks his with a suspicious eye, throwing a glance at Maureen. The woman looks down her nose, blows a bubble in her gum and walks away.

My taste buds explode when I fork a mouthful of Tortellini Alfredo. Billy examines his, moving it around, searching for signs of anything odd. He sighs and takes a leap of faith, spooning spaghetti and a chunk of meatball into his mouth. Since we eat in silence, it must have passed scrutiny and we stop only to sip on wine.

The city lights begin to blink on. Our window faces Fillmore Street and I turn my attention to jaywalking pedestrians, honking cars and storefronts casting fluorescent shadows.

Lost in the rhythm of the city, it takes a moment for my brain to register a low rumble. At first, I think it's thunder, then my view is blocked by nothing but orange.

My heart rate spikes into the red zone

Ohmifuckingword...Dean's Ferrari.

Billy's engrossed in his meatballs and doesn't notice me splutter on a half-swallowed sip of wine.

Maybe it's not him. Maybe it's just a coincidence. Surely there's more than one orange Ferrari in San Francisco?

That delusion is immediately shattered by the car window rolling down and Dean's blonde head appearing, back-lit by the interior light. He looks right at me. Our eyes lock and that adrenaline prickle spreads from my toes to my scalp.

He revs the engine, attracting everyone in the restaurant's attention. Drivers behind him lay on their horns, but he ignores them, forcing cars to drive around blasting their horns and flipping him off. The whole time he holds my gaze. And just to be a dick, he lifts two fingers and blows a kiss.

"What the hell is Melnikov's problem?"

Ripping my eyes from Dean, I stare at Billy. "You know him?"

"Of him."

My stomach plummets and I can almost feel the blood draining from my face.

Glancing up from twirling his spaghetti, he looks at me, at Dean, then back at me. And it dawns.

His cinnamon eyes get wide. "Holy fucking fuck." He jerks a thumb towards the window. "Him?"

Before I can answer, Dean blasts the horn and we turn to glare. Well, Billy does. I mainly just stare, unable to do anything else. Then Dean cocks his head, winks and pulls away.

My eye twitches, so I press a finger to the muscle and it occurs to me that if Billy recognizes him this is way worse than I thought. The question is, precisely how much worse?

"Shelley?" Billy slumps in his seat, dropping the uneaten pasta with a dull metallic thud. "Tell me that isn't him."

I stare at my half-eaten food. "It's him."

"Did you tell him you were here?"

"No." As the knowledge sinks in my head jerks up. "I didn't know we were coming here."

"That motherfucker," he growls, picking up his glass and draining it in one gulp. Those lovable eyes have changed from warm and soft to hard and cutting and I get why people were so afraid of him. "You're gonna need more than a gun."

Swallowing, I sink back into my own chair. “Probably, but a gun is a good start.”

“What do you know about him?” he asks, massaging little circles in his temples.

“He told me he was a hedge fund manager.”

“A hedge fund manager...ugh.” Billy squeezes his eyes shut and rubs more vigorously. “Kiddo, I hate to tell you this, but he ain’t no hedge fund manager. Wouldn’t trust him with my money.” Then his eyes pop back open. “You didn’t give him any, did you?”

“Do I look like I have any *to* give?”

His brows meet in the middle. “What about...? Never mind.”

Huh...what money does he think I have?

After he wipes his mouth on a napkin, he pulls out his wallet and drops a fifty and two twenties on the table. I can’t help thinking that’s a good tip for a waitress with an attitude.

“Come on, I’m gonna introduce you to an old friend.” Billy flashes a wave to Maureen then ushers me out of the restaurant, his hand resting between my shoulder blades. “Alfie’s only a block from here.”

“Who’s he?” I ask, hunching my shoulders and covering my face with my scarf against the wind.

“Probably don’t remember him but he’s from the old days. Alfie used to be our weapons man. Still dabbles a little.”

We turn into an alley next to a New Age book store and walk to the end of a small six-car parking lot. We hustle up a flight of rickety wooden stairs. Billy knocks on an apartment door that looks like the last time it saw paint was during the gold rush.

Rusty hinges creak as the door opens and a short, shrunken man appears. Wispy silver hair lifts in the wind and skinny arms poke out of a white tank top hanging over black chinos. He looks mildly familiar.

“Alfie.” Billy grips his hand.

"Billy, you fat bastard," Alfie wheezes. "What you doing here? You bring me company?"

"This is Shelley, Jimmy De Luca's girl. She's in trouble and we need your help."

While I try to place him and hide my surprise, I offer my hand. I've gotta admit, I was expecting the stereotypical large, Italian goombah, not this tiny person.

"Jimmy, the money man?" He takes my hand in his and brushes my fingers with an air kiss. "You look just like him," he says, waving us in. "Only much prettier."

I respond to his smile and step inside, boot heels click-clacking on scratched parquet flooring as I enter a time capsule from the fifties.

The furniture's minimal and boasts the typical pointy, splayed legs so popular during that time. Except for the sixty-inch flat-screen TV mounted on his living-room wall, nothing else is from this century. A scene from *The Walking Dead*'s frozen on the screen and I instantly like him.

"Remember you, always running around with Joey." He shakes his head. "Poor bastard. Shoulda kept his nose clean. Saw you at his funeral talking with Gianni."

Aha! Now I remember him. The little old dude Billy was talking to.

He turns to Billy. "Get my bag from the room while I entertain Jimmy's girl." He flaps a hand, shooing him out of the room.

"Sit with me." He points to the couch. "You like *The Walking Dead*? I got the hots for Michonne. What a woman. Kick my ass I got outta line. Like 'em a little spicy."

Laughing would be rude so I press my lips together and pull them between my teeth.

"You look like you got a lotta spice in you."

"Some would say I'm a little too spicy."

"No such thing. A man's no man he can't handle spice. Makes life interesting."

He has a point.

Billy re-enters carrying an ancient brown leather suitcase and places it on a round, faded red, Formica-topped coffee table. Alfie undoes the straps and pops it open revealing a selection of handguns, neatly laid out in sponge. Seeing the one I want, I pick it up.

"This a Sig?" I ask.

Alfie nods.

"Clean?"

"Like bleach," Alfie says. "No serial numbers. Ain't nobody gonna trace that as long as you keep it clean. No prints, no DNA."

The 9mm slide is free of rust and the grip's rough in my palm. Feels good and not so big it wouldn't fit in my purse.

I hand it over to Billy, who does his own careful examination.

"Good choice." He nods.

"Who ya gonna whack with that?" Alfie asks.

"No whacking," I answer and hope it's the truth. "Protection only."

Alfie looks at Billy, studies him for a moment, then slides his eyes back to me. "Who's the son of a bitch who smacked your face?"

My face burns. "Um...my ex."

"Ex got a name?"

"You're sweet, Alfie, but I'd rather not say."

He grunts and flexes a depleted bicep adorned with what used to be a rose. "Not so strong no more, but I still got it. Anytime you need help."

I shake my head and blow out some air. 'Thank you. I'll let you know."

Damn.

“Never mind that now. Time to celebrate your new friend.” Alfie pats my knee, pushes himself up and shuffles into the kitchen, returning with three long-stemmed glasses and a bottle of grappa. After pouring he hands one to each of us. “To Joey, your pop, may they rest in peace, and to your safety. *Salute*

It’s the good stuff and goes down smoothly. Alfie offers more, I decline, having reached my alcohol limit, but Billy accepts. We watch the last few minutes of Darryl losing his kick-ass bike in the burned forest. When it’s over, Billy pays Alfie in cash, doling out more fifties.

Jeez, how much cash does he carry? Ten minutes later we’re back in his car, heading home with my new best friend stashed in my purse.

“Let me pay you back, Uncle Billy.”

“No,” he states. “Birthday present, take it.”

“Okay, but...”

“Be doing me a favor and I’ll sleep better knowing you have protection. You have a problem you call me or Gianni. We’ll come, no questions.”

He may, but I’m not so sure about Gianni.

I’m not sure I want to involve anyone else, but he’s right. I may as well get used to my new normal.

4

YOU'RE DANGEROUS

~

Back home, even though finding parking is almost impossible, Billy insists on riding the elevator up with me, ensuring no stalkers are camped at my door. After a quick walk through, he kisses me on the cheek.

"Call you in the morning, kiddo. Make sure you lock behind me."

My cozy little apartment is freezing but no longer stinks of burnt brownies, given we'd left the windows open. I shut them, set the thermostat to seventy-five and search my phone for some music.

The Black Keys' "I'll Be Your Man" pair with my speakers and, still loose from the booze, I sing along while I undress until my phone pings interrupting the music.

Cass. My BFF and boss. *How's the flu? Need me to bring you chicken soup?*

Crap.

I hate lying to her but I can't have her checking on me. Cass disliked Dean and *I told you so's* aren't anything I want to deal with.

Me: *I'm good thanks. Love you for asking.*

Cass: *When you coming back to work? Miss you.*

Me: *Tuesday xx*

I plug my phone into the charger in an outlet in the kitchen then hit my bathroom. After a shower, I lotion up and slip into my favorite pink flannel pajamas, missing the top button. I don't care. Not like anyone's here to see me and I smell like petunias.

A girl could do worse considering my eye's improved somewhat. The swelling is down but the color's a different story. As I'm about to sip some tea and play with my new toy, a knock on my door makes me jump.

Please not Dean, please not Dean, I chant to myself.

I have no bullets for my gun yet, but the Sig will inflict enough damage if I have to hit him in the head. When I peer through the peephole, my eyebrows spring up an inch and I lose my breath.

Good God!

It's Gianni, looking intense and dressed like a biker straight off the cover of *Born to Ride* magazine. A stark contrast to the tailored suit he wore yesterday. I'd forgotten how well he fills out a pair of jeans and tonight the ones he wears mold extra well to certain male parts of his anatomy.

While he waits, he leans against the wall opposite my door, one leg bent at the knee, cradling a black helmet.

I wonder if he's still riding the Harley, because Gianni on that Harley is all kinds of hot. And I mean Habanero pepper kind of hot!

Cherry Meloni isn't wrong.

The man defines male, with the reputation to go along. No doubt a long trail of wet panties and broken hearts flutter in his wake.

I pull in a shaky breath, put on my game face and open the door, ignoring the way the needle on my hunk-o-meter spikes.

Hoo boy.

We stare at each other for several long heartbeats but I refuse to be the first to break eye contact.

"Well?" he says, straightening and taking a step forward, not letting me win.

"Well, what?"

"Hello would be a good start."

Asshole.

"Hello works both ways, Gianni."

"You gonna invite me in or stand there staring at me?" That gaze finally drops and does a slow scan of my body, stopping at my pink toenails and leaving me...well, a little flustered. At least my toes match my pajamas and I bite back a smile at my small victory. Wouldn't do to gloat, especially as I'm going to be stupid and let him in.

I step aside.

"What are you doing here?"

He ignores my question and as he brushes past me flicks my pajama top collar.

"Cute. Had these since you were...what, twelve?"

Yep. I allow myself a mental eye roll. *STUPID.*

"Wow. Still a smart ass, huh."

He smirks, and shrugs out of his leather jacket. Too bad for me that hard stomach is covered by a tight, light blue tee-shirt. I can see the valleys in between his muscles and if I had underwear on, I'd be needing to change them soon.

As it is, my stomach quivers and I'm having a hard time breathing. Like his presence sucked out all the oxygen in the room.

"Why are you here?" I ask again, cursing inwardly as my voice comes out all breathy.

"Maybe I just want to see you."

A girl can wish. However, my flirt-alert flag's a-flying bright and strong and I need to remind myself he's taken.

Off limits.

"Somehow, I doubt that."

Those gorgeous eyes narrow. "Why would you doubt it?"

I shrug, and he doesn't press any further. Instead he digs into his jacket pocket and pulls out my sunglasses.

"Thought I'd be nice and bring you these." He places them on my coffee table, slowly and without taking his eyes off me. When he's upright again, he moves a step closer. That quivery feeling's grown to a full body shiver.

"Unless you're planning on shooting me, De Luca, I suggest you put the gun away."

Only, I'm not paying attention to his words, because I'm distracted by how close he is and how good he smells. Clean and manly, but without the spicy aftershave he wore yesterday. Just him. I swallow.

"Shelley."

"What?"

"Give me the gun."

A tiny, evil part of me hopes I'm making him as nervous as he's making me. "Not sure I want to." He doesn't have to know there're no bullets in the chamber.

"I'm not your enemy, babe." He moves forward and I move back, bumping into the barstool carrying his jacket. It tips a little, trapping me between it and his thighs.

Long fingers wrap around mine. "Let go, Shelley, before one of us gets hurt."

I can't. Though his hands are warm, I'm frozen and we stand like that for what seems a really long time.

"Not going to hurt you." His breath whispers across my temple. "Relax."

I relax, but only because I think I'm melting and not from any conscious action on my part.

Big, warm hands engulf mine, then pointing the gun away and towards the corner, he uncurls my fingers. My mind can't seem to process as he leans in, reaching past me to place the Sig on the breakfast bar.

All of me is pressed against all of him and I can't help it, but I have to breathe. Which means when I inhale, I inhale *him.* This stirs me up, but in a really good, yet really bad way.

"Um..."

"Yeah?"

Remember, I remind myself, the bastard knows exactly what he's doing, looking down at me with eyes that aren't so cool anymore, but nice and warm and all kinds of playful.

One of us moves. Could've been me, but my breasts rub against him, hardening my nipples and shooting bolts of electricity all the way down *there*. That hard torso tenses as he emits a small grunt and that square, yummy jaw with all that wonderful stubble clenches.

God, I want to kiss him. Wrap my arms around his neck, grab that thick hair and pull him down and taste his mouth.

But I can't. I blink, surprised I'm not spontaneously combusting on the spot, pull my hand from his, put both to that solid wall that's his chest and push. He moves, but not enough for me to step aside.

"Move," I say, perhaps not quite as firmly as I should.

"I'm kinda liking where I'm at."

Indeed he is, if the growing ridge in his pants pressed against me is an indication, and good lord, he's tempting. Not gonna lie, but so not the point.

"What are you doing?" I whisper.

"Testing something."

Testing what? How easily I'll give in to him? If he still has that power I tried desperately to hide, but am sure he knew he always had over me? I force my eyes to get hard and push against him again. "I said step aside."

He sighs, looking almost disappointed and moves back, and only when I'm clear, I realize I'm trembling. Not from fear, however. I clear my throat.

"How do you know where I live?"

He doesn't answer immediately, and I get the feeling that, erection aside, he's not unaffected by what just happened. Like he needs a moment too.

At last, he answers. "Billy might have told me."

I'm going to kill him.

"You should've called first. You know, good manners and all that stuff."

"Maybe." Seemingly recovered, his eyes crinkle at the corners. "But if I had, I wouldn't have had the pleasure of seeing you in your little-girl pajamas."

Dammit, why does he have to smile?

In all the years I knew him before, I'd seen him smile of course. Always aimed at the women he was with and never at me. Maybe a little upturn of his lips, or a lip twitch indicating he found me funny, (probably of the peculiar kind and not the ha-ha kind), but never so it hit his eyes.

Except once. And that was the day I fell for him. At a Giants game. I caught a foul ball, beating out both Joey and Gianni. Joey was mildly pissed. However, when I looked at Gianni expecting him to be mad that a girl beat him too, instead he looked really proud and gave me *that* smile.

My heart tumbles and skips a beat at the memory. Makes me hate all those women who got to see that side of him. And there were a lot.

He only breaks eye contact when he picks up my phone from the breakfast bar and pushes some buttons.

"What're you doing?" I ask again. It seems my vocabulary is limited to a few phrases around him. I snatch at it but he's too fast and too tall, holding it above his head.

"You reading my texts? Give that back to me."

"What's your passcode."

"I'm not giving you my passcode."

"Either give me your passcode or your phone number. You choose."

"Why do want my number?"

"Don't be dense, De Luca."

"Don't be a jerk."

God, he makes me act like I'm sixteen again. If I want it, I'm going to have to move close and I'm thinking this isn't such a smart idea. So, I back off, choose the safest option and give him my passcode. It's not like he's going to remember it after tonight anyway.

He thumbs some digits, hits the green button and a moment later his phone in the back pocket of his jeans rings before he disconnects.

"You think I want to call you?"

He shrugs. "You're gonna need me at some point. May as well get this outta the way."

My eyes roll a little but not with any vigor. "What could I possibly need you for?"

"I can think of several good reasons, but shit happens in our world. And when it does, you'll need me. Or call me even if shit doesn't happen. I'm open either way."

Was he implying I should be his booty-call fuck buddy? Very, *very* tempting, but I'm not heading down that path.

Noop.

"I'm not in your world anymore. Give me my phone." I hold out my hand, but he ignores me and finishes entering his information. When he hands it back to me, I'm careful to avoid his fingers.

"Under G for Gianni," he says.

"Not A for Asshole?"

He doesn't laugh, but his lips quirk, making the muscles between my legs do a little quirking of their own.

"Speaking of manners, De Luca, where are yours? Didn't your mother teach you anything?"

Since I don't trust my voice, I simply stare.

"You should be offering me something to drink for bringing back your sunglasses."

Shit.

"I only have wine."

"That'll do."

Of course it will, he's Sicilian. I let out a big sigh and drop to my haunches to select a bottle of my best red from the rack under the breakfast bar. Ironically a gift from Dean, but it's delicious and if I'm going to be drinking more alcohol, it may as well be primo.

When I rise, he's wandered to the chest of drawers, which holds a photo of myself and my parents, taken when I was sixteen. The last family picture before my dad died.

While he studies it, his face is grave. "Your dad was a good man. You must miss him."

I nod and keep my eyes on him, watching as he works his throat. Next, he moves on to the amber necklace I left next to the photo.

He turns it over, and the way he runs a thumb over the letters that spell my name scrolled into the silver on the back seems almost tender. The hair on my arms rise, like they did when I first picked it up. Like Joey was suddenly in the room with us again.

Gianni stills and holds it for so long I wonder if he feels it too. I expect him to ask me about it. When he doesn't, I can't decide if I'm relieved or disappointed.

After returning the heart to its place on the dresser, he saunters back to me but something's definitely shifted. The air's thicker, full of that same crackly vibe I sensed yesterday at the funeral. His expression is pensive, but gives me no clue as to what he's thinking.

Confused, I push the wine over the granite towards him, along with my corkscrew. He catches it mid slide and examines the label while I reach up to grab two glasses hanging from underneath the cabinet. Thanks to the missing button, my pajama top gapes open and suddenly my naked boob is pointing straight at his face.

Crud.

It was subtle, but I heard it. The hiss that passed across his lips, but what affected me more was the way his body went taut, how he stilled.

My belly tightens in response and I'd be lying if I didn't admit I liked how he closed his eyes in a slow blink. And that it took longer than it should before he resumed twisting the cork out of the bottle.

My face flushes, but I manage to adjust my top without making too much of a big deal out of it. After all, it's not my fault he showed up unannounced catching me in my oldest and least sexy pajamas. And I'm sure he's seen more than his fair share of boobs. My meager C cups won't be starting any wars or launching a thousand dirty fantasies any time soon. Not when he has access to a pair of double Ds.

He's silent while he uncorks the wine. On the surface he looks relaxed, but something about the way he pours suggests he's not. As he passes me a glass our fingers touch and a tingle shoots up my arm. When that tingle passes over my nipples and hits my center, my teeth dig into my lip. It's a defensive move, not a flirtatious one. Supposed to suppress the little gasp threatening to escape. But that isn't how he reads it.

His gaze lifts from my lip and when our eyes lock, his have gone steely.

"Are you fucking with me, Shelley?" His words, though spoken mildly, carry a hint of danger.

"Uh…excuse me?"

"You should know by now, I'm not a man you fuck with."

"Okay," I whisper, only because I don't know what else to say, before it occurs to me to find my lady balls. The man is in my house and being a jerk, even if it is standard behavior with him. "Except you don't get to do that here."

"Do what?"

"Drink wine and be a jerk in my house."

The silence stretches while he holds my eyes, searching them for what, I couldn't say. Then, in typical bi-polar Gianni fashion he does a one-eighty.

"You're right," he capitulates. "That was rude. I'd hate for you to have a reason to want to use your Sig on me. How about we toast to Joey instead?"

I nod but avoid his gaze when we tap glasses, though I feel the weight of his.

"Rest, little brother," he murmurs. "I hope you find some peace."

Those words send a chill down my spine and I wonder if perhaps he had felt Joey in the room the way I did a few minutes ago when he was touching my necklace.

"You said you talked to him?" he asks.

"I did."

"And…?"

"And nothing."

"This isn't pulling teeth, De Luca."

"I'm not trying to be difficult, Gianni, there's really not

much to say. We talked on the phone and he asked me to dinner. That's it. What I'm wondering is why this surprises you."

Something flickers across his face and for the millionth time I wish I could read what was going on inside that handsome head.

"Never mentioned he saw you. Were you two dating again?"

For a moment I consider lying, to see his reaction, but I decide no. I'm not into playing mind games. "No, we weren't.'

"How about telling me when you got back to San Francisco?"

"Three months ago, but why does that matter?"

A muscle in his jaw ripples. "Explains a few things. Were you ever gonna come by and say hello?"

"To you?" My brow creases.

"Yeah, De Luca. To me."

I have no answer to that as I'm not about to tell him that to preserve my sanity I'd erased him from my head.

He studies me for a while, then gives a little shake of his head, like he was about to divulge something, but changed his mind.

"*Were* you seeing him again?" The pitch in his voice lowers and for some reason he seems more imposing. As if that big, solid body got bigger. "And this time I want the truth."

"I already told you no. Why do you keep asking?"

"He was my brother and if..."

"Yeah? He was your brother and you never thought I was good enough for him. Probably still think it, don't you? You were always such an asshole to me."

He puts his glass down and takes a step closer, forcing me to look up into those eyes, now stormy and clouded yet shimmering in the low light.

"Yeah, I was. I'll admit that. Was it him?" he asks suddenly.

Huh? "Was what him?"

His finger brushes my cheek, just below my eye. "Did he hurt you?"

"No!" My eyes pop wide and I push his hand away. "Why does everybody think that?"

"You knew him so well, you tell me."

"Joey would never hurt me."

"You sure about that?"

Okay. He cheated on my ass but I'm pretty sure that isn't what he means.

"Yes, I'm sure, and you're too close."

"Then back up."

"You back up." I jam a finger into his chest. It may as well have been a fly because he doesn't even blink. "What's your problem with me, Gianni?"

"Don't have a problem with you, De Luca."

"Bullshit."

"You've got it backwards, woman."

"Backwards?" This time I use both hands to shove him away. It still has no effect on him, but the heat from his body burning through my hands sure has an effect on me.

Dammit.

"How?"

"Careful." He growls. "You put your hands on me you better be prepared for what you get."

"What am I going to get? More proof you're an asshole?"

"You need more proof?"

"Nope. Got all I need."

The next second, in less time than it takes to blink, one arm snakes around my waist slamming me flat against his body. The other tangles into my hair, tugging my head back.

I gasp, my fingers curling into his tee-shirt.

"The fuck you playing at?" A pulse beats wildly in his temple as his heart thumps against my knuckles.

His anger is hot and his body solid everywhere. He lowers his head, lips hovering over mine. My heartbeat ticks up and my mouth dries in anticipation. How would he taste? Like man, sex and wine? My tongue touches the split in my lower lip and he stiffens, then sucks in a hard breath and shuts his eyes. A moment later he pushes me away.

First disappointment, then rejection wrap around me in equal measures like the cold San Francisco fog. I turn away, mostly to hide the humiliation on my face.

"You're fucking dangerous," he says in a voice that's rough and a little harsh.

My brows furrow. *I'm dangerous?*

"I made a mistake coming here tonight." Then his gaze turns flat and drops to my mouth. "I'm gonna go before I do something stupid that we both regret."

"Then why *did* you come? You could've given my glasses to Billy, or, wow...here's a concept. Stuck them in the mail."

Really, how fucked up am I that not a single molecule in my body wants him to leave?

He stares at me for a long time before he hooks his jacket and tosses it over his shoulder.

"I'll let you figure that out," he mutters, snagging his helmet then marching to my door.

Thank God I have a healthy dose of pride, and do nothing to stop him.

Damn him.

He called *me* dangerous, but he's the one who has the power to ruin me, ruin my heart again and, therefore, probably my life.

I flop onto the barstool, rest my elbows on the counter and groan into my palms.

Dammit to hell.

His wine glass mocks me. I pick it up and consider throwing it across the room. Instead I place my lips on the faint smudge on the glass indicating where his lips were, and sip. Likely the closest thing to a kiss I'll ever have from him.

The *put-put* of Harley pipes breaks through the city noise below, and because I'm an idiot, I move to the window and watch him pull away from the curb and roar down the street.

Some men look good on a bike. Gianni looks like he was made for one. His tail lights glow red as he approaches a street sign and without coming to a complete stop, he turns the corner and disappears behind a building, into the night.

I stand at the window until I can't hear him anymore and I'm not sure how long it takes after that before I become aware of the tears sliding down my cheeks.

5

WHAT'S GOOD FOR THE GOOSE

~

Saturday dawns clear and beautiful. Birds chirping, angels singing and all that shit. The same can't be said about my head. It pounds from lack of sleep, too many tears and way too much alcohol.

I'd love to waste the day in bed watching TV, wallowing in misery. Too bad my phone's vibrating on my kitchen counter with a text.

Groaning, I stick my toes out from underneath my warm old comforter, testing the air before slipping off the bed and into the kitchen. With each step my frontal lobe thumps, punishing me.

Thoughts of Gianni's rejection play on a loop in my head and regardless of what I did or how much wine I drank, (which was a lot) they were there to stay.

My phone, lying next to the Sig, vibrates again.

Billy: *Target practice at ten. Bringing breakfast.*

Crap.

According to my phone that's an hour from now. No chance

of going back to bed and sleeping today away. I blow air through my lips, making a sound that reminds me of a Harley, so I stop.

After setting my coffee pot to brew, I pop two Advil, hit the shower, then stop dead at my reflection in the mirror.

Lovely!

A hungover vampire with a shiner.

As the coffee aroma wafts through my apartment, my stomach grumbles. I pour a cup, add milk and sugar and wait for the magic to work. After my second cup, and slightly less hungover, I shimmy into skinny blue jeans, a hooded pink sweatshirt and thick-soled, clunky combat boots I bought from an army surplus store.

Billy arrives, bearing a white box full of freshly baked goodies and my apartment smells like a French patisserie.

"You're going to make me fat if you keep feeding me like this," I say, biting into a chocolate covered doughnut. It's warm sweetness dissolves in my mouth and suddenly my day already looks better.

"These are fantastic. You weren't kidding when you said Carmine did a good job."

Billy grunts as he bites into a bear claw. "Told you."

"Okay, you're forgiven," I say.

"For what? For feeding you?"

"For telling Gianni where I live. I was contemplating shooting *you* last night."

He shoots me a sideways look. "Why's that a problem?"

"He was here."

"Again...why is that a problem?"

"It depends on what you told him."

"About Melnikov?" His thick black eyebrows rise.

I nod.

"We didn't talk about him. It was before I came over. He said he wanted to return your sunglasses. Was that not why he came?" He's still eyeing me.

I shrug and look away. "I think he's curious about me and Joey." I take another nibble, swallowing it with the last of my coffee. Billy hands me his mug. I point to the pot, but he shakes his head and I dump them in the sink.

"What *about* you two?" he asks.

"There was nothing. We hung out a couple times. If Dean thought I was seeing anyone else, things wouldn't have gone down well."

"Things *didn't* go down well, kiddo."

No shit.

"Let me ask you, what did Alfie mean by suggesting Joey should've stayed out of trouble?" I wash the two mugs with a soapy sponge and place them on a wooden dish drainer.

"He had issues. Stuck his nose into something he shouldn't have."

I snort. "The whole family is into something they shouldn't be."

"Not so much anymore. Things have changed since you've been gone. Gianni's gone legit."

"Legit?" I pull my head back in surprise. "Are you kidding me?"

"Nope. Ever since the old man died five years ago."

Wow.

"He's a good man, Shelley. Don't judge him too harshly."

"What makes you think I'm judging him?"

He gives me a *don't be stupid* look.

I sigh.

"You could use one in your life."

Yeah. Problem is he's not available and he rejected me.

"That's what I have you for." I squeeze his arm. "Are you

done? Let's head out, it's a gorgeous day and I hate to waste a well-caffeinated sugar buzz."

Even if I am still hungover.

Billy chuckles and closes the pastry box while I grab my keys and sunglasses. I stash Ziggy, the Sig, in my purse and hustle Billy out my apartment door, making sure to lock the deadbolt.

"Where're we going?" I ask as I push the down button for the elevator.

"Shooting range on the Peninsula. A friend of mine runs it, so behave yourself." He gives me a look that tells me he's only half joking.

I pout. "I'll do my best."

We reach the lobby and exit through the doors, dodging a young couple coming in. The woman, my neighbor, shoots me a smile as she passes by. This must be the third guy she's brought home this week. Lucky her! I can't even get *one* to kiss me. Doesn't do much for my self-esteem.

We step outside into the late fall sunshine. There's no wind and the bay glitters like a giant blue sapphire. Seagulls are everywhere. Two screech and fight over the remains of a roast-beef sandwich someone dropped on the sidewalk.

We cross the hilly street, wait for a passing car and climb into a red Land Rover. After we merge into the city traffic I take a deep breath, bracing myself for things I may not want to hear. But if I don't ask now, I probably never will and I have to know.

"Billy, what do you remember about Dad's murder? Did they ever figure out who killed him?"

"No, kiddo." His voice carries a tinge of regret. "Just a random drive-by. Your dad was in the wrong place at the wrong time."

"Random." I shake my head and turn in my seat to face him. "You know how many times Mom said that? Just a random accident."

He takes his eyes off the road for a second, his expression solemn.

"I have issues with that."

"I get it." He nods. "I had issues with that for years. Asked around, because, believe me, I wanted to kill the bastard. Lost my best friend that day and somebody was gonna pay."

"I can't help thinking there was more to it."

"I was angry for a long time," he says, "but I kept getting the same answers over and over. Nobody knew anything and at some point, I had to let it go and that wasn't easy for me."

"Mom never shared details. What happened, exactly?"

"She didn't for a reason, honey. You sure you wanna know?

"If I don't, I'll always wonder. And if I'm always wondering, how can I move past it?"

Billy grunts, seemingly wrestling with sharing the details. "Remember Papa's brother Joseph?"

"Uncle Joe?" Joeys namesake. "I met him at the Sea Cliff house many times. Who could forget that nose?"

"Poor bastard got his looks from the *other* side of the family."

"Or those eyebrows," I say. "They were like black caterpillars. I kept waiting for them to turn into demonic butterflies and take off."

"That was him." He clears his throat and takes a moment before he continues. "Anyhow, they were in a meeting at Joe's restaurant and the bullet came from the street. Hit your dad in the throat and he bled out. There was nothing anyone could do."

"In the throat?"

"Yup."

God.

My sugar high nose dives.

"Who was in the meeting?"

"Papa, Joe and your dad as far as I know."

"Was it a hit? I always wondered if Papa or Uncle Joe knew anything."

"No." He's silent for a long moment. "That I'm certain about. I checked it out. Quietly, of course. Jimmy was valuable. Too much information went with him."

Tears burn the corners of my eyes. My father lying on the dirty floor of a grubby little restaurant. Bleeding to death, choking on his own blood is not something I visualized before.

"God, that's messed up. No wonder Mom never wanted to tell me. I guess she didn't want that in my head."

Billy nods, and digs in his pants' pocket. The Land Rover swerves a little when he pulls out a handkerchief and passes it to me. I eye it, grateful it looks clean, then blow my nose.

"Always thought it was a retaliation thing, you know," I say after a while. By now we're heading south on Highway 101, about to leave the city and I stare at the traffic, not really seeing anything.

"We all did. For a long time. The Cadoras were in a beef with the Caruso family at the time, but they weren't involved," Billy says quietly.

"The Carusos? I remember them trying to inch in on Uncle Joe's chop shops." Even though I was protected from the details of whatever went down about the encroachment, I still heard things. Like Mickey Caruso, second-in-line and son of Frankie Caruso, fire-bombed Uncle Joe's garage. He ended up with a bullet in both his legs. I never knew who put them there, but I had my suspicions. Billy wasn't the enforcer for nothing.

"Yep. Bad bunch of fuckers, most of them dead or in prison. Partnered with the Russians. Big mistake."

"I never understood why Mom made us leave so suddenly. I always thought since everyone we knew was here, it would have been safer for us to stay."

"What matters is, it made sense to her at the time. You all got settled in a new life and she didn't want to uproot you again."

"How sure are we it was random?"

"No one copped to it. Ever! And that just don't happen. I had feelers out, all my informants had their ears open. Someone always talks, they get drunk and stupid enough. But no one did."

We drive in silence while I process this. Finally, we take an exit, a left, another left, and pull into an empty parking lot. The shooting range is next to a tidal canal fed from the bay where several Canada geese have taken up residence.

A lone pair stretch their necks and honk as we select a spot. One makes a show of spreading its wings and flapping them.

"You okay?" Billy asks me, eyeing the birds, assessing the risk of getting out of the car.

I sigh and nod. "I'll be fine. All of this is new and I still don't understand why she'd never talk to me."

"Need a minute?"

I shake my head. "Let's do it. It'll take my mind off." I blow my nose again and shove the handkerchief into my purse. Then pull my hair into a ponytail.

"Right," Billy says. "Let's head in there before the masses arrive. We've a private session."

He opens the door and steps out of the car. "Jesus," Billy exclaims, side-stepping the pair of pissed-off geese. "What the hell is up with these birds?"

They honk and stalk us as we cross the parking lot until we're out of their territory, entering through double glass doors into a large front room. Posters of the Avengers and X-Men decorate drab, gun-metal gray walls, but other than that, the place is pretty stark.

A tall, muscular man in a tight camouflage tee-shirt standing behind the L-shaped glass counter recognizes Billy.

"Son of a bitch," he says, his face lighting up. "How you

doing, man?" He and Billy do some complicated man-greeting, hooking fingers and bumping fists, while I admire a bulging arm inked with a saluting soldier wrapped in an American flag.

"And who's this?" His eyebrows shoot up as his gaze rests on my black eye.

"I'm Shelley." I extend my hand.

"Okay," he says, taking it. "I get it." His grin dims a little. "You need protection from the dipshit who pounded on your face. I'm Bob, by the way."

He has moss green eyes, dark auburn hair in need of a cut and a very nice boy-next-door face. He holds my hand, still grinning until I let out a self-conscious giggle.

"Let her go, Bob," Billy interrupts, frowning, looking between Bob and myself. "She can't shoot when you're holding onto her."

"Yes sir," Bob responds, flicking Billy a grin. He indicates with his head. "This way."

Once inside an office, he reaches out his hand. "I have to inspect your weapon and ammo, check they're in good shape." He shrugs without taking his eyes off me. "Protocol."

I remove Ziggy from my purse and pass her over.

He checks her, breaking her down into separate components, inspecting the barrel and other parts before putting her back together again.

"Nice choice," he pronounces. "The Sig's a good weapon as long as you take care of her. Make sure you clean after each use."

He fits us with safety glasses and protective ear-gear and leads us down a long hallway to the shooting booth while going over some rules. "Load your weapon. Let me see your stance."

I load the magazine, slide it into the Sig, then place my left leg in front, angle my pelvis slightly and take aim.

"Not bad," he says, adjusting my hips. His hands linger a

little, which I find not entirely unpleasant. Problem is, they're not Gianni's.

"Widen your feet," Bob says, and waits until I do. "Okay, let's see what you can do."

I aim and squeeze the trigger.

Hmm.

I missed the circle, but not by much.

"Impressive. Again," Bob orders.

I repeat the process and after a little more instruction, I shoot for the next twenty minutes until my arm cramps and my stomach rumbles.

My aim has improved enough that my groupings are consistent and Ziggy and I are now close friends. So I call it a day.

"Let's go have some real food. My treat, Uncle Billy."

"Sounds good, I could use a burger."

"I know just the place down in the Marina District."

We pack up, hand the safety gear to Bob, who's back at the front desk checking in the morning crowd.

This time he hugs me goodbye and I feel his gaze following me as we approach the doors. When I look back, he smiles. He's cute and I appreciate the attention but a pair of hot blue eyes that don't belong to Bob pop into my head.

Sigh!

I force a smile and throw Bob a wave.

The parking lot is much fuller now, though it hasn't deterred the two geese standing sentinel in between the Land Rover and a banged-up Volvo station wagon.

We slow, unwilling to provoke them, but it doesn't take much. By the look in their eyes, I'd swear they've been waiting as they make a beeline towards us, hissing.

"Shit." Billy stops dead, not taking his eyes off them. "They're out to kill us! What the hell are you wearing? You got goose pheromones in your perfume?"

"What? I'm not wearing any. Maybe there's a nest nearby?"

"Nest, my ass. That one's out to do murder. I recognize that look."

As they get closer their hissing gets louder.

"You know what?" I snap my fingers and point at him. "I can run faster than you, so I'll lead them away from the car. Pick me up at the end of the parking lot."

How hard can this be?

"Good plan."

"Ready?"

"Make a lot of noise. GO!"

So I go.

"Goose...hey...goose." I jump and wave my arms. "Over here. Woo-hoo."

It works.

They turn and focus their dark pebble eyes on me, stretching and lowering their necks, picking up speed.

Gah!

To say I misjudged how fast they are is an understatement. I run towards the cross street, but I'd forgotten about my clunky combat boots. They're slowing me down and those damn assassin geese are speeding up.

"Hurry up, Billy!" I yell over my shoulder, catching sight of the Land Rover backing out of the spot. Fucking hell, not fast enough.

The lead goose gallops and bounces towards me, flapping and honking until only a few yards separate us. He snaps, getting closer by the second.

Outrunning them is not working. I change posture, jutting my hips forward while swiping an arm behind me, hoping to deflect any bites to my ass.

"Shit!" I squeal as one lands a nip on my butt. "You got me, you bastard."

Not fucking working!

"Hurry up," I shout again. "Ow, *ow*!"

Okay, time to change tactics.

I swing my purse. This might have worked if there'd only been one, but they're tag teaming me, one on either side. Just as I connect with a roundhouse kick, the Land Rover pulls up next to me, tires screeching. Billy revs the engine and beeps the horn. The two geese part and back off, but only for a second. That's all I need. I yank open the door and launch myself ass first into the car, pull in my legs and slam the door.

"Woo!" I palm my forehead. "Holy fizz pops, that was close." My heart pounds as I brush a loose strand of hair out of my face and click my seatbelt. Then lean back, breathing hard.

It takes me a moment to realize we're not moving. Instead, little piggy snorts and high-pitched *hee-hees* fill the SUV. The gear clicks and I squint at Billy. His head rests on his forearms, which are draped over the steering wheel, shoulders shaking. Tears roll down his cheeks.

"Are you laughing at me?"

"Do you have any idea," he says in between snorts, "how funny you looked?"

"I'm molested by a goose and you're laughing?" I stare at him. "He's chewing on a chunk of my ass right now."

He wipes his eyes with the back of his hands, then mumbles, "Oh look, here come the rest of them for back-up," before he succumbs to another round.

I look behind, and sure enough, several more geese are heading our way.

"Next time, you run interference," I say, punching his upper arm. "I'll go for the car. See how amusing it is!" Despite that I find this annoying, not to mention painful, my mouth twitches and I end up giggling with him.

"Let's go eat, you big lug. I owe you a burger."

~

An hour later, at my favorite joint in the Marina District, I pick at the fries we ordered to share, dipping one into a mix of ketchup and Tabasco sauce and suck on a chocolate milkshake. No more alcohol for me. The restaurant is small and intimate with black-and-white photographs of ballplayers and flags on the walls.

Billy angles his burger, trying to fit it into his mouth, before giving up and cutting it in half.

"Tell me more about what Joey was into," I ask after he takes a bite.

He chews with his eyes closed, pointing a pinkie in the air. "Damn," he murmurs, grasping a napkin, wiping his face before taking a sip of beer. "That's a good burger. The one thing Papa was adamant about was no drugs. Gianni agreed. Joey didn't."

Oh no.

Now I've opened this can of worms, I'm not sure I want to hear anymore, but Billy's bent on educating me.

"Gianni had a hell of a time with him after the old man passed." He lifts his eyes to mine. "They were at each other constantly, but what Joey did?" He shakes his head. "That was a betrayal to Papa's memory. They didn't talk to each other for a long time. Another reason why Gianni decided to get out."

"What kind of drugs are we talking?"

"Cocaine."

"Shit." I drop my fry, suddenly losing my appetite. "Doing or dealing?"

"Supplying." He exhales. "I loved that little asshole and it cut me when I found out what he was into. Heard he had a partner and things went bad, blew back in his face."

"The last conversation we had, Joey said he had a problem with a business deal. Do we know who this partner is?"

He shrugs and takes another bite of his burger. "He kept that quiet, but I'm gonna find out."

I pull the band out of my hair, run my fingers through it before tying it again. "I knew there was something different about him." Sadness washes over me and I mourn for the old Joey, not who he'd become. "God, what was he thinking?"

"Don't think he was," he continues. "He changed after you and your mom left. If you ask me, I don't think he ever got over you. There were women, of course, but none that lasted."

"*He* dumped *me*, Uncle Billy, right after Daddy died. That doesn't say love to me."

"Yeah, he was young and stupid. Didn't understand any better."

"And I did?" I sit back in my seat and tuck a strand of hair behind my ear. "He's the main reason I find it difficult to trust men. My very first boyfriend cheats on me. Kinda set me up for life." The fact that my last one did too with a co-worker at my salon, doesn't help either.

"Joey ran around on you?"

"Yep."

"Shit." Billy's shoulders drop. "Did not know that. Sorry, kiddo."

"Didn't want to believe the rumors at first but Gloria Tortino confirmed it. Was going to give him a second chance then he dumped me."

"Gloria again."

"Yep. That girl was like herpes. Couldn't get rid of her."

"You were both young."

"Still hurt." I swirl the straw around in my shake. "Anyway, moving on." God help me, but I can't help asking. "What's Gianni up to now he's gone legit?"

"Owns a construction company and a bunch of apartment buildings. Bitch of it is, the brothers got over their beef, mostly because of their mom, I'm sure. But Joey had just started working with him. That's where they found him."

"Wait, found him where? In one of Gianni's buildings?" My eyes get wide.

He nods. "In a vacant unit he's remodeling."

Oh God.

I collapse back in my seat just as my phone pings with an incoming text. I don't recognize the number but my brain lights up like a marquee sign the moment I read it.

Hey Baby, think that fat asshole and a gun can keep me from you?

Billy stills, with his burger halfway to his face.

"What?"

I turn my phone so he can read the text.

He sighs and puts down his food. "Okay, this fuck's really pissing me off. Give me your phone." I pass it to him and he enters the number into his own, pushes send and puts it on speaker.

Dean answers on the fourth ring.

"*Da.*"

Wait? Isn't *da* yes in Russian?

"Yo, Deano," Billy says. "How you doing?"

"Who's this?"

"What? You don't recognize me? My feelings are hurt."

"Who the fuck is this?"

"The fat asshole with a gun."

Dead air dominates for several moments before Dean responds. "What do you want?"

"So sensitive. I'd expect a man who's trying to fuck me to be a little bit friendlier."

"Fuck you, you fat fuck."

Billy makes clicking noises with his tongue. "See, now that's what I'm talking about. No way to seduce me. I require a little loving, a little...tenderness. Maybe some candy and roses. I'd especially love it if you'd massage my feet. I got this..."

He's interrupted by an unintelligible torrent of what sounds like Russian dotted with a few *fuck yous* (not in Russian), then Dean hangs up.

I kinda want to laugh, but bite my lip instead when I see the look on Billy's face. "Was that wise?"

"Don't know, but fuck, I just put a couple things together."

"What's that?"

"That little prick is connected. Bet my bakery on it."

"Connected? Oh my God...you don't mean...?"

"Yep. To the Russian Mafia."

6

THE RUSSIAN WHAT?

~

Good God!

The Russian Mafia?

It's all starting to make sense. I didn't see it because I live in a bubble. A pretty, shiny, *fragile* bubble that just popped and went splat.

I drop my forehead on the table and groan and immediately bolt upright again, my eyes wide. "How does he know about Ziggy?"

"Same way he knew where you were last night. He's got people following you and I don't like how this is developing," Billy says. "Because it got more serious in the last five seconds." His gaze shifts to the window, scanning the street and buildings.

Yup.

Like him, I check for Dean's car, seeing nothing. But nothing doesn't mean nothing. It could very well mean something, just something I'm not seeing. Ergo...nothing!

I scrape a tooth over my thumbnail. At this rate, I'm going to have none left, because now I'm scared.

The frigging Russian Mafia. Those assholes are mean.

"Jesus, Billy. What do I do?"

"First, keep your gun with you at all times. Make sure when you clean and load it, you wear gloves. If you need to ditch it in a hurry, you won't have time to wipe the inside or shell casings of prints and DNA."

"Got it."

"Second, I want you to come home with me until this is sorted out."

"I don't want to be baggage, least of all yours, Uncle Billy."

"Kiddo, you're not baggage, you may not be blood but you're my family. We've got no choice. This text"—he points to my phone—"isn't nothing. You *gotta* take this seriously." His big hand covers mine. "Third, we need to bring more people in."

"More people?" My eyes go round, and my skin prickles because I know what he's going to say.

"I want Gianni on this."

Dammit.

"Absolutely not." I shake my head. "Not going there."

"Why the hell not?"

"Because we have history and...well."

"And well what?"

"Let's just say he's not going to waste time on me."

His head jerks back and his dark brows come together. "What are you talking about, kiddo?"

"I don't want to go into it, but trust me on this."

"Doesn't matter what your history is. That's not how this works. Don't you remember anything?"

"I'm beginning to realize there *is* a lot I've forgotten."

"Gianni's powerful and has the resources I—we need."

"You said he's gone legit."

"Yep, so?"

"So...? I don't understand."

"Nothing for you to understand. You're in danger and he can help."

"You're scaring me more than I already am."

"Should be scared. This fuckwad"—he points to my phone again—"is psycho. And if he's only half as psycho as I think he is, you're ankle deep. We'll form a plan, be prepared to act, and if nothing happens..." He shrugs. "But we gotta be ready. Don't be complacent 'cause I got a twinge in my bum leg telling me he's gonna do something."

I scan Billy's eyes, hoping he's joking. My belly drops when I realize he's not. I blow out air and turn my face to the window. Even the weather seems to agree with him. Heavy fog banks roll through the headlands, engulfing the bridge and the wind's picked up making the yachts in the marina sway.

"I'll owe him."

"Who?"

"Gianni." My eyes swing back to Billy's. "I can't owe him."

"No, kiddo, *I'll* owe him. It'll be my marker because he'll be doing this for me."

I meet Billy's eyes and big, fat, oily tears roll out of mine.

God, I love him.

My father's gone and the hole he left in my soul begins to fill a little with this man's love. It makes me determined to be brave and not let Dean intimidate me.

"We'll go straight to my house. I'll have one of Carmine's men pick up some of your things."

Carmine has men? That makes my head tilt. What kind of men?

"Um...wait. I don't want strangers going through my stuff. If I have to do this, I'd rather we go ourselves."

"Fair enough." He sighs, scrubbing his hands over his face. "All right, let's move."

While Billy drains the last of his beer and brushes crumbs

from his pants, I wave to the waiter for our check and hand him my credit card. I sign the merchant slip, grab my purse and check myself at Ziggy's unfamiliar weight. How long does it take to get used to having a gun in your bag?

The air's wet with fog and cold enough to bite through my clothes. In order to ward off the wind, I hook my arm through Billy's for warmth, cuddling up against him as we walk the half block to his Land Rover.

Before we cross the street, I check for cars. Only one double-parked. Halfway across I hear the engine gun and the high-pitched squeal of tires.

What the hell?

The driver's aiming the car straight for us and something about it is familiar. Before I can process, Billy shoves me hard, sending me sprawling towards the sidewalk. I land, scraping my knees and palms on the asphalt, between two cars.

There's a sickening, metallic thud and when I look up Billy's on the car's hood, arms and legs spread wide like a human star. The driver swerves and Billy rolls across the windshield then lands with a meaty thwack. Over all that, I hear a woman scream.

My stomach roils. The tires skid before gaining traction, then the car speeds away and turns the corner. I scramble and run towards Billy, realizing it's me screaming, dropping to me knees as I get close.

Fuck, no.

He lies crumpled in an unnatural heap looking dead. So very dead.

"Dear God...Billy."

Blood.

No, no, no.

Blood, every-fucking-where seeps from a gash in his hip. Too afraid to touch in case I do more damage, my palms hover over his face, shaking.

"Somebody help him," I cry.

People trickle from buildings, some with hands on their heads, rushing towards us, several on the phone. A man with reddish Brillo pad hair pushes between me and Billy.

"Paramedic," he states. "Give me room." He bends and begins to examine Billy.

"Please tell me he's alive," I say between sobs, and after an endless moment, the man mumbles, "Still breathing, pulse weak, fractured..."

My chest heaves while I fight for oxygen and I don't want to look, but can't tear my eyes away. The man places two fingers on Billy's neck and raises an eyelid.

"Probable internal injuries."

"Don't let him die. Please...don't let him die," I keep chanting.

He ignores me and continues examining Billy.

Things get fuzzy around the edges of my vision and in the background, I hear a siren but it's vague and kind of wobbly. When I look up, a red firetruck with 'Paramedic' written on the side turns the corner, just a few blocks away.

"What about you?" Brillo pad asks, looking me up and down. "You hurt?"

Everything suddenly comes back into sharp focus. I shake my head. "Wasn't hit." I press the back of my hand against my mouth, to keep the bile down.

"You're covered in blood. Your knees bleeding?"

My knees?

Weird.

I feel nothing, just a strange vibration throughout my body. I look down. My jeans are ripped and bloody, but I don't care about my knees. All that matters is Billy. "Is he going to live?"

"Can't say," he says as the firetruck parts the crowd. Two men jump out and rush toward us.

Then Brillo pad man grasps the back of my shoulders, gently guiding me to the truck and indicates I should sit on the metal ledge below the doors.

"Stay here. Gonna talk to them for a minute, but I'll be back." He walks back to the medics kneeling beside Billy. One of them greets him as he drops to their level. A brief conversation ensues and after a few head nods, he returns, stopping to pick something off the ground.

"What's your name?"

"Shelley De Luca."

"I'm Randy. These your friend's car keys?" I recognize them and take them, noticing for the first time the deep scrapes on my palms.

"Oh hell," Randy eyes my hands. "That's gotta hurt. You have someone you can call?"

I nod and reach into my purse. My hands shake so much, it takes me several tries before I can enter the passcode on my phone. Then I stare at it, unable to focus on what to do next.

"Let me make the call. Who should I try?"

Oh God.

Who indeed?

Not Cass, she'll be working and probably in the middle of a highlight. Joey's dead and Billy's lying in a crumpled heap, dying. That leaves only one person.

"Gianni...with a G."

Randy scrolls through my phone, pushes the button and hands it back to me. The phone rings several times.

Don't ignore me.

Please don't, not now.

After the fourth ring, I'm about to hang up when he answers.

"De Luca." His tone is flat and not exactly inviting, and who can blame him after last night, but my breath catches at the sound of his voice.

"Gianni, I'm sorry to ask but..." My voice is thick from the lump in my throat. I stop to sniff and wipe my nose on my sleeve.

"What is it?" Not so flat anymore.

"Um..."

"Shelley, what's wrong?"

"He's hurt, Gianni. Bad. I don't know if he's going to make it."

"Who's hurt, babe?"

"Billy. Somebody ran him over with a car."

"What the...? Where you at?"

"Marina District. Near Divisadero, you'll see the lights and the firetruck."

"What about you? You hurt?"

"No...not really"

"Stay put. I'm on my way." I hear the two beeps indicating the connection's lost, making *me* feel lost. I drop my phone back in my purse and find a clean paper napkin I'd taken from the burger joint. Wipe the tears and blow my nose then toss it back into my purse. A few pieces of tissue stick to drying blood and to keep myself from freaking out, I pick them off.

Randy takes my hands, turns them palm up. Now that the shock's wearing off, they're beginning to hurt.

A lot.

"These need cleaning and treatment. When your friend gets here, have him take you to the trauma unit at SF General? They'll take your friend there."

I stare at him, then swallow.

"Shelley, nod if you understand what I'm saying."

"Yeah, I hear you...trauma unit."

The ambulance arrives and the paramedics cede Billy over. "Can I go with him in the ambulance?"

"You'd be in the way."

"But what if he… I need to…you know?"

"They're professionals. Let them work."

They lift Billy onto the gurney and slide him into the ambulance.

A tall Asian cop with perfect, pale golden skin and short-cropped black hair approaches me. "Ma'am, would you mind answering a few questions?"

God.

"Can you tell me what happened?"

"She's in shock, Dwain," Randy says, heading him off.

"Reason I need to ask her now."

I stare past him, but he's blocking my view. All I care about is Billy, and I need to see what's happening. I sway to the side.

"Dwain, not now."

"Quit it, Randy, I have to do my job."

Somehow it registers they're familiar with each other. The cop steps in front of me again. Like a pendulum I move to the other side and as the medics close the ambulance doors and prepare to leave, I see Gianni walking towards us.

He came.

His eyes are on me but he stops to talk briefly with the medics.

Watching him, and the authority in his stance, knowing he came for me, suddenly everything's too much. My face crumples, my arms find their way around my waist and I bend double.

In less time than it takes for me to let out a sob, he's in front of me. "Out of my way," Gianni orders the cop. "I need to get to her." A moment later he's on his haunches clasping my shoulders. "Woman, thought you said you weren't hurt."

"I'm not…compared to Billy. I can't lose him, Gianni. I can't. Not him too."

"Fuck me." He breathes in deep and positions himself on the

ledge next to me. "Come here." A solid, warm arm hooks around my shoulders and a big, warm hand cradles my head to his chest. My cheek's close to his heart, the rhythmic thumping feels fast, but nice. Safe...and intimate, like home, and I allow myself to relax against him.

"I got you," he murmurs into my hair while I cry into his shirt. "Told you, you're gonna need me. Wasn't expecting so soon."

The ambulance chirps and I try to move away, but his arms tighten around me, almost like he's the one who needs reassuring, but that's just my imagination. He tugs my ponytail, forcing me to look into his eyes. His gaze is intense and his voice gruff when he says, "That's the last time you lie to me."

I blink.

"You get me?"

"I didn't..."

"De Luca."

I blink again. "Gianni, I..."

"Shut it, babe," he says softly.

"Okay," I whisper back.

He stares for a few seconds more giving me one more squeeze before releasing me. "Come on, let them clean you up."

"I'd rather follow them," I say, standing. "I'd take Billy's car, but don't think I can drive." Then to prove me right, my legs buckle.

"Whoa." Gianni catches me under my armpits, then gently moves me backward, forcing me to sit again. "Take it easy. Your face has no color."

"Can you take me to the hospital?"

"After they wash your wounds we'll follow them."

"I'd rather go now."

"What did I tell you?"

"Um...?"

"Shut it, babe. The sooner they take care of you, the sooner we can get out of here."

He waits for me to nod, then steps aside as one of the firemen, followed by Randy, approaches with a plastic bottle of something.

"This is going to sting," Randy says. "Prepare yourself."

He's right. It stings like I got stuck by a swarm of hornets. I hiss, sucking in air through my teeth as he pours the liquid over the wounds then takes a closer look.

"Gravel's embedded too deep for us to take care of it. Needs removing in the emergency room."

"Let's hit it then, De Luca." Gianni helps me stand again, keeping me close with an arm around my waist.

"Wait. Mr. Cadora?" The forgotten cop, who's hovering in the background, speaks up. "I'm going to need details from her before she leaves."

"Not now, Officer...Lee," Gianni says, glancing at his badge. "You heard the man. I'm taking her to the hospital. You can interview her later, if you have to."

Before the cop can protest, he nudges me gently, suggesting I should walk. Then guides me to an intimidating white truck. As I'm wondering how the hell I'm going to get in, he opens the door and stations me in front of him.

"Put your arms around my neck and hold on."

When I've done so, he dips, grasps my hips, then boosts me up like I weigh nothing.

"Get settled," he orders when I'm in the seat. "But don't try to do your seat belt."

He pushes the door closed, and through the tinted window, I see the cop's followed us. Gianni removes his jacket while shaking his head at something Officer Lee's saying and a moment later he climbs in. That leather jacket lands on the back seat next to a white construction hat with a logo that reads *GLC*

Construction. Something about those letters intrigue me. I can't help feeling I've seen them before. Obviously, they're his initials, but...something nags.

He leans and reaches across me for the seat belt. The inside of his arm brushes against my breast. Despite the pain, a tingle radiates out from my nipple. My breath seizes while he pulls the strap and latches it. That thick lock of wavy hair falls across his face and brushes against my nose. It smells faintly of green apples.

His eyes, usually so clear and blue, are stormy gray and locked with mine. "I know you're hurting but I'm gonna need you to start talking."

How can a man be so beautiful? Those eyes drop to my mouth. His own lips part slightly and for an absurd moment I believe he's going to lean in and kiss me but he swallows and shifts away to start the engine.

"Tell me what happened," he says, his voice a little gruffer than normal, as he eases into the street.

"Well, actually, it's a little...um, complicated."

"Complicated how?"

"It wasn't an accident. Billy was run down on purpose, but I think whoever did it was aiming for me."

"Jesus," he mutters while scraping a hand over his stubble. It should be noted, he still hasn't shaved. "Does this have anything to do with what happened to your face?"

The gravity of Dean's actions weighs heavy and my breath hitches.

"De Luca, speak. I can't protect you unless I know what's going on."

So I tell him about Dean, the shooting range and the text message.

When I'm done, without looking at me, he asks, "Who is this prick?"

"His name's Dean Melnikov."

I sense rather than see him tense and that crackling thing is back. In the confined space of the truck it's intensified and a lot scarier.

Gianni's quiet for a bit, but judging by the way he clenches the steering wheel, he's by no means pleased.

"Melnikov," he states finally, and drags his hand through his hair.

"Yep."

"*That* asshole?"

"You know him?"

He cuts a look that's loaded with death and I'm not entirely sure it's not directed at me.

Duh!

Of course he knows him. All these mafia dudes know each other and I don't know what to do with that.

"All the fucking men in San Francisco, and you pick him."

"I didn't actually pick him and I didn't know who he was. Can we not go there? I don't want to argue about him anymore."

"Problem is, woman, we're not *going* there. We *are* there."

"I get it, okay. I got enough crap from Billy...oh God...Billy."

Please let him be okay.

Gianni's chest rises, then as he lets his breath out his face softens, seemingly tamping down his anger. "He'll be fine. He's tough and nobody's killed him yet."

"He saved my life." Suddenly the magnitude of what Billy did for me breaks through. My throat tightens, my voice comes out a little strangled. "He pushed me out of the way, but his leg... he couldn't move fast enough to save himself. Should've been me."

The back of Gianni's knuckles press into my thigh and I zero in on the warmth that generates. "Shouldn't have been either of you."

I turn my head to the window, pressing my head against the seat so he can't see me cry.

A few minutes later we arrive at San Francisco General Hospital and Gianni drives to the Emergency entrance, puts the truck in park and turns to me.

"Where's your gun?"

"In my purse."

He reaches down between my legs and pulls my purse on his lap, then digs in. When he has it, he checks the safety is on. "We'll stash it in here for now." He pats the black leather console between the two seats and pops open the cover. "You can't take it inside and you definitely don't want to mention it to that cop, Lee."

As a hospital orderly approaches, Gianni slides out of the truck. They have a few words and within moments, the man produces a wheelchair and parks it on my side of the truck.

"I'll see you inside," Gianni says when I'm seated. "I'll park, then be right back."

The sun, although low in the sky, indicates there's still at least two hours of daylight. Therefore, the Emergency Room isn't overwhelmed yet with the usual Saturday night shootings, drunken brawls and general mayhem that happen over the weekend.

Gianni finds me as I'm about to be seen by a young, on-call doctor with jaded eyes that have more than likely witnessed too much and probably forgotten too little.

My body's begun to stiffen and with the aid of a nurse, they lay me on a gurney behind a small, curtained-off area.

"I don't want to leave you, but I gotta check on Billy," Gianni says. Little worry lines forming that Y between his brows. "Will you be okay while I'm gone?"

"Of course," I manage to utter, as it's hard for me to speak due to the pain.

"Fuck," he mutters. Then turns to the doctor and grits out an order. "Give her something to make her more comfortable."

The doctor opens his mouth to speak but one look at Gianni's face changes his mind. He shoots instructions to the nurse instead who scurries away, eyes wide, clearly not willing to challenge him either.

"You have your cell?" He waits for me to nod. "Call if you need me, I won't be far."

Then leaning in, he does something amazing and surprising that makes my pulse skip. He kisses my temple right next to my bruised eye. It's gentle and his lips linger long enough to make it something other than a friendly kiss, leaving me stunned and disoriented.

So much so that I forget to breathe and can't take my gaze off his back while he strides past the nurses' station. I wonder if he can feel my eyes on him.

A tug at my jeans brings me back. "Let's see the damage," the doc says, cutting the fabric above my knees, turning them into shorts. He seems almost bored with my injuries until he produces a syringe. "Got to shoot you up with a local, so I can scrub you and get rid of the gravel."

My face contorts into a grimace and since I hate needles, I turn away while he jabs me. When I'm numb he scrubs my wounds with a brush and antiseptic solution. A tetanus shot later, he instructs the nurse to "bandage her."

To me, he says, "Going to give you a prescription for Vicodin and antibiotics. Fill it soon, 'cause once that anesthetic wears off, it's gonna hurt."

"Thanks," I mumble. When the nurse has done her thing I ask. "Can you show me where the restroom is?"

"Down the hall and to the left."

I drag myself to the bathroom and bend. Since my hands are bandaged I have to run cold water directly from the faucet over my face. That's when I feel the first beginnings of nausea swirling deep in my stomach.

Crap.

My reflection tells me I'm a mess. My eyes are swollen from crying, the black around it blacker than ever, hands and knees bandaged and I look ridiculous in my new cutoffs and combat boots.

Only thing I got going for me is I shaved my legs last night.

After the bathroom, I head back to the nurses' station where they hand me my prescription and instructions to take my pill soon.

Gianni's back, talking to the cop we left at the scene. As I walk towards him, my heart jumps when his impossibly blue eyes fix on me.

For the first time, I get a good look at what he's wearing. Paint-stained jeans, brown, steel-toed boots and that beat-up leather jacket. His go-to outfit it seems, unless I'd taken him away from work.

As I approach, he runs his fingers through his hair, giving off a vibe that things aren't great and suddenly I can't breathe.

"What's wrong...? Is Billy...?"

Gianni swallows and blows out air. "He's in surgery. Cracked ribs, broken pelvis, internal damage but he has a decent chance if he survives the surgery and his heart holds out."

If?

"No...no, he can't die." I shake my head feeling that first wave of panic beginning to rise and mingle with the nausea in the deepest pit of my stomach. "I just got him back."

"Ah fuck." He steps closer, grabs my upper arms and squeezes. "You gotta keep it together, De Luca. I'm here for you, babe, but there's nothing we can do here and you're on your last legs."

"I want to stay, please. Don't make me go."

"Can't do that, babe. He'll be in surgery for hours. Carmine and his mom are on their way."

It hits me then I'm an awful person for not even thinking about his family.

"Gonna take you to my place, where you can get some rest. You can't go home."

His place?

"Miss De Luca," Officer Lee interrupts. "I have a couple of questions before you leave."

"What?" I stare at him, wide-eyed, still trying to process what Gianni said.

"Do you know who would want to do this to your friend?" I glance at Gianni, who's staring at me from behind him. *His place?*

"Miss De Luca?"

Oh yeah, the cop. "Um...I can't say for sure."

"What about the car, do you remember what it looks like?"

"Uh...a station wagon, an old one. I didn't see much because it was behind us, and Billy pushed me out of the way."

"What about the model or color? Belong to anyone you know?"

I close my eyes to picture it. "Dark blue." Then my eyes fly open and I swallow. "A Volvo station wagon."

The same Volvo I saw at the range! Dean had one of his goons tailing us all morning...or longer.

That nausea that's been building suddenly becomes overwhelming. "Uh...Gianni?"

"Yeah, babe?"

"I'm going to throw up."

"What?" Gianni's brows jump an inch. "Now?" He steps in front of Lee and with those big hands clamped on my hips, shoves me to the nearest garbage bin. As I bend over, the stench of someone's left-over fish taco hits me. My ponytail flops against the side of my face as I heave, spewing the French fries I had for lunch.

Somehow, while still holding me, Gianni procures a paper towel from a nurse and wipes my mouth, but I take it from him pushing his hand away and finish myself.

"Shit, De Luca. Didn't think you could get any paler," he says when I toss it into the garbage bin. "Need to get you home and into bed."

"Yes, please," I mumble and lean into him, grateful when he wraps his arms around me because my legs are far too weak.

"You got it, babe, it's been one fucked-up day."

Indeed.

7

VICODIN DREAMS AND PHANTOM KISSES

~

"Wake up, sleepy head."

Mmm.

Big, warm fingers press into my chin, angling my face.

"Shelley?"

I open my eyes, blink and stare into Gianni's.

They're so pretty. I wonder what they'd look like with mascara on? A giggle escapes me.

"Fuck," he chuckles back. "You're looped."

"Exacketalley." I aim a finger at his chest, but somehow end up jabbing them into his jeans. "I *love* Vicodin."

"Careful, woman," he grunts. "As much as I'd love your hands in my pants, you'll hurt yourself." He gently tugs my fingers from his waistband, then sliding his hands up my arms, loops them over his shoulders. "Need your help getting you out of the truck. Hang on."

"Kay." Though I'm not sure how much help I really am, since

my limbs are rubbery and my head lolls against the curve in his neck and shoulder.

Mmm, yummy.

I may be useless in the muscle department but my nose seems to be working just fine. With each breath, I pull in his warm, slightly earthy scent as he carries me up the garage stairs and through a door into a kitchen.

My eyelids refuse to stay open for long but I capture little snapshots of his house as we pass through. I spot a room with a large cream-colored couch, and brace for him to drop me on it. Instead he continues on up another flight of stairs, into a bedroom. Gianni lowers me onto a huge bed until I'm splayed out on my back.

He slips my boots off, but leaves my socks on and suddenly my feet are cold.

"Did they give you a prescription?" The bed dips as he lowers himself and sits next to me.

"Purse," I mumble and smack my lips.

"Sleep, while I get it filled. You need anything before I go? Water?"

"Mmm." *How about you?*

"I'll take that as a yes," he says, pulling the corner of the comforter over me. I'm half expecting—hoping—he'll kiss me on the head again like he did at the hospital and sigh in disappointment when he doesn't. My mouth may even turn into a pout when I hear his footsteps walk away. I can't be sure, though, as it's the last thing I remember before I slip into the black.

WHEN I WAKE AGAIN, it's dark but I instinctively know I'm not in my own bed.

Where?

I panic and bolt upright. "Oh...shit," I cry as pain slams through me so intense it feels as if my knees have been lit on fire.

"Ow!"

"Fuck." Somebody is next to me and sounds a lot like Gianni...but that can't be. Can it?

Then I feel him move and suddenly bright light blinds me. I jerk my hands up to cover my eyes only to have more pain wash over me.

"Ow...oh."

"Christ, De Luca, don't move. Let me help you."

Only one person calls me De Luca.

Then I remember.

Everything.

My breath hitches when his warm, hard arm curls behind me nestling me against his chest. Though his heart seems to be beating faster than it should through the soft cotton of his thermal. Probably not used to having an injured woman in his bed bolting upright and bellowing like an injured cow. It's enough to startle anyone.

"It's okay, woman, you're safe," he says against my hair, stroking his hands across my back. His touch is protective as I burrow a little deeper into him. Pretty soon my breathing evens out and I begin to relax despite the fact I'm hurting.

As if reading my mind, he moves and retrieves something from his dresser. "Gonna give you your pill, for the pain." His voice vibrates through his chest and into my body. "Need you to open your mouth."

I nod and open up. He places something bitter on my tongue then holds a bottle to my lips. "Drink, it's water."

I take a few sips and stop.

"More."

"Enough."

"Shelley, more."

"So controlling."

"Good you recognize that. It'll save us problems later."

"It's annoying."

A chuckle rumbles through his torso. Again, it feels nice. I blow out air and take a few more sips. Slowly, because I want this moment to last and content to know he thinks there's a later.

"Billy?" I ask when I'm done drinking.

"Alive."

I tilt my head and catch his eyes. "Just alive?"

"Out of surgery," he answers, taking the empty bottle from me and setting it on a mahogany bedside table. "I'll call in the morning and get more details, but for now it's enough to know he's alive."

Then, sadly, he adjusts his position and helps me to lie back down on the pillows. As he eases off the bed I notice he's changed into a pair of gray sweats and a long-sleeved burgundy *Hahvahd University* tee-shirt.

"Need to make you comfortable," he says standing above me but without looking at me. "Get what's left of your jeans off and put your pajamas on."

"My pajamas?"

"Picked up a few things from your apartment."

"Uh...?"

"Need your permission, De Luca."

Oh jeez.

I'd pictured Gianni undressing me so many times as a teenager but never like this.

"I can do it."

"Nope, you can't. You'll hurt yourself."

"I...um."

"Don't have all night, Shelley."

"Fine." I nod, trying to remember which panties I'm wearing, hoping it's my good ones.

He stares down at me for a moment then blinks. "Stay still and try to relax. Gonna undo your button first."

"Okay."

It takes him an endless moment to release it from the fabric and lower the zipper. When the two sides are spread wide, he tugs and says, "Lift your hips a little."

His knuckles feel hot against my skin as he slides my cutoffs halfway over my butt. Then he stops. My eyes, which had been closed, open partially. Surprisingly, his are closed and a moment later, I realize why. He hooks the edges of my panties, and pulls them *up*. Obviously, they'd come down with my jeans.

I can't decide if I'm relieved or disappointed. My bet is option two. The irony isn't lost on me that only last night I wanted him to do this very thing in my living room. However, now he's pulling *on* my pink pajama pants and that's certainly not in any fantasy either.

"Comfortable?" He asks, pulling the comforter over me and it has to be the pills making me think his voice sounds a little gruff.

"Mmm."

"Go back to sleep, De Luca. I'm gonna work and make some calls. Be down the hall if you need me." He reaches towards the lamp but I stop him with my fingertips on his forearm.

"Gianni?"

He pauses and even in my drugged-up state, I feel the tension in his muscles. It seems forever before he turns that beautiful face towards me.

"Thank you," I say.

Our eyes lock and something moves in his before he says, "Sleep. We'll figure out how you can thank me later," he says, turning off the light. "See you in the morning."

~

Joey's late. It's cold and the wind's picking up, whipping my hair behind me, twisting it into a spiral.

Why meet him at the marina? His text said four near the Yacht Club. But it's four twenty.

Oh, finally! At a distance, he looks so much like his brother. Same build, same hair, different eyes.

I swallow as he takes his sunglasses off and instead of a warm, brown gaze, an icy blue flash lands on me.

Why are you here? Where's Joey?

Not coming.

He texted me.

He shakes his head. I did.

He stares at me for a long time before he steps forward. I should step back, but I can't move as his hands take my face, thumbs raising my chin.

He moves in slowly. So slowly, giving me time, giving me a choice. Though the wind rushes and the seagulls screech, my heart pounding is all I hear. His lips touch mine and I let him kiss me, allowing myself to taste him, to feel him.

It's soft at first, almost tentative, questioning, until I moan and melt against him. Then he claims my mouth like a starving man, hungry and desperate, unable to feed enough. I'm all his.

Gianni's.

Like I've always been.

Then he pulls away, breathing hard, his fingers entangled in my hair and staring down at me with those eyes, normally so blue, yet now cloudy and full of turmoil.

I knew it, he says. You can lie all you want. To me, to Joey, to yourself even. But you don't love him. My brother's not the man for you.

Then he's gone.

Like a dream.

When I open my eyes, it's raining. Rivulets snake down the window hypnotizing and somehow soothing.

It *was* only a dream.

The drugs are wearing off but that's not what woke me. Rolling over onto my side I groan at the sudden, red-hot needles stabbing my knees and wait until the pain subsides. The comforter is crumpled next to me and I slide my fingers beneath the sheets. There's still a faint touch of warmth.

He was here.

Is that what woke me, him leaving the bed? The absence of his presence?

I wonder what Miss Double Ds would have to say about him sleeping next to me. But I quickly banish *that* thought. I don't need to dwell on any of his women, especially now that one of them has a face.

But I can't think of them now since another, more urgent need presses and if I don't get to a bathroom soon, I'll embarrass myself.

When I inch myself up into a sitting position, I see the room for the first time.

Not bad.

Gianni has taste.

The walls are a dark beige, decorated with a series of abstract paintings in warm, rich earthy tones. The cold morning light filters through partially opened wooden plantation blinds hanging at windows trimmed with white sills.

Jeans lie tossed onto a corner chair along with his jacket. If there were any doubt before there's none now. This is his room.

Fucking hell, I didn't imagine it. I'm most definitely in his bed.

Two pill bottles with my name on them sit on the bedside table alongside a bottle of water. I chug one of each, scoot to the edge of the dark sleigh bed and slip off.

There's a bathroom, thank God. I grit my teeth and wince with each step as I move as fast as my stiff knees allow and step into a bathroom paradise.

Oh wow.

A marble oval tub, big enough for two, sits in front of a large, curved bay window. Through the rain, I can just make out the blur that's Alcatraz Island and down the way a little, the Palace of Fine Arts.

Double Wow.

I pee, then stare at the tub thinking what I wouldn't give to be in that right now, filled with bubbles and him all naked and hard and slippery...

Stop.

Can't go there.

The Gianni I remember was never a one-woman man so who is this Miss Double Ds to him? Is she someone special or just another one in a long line. And just because he's being nice to me for a change doesn't mean anything. I can't let it burrow beneath my defenses and allow myself to believe there's anything to it. But that kiss on my temple yesterday makes me *want* to believe it.

So very much.

My reflection shows I could be an extra in *The Walking Dead*. Only *I* wouldn't need make-up. Hard for any man, let alone Gianni, to find that attractive.

Sigh.

In the bedroom, I rifle through the duffle bag Gianni

brought from my apartment, checking the clothing. He's thought of almost everything.

Sweats, toiletries, toothbrush and a hairbrush. Even a clean bra and panties. The good ones too. My face burns knowing he went through my underwear drawer. Somehow that feels really intimate, but then I remember how many women he's had. No stranger to lady's underwear and probably bought his fair share too.

Shoving that aside, a little forcefully I might add, I keep looking but find no shoes.

Oh, well.

The bandages make it difficult, but I wash my face, brush my teeth and pile my hair on the top of my head in a loose bun. Then I follow my nose to the kitchen.

The stairs prove to be inconvenient and I consider sliding down on my ass, except my knees won't bend far enough for me to get on my ass. But, since the drugs have begun to kick in, it makes it tolerable, if not comfortable.

The closer I get to the kitchen, the more my mouth waters at the smell of coffee, eggs and toast. I haven't eaten in a long time and what I ate then is now married to a leftover fish taco.

Gianni butters a slice of toast at a long granite counter, hair messier than usual, like he's run his fingers through it. Which, damn him, makes it sexier than usual. Those sweatpants mold that perfect ass, showing off indentations on the side of hard butt cheeks. If my knees could take it, I would stand and watch him all day.

No man has a right to be so damn beautiful.

"Morning," he says, looking over his shoulder, hitting me with those eyes.

I smile, although I think it's a little wobbly. Stupid Vicodin.

"That smells really good."

"Sit down and eat. Unless you want me to feed you standing up?" he snarks, reaching into a cherry wood cabinet.

"Ha. He has a sense of humor."

"I have a sense of something," he responds almost to himself. "Not sure it's humor." He pulls a red mug with *Be mine* written in a white heart and fills it from the coffee pot.

I can't help wondering which one of the many gave him that. Miss Double Ds? Bitch.

"Milk and sugar?"

"Please." I nod and slide onto a bar chair at the kitchen island, which is made from the same granite as the counters. Mostly white with warm beige seams flecked with gold.

"You heard anything about Billy? Can I see him?"

"Still critical." He pushes the mug to me, before moving to a double-door fridge to pull out a half gallon of milk. "No point in going today since he's still out of it. Maybe tomorrow, depending on how *you're* doing." Gianni adds milk, then points to the sugar bowl. Using a spatula, he spoons scrambled eggs onto a plate, adds the buttered toast and places it in front of me.

I smile my thanks, then watch him as he straddles a chair opposite me, sipping from his cup. Taking in his bloodshot eyes and the darkness beneath them, it dawns on me how much I'm imposing and disrupting his life.

"Have you slept?" I ask and take a bite of the eggs. Although I'm sure they're delicious, the drugs have killed my taste buds.

"A little."

"I'll call my girlfriend, Cass. I'm sure she wouldn't mind picking me up."

His eyes meet mine and go all steely. "Absolutely not."

I swallow. "Absolutely not to which part? Calling my girlfriend or her picking me up?"

"Second."

"Gianni, I can't stay here."

"Can't or won't?"

"Well..." My mind goes blank.

Shit. How do I explain it's both? I've no desire to be around witnessing him do his thing with his women.

He's still looking at me, though now his eyes have narrowed as he waits.

"I'm not going to impose on you. I already owe you enough."

That little Y forms between his brows. "Owe me?"

"You said last night you'd think of how I could thank you."

He grunts. "I did say that, didn't I. But what does your girlfriend do, De Luca?"

"She does hair, like me. We work together."

"I see." He places his coffee cup on the counter. "So, let me get this right. The two of you are gonna keep that asshole away with a pair of scissors and hairspray?"

Pff.

I roll my eyes. "Shears."

"Pardon?"

"They're called shears," I say slowly. "Not scissors, and in case you didn't know, hairspray's flammable."

He shakes his head, eyes boring into mine like I've lost what little mind I had left.

Okay, so he knows hairspray's flammable.

"Must be all that LA smog."

"Excuse me?"

"Lack of oxygen in the air, killed your brain cells, 'cause what you're proposing is not happening!"

"Why not?"

"De Luca, do you remember anything or are you just being stupid?"

"Why does everyone keep asking me what I remember? And who are you calling stupid?"

"I'm not calling *you* stupid. I said...Jesus, never mind! Let me spell it out for you, woman." He holds up a finger. "One. You can't be alone or with people who don't know how to protect you." Up goes the second finger. "Two, I'm gonna protect you. But in order for me to do that, you gotta do everything I say, no argument, and third"—his thumb joins the other two fingers—"you're going to my mom's."

"Your mother?" I squeak. "I'm not involving your mother."

"Not the right answer, Shelley. You can waste energy and argue all fucking day if you want but it's not gonna change the outcome. You have no choice, not until this is over."

"Of course I have a choice. I'm *not* going to your mother's."

"Her house is better suited for your situation and that's where you're going. Period."

"I'm going to Cass's."

His face hardens. "Who the fuck is Cass?"

"My girlfriend, weren't you listening?"

That's when he stands. "Don't see you for ten years, then you land yourself in a mountain of shit and who do you call?"

Oooh...here it comes.

"I didn't land in it. *It* landed on *me.*"

"Same difference. Whose phone rang yesterday afternoon?" His voice is soft, but laced with anger.

"Um..."

The air's gone all crackly again, and to make things worse, he's coming around the island. When he's inches away he clamps my shoulders and swivels my stool so I'm facing him, then leaning into me he traps me between his arms as he rests his hands on the granite behind me, forcing me to either stare at his broad chest or look up. I look up.

He asks again, "I'm waiting, Shelley."

"Yours." I whisper because, truthfully, I couldn't say anything else. "I called you."

"And why is that?"

"Because I couldn't think of anyone else at that moment"

"That's right." He stares down, holding my eyes. "You thought of me. And you know why you thought of me?"

I swallow, because I do indeed know why, but I'm not going to tell him that, as it isn't the only time I've thought of him since the funeral. "You said I might need you."

"Yeah." He's really close now, just a few inches away. "You might need me. Now accept that because I'm not in the mood for your crap."

My crap? For some reason that rubs me wrong and I take approximately three seconds to think about it before I straighten my spine and snap.

"*You're* not in the mood for *my* crap?" I shove against those hard shoulders. Regretting it immediately because, not only does he not move, but my hands hurt, *dammit.* Though I'm not going to let him know that, even as it sure as hell fuels my temper.

"In the last few days, I've been beaten, threatened, stalked, molested by a fucking goose, almost run over by a car, and Billy's in the hospital because of me! So don't talk to me about not being in the mood *for my crap.* And if that's not enough, I'm gonna owe you a *fucking* marker 'cause we both know how this works. There's no freebies in this life, especially from men like you."

He straightens and folds his arms, but stays silent, going all alpha badass on me glowering down with that scarred eyebrow cocked. And because I have no sense of self-preservation, or sense in general, I continue.

"*And...*" I throw my hands in the air, "you went through my underwear drawer."

Gianni turns to face the window and cracks his jaw. "Anything else you wanna get off your chest since you're *in the mood*?"

"You didn't pack any shoes."

He sucks in those gorgeous cheeks covered in all that delicious stubble as his lips twitch. And it's a long moment before he turns back. "No shoes, huh? Well, fuck me, I didn't pack any shoes. So that's what you're really pissed about."

God.

"No! I mean...yes. Maybe."

"Good to see you still got some fight in you."

"Shut up."

"You shut up."

"No, *you* shut up."

"You're cute when you're pissed."

Dammit.

He's not supposed to say things like that. It's not fair. So I deflect. "I don't think Vicodin agrees with me."

He's not biting and deflects back. "And you have some pretty sexy underwear."

See! How am I supposed to fight against that?

"But I wanna hear more about what this goose did to you."

"No, you don't." My cheeks begin to burn, as that was not my finest moment.

"I most certainly do, especially now that you're blushing."

Damn-the-fuck-it.

"Fine." I let out a puff of air. "It bit me on my ass."

"It did what?" Then the bastard starts to laugh. Out loud. And he's got an amazing laugh that does flip-floppy things to my belly. Warm and rich and *almost* infectious. Almost, because I'm too mortified to enjoy it.

"It's not that funny," I say after a *lot* of seconds have passed.

"Yeah, it is," he says, still chuckling, but making an obvious effort to clamp it down. "I can't wait to hear the full story."

"Shut up. You're not getting it from me."

"Definitely not from you, because you'll give me the abridged version. I want the details."

No doubt Billy will share those details when he's better. "Why are you doing all this?"

I hear him take a deep breath. When he lets it out it, he's stopped laughing. "Told you before. You're gonna have to figure it out yourself."

I swallow and look up at the change in tone. All traces of that laugh have gone and his eyes are back to serious.

"This is a fuck-up, De Luca. I'm not sure you're comprehending how dangerous Melnikov is."

"Uh…hello. Look what he did to my face."

"It's much worse than that." Before I can ask how much, he keeps going, "Okay, I'll compromise. You call your girl, but you're still going to my mom's. She can visit you there."

"Only for a few days," I counter back. "I have to go back to work at some point."

Oh crap…work. How am I going work with my hands like this?

"You'll stay as long as I tell you to stay."

"Gianni, I'm not going to let Dean, or you for that matter, dictate my life."

"Ugh." He tips his head back and growls to the track lighting on the ceiling. "Do you *not* understand the conversation we just had or the depth of the situation you're in?"

"I do, it's just that I have to pay rent."

"Rent is the least of your problems."

"Um…no, it's not. I'm still building my clientele, so money is a bit tight right now and I can't afford to lose my apartment. You know what rents are like in this city."

He plants his palms on the counter and leans in towards me. "Is that why you got involved with him? Because he has money?"

My body jolts at his accusation. "You think I use men for their money?"

"Do you?"

"Wow." I blink and look away. "That's really insulting. Obviously, you don't know me."

"Stop deflecting and answer the question. If it wasn't about money, what was it?"

"Stop being such an asshole. Not that I do use men for money but what would it matter to you if I did?"

His look bores right through me, like he's trying to see past my skull, trying to decipher whatever code is written there. Find some evidence to justify his question.

But instead of answering me, he gives a quick shake of his head then pushes away from the island.

"I liked him," I say softly to his back. Maybe I saw it wrong, but I would swear there was a hesitation in his step, but not enough to make me stop. "Dean was charming and sweet at first. I fell for it. I fell for him. Didn't know he was psycho until he hit me."

He's stopped at the kitchen sink, facing the window. I assume he's staring at the view and it's a few beats before he speaks again. But those few beats carry a lot of tension.

"So...let me get this straight," he says to the window. "You want me to believe my idiot brother didn't warn you?"

As that penetrates, my head tilts. "Warn me about what?"

He turns and pins me down. "Being coy isn't gonna work on me, Shelley."

"I'm not being coy, Gianni. I don't understand what you're referring to. Warn me about what?"

After what seems an eternity of studying me with something definitely not happy in his eyes, he leans his back against the counter.

"Fuck me." His shoulders drop a little, then he rubs his face. "You don't know."

Now it's my turn to get impatient. "Know what, Gianni?"

"That prick you let put his dick in you, Shelley, was Joey's partner."

I stare at him, more than a little taken aback by his tone, because that tone sounded a lot like jealousy, but I push it aside. Filing it for later.

"You're joking," I whisper as goosebumps erupt on my skin. I don't know if it's because of the maybe-jealousy or the information he just imparted.

"Nope," he confirms.

"You mean by partner, he was Dean's supplier?"

"Yep." His eyes get narrow but remain stuck on me.

"How long have you known?"

"Not until recently when I heard them on the phone. Melnikov wasn't pleased Joey wanted to quit, wouldn't leave it alone. But that wasn't all. They were arguing about something else as well. It got pretty heated"

"About what?"

He shrugs, but the way he's looking at me suggests he knows a lot more than he's willing to say.

A chill begins at the base of my spine, moving up, as I remember Joey's words to me when I told him I was seeing someone. *Know that.* I can't help feeling they were arguing about me.

Then Gianni asks, "How long have *you* known Joey was supplying cocaine?"

"Um...Billy told me yesterday...right before everything happened." Something occurs to me and my eyes widen. "Oh jeez. You think Dean killed Joey."

"I'm working on that theory."

Good God.

I close my eyes and take a few deep breaths. This just keeps getting worse. When at last I open them again, I glance at Gianni and he's looking down at his feet.

Perhaps it's because he looks so tired, or his hair is falling across his forehead, making him look vulnerable. Or because of the mixed signals I'm getting—something that sounded like jealousy, but might not be. I rise from my chair, walk to him and slip my arms around his waist. We're joined at the hips, with my torso to his and my head just below his shoulder. He lets out a short breath then tenses, every muscle locking up. As his arms slide around me, beneath my ear I hear his heart speed up.

We stand together for a few seconds like that until I do something stupid. I can't help it, because his scent and his warmth make me lose my mind.

I kiss him.

I just press my lips to that broad pectoral plane, right below his nipple.

Impossibly, he locks up even more. "Shelley?" The tenor in his voice, low and strained, makes my belly dip. "What are you doing?"

"Um," I whisper tilting my head to meet his eyes.

"Shouldn't be doing that, babe."

I withdraw my hands from his back, sliding them across his smooth muscles, settling them on his hip. As I do, he sucks in air, making a small hissing sound through his teeth. I lean slightly back and in doing so, my pelvis presses closer to his. Our eyes lock and something in his flare.

"Don't," he says, sounding as if he's in pain.

"Don't what?"

"Start something you can't finish. You're injured and full of Vicodin, but dammit, De Luca, I'm still a man."

It's then I become aware of his erection, but can't make myself move. Our eyes are locked before he closes his and swallows.

Then he takes in a deep breath through his nostrils and with a grunt that vibrates through his torso, he pushes me away and steps to the side. Since he's angled away from me, I can't see his face but I do see the pulse beating on the side of his neck. He drags his fingers through his hair before turning to me.

"I'm sorry. That wasn't my intention..."

"It doesn't matter what your intention was, Shelley. Like I said, I'm still a man. So I suggest you keep your distance and don't put any more moves on me."

"Moves...? That most definitely wasn't a move."

"Your hands touching me and you looking at me like that? That's a move," he growls. "I'm gonna go take a shower." And the look he slides me as he stalks out the kitchen suggests he might do *more* than just shower.

Hoo boy.

I blow a strand of hair out of my face and watch him, my eyes fixed on those flexing muscles in his ass as he climbs the polished wooden stairs until he's out of sight, then I collapse onto my chair and rest my head on my arms.

I suppose it's a small victory I managed to have that effect, although I get the feeling any warm female body would do but it doesn't stop the space between my legs from tingling, because I still feel him. Feel that hard ridge against me. And that reminds me of my dream.

Joey's not the man for you.

Boy did he have that right.

Fucking Vicodin! Makes my mind and my body do stupid things.

One more day, maybe two, then I won't need the painkillers anymore. Good thing too, as being around Gianni is too damn dangerous.

Maybe Cass can help me with plan B...

I freeze as the sound of a door opening and closing sends my heart racing.

Holy cow...who the hell is that?

They're coming from down the hall. Moments later clicking heels, *high* clicking heels, echo down the hallway.

HA!

I instinctively duck underneath the kitchen island. As my knees aren't as flexible as perhaps they would normally be, I lose my balance and land hard on my butt, letting out a muffled *oomph*.

Maybe five seconds later, a woman saunters into the kitchen passing me on her way towards the counter. A black, beautifully cut bob swinging with each step.

Jeez.

Two things hit me.

First relief because it's not some dangerous killer.

Yay.

Then, as if I haven't had enough humiliation, I realize it's *her.* Miss Double D.

Only this time both stiletto heels are, from this point of view, perfect.

And she has a key.

She doesn't notice me. After placing her purse on the counter, she reaches into the cabinets, pulls down a mug and fills it with coffee from the pot.

I'm thinking I could scoot myself around the corner and out the kitchen door before she sees me. Except...and that's when the second thing hits me.

Her perfume.

My nose twitches and before I can squelch it, I sneeze.

She pivots, eyes landing on me and if there was any warmth in her face, it's no longer there.

She's beautiful, of course. On a scale of one to ten, I'd put her at a nine point nine-nine with flawless skin and eyes so dark, you could call them onyx.

"What are you doing down there?" she asks, with no warmth in her tone either.

I don't answer because...well, really, what can I say? That I fell on my ass like a fraidy-cat when I heard her coming?

"Do you speak English?"

I nod, which makes my nose twitch. Causing me to suck in a breath, gasp three times then sneeze explosively into my hoodie sleeve. That makes her take a quick step back.

When she's determined she's a safe distance from me she says, "God, I hope you're not contagious. I can't afford to get sick. Where is he?"

"Gianni?" I manage before sneezing again. Good Lord, what perfume is she wearing? Expensive for sure but it's doing a number on my sinuses.

"Of course, Gianni," she says in a tone that implies I'm not too bright. "Who else?"

Well, duh.

She inspects me, taking in my sweats and socks and untidy hair. No doubt determining I'm no competition. Dammit, even with her lips all prissy and suspicious, she's still pretty.

I point upwards towards his room and try not to wince as I pull myself up with the help of a barstool. Halfway up, another sneeze. This one comes from deep in my chest and hurts a little.

"Seems you're a little worse than I first thought. I didn't notice the bandages last time."

"Because they weren't there. These are new."

"I see." Her lips flatten and those dark eyes narrow. "I never got your name."

Oh boy.

"Uh...I'm Shelley." I pick up my mug and place it in the sink, not bothering to rinse it. "I'm just gonna...um...tell Gianni you're here."

She says nothing to that, but watches me over the rim of her cup as she sips her coffee. And I feel her glare stuck on me as I leave the kitchen.

Going up the stairs proves more difficult than coming down. I take my time, as every step's harder and interrupted by more explosive sneezing.

The bedroom door's ajar and since I'm a little woozy from the effort and the sneezes, I lean against the frame to catch my breath. It doesn't help he chooses that moment to exit the bathroom with a towel wrapped low around his hips. Maybe if I will it hard enough, that towel will loosen and drop to the floor.

Our eyes meet and his brows pull together. "You okay?" he asks.

Joy.

If he has to ask.

"Um..." I jerk my thumb towards the kitchen. "Your girlfriend is downstairs."

His head cocks and that wayward ringlet falls over his eye.

"My what?"

"Pretty brunette from the funeral. She let herself in."

"Shit." He grimaces and palms his forehead. "Gina! I forgot she was coming."

Sigh.

Although I'm kinda happy he'd forgotten about her, I'm not so happy she's downstairs now. I make little popping noises with my lips, finding something interesting to look at on my toes.

Awkward.

"We're supposed to check out a building together," he explains. "Coincidentally, one in your neighborhood." I feel his eyes on me until he disappears into the walk-in closet. Then I hear hangers moving, a zipper being pulled and a moment later he exits in ripped jeans that hang just as low on his hips as the towel did. Leaving that sexy V with just a hint of his happy trail showing. The man's determined to torture me.

He walks towards me pulling a tee-shirt over his head. That's when I notice the scar, about the size of quarter, just up and to the left of his heart.

There's no time to think about it as he stops a foot in front of me, takes my chin between his thumb and index finger and tips it. His eyes are soft as they stare into mine for what seems like a really long time. "You don't look so good," he finally announces.

"Mmm."

"De Luca?" His other hand joins his first and they both cup my face and the warmth from his touch makes it hard to focus. "Don't bullshit me. What's wrong with you?"

"Pills," I mutter and swallow, trying to invoke moisture in my mouth. "Make me feel weird and...wipe me out." *Among other things.*

"Why are your eyes watering?"

"Allergies."

"From the Vicodin?"

I shake my head. "Her perfume."

"Right." Those hands move from my face and I miss them, but they continue to move slowly down my neck, and that feels nice. Then even further over my shoulders and that feels *really* nice. For a man who doesn't want me touching *him*, he sure doesn't mind touching *me*.

It's confusing.

When his hands reach my upper arms, he clasps them and walks me backwards, until my calves bump against the wooden edge of the bed.

"Lie down for a few, until you feel better. I'll deal with Gina."

What exactly does *deal* with Gina mean? Boot her ass out or deal with her in another, more intimate way? I'm not sure I want to know.

I sit, or rather drop onto the bed. Snatching a Kleenex from the box on the side table before I let myself fall sideways, my head landing on his pillow.

Somewhere in the middle of my haze, I realize he's lifting my legs onto the bed, then he's pulling the comforter over me. Despite the coffee, my eyelids feel heavy and I really, really need to nap.

Whoo.

Just a few minutes. When my head burrows deeper into his pillow, I catch a whiff of green apples, inhale it, absorbing it into me and before I know it, I'm gone.

~

FINGERS BRUSH my hair back from my face, then a thumb moves over my lips.

Dammit, DeLuca.

Shelley, your father's dead.

Daddy...Daddy's gone?

We have to go.

Don't want to go.

We have to, Shelley. We can't stay. Dangerous.

Need to see Joey. Need to understand.

No! We have to go.

Daddy...

Tires squealing.

Screaming.

~

"JESUS, SHELLEY."

Billy! Fuck, fuck.

"Shit, De Luca, wake up."

My eyes fly open and I stare straight into beautiful icy blue ones.

"Fuck, woman." Gianni, crouched next to the bed with hands cradling my face, holding me firm. "Look at me."

My breath hitches as I fight for control.

"Babe, look at me. You were dreaming, but it's over now. You're safe."

"My dad..."

He slides onto the bed and gathers me in his arms, kissing the side of my head. "It's okay." His breath against my hair somehow is the one thing anchoring me, keeping me from spiraling down. Just to be sure, I cling to his tee-shirt.

"Shh...I got you...I got you."

Is it strange his heart's beating so hard against my ear? Or is it *my* heart beating so hard? I can't tell.

He adjusts himself, then slides an arm under, pulling me closer. "Talk to me, De Luca, what's your dream about?"

"My dad..."

"What about your dad?"

"The day...the day he was shot. Billy told me things I hadn't heard because Mom refused to talk about it, and hearing things she kept from me...I guess I'm still processing."

He stills and the slight increase in the tension of his arms is my first clue.

"What did he tell you?" Something's so subtle in his tone I almost don't catch it. But it sends a chill through me. I begin to pull away. At first, he doesn't let me. When I insist and look into his face I sense something I never thought I'd see coming from him.

Fear.

My forehead wrinkles as I search further. "A bullet ripped his throat out...and he died choking on his blood."

Gianni shudders. It's honest and visceral, almost as if he was experiencing it. Like he was there.

Impossibly my heart, still beating fast from my dream, speeds up. When he swallows, I gasp.

Like he was there!

"You were there."

His lids close, then reopen slowly and suddenly, in my gut, I know it's the truth.

"You *were* there," I whisper.

He drags in a deep breath and lets it out slowly.

I scramble backwards, ignoring the biting pain as my hands scrape against the bedding. "You were *there.*"

"De Luca..." He reaches for me.

"You were fucking there!" I yell, kicking and slapping. Warding him off.

"I was," he mutters and makes a dive for me.

Fuck.

Fuck!

"You saw him die?" Horrible thoughts race through my mind. Horrible *mafia* thoughts as big, hard hands capture my wrists and using his body he pins me to the bed.

"Let me go."

"Babe...I'm trying to stop you from hurting yourself. Calm down."

"*You're* the one hurting me," I cry. "Let me go."

"I'll let you go, but I need you to look at me."

"No." Sobs wrack through me, interrupting my breathing.

"Please." His hands squeeze lightly. "Look at me."

I don't want to, but the pain in his tone demands I do. What I find surprises me. I expected something—grief, guilt—and I see both of those, but what's even more remarkable is I see the one I suspected. Fear.

And that makes me fearful, because what would a man like

him, groomed in a world of violence, have to fear? Only the truth.

But what is the truth and because I have to know, I ask, "Did you do it?"

He flinches and shuts his eyes.

"Did you kill my dad?"

"No," he whispers.

Relief punches through me like a heavyweight boxer pounding a sparring bag.

"I can see why you'd think that, but I swear to you, De Luca, on all that's holy, I didn't kill him."

Then what's with the fear in his eyes? What's he hiding?

"Is there anything else I need to know about that day?"

He hesitates for a long moment, then shakes his head. "No. But I need you to know there was nothing I could do to save him." The muscles in his jaw ripple, then he swallows. "I wish to Christ there had been, because, believe me, I live with it every single fucking day."

8

DOGS, DOGS AND MORE DOGS

~

The next twenty-four hours are a blur, and I spend them sleeping or zoning out watching reruns of *The Walking Dead*. This is mostly because I decide that gobbling a Vicodin (or two) and living in la-la land is preferable to having to face Gianni and what his revelation means.

Beyond that first night when he slept next to me, he's left me alone. Though grateful for the time to get my head sorted, and I have much to think about, I've missed him.

His presence is everywhere. I've smelled his body wash when he's showered. I've heard him in his office, or downstairs puttering about or talking on the phone, but except to ask me if I want food, he's stayed completely away.

Should I be angry with the man who happened to be with my father when he died?

Or.

Should I be furious with my mother, who kept that information from me?

Why?

After vacillating between the two I decide on the second as it isn't my mother who's taken me to the hospital to visit Billy or promised to protect me. Granted, he's expecting something in return, his marker if you will, but I'll deal with that later.

And it isn't my mother who sets my heart fluttering or my belly whooshing every time I look at him. Or when I feel those intense eyes on me. Like they are now.

"You good?" Gianni asks, as we pull up to a high, white wall with black ornate iron gates.

"Sure, just hurting a little. I took my last pill last night."

"We can get you more."

"Still have some. Just don't want to take any more."

He enters a code on his phone and while we wait for the gates to rumble open, his eyes are back on me.

We navigate a long driveway squished between two houses lined with palm trees and Japanese hydrangeas.

"Oh, my God." Despite myself, I start to giggle. "I'm remembering the crazy parties your parents used to hold. How loud and in-your-face they got."

"They *were* something." He smiles, and if those little laugh lines aren't enough to send my heart thumping, the grooves in his cheeks sure are. "Nobody eats or argues like us."

"Think I missed that most of all," I mumble, the laugh dying on my lips.

The family lived hard, but they loved harder and when Mom and I moved, we left all that behind. Even after she remarried, my stepdad's family were too Bel Air to consider arguing at a family soirée. At least not in public. Instead they stabbed each other in the back behind closed doors with their little escargot forks. Needless to say, I avoided said soirées like the Ebola virus.

"That crazy Thanksgiving when Uncle Joe drank too much grappa."

Gianni chuckles. "You mean when he dropped to his knees in front of my aunt?"

"Yeah, what was so funny about that song anyway?"

"You don't wanna know."

"Oh c'mon. Can't be that bad."

"Depends on how dirty your mind can get about a lonely farmer and his goat...and his dog."

"Oh, *gross*."

"I did warn you." He smiles.

We arrive at the house, which is set on a pinnacle of land in front of several others. Gianni drives past a large queen palm set in the middle of a grassy patch and parks the truck in front of double wooden church-style doors.

Looking around, I realize he's right. This house *is* a fortress. It's on the edge of the cliff and is higher and more than twice the size of the average lot in Sea Cliff. There's only one, easily protected, point of entry.

The neighborhood is one of San Francisco's most affluent and the majority of the houses, although large, are built very close to each other and all have their own security systems.

The Cadora family has owned this piece of land and the two houses on either side of the driveway since the early nineteen-hundreds. They've survived several family skirmishes and two major earthquakes.

Gianni twists in his seat to face me, resting a forearm on the steering wheel. "Speaking of dogs. Don't move unless you wanna be accosted."

That sets my heart hammering. "Excuse me...did you say accosted?"

He answers with a grin so sexy, I have to press my legs together.

That's when I hear them and wonder if the remnants of the drugs in my system are still affecting me. When I realize what it is, I'm hopelessly disappointed he wasn't talking about him accosting me. It's a small pack of canines. Four to be precise, creating a commotion worthy of ear plugs ranging from a deep woof to a high-pitched yip. They circle the truck like frantic little warriors.

"I forgot to ask you, I hope you like dogs. My mom's obsessed with them. Keeps rescuing the damn things. In fact, I think she's determined to turn the house into a shelter."

There's a softness in his face and by the goofy (yet sexy) grin on his face, I suspect he might be too. I find that I like this side of Gianni a lot.

"Stay in the truck," he says, opening the cab door. "Let me get these critters sorted first." But before he can unfold those long, hard thighs and climb out, enormous paws land on his shoulders, then a black and tan head is pressed up close to Gianni's.

"Fucking hell, Tink...let me get out the damn truck first," he grumbles, but it must be said those grumbles are interrupted with chuckles.

The dog obeys, backing up, allowing Gianni to exit. He bends, though not very far, to rub the dog's ears and head. "Good girl. Now you can kiss me."

"This monster's Tinkerbell," he says over his shoulder, lifting his face above the onslaught of the dog's massive tongue. "She's still a puppy and needs some training."

He greets each animal with equal pats and ear-rubs, leaving me both envious, charmed and unable to do much about the silly smile on my face.

Finally, he makes his way around the truck, surrounded by the quivering entourage of canine muscle.

"Sit," he points to the ground, at which they plant their doggy butts on the asphalt, ears pricking attentively expecting his next command.

"Stay." He waits a moment, ensuring their obedience before opening my door.

By now we've established a routine on getting me in and out of the truck. My arms automatically slip around his neck as soon as he unclasps my seatbelt and his hands grip my hips. Since it's a fair way down, and my arms are wrapped tight, as he lowers me, my breasts scrape against his chest. The friction causes my nipples to harden and I can't stop the gasp escaping my lips.

It's not lost on me, on account my sight is in direct line with his neck, that he swallows. Not once, but twice.

"You need to take your pills," he mumbles to the top of my head. I can't miss that his voice sounds a little husky. "No need for you to be in so much pain."

"I'm fine." I avert my eyes as what I'm feeling has nothing to do with pain and everything to do with what's happening between my thighs.

After clearing his throat, he lets me go and scoops up the chihuahua. "Hold out your fingers. Let him smell you."

I do, and the little dog shoves his cold nose into my palms, sniffs then licks them.

"Meet Rambo. He's the old man of this mangy bunch."

The little black and white dog shivers while tasting my fingers and soon after that his tail wags. I know I've been accepted when he grins, revealing two broken teeth and a few missing ones.

"Mom found him in an alley behind some garbage cans. Poor thing was nothing but sores and bones."

"Aww...poor baby," I say to Rambo. While I scratch his chin, he aims his tongue at my nose.

"Since there're no grandkids yet for her to spoil it's been good for her to have them to baby, especially after my dad passed."

Something about how he says grandkids *yet* with his eyes

caught on me makes me warm all over and shiver at the same time. And then the reality of that statement hits me.

Gianni and kids, which means at some point he's thinking of settling down. That doesn't feel so warm and shivery anymore. My belly hollows but fortunately I don't have time to ponder that as the next second, the double church doors fly open.

"Shelleyyy!" A deep, rumbly voice echoes off the truck.

I swing my head towards the stairs and squeal at the large bald man jogging my way.

"Oh, my God." I launch myself at another member of the Cadora clan, Gianni's cousin.

"See you remember Marco," Gianni mumbles, stepping out of the way and folding his arms. "This scary fucker's the other half of your protection detail."

Marco bear-hugs and twirls me, scattering dogs and eliciting a grunt from Gianni that doesn't sound exactly happy.

"Hmm. Didn't know you were *that* friendly."

"You know this girl had the balls to turn me down for senior prom?" Marco says as he deposits me back on the ground then taps my butt as he steps away. This gets him a hard glare from Gianni.

"That's only because Joey threatened to shoot you *in the balls* if I said yes," I respond. "You should be kissing my ass as I'm the reason you're still a man."

He laughs and reaches to squeeze me one more time. "Damn, girl, good to see you and despite those nasty bruises you're as hot as ever."

I giggle when he plants a kiss on my cheek. "And you have more piercings and more muscles." I point to the barbell in his eyebrow and he cocks it in the most adorable way.

The slamming of the truck door draws both our attention. "You two done?" Gianni, looking annoyed, tips his chin at Marco. "Help me get Shelley's stuff upstairs." Then he grabs two of the three suitcases he insisted I pack. Each time I thought I had enough clothing, he pulled more from my closet.

"I'm not moving into your mother's house permanently, you know," I'd protested.

"You are for now," he'd responded in a tone that cut off any argument. "Until this thing is over with Melnikov and I say it's safe enough for you to go home, consider your stay permanent." I figured I'd let him have his way for now.

The way he lugs those suitcases, like they weigh no more than the chihuahua, makes it difficult for me to pull my attention away from those corded forearms. Until I hear Marco sniggering. When I slide my gaze over and catch his eye, he gives me a smile that sends heat straight to my face. The bastard caught me ogling.

Gianni's already inside flanked by two of the canines. Tinkerbell in the lead, Rambo close behind.

Marco hooks an arm around my neck and plants another kiss on top of my head. "Let's get this out of the way before numbnuts loses his shit," he says, picking up the remaining bag.

I follow them into the large, marble-floored foyer and my mouth drops at the spectacular view. Through floor-to-ceiling windows, you can see the Pacific Ocean.

The house has been remodeled since I was last here. The change is dramatic, from early-twentieth-century to luxurious and modern. A round, polished ebony table sits in the center with a huge display of pink and white oriental lilies. Their scent mingles with the ocean air, infusing the room.

I follow Gianni and Marco up a crescent-shaped wooden staircase with a wrought iron banister, a dog on either side. A panting, overweight English bulldog, tongue hanging out the side and a floppy-eared Doberman, showing more than a casual interest in my knees. I eye it, hoping it's not considering them as a snack.

My room is to the right at the end of the landing. The men deposit my suitcases on the floor in front of a huge walk-in closet. Gianni opens French doors, letting the dogs out onto a large, wrap-around balcony overlooking the water.

Marco glances at Gianni, gives him a chin tip and rubs the top of my head. "I'll see you downstairs in a bit and we can catch up. I've a few things to take care of."

The vista of the Pacific Ocean suffused in silvery light is stunning, although the water's choppy from the recent storm. To the right is the western span of the Golden Gate Bridge. A fully loaded tanker, riding low in the water, glides beneath, steering into the bay presumably on its way to the Port of Oakland.

"Will this room work for you?" Gianni's eyeing me, and I'm struck by how much this house suits him. It should, considering he was born here. "If not I can have Connie fix up one of the other guest rooms but this one has the best view."

I let out a puff of air and glance around the spacious bedroom, beautifully decorated in warm, rich desert tones.

"How could I not be happy here?" I cut a glance at him. "This is...was Joey's room, right?"

He acknowledges with a sad smile.

Though Joey had long since moved to his own apartment, I could still sense his presence. Almost as if the furniture had absorbed, and then re-emitted his energy.

"It's so surreal to be back here. I feel like I'm in a dream, almost like the last ten years didn't happen."

I step outside and walk to the edge of the wrap-around balcony, which is decorated with tall terracotta pots. They overflow with orange and white impatiens and deep blue lobelia. At the southern end is another set of double French doors.

Gianni follows me and sits on the white balustrade with his back to the ocean, palms curled over the edges on either side of him.

"I forgot how amazing this view is," I say. "You're fortunate to have grown up here."

"Wasn't without its challenges." There's a touch of melancholy in his voice and, curious, I turn to look at him.

"I bet. Growing up in your father's shadow, being groomed to take over must have been difficult, to say the least. Especially if that wasn't what you wanted."

"That too." He murmurs, then holds my gaze for several heartbeats and something about how his eyes have gone dark then drop to my mouth makes me feel dazed, like I've overdosed on Vicodin. Then they drop further and linger on my nipples. It's almost physical, that look, as if his hands and not his eyes are touching me.

It's exciting and nerve-wracking all at once. I force myself to look away.

Those fucking mixed messages again...I'm not going to fall into this trap, having made a fool of myself twice already. Though my breasts, the little traitors, still tingling from our earlier encounter by the truck, disagree.

"Is that your mom's room?" I point to the balcony above our heads hoping to steer the conversation in another, safer direction.

He lifts his gaze and nods.

"I'd like to say hello if she's available."

He stands with that easy, lazy grace I've come to associate with him and takes a step away from the edge, bringing him closer to me. "She's not here."

"Um...what?"

"She's in Italy, with family. This thing with Joey...I want to make sure she's safe and out of the way should anything happen."

My first thought is what is he expecting to happen? Then

another one occurs to me. "When were you going to tell me I'd be here alone?"

He exhales on a grunt that could be also be construed as a swallowed laugh. "You're not gonna be alone, woman. I'll be here and so will Marco. And Connie, the housekeeper, the gardener, the dogs and..."

"Okay, I get it." I laugh, grateful I've managed to divert a situation where perhaps I'd make a fool of myself again and turn to face him. But stop short at his expression.

"You shouldn't laugh, De Luca," he says softly.

Uh-oh.

"And why is that?"

"It makes you far too irresistible."

Irresistible? After he's rejected me twice?

I'm not sure due to the blood suddenly buzzing through my head. That crackly thing begins, the way it does when he gets intense, making my breath catch in my throat and my belly tighten. And then his hand comes up slowly and circles behind my neck.

"And right about now, I'm thinking you owe me a kiss." This is said low and a little raspy as he pulls me to him.

"I do?" I whisper back. A thrill of anticipation rushes through me at the same time as fear. Fear I'll be irretrievably lost if he does kiss me, for there'll be no going back for me once I've tasted him.

"I'm done waiting." Fingers slip into my hair, grabbing a handful and tugging, while the other hand slides around my waist and crushes me to his torso. "And I'm done with your teasing."

"My teasing?" I repeat, not sure why my brain is finding his words so hard to process.

"Yeah."

"I think you're mistaken...I never...ah."

My mind goes blank when his lips touch my neck and that bristly stubble grazes my skin. Goosebumps prickle all the way down to my nipples, making them ache and I pull in a quick breath. I allow myself this one tiny moment.

Because it feels good.

So, *so* good.

Liquid desire pools between my legs with an intensity that thrills me way too much, and when I feel him hardening my insides quiver. And I capitulate. Because I have no willpower to do anything else.

When my head drops back, he groans softly deep in his throat, trailing kisses up my neck, along my jaw and to the corner of my mouth. Each one, combined with his scent, the heat of his breath, his heart thundering next to mine, makes me want more. Then his mouth moves over mine, demanding... sucking on my lower lip...coaxing my mouth open. His tongue begins a slow, sensual slide across my lip that deepens, getting wilder, hungrier and hotter.

I'm lost.

Years of pent-up want and yearning, every fantasy I ever had I realize now is wrapped up in some version of this man. And he's kissing me.

More than that.

He's devouring me, like he's wanted this too. Like he's *craved* this too.

His taste, his touch, everything about him I absorb. Aware I'm stepping off a cliff, about to fall into the deep abyss. But I don't care. His hand moves under my top, sliding over my skin, over my ribs sending electricity coursing outward. When that big, rough palm captures my skimpy breast and scrapes over my nipple, it hits me.

Miss fucking Double Ds.

Fuck.

Fuck!

That's when I begin to fight, like I should have before. Gathering the very last vestige of control, I turn my head and break the kiss.

"No!"

I'm panting and aroused and it's the last thing I want, but I have to. I refuse to be just another one of his conquests. One of his women he can tap anytime. I can't deal with that so I push against him.

"What's your game, Gianni?" My voice is thick and breathy and I'm terrified of what he'll say, but I need to hear him say it, setting whatever illusions aside.

"My game?" His brow creases and he pulls back, but keeps one arm locked around me, though the hand on my breast drops. He blows out a shaky breath.

"I'm not one of your toys."

He blinks and clears his throat. "Toy? What're you on about? That was no game."

"What about the woman who came to your house, your girlfriend?"

"Gina?"

I push again, harder, using the back of my forearms. He releases me and takes a step back.

"Yes, Gianni," I snap. "Her."

"What about her?" He reaches for me, but I take another step back. "She's nothing."

"Nothing? Is that how you think of women you sleep with?"

"Jesus...no. That's not what I meant."

"So, you have slept with her?"

"Shit." He closes his eyes and runs a hand through his hair. "Yes, but...that's got nothing to do with this."

My stomach plummets. Is he going to lie to me? Does he lie

to women in general? "She can't be nothing, Gianni. A woman who comes to a funeral with a man isn't *nothing*."

"That wasn't what you think, De Luca. Her car died. We picked her up on the way."

"She has her own key, explain *that*."

He doesn't, instead he stares at me intently, looking for what, I couldn't say. "We're not together. Don't overthink this."

"Overthink it? Despite the fact that you think I use men for money, which, by the way I don't. You should also know, unequivocally, I don't poach another woman's man."

"Were you listening? I said we're not together." Something moves across his face, and if I didn't know better, I'd say it was resignation. But that's also when I realize I'm making way to big a deal, giving him too much power over a kiss that means nothing. To him.

It's not his fault I responded the way I did, wanting more than I should expect. But it's my feelings getting crushed, my heart that will undoubtedly get broken.

So I dig deep, searching for my inner mafia princess, that lazy bitch, and summon her the fuck up.

"You're right." How my voice doesn't waver is beyond me. "I am overthinking. You're a player, looking for someone to play with. But I'm not it."

"Shelley..." He reaches for my wrist.

"Don't." I jerk away and get a small sense of satisfaction when something washes over him. Something that almost looks like pain when he swallows, but then I remind myself who I'm confronting. Gianni-fucking-Cadora.

"Uh...you two." Marco steps out onto the balcony, with a look that says he probably saw more than he should have. "I hate to interrupt, but..." He stops.

"What?" we both say at the same time when he doesn't continue.

He grins, then shakes his head at Gianni. "Smooth, man."

"Fuck off." Gianni glares back.

I glare at them both. "Well?"

"There's a really hot blonde here to see you, Shelley."

"Oh...Cass."

Thank God.

"Give us a second," Gianni says to Marco, with a pointed look that would make lesser men scurry away. But Marco tips his chin and winks at me before turning to walk through the French doors.

My face turns hot.

Gianni cages my jaw with his big palm before I can move out of his way, his eyes boring deep into mine. I can tell he's searching for something.

"We're not done here, Shelley."

"Yeah, we are. There's nothing more to say."

"The hell there isn't."

Before I can argue further a tornado in the form of a blonde with flashing green eyes sweeps through the door.

"Oh, my God!" Cass cries, marching her curvy form, followed by Marco, into my new bedroom, dropping her purse on the bed. "Why didn't you call me sooner?"

She grabs my wrists and studies my hands before focusing on my face. "And what the hell happened to your eye?"

I embarrass myself by bursting into tears.

"What is going on?" She turns her stare to Gianni and Marco. Mostly at Gianni. "Why's my girl crying?"

Neither man answers her but both stare back, looking like they're not sure what to do with her.

"Okay, enough." Cass takes charge. "I don't mean to be rude in your home, but Shelley needs girl time." Through my fingers I catch a glimpse of her waving her hands, shooing them.

"Out...out. Let me handle this."

If I wasn't so messed up, I'd find it funny. Two alphas shepherded by a bossy blonde, followed by three dogs.

Dog number four, the overweight bulldog, plonks himself down on the floor at my feet, legs splayed, panting and almost looking like he's grinning with that pink tongue protruding from a slightly askew under bite. Now that I've had a chance to really look at him, I'd swear on a stack of hair foils he's Truman Capote reincarnated.

Marco shuts the door, but not before smiling at Cass. Though I'm not sure she notices as she's rushing back to me, wrapping her arms around me, pulling me close.

"I'm so pissed at you," she says, rubbing circles on my back. "Why didn't you call me? What are girlfriends supposed to be for?"

She steps back, keeping a hold on my upper arms. Her gorgeous green eyes shimmer with worry.

"I'm sorry," I mumble. "I was embarrassed and couldn't deal with all the questions."

"Tell me that glorious-looking man with those sexy blue eyes isn't responsible for any of this?"

"God, no! This is all Dean."

"That motherfucker," she yells. "If he comes near you again, I'll sit on him while you use your hair-clippers on his balls."

Trust Cass, she always knows what to say. We stare at each for a heartbeat, then we both burst into giggles.

When we finally get it together, she asks, "So, what's the story with those two?" She points her chin in the direction of my bedroom door.

"Gianni's helping me."

"And who is this Gianni and why haven't I heard about him before?"

"Long story."

"I have time. I'm here for you baby...tell Momma."

"Okay."

"Excellent. Because I brought wine." She points a finger at me. "I want every lurid, dirty detail." A bottle of Chardonnay and a corkscrew appear out of her thousand-dollar, mint green designer bag. "Start at the very beginning." After popping the cork and pouring the wine into glasses she found in the bathroom, she toes one shoe off at a time and hops onto the bed.

Careful not to spill the wine, I lower myself into a plush, over-sized armchair upholstered in velour the color of burnt sienna.

As I sip and unload, I realize I'm an idiot for not telling her.

"I'm gonna need some time off," I say when I'm done. "You know...while my hands heal."

"No worries, hon." She shakes her head and brushes angular bangs from her face. "Take as long as you need. Your clients will miss you but they'll be fine. However, I'm still trying to wrap my head around this mafia thing. How come you never told me?"

"That my father hid money from the government?"

"Uh huh."

"Well, it's not exactly something you speak openly of. I loved my dad, but I'm not exactly proud of what he did."

"Yeah, I can see that." Cass swirls her wine, takes a sip, then peeks at me through her lashes. "And you and this Gianni?"

"What about us?" I ask warily, wondering how much to divulge. Not that there is much to divulge.

"There's gotta be something there and I don't mean because you dated his brother."

"He thought of me as an annoying pain in his ass, not worthy of his brother."

"That was then. What about now?"

"Now he wants to play. Thinks I'm a toy."

There's a skeptical slant to her beautiful cat eyes. "Mmm... not buying it. I had about two seconds to examine him, but that's not the vibe I was getting. Not the way he was looking at you. He's got an agenda beyond playing, hon."

"That's what I'm afraid of."

"You're gonna be all right? You can always stay with me."

"Thanks," I murmur, thinking I might need to take her offer.

"And Dean, that bastard. He's fine-looking, dammit, but I knew there was a reason I didn't trust him. He was always so damn possessive. He came to the salon looking for you."

"I suspected he might."

Cass pulls her lips in between her teeth and nods. "He got this really odd look on his face when I told him you had called in sick. I couldn't understand why, I mean"—she throws out a hand—"wouldn't he know you were sick? Anyway, I should have figured something was up and checked on you. I'm sorry, Shelley, I'm not a very good friend, am I?"

"Don't you do that. You're the best I've got. Anyway, I don't want to talk about him anymore. Will you help me wash my hair?"

"Of course, on one condition." She slides her bottom off the edge of the bed. "Damn, these wood floors are beautiful. I need to ask that man of yours who did them."

"He's not my man, Cass. What condition?"

"You have to tell me about baldy. Is he single?"

"Say what?" My eyebrows shoot straight up.

"He's kinda hot in that bad boy, biker sort of way." She blushes and fans herself as she pulls up a chair to the bathroom sink. "I'd love to get a closer look at all that ink."

"Cassandra Jones!" My face splits into a grin. "Marco? Really? You're stepping out of your fancy white-bread-Wall-Street comfort zone?" I smirk as I get comfortable in the chair.

"I know," she giggles. "There's a lot yummy about him, all those muscles and tats. If I dated him, my parents would *die.*" She fills up a decorative pitcher with warm water. "Tip your head back."

"Mmm," I groan as the warm water saturates my scalp. "That feels good." She pours a dollop of shampoo onto her palm. I get a familiar whiff of green apples as she massages it into my scalp working up a thick, foamy lather. I smile thinking it must be the same stuff Gianni uses.

Suddenly a more pungent odor breaks through.

"Ugh!" Cass wrinkles her nose and sniffs the bottle.

"God. What's that smell?" I ask, almost gagging.

"Well, it's not this...OH! Jesus. That fucking ugly-ass dog just farted."

Gak.

I push myself out of my chair, ignoring the pain shooting through my palms. Must. Get. Outside!

"Open the window," I yell, hitting the fan switch and scrambling to get out of Cass's way. We do one of those move to the left, move to the right things before she holds me still and steps past me, then flings the window wide. I shuffle out of the bathroom, covering my nose and wiping shampoo from my eyes. Almost tripping over the damn dog in question, who's running circles around my legs probably thinking it's a game.

Cass is right behind me waving hands in front of her face when we spill out onto the balcony.

We gulp lungfuls of ocean air, then look at each other. For the second time since she got here, and this time fueled by wine, we burst into giggles.

"What the hell do they feed you?" I say to the dog, who I've decided to name Truman.

The dog sneezes and hangs his head. Big droplets of drool fall on the tile and I have to be more than buzzed because I swear his lips turn pink.

"Oh boy, buddy. How can something so ugly and farts like you be so damn cute?" I scratch the top of his flat, blonde head and this seems to please him. He snorts and smiles, turning on his canine charm. And just like that, I fall in love with the little bastard.

"You know, Truman, you and I can be really good friends as long as you don't keep doing *that*."

AN HOUR LATER, after Cass has blow-dried and styled my hair, I'm still buzzed from wine and grateful it's not from Vicodin for a change.

Before leaving, Cass helps me unpack and hang my clothes in a closet the size of an extra-large storage container. They look lost in there.

From my limited wardrobe, I choose loose black palazzo pants, and a matching low-cut, V-necked sweater and since I can't navigate the hooks, forget the bra.

My hands and knees are scabbing, but they're still tender and currently unbandaged as I'm airing them out from my shower.

Just as I'm slipping on a pair of sandals my cell phone pings.

Dean: *Miss you Baby. Can't hide from me. Know where you are.*

Ugh.

Dean: *Can't stop thinking about you. All the things I'm going to do when we're together again. Just thinking about you makes me hard.*

Then the asshole sends a dick pic.

Dean: *This is what you do to me.*

Fuck.

I need a new phone.

I'd be lying if didn't admit I was scared. But really, I'm more disgusted and annoyed. I should tell Gianni, maybe...no, definitely, minus the dick pic, but I'm not ready to face him yet.

I am, however, fortified with alcohol and perhaps my judgement is lacking but I've had enough of Dean's crap.

Me: *Fuck you, Dean. I hope it falls off.*

The moment I press send, I realize my mistake. My insides dip as I toss my phone onto the bed.

Stupid, stupid, *stupid.*

When are they going to invent the technology to *unsend* a text? I'd invest.

Shaking my head at my stupidity, I wander over to the French doors and lean against the frame. In the failing light, a small sailboat skims over the choppy ocean and a tiny crewman dressed in yellow ducks under a shifting boom.

Dean aside, I have a bigger problem. A rather large, man-sized one and it's taking every cell in my body to fight this attraction and I have no real defenses. I've never had any defenses against him.

As a teen, I would have given anything to be seduced by Gianni, no matter how selfish or inappropriate.

Okay, since I'm being honest, I'll admit I went out of my way to attract him. Pretending to myself I was dressing for Joey in sexy tops, showing lots of skin. I didn't make it obvious (at least, that's what I hoped) and I didn't exactly throw myself at him because that would have pissed Joey off and caused a fight. Not that they needed a reason to fight. But I put myself in situations where I *might* have brushed up against him. Or my bare leg touched his briefly under the table. I'd pretend it was an accident or I didn't notice.

The summer before my dad died, I'd overheard Gianni making plans to attend a concert at Crissy Field. I convinced Joey and some other friends to go and I dressed in low-rider jean shorts and a tank that exposed inches of my midriff and my belly ring. I thought I looked hot. Joey agreed but Gianni lost his shit when a girlfriend and I *accidentally* ran into him and his date on the way to the bathroom.

He looked me up and down, wrapped his hand around the inside of my arm, his knuckles grazing my breast. I barely noticed him pulling me aside as I was fixated on the electricity buzzing through my nipples and body.

Then his mouth got close to my ear and he growled. Not *hello* or *how's it going*. Instead, I got *What the fuck you doing? My brother lets you dress like that and walk around alone? You looking for trouble, Shelley?*

I didn't know what reaction I expected, but it wasn't that. It was the first time he put his hands on me and the first time I experienced raw sexual need in a way that left me edgy for days. I didn't even mind he was pissed because he *noticed* me and I got *that* reaction from him. Like he cared a whole lot.

When I looked over my shoulder as we marched away, he was watching me and I won't deny it thrilled me.

If he decides to seduce me now, how long will I be able to hold out and what happens if I no longer want to?

For him, it'll be just sex.

For me, something else entirely.

The thought is profoundly depressing. Problem is, there's a part of me that wants to be one of his women. That's willing to take what I can get. Good thing the rest of me—the saner, smarter part isn't—and that's what I'm clinging to.

A knock on my door sounds. "Come in," I yell over my shoulder, thinking it's probably Cass being her usual forgetful self and come back for something.

As soon as the door closes, the skin on my neck reacts, as if a breeze passes over it. I whirl around and my heart stops, then resumes pounding at double speed.

His hair is damp and curling over his ears. A clean pair of jeans hug those lean hips, complemented with a light blue, button-down flannel shirt. It's partially open, allowing a glimpse of hard chest muscles.

"You have a moment?"

He enters without waiting for my answer, but it wouldn't matter, since his hotness has fried all the synapses in my brain and I can't seem to formulate any words. One more layer of my defenses crumble and falls like confetti to my feet.

On his way towards me, he drops something onto my bed, though his eyes never leave my face. They're searching, like he's trying to see inside my head, read my thoughts, gage my reaction and therefore determine how to deal with me. I find this all unnerving, yet strangely empowering. It seems I may have him on uncertain footing.

Then he one-ups me.

"You look beautiful," he says.

The muscles between my legs clench. It's bad enough he's in my room, filling my space but then he has to throw words like that at me? Not only does it confuse me, but I'm immediately suspicious.

"I took advantage earlier, when I kissed you," he says.

My eyes widen and I'm thinking what the hell? When he says nothing more, it occurs that although he hasn't actually said he's sorry, at least he's acknowledging it. Since he broached the subject, I may as well call him on it.

"I'm not at your disposal, Gianni."

"I know." He takes another step, stopping only a foot away.

Dammit, he's too close.

I drag my gaze away, afraid he'll see more than I want him to and focus on the little sailboat that's almost below the bridge now.

"I don't want you to think it's the reason I brought you here." His voice is soft. "To take advantage of you." He reaches out a hand and wraps it around my forearm. I manage not to react. He cannot know he has any power over me.

"Shelley?"

I ignore him.

"Will you look at me, please?"

I steel my nerves and meet his gaze, careful to keep my expression bland.

It's not easy. It's not fair, the advantage he has, and though his touch on the surface may look impersonal, it feels possessive.

"Are we good?" he asks.

No, we're not. But I shrug as casually as I can. "Sure," I say, then turn my eyes back to the water. "It was just a kiss."

Those fingers around my arm tighten almost indiscernibly. "Right," he says after a beat and lets go of my arm. I hate that the warmth is gone. I want it back.

"Come inside."

"Why?" I hold my breath and glance at him, noticing he's gone cool again.

"Time for fresh bandages." He points to the little bag on my bed and indicates with his head that I should precede him.

I hesitate, not sure I want him touching me while my body's humming the way it is. Except he leaves me no choice by stepping behind and herding me towards the bed.

"Take a seat."

I continue to stand while he scoots that comfortable armchair closer, placing it in front of me then eases into it.

"De Luca"—he catches my eye—"sit."

It's fruitless to argue, so I sigh and drop onto the bed. He begins to roll his sleeves and I'm spellbound by his arms, not too bulky, but strong and beautiful. His muscles cord and flex as his fingers manipulate the fabric, making my stomach tighten. I'm thinking I'm doomed as a wave of arousal washes over me.

When he's done, he reaches for my leg, cupping my foot and lifting it, situating it on the chair between his thighs.

I force myself to keep my breathing steady, even as his warmth lingers around my ankle.

But then his other hand captures the fabric of my pants, sliding slowly up my calf and the back of my knee. Trails of fire follow, which burn brighter the higher he goes. Those palms are rough and calloused, like a man used to hard work, but they feel good moving over my overly sensitive skin.

So, so good, I don't want him to stop.

That hand shifts to the inside of my thigh. Every single muscle tightens and it wouldn't take much for me to climax if he'd just touch me *there*. I bite harder to stop from gasping and squeezing my legs together.

It would be so easy to give in. To spread my thighs inviting him further.

"Gianni?" My voice is breathy and little more than a whisper.

His hand stops midway and it's not lost on me that he's breathing harder than he should. I search his face, but his eyes are focused on the spot where my thighs meet.

"Gianni?" Stronger this time.

His gaze shifts to mine, and it's hot, glazed, like a man really turned on.

"What are you doing?" I whisper and it's odd to me that it's me asking this time.

"Whatever the fuck you want me to."

"You need to stop."

"Jesus, De Luca," he says it like it hurts. "You can't look at me like that and expect me to want to stop."

I blink and his hand inches a little bit higher.

I swallow, because I want him to keep going but he can't. He just can't, and it takes everything in me to say, "Please stop."

He stills and shuts his eyes. Then a moment later he sits

back in his chair, taking a deep breath through his nose. When he looks at me again his face has gone hard.

"You're a piece of work."

"What?"

"The fuck you doing pulling a stunt like that?"

"Me? What are you talking about?"

"Don't pull that shit with me. Your voice says stop but your eyes say something else."

Oh *God!*

"Are you kidding me? You're calling me a cock-tease?"

"Your words, Shelley, not mine."

"You're the one who had *your* hands on *my* legs. I did not ask you to put them there, so how does that make me a cock-tease?"

"Yeah, that was me." He leans forward and gets in my face. "You don't look at a man like that, look at *me* like that, if you don't want to take it further."

"What are you talking about? Look at you how?"

"That's the way you wanna fucking play it?" He holds my gaze for a long moment. "Warning, De Luca. I'm not one of those little boys you've fucked before like my brother and I'm sure as fucking hell not Melnikov. Next time you play with me, expect to get what you get."

Excuse me?

Oh!

"That's a really fucked-up thing to say to me." I rise up and plant my hands on my hips. "I can see you haven't changed at all. You're still a giant asshole. In fact, I think you are an even bigger asshole than you ever were. This is the way I look, Gianni Cadora, and I'm not the one doing the playing. Believe me, I'm very aware you're not Joey and I'm also very aware you're not Dean. But guess what else I'm aware of?"

"I can't fucking wait to find out."

"Ugh! That, right there." I point at him. "It's men like you that make it difficult for a woman like me to trust. You never explained how someone"—I make air quotes with my fingers —"you're not in a *relationship* with has your goddam front door key. Don't you dare tell me I'm a piece of work. Apologize for insinuating I'm a cock-tease, or I'm packing up my ass and heading to Cass's."

"You're not leaving."

"Then apologize."

"Fine." His jaw sets into a hard line and those eyes are back to ice "You're not a cock-tease."

"And?" I tilt my head.

"And Gina used my house to entertain some of her real estate clients since her apartment was under construction. I forgot she still had the key."

"Hmm."

"Yeah, hmm. Now sit your ass down and let's try this again."

I open my mouth. His answer, however, was more than I expected, so I shut it. I'm angry and frustrated but mostly with myself that I allowed myself to be so exposed.

I'm also intrigued with the tiny kernel of knowledge I gained. It's the second time I've gotten the impression he's jealous. But I sweep it away because no damn good can come of me thinking like that. Thinking I may have some effect on him other than just a primal, basic one of a dog chasing a bitch in heat. Past experience has taught me how often I've been wrong about a man. Particularly as he wasn't honest with me about being with my dad when he died and I'm still not entirely convinced he's told me everything.

Since I can't look at him, because him being angry somehow makes him sexier, I focus on the snoring dog at my feet instead.

By the time he's finished bandaging my knees, I've calmed enough to resolve I'll stand firm and *not* give him any more power over me. I won't be his toy, no matter how persuasive he is or how much I want to.

My phone buzzes again. I glance at it and groan inwardly. Another text from Dean.

"What?" Gianni asks. Though he's calmed a little too, I get the impression he's not exactly lollipops and rainbows.

"Nothing."

"Hand me your phone, De Luca."

"It's nothing."

"Hand me your fucking phone, Shelley." He says it slowly, punctuating each word.

Okay.

So, he's still angry.

He sticks out his hand, palm up. I sigh and give it to him.

Dean: *Coming for you, baby.*

I watch him as he works his jaw, the muscles bunching as he scrolls through all the messages and figure the exact moment he sees the picture of Dean's erect penis. It isn't hard to miss because every muscle seems to solidify then vibrate.

When he's done reading, he lifts his gaze. His eyes are hard and glittery, making my skin prickle. I recognize that look. Joey had the same expression just before he blew.

"When were you going tell me about these?"

"I was going to..."

"I'm not fucking around here, Shelley."

"I..."

"*Do not* antagonize him. From this moment on, I want to know the second they come in. You forward them to me immediately. You get me?"

"Gianni, I..."

"Simple question, De Luca. Do. You. *Get*. Me?"

Shit, I'm in trouble.

I can take a lot of things, but I'm not sure I can take this.

Tears prickle at the back of my eyes and I blink several times, then nod.

He hands my phone back. Our fingers touch and that electric buzz runs through my hand. The way his jerk, I know he feels it too but he avoids my gaze and pulls the zipper on the first aid kit like it's the most important thing in the world in that moment.

"I've got work to do," he says. When I look up, I see what anyone who's ever fucked with a Cadora must have seen, right before they died. Pure, lethal, unadorned violence.

"Help yourself in the kitchen. If you need anything, ask Marco. I'll see you tomorrow."

Then he's gone. Five minutes later I hear the door on the truck slamming and then him leaving. The mutt hears it too. Truman raises his head, ears twitching. Then he turns towards me, blinks and farts.

Gah.

"Couldn't have said it better myself, buddy, but you are so not sleeping in my room tonight," I say, burying my head in the pillows.

9

GAME ON

~

The following evening, I enter the kitchen with a steadfast Truman in tow. Except to eat and do his business he hasn't left my side and truthfully, I'm grateful. It's been lonely.

Marco stirs something in a large pot on a stainless-steel gas stove. My senses detect garlic and tomatoes and my empty stomach celebrates.

When he hears me, he turns and I burst out laughing. Always the comedian, his head is freshly shaved and he's dressed in jeans and a black Henley, covered by a frilly pink apron with *Viva Las Vegas* stamped in rhinestones on the front.

"Look at you in your pretty little apron. How could I forget what a goofball you are?"

Without a doubt, he did it to cheer me up as he's laughing his big, warm laugh with me. The panty-dropping kind that comes from the gut and lights up his eyes. I see why Cass is so interested.

Gianni is missing in action...still. In fact, I'm not even sure if he came back last night. What if he went to Gina? Awful thoughts of them ran through my head on replay all night.

And all day.

I have no right to be jealous, but of course I am.

"What's cooking, good-looking?" I ask Marco, faking good humor and peeking past his shoulder.

"Spaghetti and meatballs," he says, hooking an arm around my neck and kissing the top of my head. "Want wine?" He points a wooden spoon to a crystal decanter of red on a large, polished farm-style table, with places set for three.

Three.

My pulse jumps. "Just a little," I manage to say without my voice shaking and betraying my excitement that Gianni's joining us. At least I hope it's Gianni, unless Marco has a date.

"Watch out for this one." Marco taps Truman's rear with a scuffed motorcycle boot, sending him out the kitchen door to join the rest of his pack in the backyard. "Go on, Dog. Go get your dinner." To me, he says, "He has a nasty habit of stinking up the room."

"I'm aware. Truman and I have become well acquainted."

"Truman?" He shoots me a glance, then dumps spaghetti into a colander in the sink. After it drains, he returns it to the pot, adding olive oil and fresh basil leaves.

"As in Capote. What's his real name?"

He lifts a shoulder. "Usually refer to him as Dog."

Hmm. I put my phone on the table, and contemplate why no one's bothered to name the poor mutt. He may be ugly, but he's clearly loyal. And to me that's far more attractive than good looks. After I've poured the wine, I carry a glass over to Marco.

"Salute." We tap glasses as the kitchen door opens. Before even looking, I feel him enter and everything stops. My heart, my breath, even my blood.

What doesn't stop, however, is the ability to take him in with that laser-focused giddiness of a schoolgirl. Sporting more stubble than yesterday and hair still wet from a recent shower, he looks predatory and dangerous, and so damn sexy it sets my nerves buzzing.

Our eyes catch for a long moment and it's a miracle my legs hold. Even when the dogs threaten to bombard the kitchen and he throws a leg across the door, blocking them from following him. Only when he turns to shut it, am I able to drag my gaze from him but not before I notice he's carrying an empty bag of dog food. Something about that, how he cares for those dogs, rushes through me, compounding that persistent, needy ache between my legs. He makes me want to breed, have babies with him.

In my peripheral, I covertly watch as he rolls and tosses the empty bag into the garbage then moves to the sink, pumps a soap dispenser, flips the faucet lever and lathers up.

Lord.

Even the way he washes his hands is hot and I'm rethinking my decision to keep my distance from him. He snatches a kitchen towel hanging from the oven handle, dries himself, then places it back in its original place.

"Would you like some wine?" I offer because one of us has to break this ridiculous tension.

He turns to me slowly, as if planning his next move. That handsome face is intense and those eyes are now a dark blue and...determined. Like he's made a decision and he's going to stick to it, while stalking the few steps from the stove to where I'm leaning with my back against the table. Next thing his feet straddle mine and I'm trapped against his warm, hard body. I can't move, not even an inch, even if I wanted to, which I don't.

Pressing a palm on the table behind me to support himself, he angles in, forcing me back and tilting his head. My lungs seize. Then the bastard smirks when my eyelashes flutter from his breath skating across my face and stopping at my ear. Shivers rush through me and I know he feels them because he tenses slightly and I see him swallow. The decanter clinks against a glass, I hear wine pouring and then slowly, so very fucking slowly, he pulls back, capturing my gaze.

Okay.

He wants to play dirty.

Well then. Before I think twice about the consequences, I touch the tip of my tongue to the corner of my lip, then drag my teeth across the bottom one.

He hisses, closes his eyes. It's a long second before he murmurs in my ear, "Careful, De Luca. Don't be starting any fires."

Fires indeed.

Fires everywhere: in my body, in my blood and in my heart.

"You two done?" Marco asks.

Crud.

I squeeze my eyes shut and pull in my lips; I'd completely forgotten we weren't alone. That's the power this man has over me.

"For now," Gianni answers, but to me he mutters, "Game on, De Luca." As he pulls away I can't help feeling a tiny victory when I notice the semi bulge in his jeans.

"Good, 'cause dinner's ready, dude. Help yourself, I'm not serving your ugly ass." Marco grins as he unties the frilly apron and tosses it onto the back of a chair.

He sets a plate loaded with spaghetti and several meatballs on the table and pulls out a chair, motioning that I should sit. If he notices my flushed face, to his credit, he doesn't show it.

Once everyone is seated, we dig in. I sprinkle freshly grated Parmesan on my meatballs and taste.

Mmm. "Whose recipe is this?"

"My mom's...family secret," Marco says. "I could tell you, but then I'd have to marry you."

"Ha! Somehow, I don't think I'm the girl for you." I send him a coy smile. "I think you might prefer blondes with pretty green eyes."

He nods but says, "Well, then numbnuts here will have to marry you." He ticks his head and flicks a thumb at his cousin.

That comment makes me almost snort wine out my nose, but I manage cover it with a little cough.

"My nuts are certainly not numb," Gianni counters, looking at me. "Blue, maybe." It takes everything to keep my face blank and not allow myself to hope his blue balls are because of me. If I think I'm going to one up him, I'm an idiot. This game he wants to play is too dangerous. *He's* too dangerous and too experienced at getting what he wants.

I take a sip of wine, savoring it, allowing time to compose myself then steer the conversation elsewhere. "I'd like to see Billy tomorrow."

"Marco will take you. Unfortunately, I have commitments I can't get out of."

"I can go on my own."

"Not happening," Gianni says.

"I know you're busy too, Marco. I'll take Billy's Land Rover. You guys don't need to babysit me every moment of the day."

"Yeah, we do," they say together, then look at each other and shake their heads.

Ooo...kay.

"You can't drive anyway," Marco says, registering the look on my face. "Not with your hands like that."

Gianni only glares. "And don't think about pulling any more stunts like you did yesterday. He wants you to engage with him. Don't give him that."

"What did you do?" Marco asks, cocking the brow with the barbell.

"Um...I kinda told him to fuck off."

"Ah, shit."

"He sent me a dick pic. I was grossed out and had a momentary lapse in judgment."

"A dick pic?"

Gianni lets out a feral growl at the reminder. Marco tenses and there's a similar deadly expression in each of their eyes, leaving no doubt to their family connection. I suspect they got lessons from their dads, *how to look badass 101.*

Although, probably wasn't a good idea to remind him about the photo.

"That fucker's gonna make a move," Marco says. "I can feel it."

"Yep." Gianni nods. "Question remains how far he's going to go."

"Okay, so..." I ask both of them. "What should I prepare myself for?"

"Could be anything," Gianni answers. "Just be aware of where you are and who you're with."

As I'm taking another bite of meatball, my phone pings with a new text. I jump and everyone else freezes. First, I'm relieved when I see it's from Marshall, my building manager, then my head jerks back, when I read it.

Are you okay?

Why's he asking me if I'm okay? Suddenly a cold and tingly feeling touches the back of my neck.

"What's up, De Luca?"

"I don't know. Need to make a call."

Both men stop eating and watch me as I rise from the table and walk out the kitchen to the hall. The meatballs feeling suddenly heavy in my stomach.

"Shelley?" Marshall answers after the first ring. "Jeez, girl, you almost killed me, I've been so damn worried."

"Marshall, what's going on?"

"Tell me you're okay? If you're not say *up yours, Marshall.*"

I almost want to laugh, but he doesn't call me out of the blue for nothing. "I'm good but you're starting to freak me out."

"Girl, your apartment was broken into."

Good God!

Coincidence?

"I was worried after what happened, you know, the other day. Thought that punk came back and hurt you. You don't have anything of value in there, do you?"

I'm stunned and can't speak, except for a whimper.

"Your neighbor called me a few minutes ago. She was gone the whole weekend and when she got home noticed your door had been drilled open. I'm here at your unit now. What you want me to do? Call the cops?"

"No!" My voice comes out a little louder than I intended. "Please don't call the cops. Can you wait inside until I get there? I'm on my way."

"Shelley...?"

"I'll be there in thirty. Please, Marshall, let me see what's up, then if I need to call them, I will."

I hear him sigh into the phone. "Sure. I'll wait. But I'm not happy about this."

"I know and I appreciate you worrying about me." I let out a little sigh of my own. "Thank you. I'll be there soon and I'm bringing backup."

When I re-enter the kitchen Gianni looks up, takes a look at my face and says, "Sit and start talking."

"Ah..."

"De Luca...?"

"Um..."

"Fuck," he grumbles, looking at Marco. "Why is it when you *need* women to talk, they can't?"

"Uh..."

"Spill it, Shelley."

So, I spill.

"Why would he break into your place?" Marco asks when I'm done. "Do you have something of his?"

I gasp. "Oh God." I slap a palm on my forehead. "The night of Joey's funeral he came to my apartment. Said he'd left something there and needed to get it. I didn't believe him. I thought it was an excuse to get me to open the door, but maybe there really is something."

"Need to check it out and we need to go now." Gianni pushes the remnants of his food away and rises.

"Bad, bad fucking feeling about this," says Marco. "Asshole could have planted something you wouldn't want the cops to find." Another look passes between them and my knees tremble.

"What do you mean?"

"Drugs...or something," Gianni says, his eyes getting hard. "What *do* you know about this piece of crap you fucked, Shelley?"

"Dude." Marco shoots Gianni a glance. Gianni ignores him, continuing to glare at me

I chew on my nail, and though I don't like what he says, I don't know what to say in response, because he's right. What do I know about Dean?

Nothing; that is the truth.

10

LIGHTS, CAMERA, ACTION

~

Half an hour later, as we exit from the questionable elevator in my building and step onto my floor, my palms begin to sweat. My front door is shut, but not secured. So much for my new industrial deadbolt. I realize now it gave me a false sense of security. If Dean had wanted in, there wasn't much to stop him.

Gianni blocks me with his arm as I aim to push it open and steps in front. "What does Marshall look like?"

"Big, muscular black guy, about fifty."

"Stay back," he orders then nods at Marco. They both pull weapons from the back of their jeans.

What the...?

How did I not know they were carrying? More bad ass 101? Then they enter with Gianni in the lead and I can see past them down the hall where Marshall is sitting on my couch with the remote resting on his leg, watching TV.

He stands, tips his chin at them, ignoring their weapons and moves to engulf me in his big arms.

"Damn, girl. I was expecting to see your body lying on the floor when I first came in. Who're your wingmen?"

After introductions, they stash their guns, shake hands and size each other up.

"Army?" Marco asks.

"Marines," Marshall responds. "You?"

"Hooah!"

The two bump fists and Gianni watches, legs spread, arms folded and looking no less intimidating.

With the pleasantries done, he asks, "Tell us what you know."

"Just what I told Shelley on the phone," Marshall says. "Nothing more."

"Talk to the neighbor," Gianni says to his cousin. "See what she has to say." Marco nods and wastes no time following orders.

"I'll get my tools in the meantime," Marshall contributes, "and fix the lock for you, unless you're calling the cops?"

"No!" I say. "No cops."

He cocks his head, but says nothing then catches Gianni's eye. I hear Marshall mumble something to him, but I'm not paying too much attention, because I've moved away and am surveying the damage to my apartment.

When he's gone I check under my mattress for the envelope in which I keep my tips. It's still there, all fifteen hundred dollars. Almost dizzy with relief, I shove it into my purse. No way I'm leaving it here now as it's my only means to pay rent and it's not even all that's due.

I cast an eye around for anything missing. Things have been moved, some drawers are open and my bed looks rumpled. But I don't notice anything obviously gone or any damage. I check my jewelry box and my collection of silver is intact. And so is my amber heart. Obviously not a burglary, which leaves no doubt this is Dean's work.

Then I go to check the bathroom, but Gianni blocks me.

"Don't go in there, Shelley."

"Why not?" Something about his voice, low and cautious, makes my tailbone tingle, but conversely more determined to see what he's blocking.

"Just don't, you don't need to see it."

"Dammit, get out of my way." I duck under his arm and flip the light switch. The noisy extraction fan spins to life and my heart stops as all the oxygen is punched from my lungs.

Lingerie Dean bought is scattered all over the counter, tub and hanging from the clear glass shower doors. Thongs, panties and two sexy teddies. None of which I had worn, still sporting their price tags. For some reason, even before Dean hit me, I couldn't bring myself to wear them.

Now they are a statement in my bathroom and written in my red lipstick on the white tile of the shower enclosure is *MINE.*

MINE. MINE. MINE.

Repeatedly.

But worse, much, *much worse*. A pair of my sexiest and most expensive lacy panties lie on my vanity. I'd worn them the day before the funeral and discarded them to join the rest of my dirty laundry in my hamper.

They're covered in a white sticky substance. My brain seems to have stopped working as it takes me several moments to register. I'd heard dirty stories of men, *stalkers*, doing things like this but never thought I'd see the day it happened to me.

The asshole jerked off and came on my panties.

I gasp, take a step back and slam into Gianni. Our eyes meet in the vanity mirror.

He knows what I've seen. His fingers digging into my upper arms are a clue, and the rage vibrating off him is palpable.

"I'm gonna fucking kill him," he grinds out through that hard, clenched jaw.

Above all, Dean's cologne lingers, clinging to the lacy bits of fabric. I'd venture a guess on my panties too. I picture him sniffing them while he jerks himself off. Maybe in another universe I'd find Gianni sniffing my panties hot, but not Dean. Never Dean.

I gag and stop breathing, not wanting to absorb his smell. An overwhelming sense of violation washes over me and my mouth opens and closes, but no words come out. Seeing me struggle, and with his fingers still digging into my arms, Gianni pivots and pushes me out of the confined space.

Outside, every attempt to suck in air falls short. No matter how many breaths I take, I can't seem to get enough.

Gianni's right behind me, wrapping his arms around my waist. Despite his own fury, he seems to know what I need and mutters in my ear, "Keep it together, babe. I got you." His breath against my hair, his warmth against my body and his voice begin to break through. "I got you."

I twist in his arms and slump into him, shaking, feeling his rage vibrate through him and nudging my nose into his armpit, pulling in his scent. If I could just smell *him*, the clean scent of his deodorant and that slight musky man smell, I might get through this. It's primal, base and strangely comforting.

To both of us.

"Come on, babe," he says after about a minute, and half carries, half leads me to the couch, helping me sit. Funny how I feel like a stranger in my own apartment. As if Dean's vile acts and presence have made it something other than my home.

Gianni drops to his haunches in front of me. "Look at me," he says, taking the tips of my fingers, squeezing them till I meet his eyes. "This fuck is gonna pay. That I promise you." His words are not light. They carry the weight of generations of mafia vows made in times of war.

"I feel so violated," I whisper shakily. To stop my teeth from rattling, I clench my jaw. "So fucking defiled."

He drops his head and looks at the floor and I hear him take a deep breath. When he meets my eyes again, his expression is a mix of conviction and anger, yet lying beneath both of those emotions, I see concern for me.

"He's fucked with the wrong people, Shelley. This will not go unanswered. But right now, I have to focus on what's important. That's dealing with this and keeping you safe. I need you to help me with that. You get me?"

I swallow down the hard lump in my throat and tamp down my anger. Then I nod.

Gianni's expression is uncompromising and solid, but his Adam's apple bobbing and the barely noticeable twitch in his eye are things he can't hide. I wish I knew how he stays so damn calm. Years of watching his father, I suppose, and not reacting as expected when provoked.

I should take lessons.

I want to slash pillows or swing my softball bat at something. Maybe target practice with Ziggy, preferably aiming at Dean's knees, but because Gianni's holding my gaze and my fingers, anchoring me like a tiny boat on the ocean in the face of a hurricane, I don't.

"You good?" he asks after a long time.

I tip my chin, and after studying me, it seems he's satisfied that I am. "Okay, babe, sit tight."

He stands, letting my fingers slip slowly out of his. Then takes a small step back, turns and walks to the bathroom. Pulling his phone from his back pocket he videos my apartment, bathroom and the drilled-out front-door lock. It has a calming effect, watching him move, his strength filling my space and knowing he's here doing this for me. Calming because I'm no longer shaking. My anger, however, that's entirely a different matter. But pretty soon my pounding heart slows to its normal beat.

As he's finishing, Marco returns from next door. "Neighbor doesn't know anything else," he says. "Didn't see…whoa."

His eyes slide from the bathroom, to me on the couch, then to Gianni. "Shit." This comes out long and low as he points to my bathroom.

"Yup," I say, chewing on my thumbnail and bouncing my foot.

"That creepy motherfucking fuck."

"Yup."

"You okay?"

"Besides feeling sick and ready to slice his balls off? Yeah, I'm just fine and dandy."

Cass's suggestion of taking my hair clippers to his testicles sounds really attractive about now. I'm not a violent person despite my family history, but with Dean I could indeed engage in doing bodily harm.

The sound of a toolbox clanging on the floor snaps me out of my dark fantasy. Marshall is back.

Good.

We can blow this fucking joint. "I don't want to be here anymore," I yell to everyone in general. "Can we go, please?" I rise and hook my purse from the floor.

"Not yet." Gianni pokes his head out of the bathroom. "Need to clean up here first, babe. You don't want to come back to this. Where are your cleaning supplies?"

"Under the kitchen sink, but don't you have people for this?" I rise to get them. "Cleaning up messes?"

"I do, DeLuca. But I'm not asking anyone else to do this, so sit." He stalks towards me. "Let us handle this."

"I can do it," I snap.

"I said sit."

I tilt my head up and level a glare at him with my fists balled on my hips. "And I said I can do it. I'm not one of your dogs, Gianni Cadora. Stop ordering me to sit."

He stares back, tips his chin down then those ridiculously hot lips twitch.

"What the hell's so damn funny?"

This gets me a full-blown grin. "There you go again, being all cute with your spice."

"Shut up."

Now all three men are smiling. What the hell?

"Fine." I release a puff of air and roll my eyes. "Let's get this done already." I barge past him, roll into my kitchen, grab a sponge, yellow rubber cleaning gloves, bleach and 409. As I march back he blocks me by placing hands on my shoulders, making soothing little circles with his thumbs.

"De Luca," he says quietly.

"What?"

"You can't get chemicals on your hands, babe."

"That's what the gloves are for."

His eyes go soft. "You think those are gonna fit over your bandages?"

My brow furrows as I eye my gloves, then my hands.

Dammit, he's got a point.

Those thumbs have moved to the base of my throat and are distracting me, making my pulse flutter.

"Hand them over, babe. And there's no point in wasting energy fighting, because the end result is gonna be the same."

"You keep saying that to me."

"Because it's the truth. There *is* no point in arguing. Not about this."

I sigh and hand the supplies to Marco, who takes them back to the bathroom. Then I go in search of a garbage bag which I also keep under the sink. "Can you get rid of those...things?" I say, passing it over trying to suppress a grimace. "I can't touch them."

"Sure," Gianni says softly and takes it from me, our fingers grazing. Even under these horrible circumstance, my stomach flips.

Both men disappear behind the door. I blow a strand of hair out of my face, and begin to straighten my bed and I'm about to push back the drawers on my dresser when I hear them.

First Marco, and it's nothing unusual because that's the type of man he is. Goofball extraordinaire.

But then Gianni joins in and my head jerks up.

Buona sera, signorina, buona sera...

Good God, they're singing. How could they be singing at a time like this?

It is time to say goodnight to Napoli...

A moment later Marshall's smooth, dark chocolate voice accompanies with trumpet sounds.

Though it's hard for...

More trumpet noises, and now one of them is whistling.

Despite it all, I drop my head and giggle because there's nothing else for me to do and I know what they're doing.

This is for me.

Our parents used to goof around and sing this song and other old, much raunchier Italian classics.

And by the little jewelry...

As kids, it was uncool and embarrassing, which of course only made them sing louder. Now, it's just funny.

Marshall finishes up with the lock and steps over the threshold to give me a new set of keys, still trumpeting along.

They wrap up the song and Marco, sporting a cheesy sideways grin, steps out of the bathroom and bows with a dramatic flick of his wrist. I clap delicately with the tips of my fingers and blow kisses.

"Shelley?" Marshall calls. "How long has your bathroom fan been making that noise."

Huh.

"Um, I'm not really sure. I didn't notice it before."

He lifts his brows, then his eyes slant back to the fan. "I'm gonna check it since I'm here. Got something for me to stand on?"

"Yeah, there's a step-stool in the hallway closet."

He retrieves it, then pulls a screwdriver from his bag, situates the stool and unscrews the grate from the ceiling.

Gianni holds up the garbage bag filled with the unsoiled lingerie. "What do you want to do with these?"

"Give them to my neighbor. She dates a lot. Maybe she can use them."

"She a hooker?" Marco asks.

I wrinkle my nose and think about his question. "I don't think so, but why would you ask that?"

"She's not that hot. If she's dating as much as you say, maybe something else is going on. And she thought I was there to see her when she opened the door."

Say what?

But I don't have much time to think about it because Marshall interrupts.

"Uh...Shelley? You need to see this."

Crap. What did I break?

"What's the matter?"

He scratches the back of his head, brown eyes wide. He's pointing to the hole in the ceiling with his screwdriver.

"What am I looking at?"

Gianni follows me in, his eyes focusing on a small dark object attached in the corner of the square hole. Instantly the energy changes to something dark and dangerous a second before he emits a long, low growl and slams his fist into the bathroom tile.

The sound echoes above the noise of the still-running fan and I'm surprised the tile didn't crack.

"That fuck is dead."

Obviously, I'm missing something and I'm almost afraid to ask. "I don't understand." I glance at Marco whose nostrils flare. "What's he showing me?"

"That, De Luca," Gianni grits out, pulling my focus back to him, "is a camera. That pile of rat shit's been perving on you in the shower."

A camera?

A fucking *camera*!

I close my eyes. A shudder vibrates through my body as the words sink in. My legs buckle and I drop to my haunches, ass on my heels. First the panties and now this. I take three deep, hopefully calming breaths before I open my eyes.

In my peripheral vision, I catch sight of Gianni's hands, which are shaking and white, the skin on two of his knuckles split and bloody.

"Stay with her," he shoots to Marco, his fury obvious in his voice. "Gotta get some air."

Then he's gone and my door slams behind him, making the walls in my apartment quiver.

"Should I go after him?" I make a move to stand, stumbling a little as my legs are shaky.

"No!" Marco's arm snakes across the front of my shoulders and stops me short. "Let him cool down."

I press my injured palms against my forehead until they hurt. *Shit.* They're shaking too. However, I'm more worried about Gianni. I've never seen him so angry and wonder for a moment if I've broken him.

"He's not going to do anything stupid, is he?"

"My cousin's many things, but stupid isn't one of them." Marco's expression carries none of his earlier antics when he tried to cheer me up. Instead his usually warm brown eyes are hard and if I didn't have a clue about how serious this is before, I'm getting it now.

"Just give him space."

I blow air through my lips trying to pull it together. A fucking camera?

In the bathroom, I watch Marshall disconnect the tiny spy-cam from the fan and he hands it to me along with its battery. Who knew they made them so small.

"The day before Dean hit me," I say to Marco, "he'd said his stomach was upset. I left him alone in my apartment to get him something from the drug store down the street. I bet that's when he installed it. I wonder why he didn't fix the noise?" I dangle the camera between two fingers. "If he had, we would never have found it."

"Probably 'cause he was interrupted," Marco says. "We should check around for any more devices that fuck may have planted."

"You all need help?" Marshall asks, finishing up and screwing back the grate.

"We're good," Marco answers. "Appreciate it if I could borrow your tools?"

The men lock eyes, some silent battle passing between them until Marshall nods. "I'll leave them here for you and when you're done, drop them off at my apartment."

They shake hands, then Marshall hugs me as I see him out the door. "I'm glad you're good, and you have a crew to take care of you."

"Thanks for understanding, Marshall. When things settle down, I'll buy you lunch."

"That, I'll accept."

When I close my door Marco's already pushing open my windows and shining a flashlight over the metal fire escape. Then he scrutinizes the light fixtures, the smoke detectors and even the carbon monoxide alarm while I go through my cabinets and closets.

We search every obvious and not-so-obvious place but there's no sign of any additional spying devices.

Half an hour goes by with no word from Gianni. Worry begins to gnaw at my gut while I imagine all sorts of mayhem he's committing on the city when, at last, Marco's phone chimes with a text. He dips his head to read it.

"Where are your car keys?"

I point to them on the breakfast bar.

"Come on." He snags them and the camera. "Time to blow this joint. Bring whatever you need with you. Not coming back for a while."

I snatch up my jewelry box and the amber necklace and shove them into my purse. I can't believe I forgot my silver or my tips the last time I was here.

Stupid Vicodin.

We dump the garbage bag full of lingerie at my neighbor's door and return Marshall's tools. Curiously, the soiled panties have disappeared and I wonder which one of them took care of them for me. It doesn't matter who, I'm just glad it didn't have to be me. And last, we head out through the lobby into the cold night air.

Gianni's waiting at the bottom of the stairs, a thumb hooked into his jeans pockets. His expression is dark and brooding and still dangerous as he watches us walk through the double glass doors.

As Marco opens the door, holding it for me to pass first, a Nissan Centra with teeth-rattling hip-hop echoing off the buildings drives by. Two drunk girls hang out the rear windows.

"Yoooow," one of them calls.

Gianni turns his head towards the noise and the girl closest to us lifts her top and flashes her enormous naked breasts at the men. Gianni shakes his head, then focuses them back onto me rolling his eyes.

"Life in the big city," Marco murmurs as he tosses my keys to Gianni.

He snatches them out of the air and shoves them in his jacket pocket. When he takes the spy-cam from Marco, his jaw's still tight but he's calmer and his breathing is even.

"Hopefully you didn't kill anyone?" I lay my hands on his waist. He tenses. It takes a moment for his eyes to hit mine, but when they do, I swallow.

"Not yet."

In that instant I realize, he may have gone legit, but the blood coursing through his veins is still mafia, and always will be. Leaving no doubt that he *would* kill. What's more, and this may have more to do with that honor thing Billy mentioned, but I believe he'd kill for me. I must be a sick person because although the knowledge is unnerving and frightening, it's also strangely satisfying. Perhaps *I'm* more mafia than I realize.

"Where's your car?"

I point in the direction of my convertible. "The little blue Mini down the street."

"A Mini?" His scarred brow hikes up.

"What's wrong with my Mini?"

He doesn't smile, but his eyes warm and soften a touch. "Of course you drive a fucking Mini. Your marker is growing, De Luca."

Crud.

My marker.

I'd forgotten all about it

"Um...yeah." I bite the corner of my lip. "We still need to talk about that."

The look he gives is both cryptic and hot enough to melt my bones.

He dips to mutter in my ear, "I know what I want from you." His voice is rough and his breath against my skin sends tendrils of need shooting through me. But before I can question further, he lifts his head and says, "Marco will take you home in the truck. I'll see you later."

"Wait." I shift my hand to his arm. "You can't say something like that and leave me hanging."

"Trust me." His eyes close momentarily. "Neither of us will be left hanging."

Oh my God.

"Are you suggesting...?"

"Later, Shelley. I gotta go."

"Where to?" Marco asks.

"Carmine." They exchange looks, conveying the sort of non-verbal information that only two old friends would understand.

"Billy's Carmine?" I ask. Why would he go there?

Gianni says nothing, then snakes an arm around my waist and pulls me hard against his body. "Behave. No more snarky texts."

My eyes widen. "You think he did this because of my text?"

"Not the camera, but the other shit." He tightens his arm, bringing me even closer. "You challenged him and maybe he didn't like being challenged." Fingers slide across my cheek, into my hair. "Just so you know, I do." Then he grips a handful, holding my head captive and brings his mouth down onto mine.

It starts off gentle, him sucking on my lip, teasing. When I open it gets deeper, hotter, more possessive and definitely more carnal. My body ignites and hums in response, but after a few seconds and way too soon, he breaks it. His fingers, however, remain tangled in my hair. When I open my eyes, his are peering into mine. "Later, Shelley," he whispers.

Next second he spins on his heel and walks towards my car. I watch his long-legged strides down the hill, back-lit by the streetlights before he vanishes into the mist and shadows.

Good Lord, the man can kiss. One more minute and my panties would combust.

At some point, I realize Marco has come up behind me. His chuckle snaps me out of my trance. "Close your mouth, Shelley."

"Shut up." I slap his arm, immediately regretting it.

Shit-dang-it. I need to remember my hands hurt.

"Damn, that was a hot one..."

"Shut up," I repeat, only louder. This time I aim for his bald head, knowing he'll dodge me, which he does. "What are you...seven?"

We're still laughing when he boosts me into the truck, with one hand on my butt cheek. If it was anybody other than Marco, I would have elbowed him. But he's like the big, goofy brother I never had and I know it means nothing.

"Why's he going to Carmine?"

His smile disappears and his expression turns serious. "You don't wanna know."

"Why don't I want to know?"

He gives me a *don't ask me that shit* look and shuts the truck door. I have to wait for him to open the driver's side before I can speak again.

"I thought you guys weren't doing the mafia thing anymore?"

"Mostly not, also doesn't mean we don't know people."

Mostly not? What the hell does *mostly not* mean?

Crud.

And what kind of bakery does Carmine run? I'm beginning to suspect not the usual kind. Perhaps a front for something more sinister? Which leads me to wonder how forthcoming Billy was?

Regardless, Marco's keeping it zipped and clearly I'm not getting any more information out of him. Instead he turns on some music. The opening riff of "Under the Bridge" by the Red Hot Chili Peppers fills the cab.

Tomorrow, if Billy's awake and up to it, I'll ask him.

I try another tactic. "Okay, so answer me this. Why did Gianni take my car?"

He slices a sideways glance at me while strapping himself into his seat.

"You think Dean did something to it?"

"Could have installed a GPS tracker."

Jeez.

"So, Carmine's some kind of techie who knows about surveillance stuff?"

"You could say that." He shrugs as he checks for traffic in the side mirror before engaging the gear and pulling out. "What I wanna know is how you got involved with this dipshit."

"I cut his hair once, then he kept coming back to the salon asking me out until I said yes."

"You didn't pick up on who he was?"

"No, why would I?" *Unfortunately.* "I've been gone a long time, Marco. *And* he lied to me. I also had no idea he knew Joey."

"Speaking of, how did you hook up with *him* again?"

"Pure chance. One afternoon outside work, he saw me on the street and called my name. I was...shocked at first, but once I got over that, I was glad to see him again. I realized I'd totally forgiven him."

"For what?"

"He pulled a dick move on me...didn't have the balls to break up with me in person. I'd also just found out he was cheating on me with that chick Gloria with the really huge boobs. Remember her?"

"Gloria Tortino?"

"Mm hmm."

"Shit."

"Yeah. Well anyway, he gave me a present one day and then sent a card saying he needed to get his head together."

"Huh."

"It's because of him, I have trust issues. Anyway, I was devastated, and then later really pissed off. My dad dies and my cheating boyfriend dumps me."

"Shit, Shelley, that must have sucked donkey balls."

"I don't really remember anything else about the funeral, though. Just that he wasn't there. Mom dosed me up on valium and I guess I suppressed a lot. After that, we were in Los Angeles and life went on. Now I'm here."

And with no clue who the players are. It appears I have some catching up to do.

For the rest of the drive home, we're silent, listening to the music, deep in our own thoughts. Or at least I am and I'm beginning to wonder if it was a coincidence that I started dating Dean shortly after I found Joey again.

Jeez, I'm getting paranoid.

Back at the house, Marco kisses me on the top of my head and we head to our separate rooms. But it's another kiss I'm thinking of.

What's he up to?

Is this what's it's like to be a mafia wife? What my mother went through, with all the late nights wondering where my dad was and if he was safe?

I slip into light blue cotton pajama shorts and a ribbed tank top, brush my teeth and settle down on the bed, aimlessly flipping through channels. Finally, I choose *Game of Thrones*, but a scratching at my door interrupts just as I'm getting settled.

Truman, tongue hanging out one side, stares up at me when I open. Giving me no chance to deny him, he nudges his flat, wrinkled nose between the door and the frame. Apparently, he's an expert at manipulating women like me.

"No farting, buddy," I say, opening the door wide for him to enter. "Otherwise I'll have to eighty-six your ass. Got it?"

He sneezes and I scratch his stubby ears. After a grunt, he waddles to the end of my bed, turns back and stares at me.

"What?"

He emits a low whine.

"You want on my bed?"

Another whine.

I sigh and look at my toes. What harm can it do? It's a big bed, so I relent and lift him up. He circles three times one way and then three times the other before lying with this head between his paws. I climb in and watch TV for a while, with one ear listening for the sound of my Mini but all I hear are baby dragons screeching and Truman snoring.

Next thing I know, it's early morning and the TV is still on. The light is only just beginning to change, peeking through the drapes.

Truman whines and dances at my door, lifting one back leg, then the other in a canine version of the polka.

"All right, buddy, I'm coming." I stretch, yawn and roll out of bed, wincing at the ache in my knees, and open the door. The dog launches out of my room and races down the stairs.

Jeez.

Sure can move when he wants to.

Unless he's doing his business in the kitchen, I'll have to venture down and open the door, but I'll never make it if I don't take care of my own urgent need first.

That done and my face washed I head down, expecting to see all four dogs. My heart lurches when I see Gianni instead. In sweatpants, no shirt, gleaming and delicious.

He leans against the granite counter drinking from a frosty water bottle with his eyes closed. I step inside, fascinated with how his throat moves as he swallows. It's strong and sensual and I have an overwhelming urge to nip at it.

Having had his fill, he lowers the bottle and uses his balled-up tee-shirt to wipe his face.

As if sensing me watching him his eyes open. "De Luca," he says, blinking. "What are you doing up so early?"

"Letting the dogs out, but it seems you already have."

"I usually do when I'm here, before I run. Noticed one missing this morning. He spend the night with you?"

I nod and reach behind my neck to twist my hair into a coil and drape it over a shoulder.

His eyes follow my movements, dropping to my breasts, which pucker under his gaze.

"Lucky dog."

Um.

"You make it back last night?" I ask, proud my voice doesn't reflect my sudden inability to breathe. "I didn't hear you come in."

"Not till late. Why do you ask?"

"I was worried about you."

There's a long pause before he speaks. "Were you, Shelley?"

God, he's beautiful...and hazardous the way he looks at me.

A thin layer of sweat augments the valley between his chest muscles, darkening the silky line of fine hair separating the two sides of his six-pack. Down to where his pants, hanging low, meet that sexy V. Makes me want to run my tongue over his skin and taste the saltiness.

"Why?"

"Billy told me you'd gone straight." Or *mostly* straight. "I don't wanna be the one to screw that up for you."

"Is that all?" His voice is soft as he places the water bottle on the counter and curls his fingers over the edge of the granite. Opening himself, inviting me to come closer.

Like a honeybee to nectar I'm drawn, and take another step.

"I don't want you getting hurt or to do anything illegal for me."

"Little too late for that, Shelley.

I'm within touching distance. My lips feel dry, so I flick my tongue along the seam to moisten them.

He swallows and the pulse at the base of his neck jumps. I so want to believe there's something more there. But with my track record?

"What have you done?" I ask.

He shakes his head and dodges my question. "I've gotta know something."

"What's that?"

"You fuck him?"

"What?" My head jerks back. "You're serious?"

"Need to know, babe."

"Gianni, it's none of your business, besides I think you've already made up your mind."

"Answer me, De Luca. You owe me that."

"All right…I'll tell you, if you tell me why you want to know."

In less time than it takes for me to take a breath, he grabs my hips and spins us around to trap me against the counter. Using a foot, he kicks my legs apart, far enough to step between mine.

I gasp as he situates himself, adjusting his position so he's rubbing against my most sensitive place. Sensations shoot through me causing my nails to dig into his shoulders.

He grunts and takes a moment before insisting, "Did you, or didn't you?"

"You don't scare me...mmm." My head drops forward to his chest when he flexes again because he's right *there.* Goosebumps erupt everywhere. God, he's going to make me come.

"I wonder why that is?" His pupils are dark and greedy and he's breathing almost as fast as I am.

"I think...I scare *you,*" I whisper between breaths. My fingers develop a mind of their own moving over the ridges and muscles of his shoulders and down towards his chest. He sucks in air through his teeth then grinds again. My body responds, with heat pulsing through my veins, liquefying between my legs. I throw a leg around him, availing myself. I'm so primed from wanting him, from his teasing, that when he hits my clit again just right, I spasm and shatter around him, crying out.

Oh my God.

"You're fucking killing me." His voice is thick and hoarse as he circles his hips against mine. Fingers slide across my face, tilting my head with his thumbs under my jaw. Our mouths collide. It's urgent, wet and deep. Tongues clash and stroke, unable to get enough as we devour each other. I arch into him, still riding my climax, and slip my arms around his waist, pulling him closer. He's rock hard and I grind my hips against his milking it for as long as I can.

But I want more and I must have lost my mind because I don't care we're in the kitchen. I want him in me and reach inside his pants, intending to get my hands and mouth on that beautiful, pulsing cock. When I do, I circle my thumb over his tip and find it's moist.

"Fuck," he growls against my mouth. "Not like this, not here." He rips his mouth away and pulls back. But his eyes are blazing and hungry. Dragging air in quick hard breaths, he buries his face in my neck. "We need to stop."

At first it doesn't register.

He just gave me an orgasm, and it was amazing, mind-blowing even. Doesn't he want me to give him one too? I'm aching and empty, needing more, needing to taste him. For him to fill me because he's the only one who can and he wants to stop?

The depth of that thought is something I don't like at all.

In fact, it sucks.

My breath hitches as I pull my hands out of his sweats and push my forearms against his chest. He captures my wrists and crosses them behind my back, keeping me trapped and close.

"You're not going anywhere."

"You told me to stop." My face is burning with the lingering effects of my climax and humiliation as I struggle to free my arms, but he tightens his grip. "I'm stopping. So let me go."

"That's not what I meant."

"Then what did you mean?"

"De Luca, the first time I take you, isn't gonna be in the kitchen up against a counter," he says, nipping the tendon in the crook of my neck. A shiver races through me.

"It's gonna be in my bed. You're still injured, babe. I don't want to hurt you because I can't promise I'm gonna be gentle."

My chest rises and falls and everything inside clenches. It's a really good thing he's still holding me, because my knees threaten to buckle when he drags his teeth and stubble along my skin to my shoulder, making it erupt along the way.

God, he's lethal, throwing words like that at me. Maybe because I'm coming down from my orgasm, or maybe it's because of who he is and just how damn good he is, but reality hits me. The universe just threw me a wake-up call. I need to pay attention to its warning. Protecting me from Dean is one thing, but getting me into his bed is another matter entirely.

"You can't say things like that to me. It's not fair."

He pauses, then those eyes hit mine and his brow furrows. "What do you mean?"

"I can't do this."

I really want to, but if I give myself to him, it'll be the end of me. "I can't play this game with you. You win."

His body locks up and he blinks slowly. "That doesn't sound like me winning."

At that moment, the kitchen door flings open and bounces off a door-stopper. We flinch and turn our heads. All four dogs rush in and surround us, panting and bouncing off their front legs, their toenails clicking against the tiled floor.

Tinkerbell shoves her nose in between our torsos while Truman growls and nips at Gianni's ankles.

"Shit," he murmurs in my ear. "Canine interruptus."

It happens to me sometimes. The effects of adrenaline, hormones or maybe my frazzled nerves but that strikes me as funny. I burst into giggles.

He rests his forehead against mine and snorts, which makes me giggle even harder. Because I'm laughing, he is and we stand together with a giant, slobbering dog's head squished between us, shaking. I've only ever heard him laugh once before, in his kitchen when I mentioned the goose incident. I wonder how often he laughs and for a second I'm really glad it's me that's making him.

"Ai." A shrill voice makes us laugh even harder. I peer round Gianni and through the tears in my eyes see an attractive, plump, Hispanic woman in her late fifties covering her eyes and holding up her other hand, palm forward.

"Mr. Gianni! *No en mi cocina! Tu madre* will kill me."

He pulls himself together with an effort and, letting out a deep sigh straightens, releasing my hands from behind my back.

"Shelley, meet Connie, Mom's housekeeper."

11

CASUAL DRIVE-BY PIECE OF ASS

~

"*Hola,* Miss Shelley," Connie says. She has lovely, rich brown eyes like stained mahogany that reflect her smile. Which is shy. I can't tell who's more embarrassed, her or me. I wonder what she's got to be shy about. I'm the one who's been acting like a bitch in heat, grinding myself against Gianni.

Even as I answer with a smile of my own, my cheeks burn and I feel Gianni's gaze on me. Orgasm and giggling fit aside, something has shifted between us. If only I could allow myself to trust it. To trust him.

"Let me know if you need anything." Connie glances between me and Gianni. She scoops up Rambo and dumps him into the front pocket of the frilly Viva Las Vegas apron. The one Marco borrowed last night.

"Thank you," I mumble.

Truman head-butts my ankle and, glad for the excuse to avoid looking at Gianni, I bend and scratch his ears. The floppy-eared Doberman sitting next to him cocks her head. I take my time petting her too.

Connie walks into the pantry, exiting a moment later with a large, unopened bag of dog food.

"*Un momento*, Mr. Gianni, I feed the dogs. Then I make coffee and breakfast."

As one, the three still-grounded dogs storm the door as soon as she opens it. Rambo hooks his paws over the rim of the pocket.

"She needs hazard pay for that job," Gianni says almost to himself.

Indeed.

I take the opportunity to make my escape. However, when I turn to leave the kitchen, his fingers hook around my wrist. "What just happened, Shelley?"

I squeeze my eyes shut and hope my voice won't betray me. Then I turn back and face him, keeping my eyes on his face and off all those delicious muscles. "You're right."

"About what?"

"This has to stop."

"I disagree and I'm gonna be a dick and remind you, I didn't start it. You did."

"No, I didn't."

"Yeah, you did."

"How did I start it?"

"You put your hands on me."

"You trapped me against the counter first."

"That's because you walked into the kitchen dressed like that. So you see, you started it."

Gah!

Then he grabs my chin, forcing me to meet his gaze. It's flaring, and not in a good way. More like a pissed-off, frustrated way. "What changed?" he says slowly.

"I don't do casual, Gianni. That...um...what just happened?" I swallow, looking for the right words. "That's not going to work for me." I push his hand from my chin and back up a step.

His brows come together. "There's nothing casual about that. You just came when I barely touched you. That's the most beautiful thing I've experienced in a long time, De Luca, and from where I stand that more than worked for you."

Those words again, the ones that will kill me. Shit, I may as well own it because he has me there.

"You're a very good kisser...and you were in the right...um... place. But it can't go on, it will lead to something we'll regret."

"*Don't* demean it like that. There was much more to it than me just being in the right place and *I* won't regret it."

"Maybe not, but when you're done in a week or so you'll move on to the next. That's not how I operate."

"Is that what you think? That you're a casual, drive-by piece of ass?"

"You forget, I know who you are. Your reputation, Gianni Cadora, goes all the way back to high school. You nailed every girl I knew and all the ones I didn't and I don't believe that's changed."

"Not all of them." He steps back and folds his arms, making those biceps bulge.

"You don't have to split hairs. And just to clarify, you're not denying it. Have you ever had a relationship for more than a few weeks?"

"No, can't say I have." He lets out a long breath.

"Why not?"

"I never wanted one."

"Uh huh." It's my turn to fold my arms. "My point exactly."

"And that is...?"

"I'm just wondering if you're capable of feeling anything more for a woman other than she's *just a piece of ass*."

"Careful." His eyes turn stony, the blue changing to gray. "You think I'm a heartless bastard, Shelley?"

"Hey. Those are your words." I toss what he said to me yesterday back at him. "And that is *not* what I said." I put my hands to my forehead and blow out air. "I don't want to do this now, in here." I cast a glance at the door. Connie could return any second. Who knows, she might even be listening at the door.

"We're doing it, De Luca. And perhaps now is a good time to talk about your marker."

I blink several times, holding my breath.

Holy shit.

"What's it going to be?" I whisper.

"It's going to be what I say it's going to be. In my bed, when I want, for as long as I want."

What?

"Are you nuts? You're going to make me sleep with you?"

"I'm not going to *make* you, De Luca, and there will be very little sleeping involved." He leans in close to my ear. "Based on what I experienced earlier, you're going to *want* to."

My head explodes, every synapse firing at once. My jaw drops, I slam it shut, then it drops again.

"You said we'd work something out. We haven't discussed this."

"We're discussing this now. Those are my terms."

"I have a say in this, don't I?"

"Nope."

"What do you mean *nope*?" I yell.

"Be honest with yourself for once, Shelley." His fingers clamp around the back of my neck. He pulls me close to him, our faces inches apart. "Ten minutes ago, you were hot and ready with your greedy hands on my cock. If I hadn't slowed things down, we'd be giving Connie a show fucking in the pantry up against that wall right now."

Gah!

He's right. He's so, so right but I'm not willing to concede. Not one tiny bit. But it doesn't stop the blush from moving up my neck.

"This isn't happening." I shake my head.

"It's happening."

"I'm not having sex with you."

"We'll see. But for now, you and Connie get acquainted. I need to get ready for work."

Halfway out the kitchen he stops and turns to face me. "You didn't answer my question, De Luca."

My brain's frazzled and at first, I don't know what he means so I simply stare at him. Then it clicks.

"You didn't tell me why you want to know," I fire back.

He glares at me for several long beats before he speaks again. "Either way he's staked his claim with his little stunt in your panties. If you did, it makes him more dangerous. In his mind, you're his property and the fact that you're here, under *my* protection, doesn't make him look good to those that matter."

Oh.

Wait. His property?

"You mean like he literally thinks he owns me? Like...like one of his girls?"

"Yep."

My brain is refusing to process. "Um," is the only word my mouth will utter.

He hasn't moved. His eyes remain locked on my face, except now there's a strange look in them, almost like disappointment.

What's he got to be disappointed about? Who the hell is he to judge me, Mr. I-banged-every-girl-in-town?

When I refuse to respond those eyes change to something else. Something that looks a lot like hurt.

"I guess I have my answer," he grits out, jaw tightening as he spins to leave the kitchen.

No way I saw what I think I saw. I shake it off and focus on what he said.

Sleep with him?

Shit dang it. I can't go there either.

Even though just a few minutes ago I was going there. Like *really* going there and *would* be going there right this very minute if he hadn't given me time to change my mind.

The door opens, reminding me I'm still standing in the middle of the kitchen chewing on my thumbnail. It takes Connie washing her hands and filling up the coffee pot before I'm able to ignore the hollow in my stomach and kick-start myself into gear to actually move.

"Sit down, Miss Shelley. I make breakfast. What you like?"

"Um?"

How many times has she come across Gianni kissing someone, or doing *other* things, in the pantry? I can't even contemplate how many women he's brought here over the years.

"You want bacon and eggs?"

Whenever I was here, there was always one. I'd swear they took a number and waited in line and now it seems my number might be next, but I certainly won't be the last.

"Bagel and cream cheese?"

"Uh..."

"She makes a killer cheese and mushroom omelet," Marco says, striding into the kitchen. Though his head is shiny and smooth, the evidence of a goatee is beginning to show. "You should try it."

She looks at me, and I nod because there isn't much else I can do. My synapses haven't reconnected yet.

"You okay?" Marco asks. "You look like Bambi facing an eighteen-wheeler."

I *feel* like Bambi facing an eighteen-wheeler but I'm *so* not telling him what just went down.

So I nod again.

"Hmm!" He squints as he checks me out while getting milk from the fridge and setting it on the table with the sugar. He takes two mugs from the cabinet, fills up one from the still-brewing coffee and hands one to me.

"You and Gianni go at it?"

My eyes go wide and fly up to stare at him.

"What do you mean go at it?" I ask, panicking.

God!

Did he see us? I spin around to hide my reaction, almost spilling my coffee. I yank open the closest drawer pretending to search for placemats.

"Jesus." He gives a low chortle. "Chill, girl. I meant did you two get into a beef?"

I find them in the third one I open. "Why do you ask?"

"'Cause he looks pissed as hell, like somebody gave him a wedgie, metaphorically speaking. I'm thinking it might be you."

Ooo...kay!

I'm not talking about this. I pull out two woven ones in vibrant red-and-orange stripes and arrange them on the table, suddenly very interested in the label that says they're from Pottery Barn.

"What time can we go see Billy?" I ask without looking up.

He leans back in his chair and folds his arms across his broad chest. "You did, didn't you?" His hazel eyes twinkle as his face splits into a slow, lazy grin. "Damn. I missed it."

"Marco?" I pass him a knife, fork and a matching napkin.

"Yeah?"

"What time?"

"Fine. Any time after eleven."

"Is he awake yet?"

"Somewhat. Just spoke with Carmine and he says Billy's been asking about you."

Well, I have a lot to ask him too. Like what does Carmine really do.

Our omelets are ready and Connie sets a plate on the placemats in front of each of us along with bottles of condiments. I sprinkle Tabasco sauce on mine and take a bite. It's light and fluffy and delicious with the right amount of melted cheese oozing out the sides!

Marco reads the sports section of the *San Francisco Chronicle* while I peruse the style page and neither of us speak again as we eat, except to arrange when to meet.

When we're done, I clear the dishes and set them in the sink before I head upstairs to shower and change.

My hands are finally at a point where I can get away without bandages. Although I have to be careful and my knees will still require some sort of covering, but they're healing nicely too. Giant Band-Aids should suffice.

Dammit.

Gianni has the first aid kit!

I refuse to ask him for it so my knees are going to have to wait. I can't think straight around him, especially now and I don't know what scares me more. Dean's vile acts, or Gianni proclaiming his marker.

I may as well put my heart in a shredder and feed the bits to the seagulls, because when he's done with me, I'll never be able to glue them together to heal again. I'm pretty sure of it.

I'm going to have to figure a way to renegotiate or pull some dirty tricks of my own.

What, I don't know yet.

After a quick shower, I choose wide-legged brown linen pants that won't rub against my scabs and a rust-colored, long-sleeved tunic shirt. I pretty myself up with a little help from some mascara, eyeliner and silver and amber earrings that match Joey's necklace perfectly.

The bruising around my eye is breaking up and with any luck will be gone in a few days. I'm starting to look like my old self again, except for the freaked-out expression in my eyes. Being spied on and forced to pay a sexual marker will do that to a girl. Though, to be honest, forced might be a little strong.

Marco's waiting for me when I head back down, looking like a member of Sons of Anarchy with a black bandana tied around his head, ripped jeans and his leather cut.

"You wanna take the Harley or be boring and take Billy's car?"

"Under normal circumstance the Harley, but I'm not sure my knees could handle the wind."

"Boring it is."

Connie helps me apply large Band-Aids the size of an iPhone to each of my knees and then we exit through the kitchen door and down some stairs that lead to a ginormous garage. It houses Mama's Lexus, my Mini, a very expensive-looking BMW, the Land Rover, and, of course, Marco's badass black Harley with silver-studded saddlebags. We pull out, and in the circular driveway, sticking out like an unwelcome zit on prom day, is the truck.

What the hey?

"Is Gianni still here?"

Marco slides a guarded look at me. "He left an hour ago still looking annoyed. Seriously, what did you do to him?"

"Nothing," I say quickly. *More like what he's doing to me.* "How did he get to work?"

"Gina picked him up."

"Oh."

I'm surprised I could actually get the word out, as it feels like a battering ram slammed into my gut. I turn my face to look out the window. Marco doesn't need to see how much that bothers me.

Seriously? The asshole wants to bang me, then has another woman he's banged come pick him up?

Like, really?

Well, fuck him.

I count backwards from ten and try something different.

"You told Marshall you were in the army?"

"Yep, enlisted after high school and got out five years ago. Took over from Pop when he passed on."

"Oh yeah...your dad's chop shops."

"I converted them to motorcycle repair shops and bought a Harley dealership. I have some of Pop's old crew working for me, mostly the younger ones, but we're clean now."

"I've been hearing that a lot. What made you guys go all legit?"

He sucked in a breath and held it for a few beats. "A lot changed after your dad died. We all loved him and when *our* dads died, both Gianni and I decided we didn't want that world. There's no need for it anymore and it just invites shit you don't want. You know, to raise kids like that? It doesn't make sense. What it did to Joey...it's just sad."

"What do you mean?"

"Dude, he embraced it. He got off on the dark side and the conflict. Not to mention hanging with the Russians. Those fucking Melnikov brothers, they run girls and heroin. Man, that shit's just evil, but nobody could get through to him."

"Wait, Melnikov *brothers*? I didn't know there were more of them."

"Yep. The other one is Vasily."

"And Joey was running girls? As in prostitution?" I squeak.

"I'm talking trafficking but no...he didn't get involved in that. We *all* would have killed him if he did. He supplied Melnikov with coke which he in turn sold to his clients at his brothels. He had a connection working customs at San Francisco Airport."

My God.

Brothels.

This is so much worse than I suspected.

"I didn't know anyone did coke anymore. Isn't that so eighties?" I ask.

"Dude? You been living in a time capsule?"

"What?"

"Coke is hot again. But—whatever, it drove Gianni nuts."

"I'm beginning to feel like I never knew him. I mean, I knew he had a dark side, but to me he was mostly sweet and protective. Until he wasn't, that is. Then I thought he was an asshole."

"I loved the little fuck, he was family, but in general he *was* an asshole. After your dad died and you left, he got worse. Thinking back, you were probably some kind of moderating energy. He probably kept himself in check because of you. What's weird and even more tragic is, in the last few months, it seemed he was coming around. Like he was getting it together. He even approached Gianni to work with him."

"Billy said that. How did it go?"

"Gianni didn't trust him, of course, but let him in. If Joey needed a way out, he was gonna give it to him but keep him on a leash. For my aunt's sake."

I nod, because that makes sense.

"I just found out Gianni was with my dad when he was shot."

We've stopped at a red light and he turns to look at me. "You shitting me?" he mumbles.

"You didn't know he was there?" I ask, my eyebrows pulling together.

"No, I meant I didn't know *you* didn't know he was there."

"Oh."

My eyes catch on a dog-walker with a troupe of five crossing in front of us. One of the animals is a bulldog and my lips pull up in a smile. Marco continues to watch me like something's not making sense, but then seems to shrug it off when I turn back to face him.

"Why are you looking at me like that?" I ask.

"Nothing. Just, yeah, that was messed up," he says, rubbing his face.

"I can't believe they never found out who killed him," I say to the windshield.

Marco says nothing, but then the light changes and we're close to the hospital. As we're about to take our turn, it occurs to me everything keeps coming back to my dad's death. Why was it so pivotal to all of them? It's not as if they weren't used to violence or even on occasion involved in it. There's something missing, something they're not telling me and no one, including my mother, is talking.

"Okay," Marco says, cutting into my thoughts. He pulls into a spot and kills the engine. "Do me a favor, will you?"

"Sure...what?"

"If Carmine's here, don't fall in love with him."

I burst into giggles. "Why would I do that?"

"You'll see."

~

Billy's been moved out of the intensive care unit to a private room and when we arrive he's asleep. There are bouquets of flowers on every available surface, and the room smells like a flower shop.

Shit. I didn't think to bring any although he'd probably prefer a doughnut anyway.

His hands lie outside the sheet and I touch one of them, but get no response. His face shows signs of road-rash, but fortunately no severe head injuries, unlike his body.

White tape spans his ribs and a long metal pin sticks out of his pelvis. And stuck in the crook of his left elbow is an IV, making my stomach queasy.

Marco sits on the far side of the room and powers up his laptop.

"Work," he apologizes, pointing to it. "Gotta place orders."

"No worries." I pull out a paperback novel I'd found in Sea Cliff and get busy reading. I'm deep in a scene when my spidey-sense kicks in. My head jerks up and I stare into a pair of intelligent light green eyes scanning me from head to toe. I stop breathing.

Holy fizz pops.

Carmine?

My mouth muscles develop a mind of their own and split into a big grin. If this is him, I get why Marco warned me. He's almost as beautiful as Gianni, with dark brown curly hair overdue for a trim and sexy as hell. If I wasn't already in love, I could find myself falling for him.

He stands in the doorway, staring at me, head cocked. Looking nothing like your local baker, more like a wild, untamed Roman god you'd have a fling with, should you find yourself in Rome.

He smiles back. "Shelley, I presume?"

"I am." I move to get up, but he holds a hand out, stopping me. "Don't get up."

"I'd offer to shake but..." I show him my palms and he gives my fingers a little squeeze instead. His grip is cool and gentle and lingers a teeny bit too long.

Okay, he gets better-looking by the second and he's obviously charming. No wonder Billy's bakery is so successful.

"Dude," he calls to Marco who's watching our interaction.

They shake and do that power-patting, brotherhood thing. "I get it. Never thought I'd see it, but I get it."

Marco glances at me, then tips his chin and says, "Outside, so we don't disturb Billy." He closes his laptop and leaves it on the chair.

"Be back in a bit," he says to me.

Carmine smiles and shakes his head.

Disturb Billy, my ass. They don't want me to hear whatever it is.

What kind of mafia ninja powers does Carmine have that these men go to him for help? Maybe I don't want to know.

They leave and I go back to reading my book but can't get it together enough to focus. Too many questions run through my brain. That vibe that something's off won't go away and neither has the feeling that it has to do with my dad's death.

But what, I ponder, as I chew on my thumbnail. How did Gianni get that scar? Was he shot that day too? Surely Billy would've known if he had been and I can't imagine him keeping that from me. He didn't even seem to know Gianni was at the meeting.

Hmm.

The answers evade me. So I continue to try to read until lack of sleep catches up on me and I nod off. Until a touch on my head wakes me. My eyes pop open to Billy's smile.

"Hey." I stand and kiss him gently on the forehead. "God, Billy...I can't tell you how happy I am you're alive."

"Me too, kiddo." His voice is scratchy from disuse.

"I'm so sorry he did this to you." Tears form and drip onto his sheets.

"Shh..." He swipes a thumb across my cheek. "Nobody's killed me yet. Least of all that piece of shit."

"I just got you back, I can't lose you again."

"Not losing me. What about you? You okay?"

"Just a few scrapes on my hands and knees." I show him my palms. "You saved my life and almost got killed doing it. You aren't allowed to do that again."

"I'll try to avoid it next time." He lets out a chuckle, then winces. "Ugh." He presses a hand to his ribcage. "That hurts."

"You need me to get a nurse?"

"I need you to get me the hell out of this place. Wanna kick some Russian ass."

A little half choke, half laugh escapes. "You big, lovely old fool. You've got to stay here until they're able to move you. Besides, Gianni and Marco have it. And Carmine too, I guess."

I fill him in on the last few days and as I'm finishing, Marco returns minus a certain hot Roman god and I can't help feeling a little disappointed. He and Billy shake, then he pulls his chair next to mine.

"Carmine informed me they found the Volvo," Marco says. "It was left in a parking lot at Crissy Field, reported stolen. The cops are checking for evidence but I doubt they'll find anything they can use."

"How does Carmine know all this?" I ask.

"He knows the cop that got the call, Lee. He shops at the bakery."

"Okay, you two have to level with me, what does Carmine really do?"

Billy and Marco exchange a look. Billy dips his chin. "She's in it now. Needs to know."

Uh oh.

"Let's just say he's skilled at finding and fixing things for people," Marco says. "The bakery's a front. When people need a certain kind of help, they go to him."

"Like what's happening with you," Billy says.

My eyebrows shoot up. "You mean he's a fixer? Like that

show *Ray Donovan*?" Apparently, I watch way too much television.

Silence.

Of course he is.

My mother would be so disappointed. She dragged me from San Francisco to keep me from all this, and here I am, smack bang in the middle of my very own episode.

A Fixer!

I'll be owing haircuts to these men forever. And jeez, never mind what Gianni's expecting. I press my thighs together, remembering this morning. I have to admit, I *enjoyed* what happened in the kitchen, maybe more than I should so perhaps that won't be so bad after all.

Noop, noop, noop. Can't go there.

"Um..." I clear my throat and squirm a little. "What's Carmine going to do?"

"Dunno." Marco shrugs. I look at Billy. He shakes his head.

Crud...they're not talking.

Before I can ponder that Billy lets out a long yawn. "You two have pooped me out. Gonna need my beauty sleep now."

"No amount of sleep's gonna pretty up that ugly face, man," Marco chuckles.

Billy extends his middle finger and wiggles it in a wave.

I smile because I love their banter. Despite the irreverence, it's honest and real and there's a level of respect all these men have for each other.

After straightening Billy's sheets, ensuring he's covered, I fill up his water glass and kiss him on the forehead.

"See you tomorrow, kiddo?"

"Of course. You want anything?"

"Just yourself...and your smile. Good to see that bruise on your face is going away."

We're walking out the main hospital door when an incoming text pings.

Cass: *You up for lunch?*

As I still have a little room on my credit card and I definitely owe Marco food, I may as well go for broke. When I finally get back to work, I'll make up for it with longer hours.

"Marco, you hungry?"

"I could eat. What you thinking?"

"Mexican?"

"Always."

I text Cass back. *Tony's?*

HALF AN HOUR LATER, we arrive at Tony's Taqueria. The lunch rush is over and Marco drives the Land Rover into an empty spot in the back.

The place is a few doors away from the salon and a frequent after-work hangout for most of the stylists. It's Monday, a regular day off, so there's little chance of bumping into any of the staff.

Perfect.

I have no desire to explain my injuries.

We enter through the back door and pass through a hallway off the kitchen.

"Yo." I throw a peace sign to the kitchen staff and they respond with a chorus of *Yos* of their own.

Cass, dressed in jeans and chunky black sweater sits at the dark blue-and-white tiled bar drinking a watermelon margarita on the rocks.

She's talking to Tony who's shimmying to Earth, Wind and Fire's "Fantasy" blaring over the speakers. He inherited the restaurant, that's been in business since the seventies, from his father, also named Tony, and restored it to its original condition.

The only difference is the color scheme, which is now orange and turquoise, instead of orange and brown.

"Woo-wee," Tony calls, chucking a skinny, silver-lamé-clad hip to the side. "And who's this handsome fella?" His wardrobe is reminiscent of Steven Tyler's, except he doesn't do hats.

Cass swivels in her chair, eyes widening when she sees Marco. She shoots me a *you could've warned me* look which I, of course, pretend not to notice.

"Marco, this is Tony," I say.

Marco reaches over the bar. Tony drapes the towel he's using to dry glasses over a purple-sleeved arm and extends a hand. He has a standing mani–pedi appointment every other Tuesday morning at the salon. This week his nails are silver. I believe it's the only time he leaves this place. Unless he's browsing vintage clothing stores.

"And you've met Cass."

Big, tough guy Marco blushes as he takes Cass's hand and she reciprocates with doe eyes.

I smile. My work is done.

Now, if only Gianni were here.

Noop. Can't go there.

Probably still with Gina anyway. I sigh and try to ignore the black hole in my chest as I maneuver onto a barstool, leaving one open between myself and Cass, which Marco takes. Good man.

"You want a margarita?" I pick a tortilla chip from the basket on the bar and dip it into the house salsa.

"Don't like fruit in my alcohol. I'll have a beer. Amber ale?"

"Coming up," Tony purrs. "And for you, lovey? Mango or watermelon?"

"Mango, please." Tony minces in time to the music to the other end of the bar and fires up the blender.

"Dude," Marco asks, "where did you bring me? There's a fucking disco ball hanging from the ceiling."

"I know," I giggle. "Great, isn't it?"

"Shit." He shakes his head and tilts it back, taking in the glittery stars on the ceiling.

"You should see this place on karaoke nights," Cass says. "It jumps. Shelley and I kick ass with 'Wannabe'."

"'Wannabe'?" That barbell in his brow takes a hike north.

"Yeah, by the Spice Girls? On a good night, we bring down the house."

Marco turns to me with his brow furrowed. I nod. "It's all relative to the amount of alcohol we've consumed."

The music changes to "Boogie Wonderland" and Cass and I bop and sing along, like we've done dozens of times before.

"Be happy my knees hurt, otherwise we'd be doing the electric slide."

Marco's head disappears behind the menu. It takes me a few seconds to realize his shoulders are shaking.

"You're still a fucking nut, Shelley," he says when he stops chuckling. "You haven't changed. I get the feeling this isn't going to be *just* lunch."

Tony serves our drinks and takes our food order.

"Cass and I haven't done this in a while. Dean didn't like hanging out with my friends."

"Asshole," Cass mumbles.

"Amen," Marco says and we all clink our drinks together.

Besides us, there're two middle-aged businessmen sitting at the bar having a lively discussion, gesticulating in the air. And a table with five rowdy women who look like they've been there since opening. One looks familiar and at least two are checking out Marco, looking ready to pounce.

Cow bells on the wood and glass front door jingle and a cool breeze shoots through. A moment later a tiny figure with wispy, wind-blown white hair climbs on to a stool next to me and steeples his hands in front of him.

I do a double take. No freaking way!

"Hey," I say to my gun dealer. "How are you, Alfie? Do you remember me."

"Of course I do. Jimmy's girl," he wheezes. "And if that ain't my distant cousin Marco Cadora, then I'm John Travolta."

What the hey? Alfie's related to the Cadoras?

"Hey, Alfie." Marco nods. "How're they hanging?"

"To my knees. Who's the pretty blonde?"

"That's Cassandra Jones," I answer. "She owns the salon down the street."

Cass smiles and waves.

"That used to be a barber shop back in the day," Alfie says. "I'd get me a good shave and a trim. Too fancy now."

"Come by any time you want, Alfie," I say. "I'll cut your hair for free."

He smiles and pats my hand. "That's very nice. You're a good girl. It'll take you two minutes."

"I've never seen you here before," I ask. "Do you come here often?"

"I knew his pop," Alfie says, pointing with his chin to Tony.

Say what?

"Came here when I was a young man. Still do. I'm all caught up on *The Walking Dead* so I thought I'd get some fresh air and a margarita." He nods at Tony and holds up a gnarled finger.

Is everybody in this town I know connected? Including Tony? How did I not know this?

"How's Billy doin'?" Alfie asks.

"You heard?"

"Everybody's heard."

Everybody, huh? That mafia grapevine must be buzzing.

"He's got a long road ahead, but he's alive and doing better," I say. "I bet he'd love to see you."

"He's a tough son-of-a-bitch. He'll be good."

"That's what everyone keeps telling me."

Alfie's mango margarita arrives and I clink glasses with him. He removes the straw and slugs it back in several gulps. Then holds up his hand to Tony, who nods and takes his glass. I gape and then start to giggle.

"Only fruit I get. Things don't work so well no more." He taps his yellowed dentures with his fingernail, then studies my face and says, "You have your pop's eyes. Like a good cognac."

"Did you know I was here, Alfie?"

He grins. His own watery nut-brown eyes twinkle.

"You're as smart as you look. Word's gotten around about you. Us old fellas, we ain't got nuttin' much to do no more. We loved your pop. Took care of us, now we take care of you."

"How many old fellas are we talking about?"

"Enough to kick some scumbag ass."

Oi yoi yoi.

"Please don't be kicking scumbag ass on my behalf. I couldn't forgive myself if anyone else got hurt."

"Eh." He waves a hand at me. "Ain't much that hasn't already been done. Besides, I like a little fun."

"Fun?" My mouth drops open again.

He cackles, and accepts his second drink from Tony. This time he sips it through the straw.

"Miss the action. We're all rotting away doing nuttin'. Better to go out like a warrior."

"Thank you, I think. But I don't understand something. What do you mean that my dad *took care* of you?"

"He was good with the money. Cleaned it up and taught us where to put it."

"Uh huh." I nod my head and chew on my thumbnail. "That's another thing I keep hearing."

Hmm.

How come he wasn't so great with his own money then? This is something else that's not adding up. While my fingers run circles through the condensation on my glass I decide I need to call my mother.

"Did you tell Alfie I was here?" I ask Tony when he shimmies back to our side after serving the two men fresh beers.

He smiles and does a little head bobble. "Of course I did."

When I glare at him, he makes little huffing noises. "Lovey, there isn't much that goes on in this town that I don't know about. As soon as Cass told me what that dingleberry did to you, I blew my trumpet."

I swivel to aim my glare at Cass, but she's engaged in a grin-off with Marco and ignores me.

No help there.

Fine.

I plop my elbow onto the bar, drop my head into my palm, and suck a huge sip of my drink through my straw.

Aaah...jeeez!

Brain freeze.

While I wait for the pain to pass another thought creeps into my head. "Wait...Tony. How did you know I'd met Alfie?"

"Oh puh-lease." His eyeballs roll back, then he looks at Alfie. "You're one of us. It's my business to know."

Bloody hell. I've become a project.

The cowbells jingle again and I turn to see two men enter. One is a distinguished elderly black gentleman with a gray goatee and a dated chauffeur's hat who stands by the door.

"Ah! My ride's here," Alfie says and sucks up the remaining margarita. "Gotta go. I ain't as tall as I used to be so I can't reach the pedals no more. Just wanted to stop by and say hello."

He slips off the barstool and pulls a wad of cash from his pocket and tosses a fifty onto the bar.

"Lunch on me. Ciao, girly."

"Alfie, no..." A hand on my wrist stops me. I eyeball Tony, who's shaking his head.

"Accept it," he says. "He'll be hurt if you don't."

"But...?"

That gets me another head shake.

By the time I turn around again it's too late anyway. Alfie's sliding into the back seat of the biggest car I've ever seen. A double-parked nineteen-seventies black Cadillac. I catch a glimpse of the top of his wispy hair through the passenger window.

"What the hell?" I ask Tony, holding both hands palm up.

"Oh, don't get your titties in a twirl. You need a lesson in mafia etiquette. You never turn down an offer like that. It's not done. Didn't your momma teach you anything?"

"Tony, I've been to his apartment. The poor man looks like he's barely making it on his social security."

"Ha!" One hip skids off to the side while he flicks his hair back with a head flip. "Shows how much you know. Didn't you see the wad of cash on him? Alfie has more than enough, probably thanks to your dad. You don't need to worry about his finances."

"All right." I sigh. "Well, I've got to visit the ladies." I nudge Marco. "I'll be right back."

He nods but doesn't take his eyes off Cass.

Pff.

Seems I've done my job too well.

A happy little tequila buzz flows through my veins as I follow a man in a windbreaker with the collar up and a baseball hat pulled down low. I can't see his face but who needs to, as he has an amazing ass, and I can't help thinking how it would measure up to Gianni's.

He passes two of the kitchen staff, stacking dinner plates on a cart before exiting through the rear door. I take a right and enter the bathroom at the back of the restaurant.

One of the women from the table of five is right behind me. The Bee Gee's "More than a Woman" plays and I sing along as I take care of business. The other woman joins me and we do a little harmonizing through the stalls before we burst into giggles.

"Wow, you can really sing," I say to her when we meet at the sink to wash our hands. "I remember you now. You work at Provocative, the lingerie store."

"Yeah, I'm Terra. Funny, I've been meaning to stop by to make an appointment with you."

"And I've been meaning to buy new lingerie. You've gorgeous hair, I'd love to get my hands on that."

We chat for a moment longer then swap cards. "See you in there," Terra says as she opens the door. I smile and finish touching up my face. After which I apply a little lip gloss, zip my purse, step outside into the hallway and freeze.

Fuck.

The base of my spine tingles as it hits me.

The dude with the sexy ass.

That was Dean!

I know because that ass was one of the things that attracted me to him.

Goosebumps erupt over my skin. I swivel around, frantically searching for him.

God!

Is he hiding somewhere? Fear squeezes my heart and I struggle to breathe.

Get a grip...get to Marco, fast.

As soon as I arrive back at the bar, Marco's brow creases and Cass's eyes widen.

"What happened?" They say simultaneously.

"Dean."

Marco jerks to attention. "What, where?"

"Out the back door. But I think he's gone now."

"Stay here." Marco slides off the barstool and sprints through the passageway.

"Shit, Shelley." Cass clutches my hand. "You're paler than platinum blonde number ten."

I swallow and bend over, putting my head between my legs, sucking in air and trying to get some blood to my brain.

"What's going on and where did that fine specimen disappear to?" Tony asks.

"Dean's outside," Cass says.

"What? Oh, *hell* no!" He dips behind the bar and comes up a moment later with a shotgun. Everybody in the bar halts.

Tony jumps butt first onto the bar, swings silver glitter platform boots over my drink and slips off the other side. He points the shotgun at the ceiling and pumps it as he trots towards the back door after Marco.

The only sound is the song "How Deep is your Love". I sit back up and glance around. Except for the music playing, it's like the giant clock of the universe stopped ticking. One of the gesticulating men still has his hands in the air, mouth hanging open and the women are silent for the first time since we've been here, staring after Tony.

It stays like that for a second longer, then suddenly the spell breaks and everybody's back to what they were doing.

No big deal, just another day at Tony's.

I look around the room then at Cass. We both shrug and I suck up more of my margarita. Now is definitely the time for liquid courage.

Marco jogs through to the front door, motorcycle boots clomping on the tiled floor. The women stop talking again, drop their jaws and follow him with their eyes. I think a couple even squirm in their seats.

Marco pulls open the door and steps outside. He's gone for at least a minute, while Cass grips my wrist. When he enters again, he shakes his head, his eyes sliding from me to Cass.

"He's gone." He pulls his cell from his pocket, punches a number and heads back out to the parking lot, passing a re-entering Tony on the way.

"Jesus, Tony," I say. "You surprised the crap out of everyone. Who knew you were so macho?"

"Just 'cause I'm a fairy, lovey, doesn't mean I'm not ready for action. Pop taught me well. How else do you think this bar has managed to maintain peace over the years? I've got a reputation in this town."

Good point.

He returns to behind the bar taking the long way around then squats for a moment as he sets the shotgun back in its place.

"Woo-wee," he says when he rises. "I'm jazzed." He shimmies those skinny shoulders and shakes his hands.

"Who's for another round? On the house!" There's a chorus of *Yays* all round and he slices up more mangos, tosses them in the blender and pushes the button. After he adds a double dash of tequila, he shakes the container, then pours. Just as he places our drinks in front of us, the front door jingles again. Tony follows the sound of the bells, then his face goes slack.

"Sweet Holy Jesus!" he murmurs. "I must be dead because I'm seeing angels."

I turn around. My stomach whooshes and that poor abused thing in my chest called my heart starts dancing the hustle.

Gianni-fucking-Cadora.

Looking fantastic, a little flushed and windblown. He's dressed in a dark blue, slim-fitting suit, crisp white shirt and an icy blue silk tie, the same color as his eyes. As he walks towards me running a hand through his hair he passes the five women. A few hands fly to their throats including Terra's and all their eyes pop wide open.

One of them announces loudly, "That's it! I'm going home to jump my man. Too much hotness in one room." The rest of them burst into nervous giggles.

I have to agree.

"You good?" he asks, running his hand up my arm, eyes searching mine and breathing hard.

"I'm good," I mumble 'cause that's all I can manage. "Why are you so out of breath?"

"Ran here."

"What? You ran here?"

He nods and scans the room. "Was a couple blocks away. Where's Marco?"

"Out back."

He ran?

For me?

"Stay here." He turns to Tony and stops with a jerk as he takes him in. Then drops his head and pulls in his lips. After a moment he asks, "You and your shotgun got this?"

Tony's mouth's still hanging open, head cocked to the side. He nods once, slowly.

"Okay, then," Gianni says. "Nice pants."

He squeezes my arm and touches his lips to my temple before moving to the rear exit.

Tony's eyes, wide as margarita glasses, follow him until he's gone then keep staring for a few moments more as if hoping he'll come back.

"Woo-wee," he says finally, but it comes out weak and a little shaky. "If you ever break up with that man, I want first dibs."

"I'm flattered, Tony, but he's not my man."

"Oh, sugar pie, he's yours, don't doubt it. 'Cause if you do, I'll come right behind you and swoop him up."

"I don't believe he's turnable, Tony." Cass giggles. "But it would be all kinds of fun watching you try."

"Hallelujah, sisters," he yells, holds his margarita glass in the air, then tosses it back. First his eyes widen, then they cross and his mouth puckers.

Placing his glass on the bar with deliberate slowness, he squeezes his temples with his silver fingernails and squeals out a high-pitched, "Oooooh."

It's too much. Cass and I burst into gales, snorting margaritas out our noses, which, of course, makes us laugh even harder until we're doubled over.

"How the hell did Alfie do that?" Tony asks after he recovers.

"He's got dentures. Maybe that helps." I say, wiping tears from my eyes with my thumbs.

"I suppose. My nuts retracted all the way up into my eye sockets. Explains why Alfie never had children."

This sets us off again and I'm laughing into my arms resting on the bar when Gianni and Marco return. I know this because the noise level at the women's table drops to a hush. I sit up and try to pull it together.

"We gotta go," Gianni says, taking a look at me. "What's the damage?" He looks at Tony, making a little circle with his index finger over the drinks.

"Buuuh," Tony utters, his face going slack again. It's a thing of wonder, the reaction people have to Gianni.

"I think what he's trying to say," Marco says, grinning, "is Alfie took care of it."

"Yaaaa..." Tony nods, his pale complexion turning bright pink. Good to know it's not just me.

Cass and I collect our purses and blow kisses at a slack-jawed Tony, then I wave to Terra. The men flank us, Marco in front, Gianni behind me.

In the parking lot, Marco tosses the Land Rover's keys to Gianni, then follows Cass to her Audi Q7.

Gianni opens the passenger door, removes his jacket and tie, then tosses them onto the back seat. When I'm settled, he pulls the seat belt across me, leaning into me as he snaps it into the slot.

Mmm.

He smells delicious. A little bit like his spicy aftershave and a lot like man. Our eyes lock and I stop breathing. His flare and when he swallows I know he's remembering this morning, but he pulls back and the moment is gone. What's not gone is the tingle between my legs that started the moment he walked into Tony's.

Suddenly, I make a decision.

I accept his terms.

It may be the tequila talking or (and this is the more likely reason) because I'm weak and apparently a slut, but I need to know where this is going.

I want him.

I want more of those orgasms he can give me and I'll take what I can get. As long as I remember what it is I'm getting.

"Marco not coming?" I ask after he starts the engine and he's backing the car out of the slot.

"Driving Cass home."

"In what?"

"Her car."

Oooh.

God, I'm in deep shit.

Alone with Gianni in a confined space after a double dose of tequila? How am I going to keep my hands off him with all these dirty thoughts running through my head? Whatever morals I had have drowned in a mango margarita.

All I can think about is that moment in the kitchen and how desperately I want another one.

I squeeze my legs together, but it doesn't help, instead it intensifies. I never got how in the movies a woman would want to have sex with a man while driving. Well, dangit, I'm getting it now.

I unsqueeze and sneak a sideways glance, but he's focused on traffic or deep in his thoughts.

Either way, that's good. That's very, very good.

"How's Billy?" he says, breaking into my fantasies.

"Feisty."

"As soon as he's able, I'll have him moved to the house. Hire a nurse."

We've hit some congestion and come to a stop and he must feel my stare, because he turns his head and looks at me.

"You'd do that?"

His gaze moves slowly over my face. "Of course. Billy's family. I love that bastard."

Wow.

"I'm pretty sure he loves you back, but that's beyond generous."

He shrugs. "He'd do it for me."

He would indeed.

"Thank you." I swallow back the lump in my throat. "You should know, I never thought you were heartless. Cold and a jerk and insensitive maybe, but that was before all this. I'm sorry."

His eyes go all soft and then they go all hot, making it difficult to turn away. "Careful, De Luca," he says in a gruff voice. "There's that fucking look again."

Oh lord, I can't hide from him. Luckily the cars in front start moving again. He clears his throat and goes back to focusing on the traffic.

For the rest of the way we're silent while I check Facebook on my phone to distract myself. But instead my thoughts wonder to what Dean's deal is? Was he there to do something or was he there just to fuck with me? Let me know he can get to me whenever he wants?

At the house, Gianni triggers the remote to the garage. The large doors slide open and the light sensor kicks in as we drive in. He pulls the Land Rover into its spot and cuts the engine.

"You sure you're good?" he asks quietly.

"I'm fine." Those blue eyes narrow, brows coming together until the Y appears. Instead of opening the door, he twists in his seat to face me.

"What is it, Shelley? I can feel those wheels turning in your head."

"I'm trying to figure out Dean. Why would he hurt Billy? Is it to hurt me?"

"Men like him don't need a reason. We've established he's fucked in the head, doing the things he's done."

A shudder moves through me at the memory of my panties and the spy-cam in my bathroom. "He's really running girls?"

"His crew is, which means he is."

"I can't believe I'm such an idiot. I mean, I liked him...until I didn't. What does that say about me?"

Something flickers across his face and he takes a moment before he answers.

"He's charming, I'll give him that. Convinced Joey to partner with him. Don't beat yourself up too much."

"Do you think...? God." I look away and swallow. "I can't even contemplate this...that he was...?"

"Going to make you one of his girls?" He shakes his head. "He wants you for himself."

"That scares the hell out of me," I whisper.

"It scares all of us."

"How's this going to end, Gianni?"

He shrugs. "It'll end the way it ends. Mostly depends on Melnikov, what kind of moves he makes. That's all I can say for certain."

"What do you and Carmine have in mind?"

He slides me a look, then shakes his head. "Can't talk about that, babe."

Shit.

He opens the car door, steps out and helps me out of my side by offering me a hand, which I take. "Come on, I want to show you something."

When we enter the kitchen, Truman's waiting, doing his little polka dance and each time he huffs in excitement, his front legs lift off the ground. It makes me happy that this funny dog's excited to see me. I rub him and squeeze his ears.

"That's another one obsessed with you," Gianni mutters softly. So softly I'm not sure I was meant to hear.

"You, Dog," he says louder, and points at Truman, "stay here."

The dog sits and stares at him, red-rimmed eyes blinking and darting between us, like he's waiting for me to contradict Gianni.

"Stay here, Truman. I'll see you soon." Truman drops his head, nose pointing to the floor.

"Truman?" Gianni cocks that scarred eyebrow.

"Yeah, what's his real name?"

"Dog."

"Not anymore."

"Fuck me," he says, placing his hands on the back of my neck and guiding me out of the kitchen.

As we walk down a long, hardwood hallway decorated with oriental carpets and paintings of descendants of the Cadora family, his hand drops to my lower back and stays there.

One little touch. It's more intoxicating than the tequila and sets fires in my lower spine.

At the end is a small flight of stairs heading down, then a door which he opens and we step inside.

Odd. I never knew this was here before.

Six large-screen monitors are mounted on a wall displaying footage of every angle of the house, gardens and driveway.

A beefy guy of about twenty-five with a buzz cut and headphones monitors footage behind a rectangular desk against the wall. He looks away from his computer and flashes a white, gap-toothed smile.

"This is Thomas."

I wave, he tips his chin.

"A surveillance room?"

"Don't miss much, do you." Gianni grins.

"Shut up." I bump him with my shoulder.

On the other side is a window facing the bridge, shuttered by partially open wooden plantation blinds.

"What are those focused on?" I point to four more screens. Only one's turned on, displaying a picture that seems familiar.

"The first three show the inside of the house. For when we have functions or meetings. I entertain here instead of at my house. But we can also direct feed remotely from other locations when we need to."

"For instance...?"

His eyes land on mine. "Your apartment."

Say what?

"Carmine and I installed wireless cameras last night."

On closer inspection, I realize the familiar picture is the hallway outside my apartment door. My jaw drops. Are the other screens for inside?

"Are you fucking kidding me?" I sense him stiffen.

That's why he wanted my keys.

Fuck. My blood's heating rapidly, racing through my veins. No doubt aided by the tequila.

"Who's running this?"

"Carmine. Shelley…?"

And that's why Marco and Carmine didn't want to talk in front of me.

Bastards.

"You should have told me about this before you began to surveil my apartment."

"Wasn't time."

"Bullshit. You had plenty of time last night to inform me you were going to do this. Or how about a text or a *hey Shelley we're going to do what Dean just did*? But *nooo*…" I jab a finger into his chest.

"Shelley," he growls and grabs my wrist. "Don't do that."

"You could've told me this morning. You had plenty time then instead of doing *other* things." I kick his shin, which probably hurts me more than him, but I refuse to show the pain jolting from my knees.

"Fuck, woman…"

"Shut up, asshole," I yell and yank my wrist from his grip.

Thomas stares, wide eyes darting between us, his mouth hanging open.

Ha! Probably never seen anyone who's not Isabella Cadora yell at him before.

I storm out the room, hearing "Dammit, De Luca…" before I

slam the door behind me, not caring how much my knees hurt or if I hit him in the nose. I hope I broke it.

As I'm not paying attention to my feet, I almost trip over Truman, who's defied Gianni's order and is waiting outside.

"Come on, Truman. Let's get the hell out of here." He grunts and follows me back up the four stairs and down the hallway. While I struggle slowly up the other, much longer flight of stairs, he jumps ahead, then stops to wait for me to catch up.

"Isn't there an elevator in this damn house?"

Truman sneezes.

When I finally open my bedroom door, out of breath, I'm pleasantly surprised, but it doesn't last long. Connie's cleaned and vacuumed. Everything looks pristine but it doesn't do much to help my mood. If I were a cartoon, steam would be coming from my ears.

Who does the jerk think he is? Dean?

Fuck, no, not Dean.

I toss my things on the bed, and use the bathroom before I fling the French doors open. Hoping the cool, salty air on my face will calm me down. I close my eyes and stand on the threshold.

There's no wind and it's still a beautiful day with a slight haze off the coastline, the sun is about a foot above the horizon.

A movement to my right catches my eye. My heart lurches in my chest and my stomach gets that whooshy feeling. Because isn't my fucking luck just fantastic? The asshole's on the phone, with his back to me.

How the hell did he get there?

Then it occurs to me, the other French doors are open.

Oh, my word.

That has to be his room, right next to mine. We share the frigging balcony. That Vicodin really did a number on me.

He paces as he speaks, running one hand through his hair.

When he reaches the end of the balcony and turns, he stops when he sees me. Then gives me that lazy smile making my heart beat so loudly, I'm convinced he can hear it.

Asshole.

Determined to stay mad, I glare at him, hoping at least one of the daggers shooting from my eye hits the target. Just because he's perfect doesn't mean I'm going to let that get in the way of chewing him out.

He keeps talking and holding my gaze until I look away. I walk to the edge of the balcony and lean against the balustrade.

A pod of white pelicans circles just off the edge of the cliff. Some dive, while others float and scoop up fish in their long, pointy bills. From a distance, they look like pterodactyls, graceful and hypnotizing.

Footsteps and a shadow alert me to Gianni's approach, but even if I hadn't heard, I'd sense he was behind me considering the way my skin prickles.

"Talk to me, De Luca."

"Who the hell do you think you are?" I spin to face him. "You had no right to wire my apartment and you most definitely should have asked me first before you took Carmine there."

"Shelley..."

"Dammit, Gianni, don't you think I feel violated enough? Does it matter that I have to deal with that freak stalking me, going through my things, my dirty laundry? And now you doing whatever the hell *you* want with my privacy?"

"Shelley..."

"And why didn't you tell me this morning?"

"If you'd shut your yap for a minute, woman, I'll explain."

"My yap?"

"Yep."

"You don't need to be a jerk."

"Now I'm a jerk again?"

"You're always a jerk."

His mouth quirks. The corner of his eyes crinkle in that way that slays my heart and *poof*. There goes my anger in a puff of fairy dust that would make Tony proud.

I plant my hands on my hips. "What's so damn funny?"

"You are. Come here, woman." His arm snakes behind my back and crushes me hard against him. Then he walks us a step back, until my butt's against the balustrade, trapping me. Again.

Not good.

But oh, so, *so* good.

"You got a thing about trapping me?"

"Yep. It keeps you where I want you."

"Asshole."

"I was gonna ask if you're done bitching, but I see I might be premature."

"Shut up."

"Mmm. There's that attitude I love so much."

"Um..."

Okay.

The tingling between my legs that never completely went away gets stronger, making my knees weak. Leaving me no choice other than to cling to his upper arms for support.

"Said it before, but you're kinda cute when you're pissed. Your eyes spark and you get this sexy little flush in your cheeks."

Great.

Now I *feel* myself flushing.

"You can't charm your way out of this, Gianni Cadora." I loosen my grip on his arms and wriggle against his solid chest but he doesn't budge. Not even a little bit.

"Keep fighting me, De Luca," he whispers, tightening his arms around me. "I wanna kiss you right now and the more you wriggle, the more I want it." He dips his head and nuzzles my neck.

I have to bite my lip to stop a groan from escaping and it's getting really, *really* hot in the south.

"You know this is happening, sooner or later." His five o'clock shadow and breath on my skin makes my belly tighten and my core spasm. "I'd prefer sooner."

Oh...God!

I stop wriggling and melt instead. Because I give in. I surrender everything.

"But, you're right." His lips capture my earlobe and tug. "I should have asked your permission. Wanted to get in fast, in case he came back. I had your keys, we took advantage."

"I'm still mad at you," I whisper, lying.

"I *was* going to tell you this morning."

Those lips have moved on to my jaw, inching closer to mine. "But then I got sidetracked." A hand slips under my top, sliding slowly up my side, leaving a trail of fire on my skin. I whimper and drop my head back.

"I blame you," he says.

Mmm. God, the things he makes me feel.

My naked nipple pebbles when he flicks his thumb over it, sending shudders through me.

Gianni hisses when he feels it. "Christ, De Luca. You do things to me." Then so softly, I think I'm imagining it. "You always have."

Fingers slide higher, scraping over my breast, then his other hand moves up the back of my neck. Fisting my hair, tugging my head back before his mouth slams onto mine. A deep, wet, sensual, tongue-twisting, mind-blowing kiss that leaves me even weaker and begging for more. Because now I know what *more* is with him.

My arms find their way around his neck while I press against him. Still kissing me, he slides his palms over my ass, lifting me up. My legs lock around his waist. Then he carries me to his room, lowering me next to the bed. Gianni undoes the top buttons of his shirt, yanks it over his head before tossing it aside to reclaim my mouth.

I can't get enough of him, or he of me. Our hands are everywhere, his under my top, thumbing my nipples. Mine tracing the ridges of his abs and back muscles.

"Get rid of this," he growls, his voice hoarse. "I want to feel your skin against mine." Up goes my top and when it's gone, he stops for a moment, raking his eyes over my body. They're burning but when they hit my swollen nipples, they flare even hotter. A quick shove, and I'm lying flat on his bed. Shoes are next, then he drops his trousers and boxers to the floor.

Holy fizz pops, how can a man be so fucking perfect and hot naked, and right now, he wants me.

Me!

Before I have a chance to feast my eyes on his beautiful, hard cock, he unbuttons my pants and removes them, then grabs my ankles, pulling my legs apart, wide enough to settle himself between my thighs without hurting my knees. A nipple disappears in his mouth and he sucks, building tension one lazy lick at a time. Crazy, exquisite sensations shoot through me and culminate between my legs.

God!

This is so, so good. He sucks again, I arch my back, moaning and opening my legs further, needing to be filled. Needing *him* to fill me.

"Your first installment is due, De Luca," he says, eyes hungry and demanding as they blaze into mine.

First?

That implies more than one.

Yippee.

"Shut up," I whisper urgently. "And get busy."

The little chuckle tells me he likes my answer while he rips the wrapper of a condom and rolls it on. "Gonna be fast and dirty the first time, babe. Waited too fucking long for you, I'm not gonna last."

He's right about that, because I can't wait any longer either. I twist my fingers in his hair, pull his head to me, and devour his mouth while his hand slides between my legs, finding my swollen clit. I'm soaked and primed and in just a few strokes he brings me to climax. I'm still coming when his cock eases into me. To say he's barely controlled would be understated. As he enters, his breathing gets harsher and with each thrust I sense him get closer to losing it.

"Christ, you feel good." His voice is thick and growly. "So much better than I ever imagined. And believe me, I fucking imagined."

Well, shit.

He *imagined*.

After that, it gets a little crazy. He pounds and I arch, meeting him, trying to get closer while it builds and builds. I'm so close, that when his stubble scrapes over my nipple, I shatter around him again, heels and nails digging in. And it's a moment after that when his thrusts get faster and lose rhythm. As he reaches his own climax, one hand cups my face while he groans into my neck, calling my name.

He collapses but we stay connected, tangled up with him still inside me breathing hard for a long time until we come down and our heartbeats slow.

I expect him to rise, thinking he'd be done with me for now. Instead, he shifts his weight so his stomach lies against my side and drapes an arm over me. Then he rains soft kisses on the round of my shoulder. His lips are still on me when I fall asleep.

12

DAMN CRICKETS

~

T*here's a cricket in the room.*

It takes a moment for me to get my bearings when I open my eyes. If it weren't for his body heat I'd think I'd been dreaming, but the tenderness between my thighs confirms it's no dream.

My belly tightens and heat rises up in me. We're in the same position, his face buried in the side of my neck and the soft rhythm of his breath fanning my shoulder.

Excellent. I get to check him out. A naked Gianni is a fantastic thing to behold. The man is nothing but muscle, ridges and pure male beauty with a sprinkling of just enough hair to keep him real. Only one tiny imperfection, the scar on his shoulder. I need to ask him how he got it.

The French doors are still open and a gentle, ocean breeze blows through. It's grown dark, but there's enough ambient light from the patio lamps outside, which I'm assuming came on automatically. At some point after I fell asleep Gianni dealt with the condom and pulled the comforter over us.

Crickets?

Really?

I lift my head and try to move his arm, but it tightens.

"Un uh," he mumbles and sucks on my shoulder while shifting his position. "Not going anywhere." He moves his leg from between mine, then slides his hand slowly up towards my breast. "Not done with you."

God. I shift restlessly, aching for him again.

He's not done with me!

This does insane things to my heart, but it's nothing compared to the sensations flooding my body. If it's anything like what we just had, I definitely want more. I grasp his hand and guide it until he finally reaches the place I need him to be. His breathing grows steadily more ragged as he cups my sex.

Then crickets again.

"Gianni," I say, barely able to contain a groan. He's already hard and throbbing against my hip.

"Either there's a cricket in the room or your phone's blowing up."

"They can wait," his voice is gruff. "More important things to do. Like watching you come." His thumb finds its way to my clit and begins a slow rhythm.

"Ah!" My body jerks, and I push more of myself into his hand, like a bitch in heat. It's building fast, curling my toes. When he slips two fingers inside and strokes me, working me both inside and out, it's only moments before I come undone. "Oh, God," I cry out, throwing my head back while fisting my hands in his hair as the spasms rock my body over and over.

"Fuck." His voice is rough and full of wonder. "So beautiful watching you, knowing I did that." His fingers vanish and I immediately miss them while he rolls on another condom, but then his knees are between mine, shoving them further apart. I feel pressure at my entrance as he whispers in a voice that's a little shaky the words I so desperately need to here. "I'm gonna take you hard one more time, babe. Next time, I promise it will be long and slow."

I'm unable to speak but manage a small nod before he claims my mouth and our tongues do battle.

I want him inside so much it's an ache that only he can fix. I lift my hips to meet him as he nudges in part way, allowing me to adjust to his size. Then withdrawing a little before rocking deeper, repeating the process until he's all the way in.

The tension in his torso, tells me he's holding back as he withdraws. Touching his forehead to mine, he asks, "You good?"

"So good." I barely get the words out when he slams into me, hard.

So, so fucking good.

And again, it gets wild, almost brutal and a little out of control. He's woken feelings and sensations in me I never knew existed and I can't get enough or take enough. Before I know it, I'm building again. The familiar tightening grows with each thrust, filling me to the point of overflowing. My legs and sex clench around him as I get there and I cry out his name.

"Jesus, fuck, Shelley. What you do to me." His breath is ragged and hot in my neck as he slams, once, then again and once more to the root before he stills, groaning as his own climax takes him.

Then he collapses on me and I lie beneath him, absorbing each shudder and his weight while I come down from the most amazing high ever. Both of us are slick with sweat. All too soon he lifts himself off me, moving to the side, but slipping an arm under my neck and curling his elbow while the other slides over my stomach. Lips against my temple, he mumbles, "There're no words. I always knew we'd be good, but you blow my mind."

It's beautiful hearing him say it. My heart swells to the point

I think it might burst and I'm grateful it's semi-dark because I push back the tears and swallow the lump that's forming.

I've wanted this for so long and to know that he got off on it as much as me means everything. Truthfully, it's the best sex I've ever had, but I'm not so much of an idiot that I'm going to ask him if it's the same for him.

Hell no.

But blow his mind?

"Always?" I tease. "It's barely been a week since I saw you again."

"Known a lot longer than a week, babe."

And...boom.

He just blew mine.

I stare at him, blinking and wondering if I've developed a hearing problem.

"This marker thing...I..." Then his stupid phone starts chirping again. "Dammit." He slides his arm from under me and rolls onto his back, dragging a hand over his face before flipping on the bedside lamp. "Hold that thought. Must be important if they keep trying. Sorry." He shields his eyes from the light, then fumbles for his phone in his discarded pants on the floor.

As he reads the text he bolts upright. "Shit."

Uh oh.

"What's wrong?" I ask.

"Shit."

He leans over, lands a kiss on my lips. "One sec." The bed dips slightly as he swings long legs over the side, pushing a button on his phone.

"What happened?" he says into his cell. When I make a move to get up, he snaps his fingers, then points at me. "Don't move," he mouths.

Two little words compounded with his others make my stomach flip and my chest fill. Unfortunately, I have certain needs that have to be taken care of along with taking a personal moment to *freak the shit out.*

"Bathroom," I mouth back not trusting my voice.

I step out of bed and slip on Gianni's discarded shirt, pulling the ends close and inhaling and his scent while I stride into the bathroom feeling him watch me.

It's almost as spectacular as the one at his own house. The shower is big enough for four and encased in a creamy marble with frosted, etched glass doors. Accent tiles, the color of sea foam match slightly darker towels and rugs. It gorgeous and luxurious and if I didn't know I was in Gianni's room, I'd swear I was at a swanky spa. But really, I'm not paying any attention to the bathroom because *I'M FREAKING THE SHIT OUT.*

Did he just admit to wanting me all those years ago?

This is information I'm not sure how to process and while my mind is running in circles, I check myself in the mirror. My lips are puffy and my hair has that *just done it* look—all wild, kinda like what my eyes look like. My poor heart is thumping a thousand beats a minute.

When I have it somewhat together again, I exit the bathroom. Gianni's fully dressed in faded jeans and a blue sweater.

Crap.

My bubble deflates. Well, it was magnificent while it lasted.

He laces steel-toed ankle boots, shoves his phone into the back pocket of his jeans, then walks towards me. One arm catches me around my waist beneath the shirt, the other cups my face with his thumb under my jaw. When his mouth finds mine, he kisses me until I'm weak-kneed and panting again.

God.

I feel it *everywhere.*

"I gotta go," he says against my mouth, his tone full of hunger and regret. "We've got some talking to do, some things to clear up. But there's a fire at one of my buildings."

Whoa!

I swallow. "Anybody hurt?"

"Don't know yet." His nose traces the curve of my jaw. I feel him inhale before he says, "Promise me, De Luca, you'll be in my bed when I get back."

Oh, thank God. Yes.

"I promise."

"All right then." Waiting for him to let me go, I'm surprised but secretly overjoyed when he doesn't. Instead, he slides his shirt off my shoulder, exposing my breast as he lays his lips on the bend in my neck. "I'll see you later."

My nipples react and harden at the prickliness of his stubble and hot breath on my skin. Seeing it, he sucks air through his teeth then cups me, pushing my breast up high. Gianni dips, then sucks one little peak into his mouth, circling it with his tongue until I whimper.

"Damn," he mutters.

Damn, in-fucking-deed.

Before he pushes me away, the ridge of his erection pushing through his jeans against my leg tells me he really doesn't want to go.

Gianni lets out a shaky breath. "You're like fucking heroin. Can't get enough." He adjusts his jeans and clears his throat. "But I have to go, babe. Thomas is here. Marco will be soon. You won't be alone."

"Be careful?"

"You bet." A last quick kiss, then he's gone and the second he closes the bedroom door, I already miss him.

I collapse onto his bed and squeeze my legs together. I'm tender, but the ache he just left me with is far worse, and I can't wait for him to come back.

The thought sets my heart thrumming and my face flaming.

The best part about it is I know he wants to do it at least once more. And so do I.

Holy fizz pops, do I ever!

And about what he said. Can I afford to let myself trust it? Just this once?

God!

I want to. So freaking much. I blow out air through my lips, making little popping noises. What to do to distract myself until he gets back? To stop myself from fantasizing about what I want him to say. Because what I want isn't necessarily what I'll get. Not in my experience.

I glance at the clock on his wall. It's only seven p.m. and he'll probably be gone for hours.

Maybe a little sightseeing is in order. I wander around his room, touching a few knick-knacks. One being a baseball signed by Willy McCovey and a football, by Joe Montana.

Some photos on the wall of a teenage Gianni and Joey in baseball uniforms. They look happy, laughing, perhaps at something the photographer said. I remember Papa was a Joe DiMaggio fan and hoped one of his sons would make it to the big leagues. I'm suspecting that scar on Gianni's shoulder may have killed any dreams he might have had.

Another photo taken on a sunny day at AT&T Park, shows him, Joey and Papa at a Giants game, enjoying happier times. But when I look closer, I can see the smile doesn't quite reach Joey's eyes. The date on the bottom right corner says it was taken eight years ago. Two years after I left.

Having done a full circuit of his room, it's time to take a shower and freshen up for round three. I meander back over to my own room.

My blood is singing through my veins and I can't stop smiling while I shampoo. I lather up with a dollop of my favorite petunia-scented lotion then pull on wide-legged black yoga pants, a long, hot-pink sweater and my Uggs.

My stomach dictates where I'm going next. It's only when I'm halfway down the stairs, I realize Truman isn't following me.

Huh.

Maybe he's outside with the rest of the dogs. I wonder if they've been fed? They don't seem to be complaining, so I guess so.

Connie left the first aid kit on the kitchen counter and I change the Band-Aids on my knees, tossing the old ones in the garbage.

It feels weird that Truman isn't by my side and I miss him. First time the funny thing has left me since I got here.

I open the back door. No sign of any of the dogs. Strange.

I step outside and whistle, then call, "Truman."

Nothing!

Not even a whimper.

I step out further. The next instant, someone grabs my wrist, then my elbow. "Hello, Shelley."

Before I can react, even scream, something fast and blurry hits me behind my ear. My knees buckle and the world goes dark.

13

SOMEWHERE OVER THE RAINBOW

~

Everything's rocking and moving. My cheek rubs against something coarse and gritty that smells like stale cigarettes and motor oil.

I can't see anything, other than a thin sliver of light and scuffed tennis shoes at the bottom of my vision. A loud droning vibrates in my eardrum.

My arms seem to be stuck behind my back and something digs into my flesh if I tug too hard. The same for my legs. I can move them a little, but I can't separate my ankles.

Someone, a man, is speaking. Sounds like he's in a tunnel, and I can't understand anything he's saying.

Through the fog in my brain, it takes a moment to figure it sounds like Russian.

Oh, fuck...no.

Dean, or rather one of his goons, since I don't recognize the voice.

How did he get past Thomas? Oh God...Thomas. And the dogs!

A million questions fly through my brain while my heart pounds so loudly, I can hear it over the droning engine.

Panic sets in and I begin to squirm, trying to kick my legs. I land a blow on dirty tennis shoes' thigh.

The man emits a loud grunt before something, I'm guessing an arm, coils around the front of my neck. I know this because I can feel its hairy roughness under my chin.

My head is yanked back at the same time two calloused fingers pinch my nostrils. As I open my mouth to breathe, a cold, bitter liquid is poured into it, then my jaw is slammed shut. If I want to breath I have to swallow.

I buck and thrash until the fingers let go, allowing me to suck in lungfuls of foul, cigarette air. Gagging, but grateful to be breathing again, I yell, "What did you give me?"

"Shh, shh, shh." The man, definitely not Dean, whispers in my ear in a thick Russian accent. "Don't panic."

Don't panic? Are you fucking kidding me? I squirm in his arms and his forearm tightens around my neck.

"Don't panic, won't grab tits."

Did he say tits?

He won't grab my *tits*?

Not what I wanted to hear, but it works. Since I definitely don't want my tits grabbed I stop squirming.

"Da. Good girly."

Calm down.

Don't get tits grabbed.

I repeat this to myself over and over, until a few minutes later, I'm groggy. Soon after that, it all goes black again.

~

THE NEXT TIME my eyes open, it's daylight. My head throbs and the thing I believe is my mouth feels like I swallowed a roll of paper towels. Worse, my vision is double *and* blurry.

I blink until it finally clears enough and realize I'm in a room with a large window, set in a wall made of logs. It's eerily quiet. No traffic noises or rumbles of construction. Nothing at all to indicate I'm still in the city.

It's then that I remember my joyride in a van that smelled like an ashtray in a dirty garage. Except the only thing that smells like an ashtray now, is me.

I push myself into a sitting position and press my fingers to my temples, waiting for the wooziness and nausea to pass. At least the shackles are gone and I can move my arms and legs.

Where in hell am I?

Doing a sweep of the room I search for something, *anything* that looks familiar. Nothing does. Not the four-poster king-sized bed nor the plush duvet or even the shaggy brown carpet.

Not a damn thing.

Okay.

Use your noodle and keep calm.

Dropping my feet over the side, I stand and grab the bedpost for support until the world stops spinning and my legs begin to cooperate. Lack of saliva forces me to constantly swallow, not that it does me any good.

Need water, and soon.

On the bedside table, underneath a tiffany-style lamp, is a bottle. My first impulse is to gulp it, but as I crack the seal, I remember they drugged me with something in liquid form. And the asshole threatened to grab my tits. What the fuck is that all about?

I squint at the bottle through one eye and squeeze, making sure there's no minuscule holes which would indicate a syringe. It seems intact, but I don't trust my vision and decide against it. I'm not taking any chances yet, not unless I have to.

There's an open door off to the side of the room and I can just make out a sink and a toilet. With one wobbly step at a time, I inch my way towards it.

The distance is short, but it takes longer than it should.

When a dizzy spell hits me, I hold onto the doorframe and wait for the starbursts behind my eyelids to fade.

Inside the bathroom, a beautiful, though blurry, claw-foot tub is situated in front of a window with a view of a lake ringed with elegant fuzzy pines. Far below, the ground is blanketed with snow.

By the looks of the scenery and lack of oxygen, I'm guessing we're somewhere high up in the mountains. Very fucking high.

Shit.

Dean mentioned a house in Tahoe. This must be it. But where in Tahoe? North Shore...South Lake?

Think.

Or was it somewhere more obscure? Ugh! Even thinking hurts. First problem I need to deal with is getting water.

The faucet's a little tight and after a yank, a few dribbles of rusty colored water trickle out...then nothing. If I had the energy I'd stamp my foot, but I glare at it instead. Willing, *daring* it to work. Does God really hate me this much?

No, no, don't think like that. I'm not going to let this beat me. Then, I hear a low grumbling in the pipe. A couple of airy bursts followed by a splattering and finally, a rusty colored stream gushes out.

A (very) dry sob catches in my throat.

When it runs clear I capture some in my hands, sucking in small sips and taking care not to compound the jack-hammering in my head with a brain freeze. After a few minutes, my head begins to clear, and stops pounding as hard.

The first thought to enter my mind is Gianni's gotta be looking for me, right?

Would he even know where to begin?

Well, that's depressing.

Need to stay calm if I have any chance of getting out of here.

Don't get tits grabbed.

Back in the bedroom, I check the door. No surprise, it's locked and so is the window, which is thick and double-paned, making it difficult to break without a tool of some kind. And since it seems I'm on the second floor, it's a long drop from here. Certainly wouldn't help if I broke something on the way down. The weather's clear, so that's good, but I can't tell the time, the sun being out of my line of vision.

Gotta be something I can use as a weapon or a tool. I search everywhere: in the closet, under the bed, in the medicine cabinet and the desk under the window.

Nothing.

Not even a ballpoint pen.

It's when I jiggle the window I hear a key turning and spin around to face the door as it opens. Dean steps in, folds his arms and leans against the doorframe.

Here we go.

His lips curve and the damn dimple in his left cheek I found so attractive appears.

"Hello, beautiful."

Except for the minor fact he's a psycho, the man isn't a dog. Thick, straight blonde hair and gray eyes. Good thing I prefer real dogs to him.

"Happy to see me?"

Not exactly doing cartwheels here.

"Why am I here, Dean?" I'm sure the pulse beating in my neck is a dead giveaway, but I act cool while he crosses the floor like a cat. I'd forgotten how good he looks when he wants to.

Fucking kidnapping asshole.

"You okay?"

No, I'm not okay! Jeez.

"Don't know, Dean. *Am* I?"

He chuckles. "Always with the attitude. That's what turns me on about you."

Fuck. Maybe I should tone it down and play the simpering little house mouse.

"Sit with me," he says, parking himself in the middle of the bed.

"I prefer to stand, if you don't mind."

"Please, Shelley." A head movement indicates where he wants me. "Sit."

Probably not the best time to piss him off.

So.

I comply, choosing the corner furthest away from him.

"Come closer." His voice carries a tinge of regret but I don't trust it. "I'm not going to hurt you."

"You did hurt me, remember?" I whisper. "You left me lying in an alley like a piece of garbage."

"I'm sorry." His voice and eyes are soft. Except for the fucking *madness* I know is lying behind that look, he's so damn convincing. "I fucked up when I hit you. You didn't deserve that."

I swallow.

He moves closer and reaches for my hand. It takes everything in me, but I resist the impulse to yank it back. Suppressing the shudder that wants to run through my body while he caresses the tips of my fingers, then turns it over and examines the scrapes on my palms.

"I sensed you were going to break up with me and...I didn't want to lose you. So when you smiled at that waiter, I lost it."

"Why did you bring me here?"

"I thought we could start over, spend some time together. Get to know each other again."

"You kidnapped me, Dean. That's not a good start to starting over."

His fingers tense. Shit. I have to watch my tone. I refuse to show fear, but I can't antagonize him either.

"Let me make it up to you," he says, lacing my fingers with his. "I want to show you I can be what you need. I can give you everything you want."

"What do you think I need?"

"You need *me*."

"Okay." Sighing, I close my eyes for a moment. "I forgive you," I say, digging deep for any sweetness left in me.

"You do?" The line between his brows deepens.

I nod. "I'll let you make it up to me."

"That makes me happy, baby."

"But if you really want to start over, you need to let me go."

"I can't do that," he whispers.

"Why not?"

"I don't trust you. Maybe you're playing me. For this to work, I need you to understand you belong to me. Only way I know how to make you understand is to keep you here until you do."

Fuck.

I didn't really think asking him was going to work, did I? But still...fuck!

He raises my hands to his lips, kisses the tips before letting them go. "You smell like Boris's van. Fucking moron never cleans it. Take a bath, relax, then we'll talk more."

He stands, his crotch only a foot away from my face and I have to fight the impulse to either lean back or head butt him. Perhaps if I let him think he's making progress, he'll get sloppy, give me a chance to escape.

"I'll bring you clean clothes," Dean continues. "We'll eat after, you must be hungry." He smiles that crooked smile, the one that finally got me to go out with him and struts into the bathroom. A moment later, I hear water running and fragrant jasmine-scented steam floats through the door.

I do want a bath. Who knows how long I'll be here and with this stink on me, I'm grossing myself out. Besides, it'll give me time to think and get a plan together.

He disappears out of the bedroom for a few seconds, then returns with a small suitcase, an apple and a can of Coke. I take the fruit from him and examine it for needle marks.

He rolls his eyes but seems mildly amused. "It's not drugged, Shelley. I want you lucid when we talk."

I peek at him through my lashes, determine he's telling the truth, well as much as he can anyway, and take a small bite.

"Would you mind if I have some privacy?" I say between mouthfuls. "I mean, this is still kinda new..."

"Let me wash your hair." His eyes bore into mine. "I can tell your hands are still tender."

Oh God. Really? The thought of his hands on me makes me lose my appetite. I place the half-eaten apple next to the tub.

"Dean, please, I have...to use the bathroom."

"Ah, of course," he says, reaching into a whitewashed antique armoire in the corner of the bathroom. He drops a couple towels onto a wicker chair next to the tub. "I suppose some things need to remain a mystery."

Mystery, my ass.

I mean, I can't forget this is the man who planted a spy cam in my *bathroom.* So I fake a smile, making sure it reaches my eyes. I got a game to play. I wish I had Ziggy. I'd plug a couple in *his* ass. But she's two hundred odd miles west, assuming I'm in Tahoe.

"I'll come back in ten minutes."

This time I don't smile. Don't want to overdo it. He knows me well enough that I'm not some simpering little wench. I'm a daughter of the mafia, for shit's sake.

And now that the initial shock of being kidnapped has worn off, I'm mostly pissed. And mentally prepared. If he hits me again, I'll fight back. It may not do me any good, but I'll fight anyway.

"I'd really prefer to do this alone. You want us to start over, you need to give me some space to sort out my head."

He's silent for a beat then he sighs. "Okay." He traces a thumb across my jaw. "I'll do that...for you." Then dipping his head, he kisses me on my lips. "Don't be long. I missed you and can't wait to catch up."

Somehow, I hide the revulsion moving through me at his touch. After he leaves and shuts the bedroom door, I resist swiping my hand over my lips, erasing his kiss. Just in case there're cameras, but I'm not going to waste my energy on looking for them. He wants a show, I'll give him one. Just not the one he's expecting.

I strip quickly, dropping my soiled clothes on the bathroom floor. The sting between my legs as I hit the perfumed water reminds me how quickly things can change.

I finally have a moment so beautiful, so profound it will stay with me for the rest of my life. However long (or short) that may be. Something I've wanted forever, with the man I've loved forever. Something to hang on to. I have no doubt Dean's going to try to kill me. If I die here, at least I'll have had that.

A small sob escapes me, but that's all I allow myself. Though I'm freaking out on the inside, I can't show it. I need to focus. What would my dad or Billy do if they were in my place? What would Gianni do?

Use what you got.

But what do I have? No tools and no weapons. All I have is me, so me it's going to have to be. I stay below the surface, but keep my knees above to spare the Band-Aids, and blow bubbles out my mouth until I run out of oxygen.

And come to terms with knowing there may be things I have to do. Disgusting things, in order to keep Dean calm. If I want to survive this, and I really do want to survive this, even if it's just to see Gianni one more time. I may as well make my peace with it now. Stay alive long enough for them to find me or find a way to get out of here.

I lie back and sip the Coke.

Think.

Before the water turns cool, I let it out and step out of the tub. I wrap one of the big, fluffy white towels around my body, the other around my head and dump out the bag Dean brought in and stare at what's on the bed.

Seriously?

My own clothes, but nothing practical, or warm. All the pieces are evening items: miniskirts, halter tops, a sequined tube-top and a short, black cocktail dress. And lingerie from Provocative, where my new friend Terra works. I can't help wondering if she sold the stuff to Dean. I hope she made a good commission.

But no shoes.

Again.

What is it with men and not packing shoes?

Are the clothes about trying to keep me from escaping or some weird personal *Dean* thing? Or something worse than that?

Maybe Gianni was wrong and this *is* about selling me. Maybe he's going to parade me in front of potential buyers. My chest rises and falls faster than it should, my breath coming in small gasps.

Keep calm.

Don't panic.

Don't get tits grabbed.

He said he wanted to talk. Hang on to that. I have to make

him believe I want what he wants to buy time. Hopefully Carmine is as good as everyone thinks he is.

When I swipe my dirty clothes off the bathroom floor, the stale cigarette smell makes me gag. Considering the clothing choices Dean's given me, I'll want to wear them again.

I run fresh water into the tub, add a dollop of the bath gel, scrub, and rinse my clothes and hang them over the heated towel rack to dry.

Better get dressed. It won't do to be naked if Dean comes back. The cocktail dress, the least revealing of my choices, falls just above my knees, but it's longer than the miniskirts he's packed.

Once my hair is combed and mostly dry, I stick my feet into my Uggs and try the bedroom door handle. I'm surprised when it opens.

Pff.

I guess I can't go anywhere in the clothes I'm wearing. They're not chains, but they may as well be. Considering all the snow outside, I'd freeze and besides, I have to figure out where I am before I know where to go.

There's a wooden staircase just off a landing decorated with gorgeous, Native American rugs and massive windows facing a small lake. This isn't a cabin. It's a freaking log mansion, like the ones you see in Aspen belonging to the rich and fabulously famous.

If I were in any other circumstances I'd take time to admire it.

The smell of roasting beef makes my mouth water and I follow my nose and growling stomach down the stairs.

Dean's stretched out, reading a dog-eared edition of *The Stand* on a long, white leather sofa in a spacious living room decorated similarly to upstairs. When he sees me coming, he rises. I cringe at how I used to think he was beautiful, now that smile makes my teeth ache. His looks are wasted on him.

"You look lovely...even with the fuzzy boots and the Band-Aids on your knees."

"You didn't pack any shoes." I cross the floor and stop a few feet away from him. "Why is that?"

His chin jerks up. "Shit. I didn't think about shoes."

Heh!

His grin turns sheepish as he approaches me. Long fingers circle my wrists, then he jerks me towards him, wrapping his arms around me until I'm flat against his body.

"Ah...now you smell good," he says burying his nose in my hair. "Like my Shelley again."

"I have a question."

"Anything."

"Why didn't you take me at Tony's? Wouldn't it have been easier than at the house?"

"I wanted to show you that Cadora can't protect you. Not like I can."

Holy cow.

Try as I might, I can't help flinching and I know he felt it, because his arms stiffen around me.

"You should remember that," he says gruffly. "No one can protect you like I can."

His fist tightens in my hair at the back of my head and he tugs it until I'm staring into his eyes. They're no longer soft and then I catch the faint whiff of alcohol.

A thousand times shit.

Please, not vodka. Dean and vodka are a lethal, unhealthy mix. Exhibit A: my face.

"But I don't want to talk about that. You're here now and it's in the past. We're moving forward."

Perhaps now wasn't the best time to ask. My one job is to stay alive long enough for Gianni to find me.

"Okay." I try a smile, the one I use when I'm in trouble and need to pretty my way out. It works, as most of the hardness leaves his face.

"Let's eat," he says and the pressure on my hair relents. "Know you're hungry."

My scalp stings but I ignore it and ask, "Did you cook? It smells really good."

"No, Shelley, you know I don't cook. It's catered. Just needs serving." He sweeps his arm towards a small square table in the open-plan kitchen.

Catered?

From where?

It's set with clear plastic utensils, which strikes me as odd, and two stemless wine glasses. Such a fancy house with no silverware? Guessing he knows I'll use them as weapons.

I hide a sigh and turn to take in the view of the lake through more floor-to-ceiling windows. The water is smooth as glass and the snow untouched by humans or animals. Since I can't see any other houses, I wonder if we have any nearby neighbors hiding behind those trees.

Something tells me no.

What I do see, though, is the sun and by its position I'm guessing the time is somewhere between noon and one. How much time does Gianni need to find me?

"Take a seat." Dean pulls out a chair, gestures for me to sit. "I'll get the food."

My stomach growls in anticipation. After placing a foil container on the table, he removes the cover, revealing a beef casserole. Saliva pools in my mouth as the last time I ate was at Tony's. A million years ago.

"Would you serve while I get the wine?" He passes spoons and another foil container with steamed rice.

I sneak a bite before piling a decent serving of rice, beef, potatoes, carrots and mushrooms on each plate, managing to swallow before he returns carrying a bottle of red wine already opened.

Dang it! No cork screw equals still no weapons. He pours and hands a glass over, then sits at the end, opposite me.

"New beginnings." He smiles and reaches across the table, touching my glass. I take a tiny sip. If this was a real date, I would think it delicious. I know from past history it's a fifty-dollar bottle of Zinfandel that he gets by the case from a vineyard in Napa. He mentioned he knew the winemaker. In fact, it's the same wine I offered Gianni the first night he came to my apartment.

Gianni.

Where are you?

I eat and for a few minutes we're both quiet, since it really is delicious. Honestly, though, it could be cardboard and I'd still find it edible. That's how hungry I am and anyway, it gives me time to figure out how I need to handle him. I decide to just go for it.

"The house and lake are gorgeous; can you tell me where we are?"

He takes a large sip and a long time before answering, eyes boring into mine, like he's deciding how much to tell me. "One of the smaller lakes near Tahoe. You like my house?"

"It's big...a lot bigger than I thought." It is, and beautiful. Pity it belongs to him.

"Could be yours."

My eyes widen, then my lids flutter. Say what?

"Why so surprised, Shelley?"

"I...um."

"I want what's mine to be yours. You just have to let me give it to you."

The hairs on my skin stand up.

Can't say exactly why, but something in his tone scares me. More than usual. I mean shit, he's not talking marriage, is he?

"By now," he continues, "I'm sure you know my business. Can't imagine Cadora would have kept it secret considering *his* agenda."

This is all crazy, but I nod anyway.

"Which means you know I have more money than the pope, not that I believe in the Church." He kind of smirks and swirls the wine in his glass, holding it up to the light. "Have a priest who's a client, so you get my reasoning."

It's a struggle to keep my expression neutral and the disgust off my face so I use what he just told me as an excuse.

"A priest? You're kidding."

"No, and I'm not bragging or exaggerating when I say I'm a powerful man."

"How powerful are we talking?"

"More than your *friends* know. I know shit about certain politicians and a couple of judges that would curdle your stomach."

"Why didn't you tell me, Dean?"

He shakes his head and bursts out laughing. Then he looks directly into my eyes. "Would you have dated me if you knew who I was?"

He has a point.

"I told you what you wanted to hear. I figured when you got to know me, it wouldn't matter anymore. Maybe you could see past all that, get to like me and like what I could offer. I got a whole fucking lot to offer you, Shelley. A whole fucking lot."

Then he sighs and it's small and quick but I see it, a flicker of pain moving across his face.

"But why me, Dean?" I whisper. "You barely know me."

"With your history...you know, your family...you're no stranger to my lifestyle."

"How do you know my history? I didn't tell you."

He smiles, but it doesn't hit his eyes.

"You have all those women...you could pick anyone."

"True, but they're whores." Dean's mouth twists a little, then he takes a deep breath, like he's about to confess something. "You have no idea how fucked up the people I cater to are, Shelley. Powerful men with shiny veneers on the outside and appetites for things that...fuck...even gross me out. They pay buckets of money to have what they want. The girls are trained, and yes, I have fucked some of them, but they're not the kind a man has by his side when he's attending some charity thing. They're just used goods. You see, I'm trying to elevate myself, get out of this cesspool and for that, I want class."

I swallow.

"That's one thing Cadora and I have in common," he continues.

"What do you mean, get out? What would you do?"

"I have so much fucking money, Shelley, I never have to do another thing. But...I have my vineyard." He smiles and holds up his glass. "Pretty good shit, huh?"

Damn.

That's his wine? He makes it? No wonder he gets it by the case. Suddenly I don't like it anymore.

"It's delicious," I mumble.

Or it was.

"But...um, I know you've dated normal women, much more beautiful women, who'd embrace what you're offering, especially a life in Napa."

He stares at me for a long time. So long I think the conversation's over. "That's where you're wrong," he replies finally.

"Wrong? About which part?"

He takes a deep breath, wipes his mouth on his napkin then tosses it to the table. "I saw a photo of you talking to Joey. I knew instantly who you were."

The band that had steadily tightened around my chest gets a notch tighter, making it hard to breath.

"Wait." *What the hell did he mean?* "You saw a photo of me *with* Joey?"

He nods.

"I'm not following."

"You see, I've known you a lot longer than you think." He sits back in his chair. "Joey...fucked his way through half of San Francisco, but he always talked about *this girl*. The one he lost. How no one else ever came close, and..." He spreads his hands and rolls his eyes. "Half the time I didn't listen, tuned him out. But whenever he talked about this girl he'd get a look on his face."

He brought a forkful of food to his mouth, chewed, then took a swallow of his wine.

"I've known Joey a while...years in fact. Then, one day, something changed. He wanted out. Didn't want to be my supplier anymore. Talked about going legit and into business with his fucking brother." He shakes his head and snorts. "That wasn't gonna happen. I needed that coke for my clients."

So, it was true. Joey wanted out.

"Apparently *this girl*, the one he'd been telling me about, was back. He wanted to fix things. Make something right."

OhmiGod.

While I push my plate away, he forks another bite, then lifts his gaze to mine.

I rub my thigh restlessly. "Make what right?"

"Don't know." He shrugs and his expression doesn't change but something about it is false. Giving me the impression he does know and before I can press him on it, he continues, "Had him followed. It took a while but ultimately led me to you. First it was just photos. When I saw them, I was intrigued enough I had to see you in person." He pauses and shuts his eyes briefly. "And when I did, I got it."

"Um...got what?"

"He always said you were beautiful, but to Joey all women were beautiful. I mean, seriously, the dude would fuck anything. I, on the other hand, am a little more discriminating. I changed how I looked and stood outside that salon and watched you work and realized you were perfect. You were class."

Oh no. He's turned me into some impossible fantasy girl. "I'm just a girl, Dean. I'm too skinny, I chew my nails and my boobs are too small." The sparse mountain air seems suddenly thick and heavy and I was struggling to keep my breathing even.

"Disagree, Shelley," he continues. "One thing I learned, though. If Joey couldn't keep you he didn't deserve you. So, then I followed *you*. Watched you, who you hung with. Saw you sing karaoke at Tony's with that bitch, Cass, and found out everything I could. I even know where you went to beauty school and where your mother lives."

Mom.

My heart stops. Is that a threat?

"I watched you for over a month until I couldn't wait anymore. Made an appointment at the salon. And when you agreed to go out with me, I treated you like a *fucking princess*." Those last two words? Well, let's just say they don't come out so friendly.

He takes a deep breath, then does this weird jaw rotating thing I've noticed him do before. Like he did the night at the bar before he hit me. "I wanted you to fall in love with me. I wanted to *make* love to you because for me, Shelley...you're the one. I've never wanted that from a woman."

Oh God.

I sip on the wine, not tasting it. Only using the action to plan a move while my heart pummels in my chest.

"Then I fucked it up by hitting you. I knew we needed more time together and you wouldn't give me a second chance, so I had to make one."

"I had no idea, Dean," I whisper. "You never said anything."

"No, I didn't. That's because I've never said those words before. Not to any woman."

The odd thing is, I actually believe him. Then he goes on and blows my mind.

"You don't know what I've fucking done for you."

I feel my eyes get big. "What do you mean by that?"

"Joey found out I was seeing you. Told me to stop." He smirks again. "Threatened me, stupid fuck. Promised to bring down all kinds of hell. Invoked his brother. Like he's some fucking superhero. *Whoo.*" He wiggles his fingers. "His family and that fat, fucking, washed-up bastard you were hanging with."

"What did you do?" I whisper more urgently.

"I took care of him, of course...in his brother's building. I thought with Joey out of the picture, you'd be mine. But the fucked thing is, you ran to the other Cadora asshole, didn't you? That's my bad. Just a minor problem I have to fix. No biggie."

My breath comes in fast, shallow gasps. "How can you be so casual about killing Joey?"

He shrugs. "The world I live in."

"And Billy?"

"He pissed me off. Boris got too close, he was only supposed to scare him, but shit happens."

The fear and rage racing through my system makes my heart want to explode.

"You say you love me, Dean? When you hurt the people I

love, you hurt me. So what I think you're really saying is you *love* to *hurt* me."

He's silent for a few seconds. "That prick? You love him?"

I don't answer, wanting to jump across the table and stab him in the throat with my plastic fork.

He must see it on my face because his eyes get hard and narrow and his expression turns ugly.

"You fucked him yet?"

I don't say anything. Instead I stare, wondering how much time I have before he kills me. Why else would he admit to killing Joey if I could bear witness against him?

"I see you have." The muscles in his jaw stretch as he rotates it again. "Doesn't matter anymore, 'cause he'll be dead soon. And so will the fat fuck. And all you'll have left is me. Then we'll see."

"You're insane." My blood is reaching boiling point. "You meant to kill Billy." Fingers grip the underside of the table as Billy's words come to me. *Use what you got.*

He starts to laugh. "Of course I did. But what do you care? You fucking him too?"

"Billy is my family," I yell.

My rage is what I've got and I shove the table towards Dean with every ounce of strength in me. He topples backwards, eyes widening as the weight of the solid wood pins him. The casserole and wine bottle slide off the surface and land on his face.

"Fuck!" he yells.

I know I have very little time to keep the advantage. I need weapons.

All I have is that useless plastic fork. Acting on instinct, I lurch for the bottle, which is rolling away from me on the floor.

"Aargh!" Dean yells and pushes the table off him. It crashes to the side. "You bitch." As he staggers to his feet, he slips in the spilled wine and goes down hard on his knees. While he's wiping food from his eyes, I swing the bottle like my softball bat, hitting him hard across his forehead, stunning him. The vibration runs up my arm like an electric shock.

As he drops again to his knees, I swing again. This one sends his upper body reeling, but still, he doesn't fall.

Shit!

One more!

The third lands across his nose. My stomach roils at the sickening crunch of bone and cartilage.

Blood spurts and his eyes roll back as he collapses, landing in the spilled beef casserole.

I don't care if I've killed him, but hope I haven't. Death is too damn easy. My breath hitches as I check his pulse and find his heart's still beating. I roll him onto his side to prevent him from drowning in his blood. I don't want him to die, but I need to survive and I know if he wakes up, I won't. I have to restrain him somehow. But with what?

OhGodohGodohGod.

I shake my hands as if the movement will stimulate my brain.

The leather in the couch!

I need a knife. I run to the kitchen and die a little when I realize all the drawers and cabinets have been locked with childproof devices, except these are more advanced.

I jiggle and try to force a drawer, but they're holding and I'm wasting too much time. That Boris goon could show any second or Dean could wake up. There's nothing usable in the kitchen. Bastard did a good job.

Use what you got.

All I have is...glass. I smash one of the stemless glasses to the floor shattering it, but the thick bottom proves to be a usable chunk with a razor-sharp edge.

Using a napkin as a buffer, I slice long sections of the couch leather into thick strips, then test it for strength. It'll do. When I have enough, I scamper to Dean and yank his arms behind him. Once his wrists have been secured, I do his ankles.

I'm really tempted to stomp on his balls, but I'd rather do it when he can feel it.

Keys.

Where are his keys and phone? I search through his pockets with shaking fingers and find both. Thank God. I press 911.

Dammit to hell and back.

No fucking bars.

The one time in my life I decide to call the cops there's no fucking cell service.

Okay, okay...don't get tits grabbed.

I go for option two. Gotta get out of here but the set of keys doesn't come with a fob for his car. Fuck. I'm going to have to walk, I just need to get to the nearest house, wherever that may be.

First, I need warmer clothes and mine are still wet. Hopefully something upstairs. I check the first door next to the room he kept me in. It's locked, but there are several keys on the keyring I took from Dean and I try them all.

The fourth key works and I push open the door. It's an office of some kind, so nothing. The second door is another bedroom similar to mine and I hit the jackpot inside the closet. I snag a white and blue ski jacket and pants about three sizes too big.

As I'm pulling on the pants, I notice my knees are bleeding, coloring the Band-Aids bright red. They're going to have to wait. Leaving this place is priority number one and I'm wasting time.

I head back downstairs with the jacket in search of snow boots. My Uggs will have to do if I can't find any. Dean's still lying on his side in the same position I left him.

So far, so good. If only there was cell service. How does he communicate with Boris?

Oh God...I'm so stupid.

The office.

Never having had a landline, it didn't occur to look for one.

When I open the door a second time I see it stuck in the corner of the desk, partially hidden behind some books.

I pick up the receiver and hear a dial tone.

Halle-fucking-lujah!

I almost start sobbing while I dial and the dispatcher answers after two rings.

"911. What's your emergency?"

"Oh my God. Please, I need help." I can barely get the words out, my voice is so thick and shaky. "I've been kidnapped. My name is Shelley De Luca and I'm somewhere near Tahoe, but I don't know where."

"Okay, Shelley, stay calm. You're calling from a landline and I can see the address of the residence. I'm dispatching a team as we speak. Can you..."

A blurry movement catches my attention. The next instant, the phone's yanked from my hand. I scream, then the chord's ripped from the wall.

"You bitch." Dean's bloody hand on my neck chokes off my air. "You broke my nose." He shoves me hard down onto the desk, rams his pelvis between my legs and against my crotch.

"You're gonna pay."

Gah.

Choking.

Bursts of white light explode behind my eyelids.

Dean pins one of my arms next to my head while his other remains around my throat. Leaving one of mine free. I thrash around, searching for anything to use. Nothing but papers and books. No pens, or anything solid.

I'm going to die.

Strangely, the only thing I can think is I'll never kiss Gianni again. And that motivates me to live. If he's going to kill me, I'll die fighting.

At last my fingers curl around something cold and hard with sharp edges. It feels like a stapler. The first attempt misses his head, landing a weak blow on his chin. Dean grunts and angles his head away. My reach is too short and I'm losing strength. So much pressure, but his hands are slick with blood, some dripping from his face.

Using everything in me I manage to twist my shoulder enough to bring my free arm up and under Dean's arm. His grip is slippery and loosens around my throat, enough for me to dislodge him. Having no support, he collapses on my chest. I'm pinned but I can breathe, and suck in deep, rasping breaths while I slam the stapler to the side of his face, catching him on his broken nose.

"Argh!"

He rears back and a flood of fresh blood spurts as he pushes his torso upright, clasping his face. "You fucking cunt."

I'm still trapped by his pelvis and try to wiggle myself free, but he's too heavy. Seizing my wrists, he grabs the stapler from my hand and throws it across the room. Pieces scatter as it breaks against the wall.

"Bitch," he growls, his face twisting into a grotesque mask. "You're gonna die, but first I'm gonna fuck you till you bleed." Capturing both my wrists this time, he pins them above my head with one hand, dripping blood from his broken nose onto my face and chest.

His grip tightens while I squirm and buck, making it difficult for him to unbutton his fly. This gives me a chance to twist my upper body away and slip out from underneath him.

For one glorious moment, I'm free!

Gasping and coughing, I scramble on my knees towards the office door.

Lack of oxygen makes me slower than I should be. A painful tug on my hair, tumbles me over onto my back, then Dean pulls the ski pants down. All that's left between him and me is a pair of skimpy panties.

Which makes me fight even harder, until Dean's hand slips around my throat again and the rest of his weight pins me immobile to the ground.

Going gray again.

Vaguely I feel the sharp tug against my hip as he rips my panties. Then his knees force mine wide and the pressure of his hard cock is against me. My only consolation is that I'll probably be dead before he's done raping me.

Somewhere in the deep recess of my mind, firecrackers explode. Must be what's left of my failing synapses. I have nothing. No air, no fight, no hope.

I'm dying.

I'm dying...but why's it so damned loud.

Someone told me once it was peaceful, like floating on a blanket of light surrounded by music so exquisite your soul rejoices.

They lied.

This is nothing like that. It's reddish gray and deafening, full of people screaming and scary.

Fuck. I must be going to hell.

No, no, I can't die. I don't want to go to hell...it hurts. I can't get enough air and the fires are already burning my throat.

Then suddenly it's silent, the only sound is my own desperate wheezing.

"Fuck, Shelley."

Yup. That confirms it. I must be in hell, because I'm pretty sure angels don't curse.

"No, no, no! Fuck, no!"

Gianni?

Can't be because he wouldn't be in hell.

"Shelley, wake up. Wake the fuck up."

The voice sounds funny, coming in and out in waves, like an old transistor radio my grandparents once had.

"Christ, Shelley, don't you dare fucking die on me. Not now!"

Okay, so maybe not dead yet, but I must be close because now I'm floating. Then my head lolls against something solid and warm.

Gasp.

"I need help here." A rumbling against my ear barely registers over my struggle to breathe. "Marco, get the medics."

Then more unrecognizable voices tickle the edge of my awareness and a swirl of fuzzy faces appear through the red-gray fog, like buzzards circling.

"She can't breathe."

"Sir, lay her down then I need you to step aside. She needs oxygen."

Something hard covers my face and I feel some relief, but not enough.

Gasp.

"Her airways are swelling. We'll have to intubate. Give her the shot."

There's a pinch and a scratch in my arm. A cold wave sweeps through my veins, into the back of my throat but those damn fires still rage.

"We don't have time to wait for it to work. This is going to hurt and she'll fight. You! Sir. Hold her head."

A vice clamps over my cheekbones. My vision momentarily clears and my eyes roll up.

Gianni's beautiful face with that lock of hair falling forward. I try to reach for it but I'm pinned

"I'm sorry, Shelley."

Something cool and wet lands on my forehead. Is it raining?

"Here we go," one of the voices says. "Keep her still."

Pressure pushes down on my arms just below my shoulders and legs. Moments later something metallic is inserted into my mouth, scraping against my teeth and my throat is being torn apart. How many more fires are there in hell?

Seriously?

My body heaves as I gag, trying to expel the thing.

"Hold her steady."

I want to rip whatever is in me out, but I can't move. Then mercifully the pain begins to fade, my limbs becoming watery. I'm swirling, then, my existence fades from gray to black.

14

MUST STILL BE IN THE MOUNTAINS

~

Nothing makes sense when I open my eyes. Shapeless forms bleed into each other, like a myriad of colors on a palette.

My lids are so heavy, as if weighed down by anchors. I fight to keep them open, and it takes me a while to realize there's something in my mouth.

A memory surfaces. Dean's face hovering over me and bloody hands around my neck. A strange noise escapes me.

"Jesus, Shelley...shh...it's okay. Don't speak, you've a breathing tube in your throat."

Gianni?

Where am I?

His hand squeezes mine. It's warm and rough and I know I'm safe. The cloud moves again and I drift off, entering that tunnel with no light at the end.

~

Voices.

Familiar enough to cut through the fog.

"They're keeping her sedated due to the trauma in her throat. Once the swelling goes down enough they'll remove the tube. She's lucky he didn't do any permanent damage to her larynx."

"Thank God you got there in time. I can't ever thank you enough."

Mom.

"I shouldn't have left her." Gianni's voice is raw, like he hasn't slept. "I should've known the fire was a distraction."

"She's alive. That's all I care about. Why don't you get some rest? You're about to collapse. I'll stay with her."

"I'm not leaving. I'll sleep in the chair."

"You need to shower, Gianni. You're still covered in blood and you'll scare her if she sees you like that."

Then I fade again, but the darkness doesn't claim me completely. At the sound of Gianni's voice, I seem to bounce, as if I'm on a trampoline.

"It's gonna be fucked but she deserves to know, Lisa."

"I suppose it doesn't make much of a difference now. I'll tell her when the time is right."

Tell me what?

This time I sink all the way down until the surface envelopes me and the blackness takes over again.

Mom's asleep, curled up in the chair next to my bed. Her dark hair, same color as mine with a few auburn highlights, is pulled up in a messy ponytail. Her face, though relaxed, shows blemishes beneath her eyes. I watch her for a while, happy she's safe.

She must sense my stare, as she stirs and when she opens her eyes, they're red and puffy.

"Oh God," she says, her voice thick and scratchy. "How long have you been awake?"

Tears spill down her cheeks. She brushes them with the back of her knuckles, stands and leans over me to kiss my forehead, gently wrapping her arms around my head.

"My baby girl." She's sobbing now. "You're alive." With her head next to mine I feel the wet against my cheek.

"Mom." It hurts to talk and it comes out like a rasp.

"Hush, honey," she murmurs into my ear.

"You're safe," I say.

"Me?" Her face pulls back as her brows pull together. "Yes, I'm safe. But don't speak...just get better. We'll have plenty of time to talk later. I'm not going anywhere."

Her familiar scent, lemon and lavender, mingles with the foggy cloud. It's warm and comforting as I slip away again.

~

THE LIGHT in the room is blue and eerie with energy that's pricklier than before. It occurs to me my vision is clear as I focus on snowflakes wafting past a windowsill.

Must still be in the mountains.

I shift my head. An array of beeping machines with blinking lights fills one side of the room. Despite multiple bouquets of flowers, the room smells of antiseptic and...hospital.

A heavyset nurse with blonde hair scraped back into a bun writes on a clipboard and the black plastic clock on the wall above her head says it's eight thirty.

"Good morning," she says, without looking up. "How are you feeling?"

"Thirsty."

I can talk.

"Well, that's a good sign. Your breathing tube's been removed so you'll be able to drink and have real food soon."

"How long?" My voice is raspy but doesn't hurt as much.

"Have you been here?" she asks, raising bushy eyebrows while spooning ice chips into a blue plastic cup.

I nod.

"Going on three days. From what I understand, you're lucky to be alive." She pushes a button on the side of my bed, raising it up until I'm in a sitting position.

"Gianni?"

"I'm assuming he's the hunky looking man who hasn't left your side?"

Again, I nod and accept the ice chips. I suck some into my mouth. It hurts to swallow, but the cold feels good.

"Well, in a moment we'll get you cleaned up. Then everyone can visit after the doctor's seen you. They've been waiting for you to wake up." She smiles as she injects something into my IV.

"You should be able to go home in a couple of days," pronounces Dr. Parks, the middle-aged doctor with a tiny squirrel on his upper lip.

After prodding and shining a light down my throat, he writes something on my chart, then hangs it on the bottom of my bed. Whatever Nurse Bushy Eyebrows injected has me feeling no pain.

Whatsoever.

"The swelling's down nicely but it's going to take a while for the bruising on your neck to fade and the petechiae in your eyes to clear. Stick to soft and liquid foods for at least another week and you should be fine. Any questions?"

I shake my head.

"Try not to talk too much, that includes the feds. They've been hovering like damn vultures but they can wait for your statement. Your voice should come back completely in a few days, but if it doesn't, I'll refer you to a specialist."

"Thank you."

"You betcha." He points his finger at me like a gun, making clicking sounds with this tongue and teeth. "I'll see you tomorrow morning."

As he's leaving Gianni appears in the doorway, towering over the doctor. All the blood leaves my head and I feel every beat of my heart in my sensitive throat. He glances at me, then follows Dr. Parks out of the room.

Exactly one minute later, according to the clock on the wall, he re-enters, but stops just inside the threshold, locking eyes with me. For an endless moment he stands there, saying nothing.

I'm struck by how tired he looks.

Scratches mar his beautiful face, and that little Y between his brows seems more pronounced than usual. He swallows, then takes a step forward.

With each step forward my anxiety grows. Why isn't he speaking? What's happened?

"Hi?"

He stops next to the bed working his throat. "Hey."

Our eyes remain anchored on each other. A thousand emotions flicker through his.

"What's wrong?"

He swallows again, then turns his gaze to the window blinking and scraping a hand through his hair. The blue light emphasizes the fine lines fanning from his bloodshot eyes.

"Can't seem to find the words...to tell you how sorry I am." His voice cracks.

"Gianni..."

"Should have been there for you."

"Sit."

I find it ironic I'm the one ordering him to sit for a change. His lips curl into a wry smile and he lets out a puff of air. Pulling the chair closer, the metal legs scrape across the vinyl floor.

Once seated he takes my hand in both of his and presses my fingers to his lips, keeping his eyes closed. His knuckles are bruised and split and my heart squeezes.

"You saved my life," I say. "Thank you."

"I should never have left you. Should've figured it out sooner the fire was a distraction."

"Doesn't matter now." Drug-induced weariness sweeps over me and I stifle a yawn. "Everyone okay? Truman?" I rasp.

"He's okay. They're all okay. He drugged them with animal sedative and almost killed Thomas, but he'll be fine."

"You?" I ask.

He closes his eyes again for a long moment. When he opens them, they're tortured. "Thought I'd lost you. Saw the blood... assumed it was yours."

He squeezes his thumb and forefinger to the corners of his eyes. My big, handsome, super badass, ex-mafia dude is trying not to cry. My belly tightens.

After taking a deep breath, he holds it, then lets it out on a long sigh. "Gotta know, babe. Did he rape you? When I got there, I thought I was in time, but...what about before?"

"No." I shake my head. "Only tried 'cause I hurt him."

His face softens, then he clears his throat, and says, "The fuck's going away for a long time."

"Still alive?" I stare at him, my mouth going dry. Now I really regret not smashing the bottle on his head until I *had* killed him.

"Unlucky for him. They're holding him in Carson City. Since his house is on the Nevada side of Tahoe, he crossed state lines and will be charged with kidnapping, sex trafficking, tax evasion, attempted murder. You name it."

"He killed Joey," I blurt out.

Gianni holds my gaze, then nods. "I know, babe. They can add murder to the charges."

"Killed him *because* of me. My fault."

"No, babe." Pain ripples across his face, darkening his eyes. "It's *not* your fault." He looks away. "Its mine. Joey's dead because of me."

"Gianni..." I insist.

"It's not your fault, Shelley."

Okay.

We'll talk about this later, I don't have the energy to fight. "How'd you find me?" I ask instead.

He lets go of my hand. Drags his over his face leaning back in his chair.

"Carmine. Pulled in his crew and dug deep. Found his properties, narrowed it down to two. Tahoe and Napa. We figured Tahoe was more likely, because of its remoteness and he'd want you alone. But he sent a team to Napa just in case. What they found there...fuck." He swallows, then clears his throat. "Carmine called in the feds and they raided Napa. A place called The Farm, 'cause it's a vineyard fronting for some sick shit. We got lucky he brought you here."

So very lucky.

"We were close, trying to figure a way in when we got a call from the cop, Lee, about your 911. Carmine had him in contact with the dispatch just in case. Heard the sirens, knew shit was going down. Marco and I got there first. Broke open the door as the paramedics arrived. Cops came a few minutes later.

"Grateful," I croak and reach for his hand. He squeezes my fingers, then kisses them. Just before I fall asleep I hear him murmur.

"Five fucking minutes I would've been too late."

15

EVERY ROSE HAS ITS THORNS

~

Two days later, Truman's between my legs on my bed at the Sea Cliff house. I stare at my phone in horror. The battery died in my absence and when I plug it into the charger it pings and vibrates with a gazillion text messages, emails and voicemails.

Including one from Carmine. All of them good, pretty much saying the same thing. They're glad I'm okay.

It's the last one, however, from Alfie, that cracks me up. *How's our spicy little firecracker?*

The man knows how to make an entrance.

The day Dean tried to rape and kill me, Alfie and his entourage arrived at the hospital in the ginormous Cadillac, blaring Frank Sinatra's "New York, New York" in the parking lot. So loud, it rattled hospital windows until the staff, concerned about the other patients and triggering an avalanche in the mountains, told them to turn it down. According to Bridget (Nurse Bushy Brows) this involved much gesticulation, ear-cupping and finger pointing. Apparently, their hearing aids were turned off due to the altitude change and something about their ears popping.

Anyhoo, Alfie, hearing I'd been kidnapped, rallied his fellas and insisted on being backup. Arriving a few hours after Gianni and breaking all kinds of federal laws transporting illegal firearms, including an improvised, shoulder-mounted grenade launcher in a false bottom of the Cadillac's trunk. Then, knowing I was safe, they spent their time entertaining the nurses, sneaking grappa to some of the patients, and gambling at a local casino. When it was time for Mom and me to leave, they tailed us back to the city and left us at the gates a couple of hours ago smoking cigars longer than their heads and blaring "Fly Me to the Moon."

Thank God for Alfie.

I thumb a response into my phone. *Thank you for the escort and grateful nothing exploded on the way! XO!*

After Alfie, I set about reading and replying to all of them. I had no idea so many people cared about me.

Truman sniffs and occasionally licks my toes. He's stuck to me like a suction cup. Even when I took a shower, he whined outside the glass doors until I let him in and shampooed him with the same stuff I used on my hair. Now we both smell like green apples.

I get how he feels because I miss Gianni. It's been two weeks since Joey's funeral and the man's caught and reeled me in like a starving little snapper on a shiny new hook.

He and Marco left early yesterday morning to deal with fire marshals and insurance adjusters while I talked to the FBI and the local police.

My phone pings, startling me. It bounces in my hand, until I get a grip.

De Luca, you home yet?

My heart beats faster than a racehorse at the Belmont Stakes and it takes several attempts to type in *Yes*.

On my way, see you soon. x

A kiss!

It's a small thing but my smile's so big my face might break. I'm willing to take a step forward and believe in what he showed me at the hospital. To trust that raw emotion in his eyes when he looked at me and take a chance it's something deeper. Almost dying has taught me life's too short to not have a little good in it. And Gianni's good is exceptional.

Truman's ears perk and a beat later there's a knock on my door. Mom pokes her head through. I offered her my apartment but Gianni insisted we all stay at the house until I'm recovered. Who am I to argue?

"May I come in?" she asks.

"Of course." My voice, although much better, is still a little scratchy. I motion for her to sit on the bed which she crawls onto, tucking her bare feet underneath herself. She scratches Truman's ears. He snorts and licks her hand.

"I was hoping we could talk in the car but you fell asleep."

"Sorry." I grimace. "The drugs make me woozy. What about?"

"You and Gianni."

"Mom..." I groan and close my eyes.

God!

I'm not ready for this. I've barely wrapped my own head around it.

"Look," she says, wrapping her fingers around my ankle. "Lord knows I'm grateful he saved you. I can't imagine what I would have done if..." She takes a deep breath and blinks away tears. "If that psycho killed you or...worse."

I shudder. "He didn't."

"Thank God."

Technically, thank Gianni, Marco and Carmine but whose quibbling.

"Look, honey, you're an adult and I can't tell you what to do, but are you really sure you want to get involved with him?"

"I don't want to talk about this. You don't need to worry."

She angles her head, and when I meet her eyes, there's something in them other than worry that I can't quite read. "I do. You're my child and it would be remiss of me not to warn you. You know he has a reputation?"

Dangit. This is what I wanted to avoid. Having Gianni's *reputation* shoved in my face. "I know you're afraid he's going to hurt me."

She swallows then lets out a breath. "Something like that. He's a Cadora. They're beautiful, charming men. But dangerous. Trust me, I know what I'm talking about. I want you to think about coming back to LA with me."

Shit. I don't need this.

"I'm making a life here, Mom, and you're getting ahead of yourself."

"Am I?"

"Uh huh." I nod.

"Still." She takes a deep breath through her nose, then lets it out. "You have the shittiest luck with men and I have to say it. All I'm asking is you be careful?"

"I will. Besides, this is stuff I already know."

I hold her gaze for a few seconds longer and a kernel of unease sprouts, but it's nothing I can grab at. "Unless...what are you not telling me?" My head cocks as I squint at her.

Her eyes widen slightly, then she shakes her head. "Nothing, honey. Just me being...well, you know."

"Mom?"

"No, no...you're right. I'm being overly cautious. I'm backing off now. Anyway, you said in the hospital you wanted to talk about your dad?"

"Yeah." I sigh and relent. Since I really do have questions.

"Ask away." She straightens and repositions her legs under her, seeming relieved to change the subject. Well, her and me both.

"I've been hearing so much about how good he was at hiding money."

She nods but her expression turns guarded.

"I'd forgotten how many people loved him." I let out a small chuckle. "He's like a legend here."

"Yeah." Her smile is sad. "He was a good man."

"But I don't understand something. He seems to have helped a lot of people, but what about us? 'Cause I remember when we didn't have a lot. That tiny little apartment in West Hollywood before you got married and we moved."

"He did take care of us." She blows a strand of dark hair off her face before tucking it behind her ear. "I had to be careful after he died. Couldn't do anything to attract attention from the government. There were foreign accounts I couldn't touch, at least not right away."

"You're saying it was all for show?"

"Yep. We lived off cash he'd stashed and what I had in the bank. Then, when I started working, I slowly converted some of the money into stocks and other forms of income."

"Were we on a watch list?"

"I can't say for sure, but I wasn't taking chances." Her lips curl into a cryptic smile.

"What?"

No response, but her smile gets wider.

"Mom?" I draw it out.

"There's an account in your name in the Caymans. Sort of a trust fund."

"Say what?" I ogle her. "Are you kidding?"

"Nope."

"A trust fund?"

She nods.

"A frigging trust fund?"

She giggles like a schoolgirl. "Your dad wanted you to learn how to handle money before you had access to it. When you're twenty-eight, it's yours."

"Oh my God. That's why you vacation there every year?"

"Mm hmm."

"How much?"

"Oh, I don't know." She waves a hand and pulls in her lips. "Probably close to a couple million by now."

My jaw drops.

"Give or take."

"I have two million dollars sitting in an offshore account?"

Holy fizz pops!

"I've been dying to tell you."

"Why didn't you?" My eyebrows are still in the vicinity of my hairline.

"Because I thought if I did, you wouldn't learn responsibility and would get yourself into debt knowing you had a windfall coming."

"Mom, I have almost no cash in my account but I also have zero debt other than the current balance on my credit card. Everything's paid off. My car, my student loans. Everything."

Except rent which is due in a week.

"Do you know how long it takes to build a clientele from scratch or how expensive it is to live in this city? My rent is ridiculous even with the break Marshall cuts me."

"I'm so proud of you." She beams, showing even, white teeth. "I taught you well."

"I guess you did." I'm in shock. My jaw's dangling and I'm still staring at her when my phone pings.

Cass: *Let me in, I'm at the gate.*

I lift my leg over Truman and roll over to push the code on the keypad next to the bed. Then adjust my black leggings and loose turquoise tunic top before shoving my feet into some flats.

Mom sniffs Truman's head. "Does he smell like apples?"

I snort and shake my head, still staring at her until I'm out the bedroom door. There's a thunk and a moment later Truman, recovering from a nose dive, scrambles behind me. We head down the stairs to the front door with my head spinning.

Two million dollars?

I could afford to buy into a partnership with Cass.

Truman beats me to the front door, bouncing off his front paws. His short legs can handle the stairs going down much better than going up.

Cass has unloaded several bouquets of flowers from her Audi when I open the huge doors. We hug, then she examines my bruised neck.

"That fucking asshole. Marco told me you smashed his face with a wine bottle."

"Uh huh. Broke his nose."

"You're such a badass." She grins wickedly at me. "Wish I'd been there to see that."

I emit a hoarse chuckle and point to the flowers. "Are those for me?"

"My God, yes! They've been arriving non-stop at the salon. The break room and your station are covered and I've run out of room."

"Put them on the table, here in the foyer," I say, picking up an arrangement of pale blue hydrangeas and white roses.

"Oh," she smirks. "We're going to need more room than that."

"Holy Toledo," Mom says, coming down the stairs. "There's enough for a pop-up florist." She smiles when she sees Cass and holds out her hand to shake.

"I'm Lisa, Shelley's mom."

Cass returns her smile, green eyes twinkling. "Nice highlights. Shelley do them?"

"Of course," she says, and hold out her hands for a bouquet of sunflowers and gerbera daisies. "Let me help you. They're gorgeous."

Once the flowers have been placed in available spots, I remove all the cards and place them on the kitchen table, touched by all the love from my clients. "That's a lot of thank-you notes to write," I mumble to Cass. "Want some coffee?"

"No time. Got a date with Marco." She gives me a lopsided grin. "I'm meeting him for dinner."

"You really like him, don't you?"

"I really do," she whispers. "He makes me laugh. Look, I hate to ask, but when do you think you'll come back to work?"

"Next week." I show her my palms. "Much better, thanks to being stuck in the hospital, they've healed nicely."

We talk for a few minutes more, then I walk her to the door, and wait while she climbs into her car.

As she circles the driveway, she honks her horn, sending the dogs into a frenzy. Another car comes up the driveway at the same time and at first I don't recognize it, then my heart leapfrogs into my throat when I realize it's Gianni.

Good God, he's hot in that car, like it was made for him. He's hot in the truck too, looking all blue-collar and badass, but in that pricy BMW, he sizzles.

Woo.

I refrain from fanning my face. He stops parallel to Cass and they chat through their respective windows.

Can't get caught ogling, so I shut the front door and lean

against it. When my heart slows, I stroll back to the kitchen to collect my get-well notes. I'm opening them with a butter knife, acting all cool, when he steps through the garage door with Truman taking his back.

Our eyes meet and all the air's sucked out of my lungs.

"There you are," he says, pushing the door closed. He hangs his keys on the little dragonfly hook before dumping a briefcase and suit jacket on the table next to several floral arrangements, never breaking eye contact. Then five steps later (I counted), he palms my face and stares down at me.

"You owe me one hell of a kiss, De Luca." Those words are spoken low and sexy, making my belly do that whooshy thing and my heart feel too big for my chest. Before his mouth comes down on mine, his eyes darken to that stormy gray that I realize now means he's emotionally engaged.

He sucks my bottom lip between his, teasing me with the tip of his tongue. Heat surges between my legs when I open my mouth, allowing him to take possession. My arms slip around his waist pulling him closer, because I can never seem to get close enough. He groans and deepens the kiss, our tongues clash before settling into a wet, sexy rhythm. He tastes like chocolate and sin. I lose myself in his incredible smell, savoring his warmth while his fingers lace into my hair and grip a handful.

"Missed you," he murmurs against my mouth, then moves to the spot below my ear and sucks on my skin.

Sensations ripple through my body and I wonder if now would be a good time to test the sanctity of the pantry, since his bedroom's way too far away.

"Oh, dear God!"

Her voice, though not too loud, penetrates and we both stiffen and pause.

My *mother*!

"I'm so sorry."

I turn my head and glare at her. Her hands are over her eyes but she doesn't look or sound sorry at all. In fact, she looks like she's trying not to smirk, having obviously accomplished what she set out to do.

Wench.

"Fuck," Gianni mutters. "What is it about kissing you in this kitchen?" He pulls in a breath and lets it out against my neck, which of course doesn't help the situation between my thighs.

"That's a curse we're gonna have to break." Then he turns his head to face her. "Lisa. Good to see you again. Made yourself comfortable?"

"Yes, thank you." Her grin is wide and unapologetic and, since I know my mother, devious. "I'd forgotten how amazing that view of the bridge is *and* you've remodeled. I love what you've done with the foyer."

I push away from Gianni whose arms tighten at first, but when I insist, he allows me to disentangle myself with a sigh. I figure I'll let them catch up, shoot the shit about the house. And *I'll* catch up with her later in a different way. Her being cautious is one thing, but deliberately obstructing is something else entirely. While I consider what I'll say to her, I rifle through the envelopes checking out the names.

One in particular stands out. The paper is of exceptional quality and embossed with an unfamiliar pattern and when I peer closely it looks much like Cyrillic.

I don't have any Russian clients.

My pulse quickens as I open the envelope and start to read. As the words sink in, my skin prickles and a light film of sweat breaks out on my upper lip. Along with the strangled little noise coming from my mouth my legs wobble and buckle. Gianni pivots, catching me beneath my arms just before I drop.

"Fuck, Shelley, what the fuck?" He pulls out a chair with his foot then makes sure I'm seated. He dips to his haunches, placing his hands on my thighs. "Babe, what is it?"

As I hold out the card for him to read, my fingers shake, the writing burned into my brain.

A Cadora killed your father. Guess which one. I love you. Dean.

That asshole! He'll never stop messing with me, even sitting in a jail cell in Nevada. You'd think he had other things to concern himself with.

I lean forward with my head between my knees to get the blood moving to my brain and silently chant.

Deep breath in.

Deep breath out.

Deep breath in.

I do this several times, focusing on something normal like my pink toes peeking through my flats. It's been more than two weeks since my last pedicure.

On my fifth inhale, it occurs. *Why's it so damn quiet?* And why are Gianni's fingers digging into my knees? It's beginning to hurt.

When I raise my head, his face, normally so robust with that gorgeous Sicilian coloring, is pale and borderline gray. His eyes are shut and I stare at him for a million years, until he finally opens them again.

"Shelley," he says softly.

Oh no.

Oh, no, no!

A whimper on the other side of the table pulls my gaze from him. The last time I heard that sound coming from my mom was at Dad's funeral.

"Oh...Shelley," her voice cracks on the sob. Her perfectly manicured hand holding the card shakes so visibly I'm amazed she's still holding it. "I'm so sorry. I didn't want you to find out like this."

It takes a moment for *that* to sink in, but when it does my hands fly to my face. All the breath leaves my body like they one-two sucker punched me.

"You know!"

"Shelley..."

"Both of you. You know." My gaze darts between them looking for any form of denial, which after several long moments, I realize is sorely missing. "Oh my God. You've always known. You've been lying to me the whole time."

"Honey, I wasn't..."

"Who was it?" I demand, cutting her off.

They both just stare, neither one seemingly willing to answer.

I slam my fist on the wooden table, blocking the pain shooting up my wrist. My mother flinches while Gianni works the muscles in his jaw. The man's going to crack a tooth if he keeps that up.

"Who, dammit?" I direct this at Gianni, praying it isn't him. "Your dad? Uncle Joe?"

"My brother," he answers so quietly I'm sure I misheard him.

Joey?

"You're lying."

"I wish I was, Shelley."

"You're fucking lying!" I jump up, pushing his hand from my leg and yell. "Why?" Hot tears roll down my cheeks. Conversely, my mother pulls out a chair and collapses into it.

"Mom?"

"It's true, honey." Her voice is shaky. "I wanted to tell you, but you were so...fragile after it happened. And then it never seemed like the right time."

"Why would Joey want to kill Daddy?"

"He wasn't trying to kill your dad," Gianni says, reaching for me, but I step out of his way. "He was trying to kill me."

"You? What? Why? I don't understand."

"Joey thought you were cheating on him." He's quiet for a long beat while I stare back.

"No." I shake my head, disbelieving. "No. None of this is making any sense. I never cheated on Joey, I wouldn't dare."

"He thought you were cheating on him...with me. He saw us kissing, Shelley."

"Us? You mean you and me? No...you're wrong. We never kissed."

"Yeah, babe, we did. That day at the marina."

The day...at the marina?

I gasp.

The day my dad died. Like random pieces of some 3-D puzzle, seemingly not connected, they begin to fall in place. Forming a picture I absolutely hate.

When he was late.

Exactly like my dream. Except now I know it wasn't a dream, it was a memory. A chill as cold as that windy day waiting for Joey spreads through my spine, turning my blood icy. Except Joey never showed. Gianni did.

"Oh God!" The noise that comes from me is halfway between a groan and a whimper as I finally acknowledge...finally *accept* what I'm hearing as truth.

Gianni swallows, and deep lines furrow his perfect, strong brow. "Joey came to the meeting drunk or high, I still don't know which, saying he was gonna kill us both. Then he pulled out a gun none of us knew he had. I got up, lunged at him and he squeezed the trigger."

Gianni stops talking, that attractive bump in his throat moving, betraying him. His voice is rough and raw when he starts again.

"One hit me in my shoulder and then he shot again as I was falling back. Your dad caught me and the second bullet missed my head, but hit Jimmy in the throat." Two fingers pinch the corner of his eyes, as if he's trying to squeeze the memory from his brain. "Next thing I knew my dad and uncle took him down before he could shoot again."

I look at my mom. She's crying silently, arms wrapped around her waist and something horrible washes through me and for one infinitesimal second, I'm torn. One part of me wants her punished, but the other, much larger part, mourns for both our loss.

Then Gianni's words pull me back.

"I don't remember much after that except my dad holding Jimmy's head. He bled out right in front of me…in front of all of us and there was nothing we could do. I'm sorry, Shelley." He scrapes both hands over his face, then up through that thick dark hair, mussing it. "It was supposed to be me." This last is said tinged with so much pain, it slices at me.

Gianni almost dying is something my mind can't—*won't*—entertain, but it doesn't stop my anger building.

"Why didn't you tell me?" I whirl in my chair to face Mom.

"We thought…you might go after Joey…for revenge. I couldn't have that, couldn't lose you too." Her voice shatters.

It's too much. "You didn't trust me? I've had this…canyon in my heart for ten years because *you didn't trust me*? You thought I'd want to kill Joey?" I sniff and fight back the tears. "You never asked me…not once…how I felt. Do you know how fucked-up I've been, Mom?"

Her shoulders slump as she shakes her head. "The more time passed, the harder it got to tell you. And you seemed better, *happier*."

I've heard enough. My legs threaten to buckle but I fight through it and stand anyway. As my chair scrapes across the tile floor, I think of one more question.

"Does Billy know?"

"No. We all agreed he shouldn't. He would have killed Joey and started a war."

"He deserves to know." I turn to face Gianni. "And you," I sob, jabbing my finger in his face, "I'm sorry you went through that but you lied to my face. I knew you were holding something back. But this? How could you? He was my father."

"De Luca...baby...I'm..."

"Don't you *dare* call me baby. I fucking hate you both right now."

He balks as if I've physically struck him, then whispers, "Fuck."

The pain in his voice reverberates through my hollow stomach and my lungs burn, but I can't be near either one. Be in any space they occupy, therefore I need to get myself gone. My car keys hang next to his on the dragonfly hook. I snatch them and push the button that opens the garage door.

Gianni's head snaps up at the sound. "Where are you going?"

"Away! From both of you."

"Shelley...wait." He moves quickly, takes a few steps and reaches for my arm.

"No!" I dodge out of his path. "Don't."

"De Luca. Stop...please."

I ignore him and wobble on legs that don't want to work down the garage stairs to my car. But he's right behind me as I pull the door open. Before I can step in, however, steely arms come around my waist and tighten, pulling my back to his chest.

"You need to listen."

"Let me go." I twist as his grip tightens, pressing his face into my neck.

"Stop fighting." His voice is hoarse and his breath hot on my skin.

I stiffen against him. "Take your hands off me," I say between my teeth.

"I can't. I'm not letting you leave like this." He's holding me so tight there's no room to wedge my palms between his arms, so I kick my heels hard into his shins.

He grunts and loosens his grip just enough for me to dead-drop through his arms, landing on my butt. It jars and my teeth clash together.

"Dammit, babe, stop. You're gonna hurt yourself." Those long arms reach for me, but I roll to the side and side-swipe him behind the knee. When his leg collapses underneath him it gives me time to scramble into my car, slam and lock the doors. But only just.

By some miracle, I manage to insert the fob on the first try and gun the engine.

He moves in front planting his hands on the hood. "You're gonna have to fucking drive over me. Stop," he growls through the windshield. I press my foot to the gas slowly, forcing him backwards before I begin to speed up.

Only at the last second, he senses I'm about to gun it and jumps out of my way as I press hard on the accelerator and barrel out of the garage and down the driveway. When I look in the mirror, he's running after me.

"Open, open, open," I curse the automatic gate as it slowly rumbles on its wheels.

Come on.

It's almost halfway open when Gianni catches up with me, slamming his hand on the car roof. I squeeze my car through the gate with little room to spare.

The last glimpse through the rear-view mirror, as I speed up out of his range, is him standing with his hands on his head, elbows splayed, and watching.

What's left of my heart shatters. But when I turn the corner I realize Truman, my faithful wingman, is sitting sentinel on the front passenger seat. It completely undoes me. I pull into a side street, find an open parking spot and yank the handbrake. When the engine dies, the last little grip on my control does too. That moan I've kept in check since they told me, since I found out Joey, my boyfriend, killed my father because I kissed his brother, finally finds its way to the fore, along with the flood of tears.

That day at the marina is now crystal clear in my head.

I'd just found out Joey was screwing Gloria "big boobs" Tortino and assumed that's why he wanted to meet me. I was ready to give him hell. But Gianni showed instead. And when he kissed me, I'd been so excited, triumphant even, riding that tsunami of teenage hormones that he'd finally noticed me, that was all I could think about. I couldn't give a crap about Joey in that moment.

But because Gianni noticed me, Joey noticed *us.* And a few hours after that, my life changed forever.

I recall Gianni's words that first night he came to my apartment. *You're fucking dangerous*. He couldn't be more right.

I'm as much to blame for my father's death as anyone. I'd blocked it out, wiped it from my internal hard drive so I could survive. But how could I be happy when my daddy was dead and my world destroyed?

Sobs wrack through me as I rest my head on the steering wheel until saliva pools in my mouth. I make it to the sidewalk before yellow bile purges onto some poor neighbor's neatly trimmed lawn.

Truman, wingman extraordinaire, follows me and waits in their driveway, guarding and panting while I heave, purging on and on until at last, when there's nothing left, I'm done.

I find a half-full bottle of water I'd forgotten in my car from two weeks ago.

May as well be from another lifetime.

After rinsing my mouth, I splash some of the cool liquid over my face hoping to revive my coloring. If I thought really hard about it, I could ignore the bloodshot, glassiness in my eyes, but the bruising on my neck remains stark, jumping out against my too-pale skin. And the dark circles beneath my eyes? Well, that's another issue entirely.

Besides, I have another problem.

I can't go home.

My apartment is still wired, my purse is at the Sea Cliff house, and ruining Cass's date is not an option.

Shit.

At least I have my phone and one place left to go.

"Okay, buddy," I say to Truman, wiping the last of the tears from beneath my eyes. "What you want to hear? Something loud and distracting?"

"Wowrowrow," he answers, eyes blinking and looking mildly apologetic.

"I hear you, bud, and *never* apologize. Loud it is." Then I stick my car in gear and pull away to Black Rebel Motorcycle Club's "Let the Day Begin."

THE WEATHER'S miserable enough that I know if I leave Truman in my locked car in the hospital parking lot with the windows cracked, he won't overheat. I can't take him with me as it's against hospital rules, and I don't believe the staff will appreciate his flatulent disposition. Or his drooling.

As I weave between the parked cars, my phone rings. My stomach clenches at Gianni's caller ID, my thumb hovering over the answer button.

No.

I'm not ready to face anyone, except Billy, so I shut it down.

As I pass through the busy hallways, I ignore the looks. I'm sure I resemble a heroin addict in search of methadone, but I'm beyond caring. My head throbs, my throat's raw from the bile and my world has just crumbled around me.

Billy's awake, fortunately, thumbing the remote of a TV mounted on the wall.

"A thousand fucking channels and nothing to watch," he growls when I enter.

"Well, hello and I love you too." I kiss his cheek and pull up a chair.

"Ah shit, kiddo. I've been in a foul fucking mood ever since I heard from Carmine that fuckwad took you. I think the nurses want to poison my food and put me outta my misery." His eyes narrow while he examines my face. "You look like shit. What's happened? Other than being kidnapped."

"There's a dog in my car so I don't have much time, but I need to talk to you."

He engulfs my hand in his as I tell him everything, stopping to snatch Kleenex from a box next to his bed every few minutes to dab my eyes and blow my noise. He doesn't interrupt, but rests his head back and closes his eyes while he listens.

When I stop speaking, he's silent for so long, I think he may have fallen asleep.

"Well, fuck me with a feather," he says finally, blinking away the moisture in his eyes. "It's a good thing I'm on some heavy-duty drugs, otherwise my heart might break."

"You're not angry?"

"Joey's dead, kiddo. And I must be getting soft and old. One thing I've learned in this hospital bed, life's too short and too damn precious to be angry about something that happened ten years ago I can't change." His thumb rubs the back of my hand, and I focus on that, instead of looking into his eyes.

"They've been lying to us the whole time, Billy. Mom always told me she never knew who it was."

"I understand why they hid it. And I made my peace a long time ago."

"Maybe you have but I'm not there yet."

You're fucking dangerous.

"Don't you see?" My voice hitches. "It's my fault. People die because of me. First Daddy, then Joey. And I almost lost you too."

"Stop." He squeezes my hand until I look at him. "Listen to me. You can't blame yourself for what other people do. They're tragedies but it's not your fault, *or* Gianni's."

"Fucking Gianni," I mumble. "How can I ever trust him now?"

"What do you mean?"

"Never mind." My voice catches again and I turn my head away. "I shouldn't have said anything."

"Ah, dammit." Billy stares at me for a long time. "You're in love with him."

"Don't want to talk about it."

"Kiddo, you got trust issues, I get that, but he's..."

"Don't want to talk about it, Billy."

"All right. But know this, he's not Joey and he has his demons, but he *is* a man you can trust."

"You don't know that." *Not when it comes to my heart.*

"Known him for most of his life so I'm pretty sure I do know that. He made a mistake but I guarantee you he had his reasons. Perhaps you should let him explain. But about Joey...it's starting to make sense now and looking back, I know it wasn't easy for him. The last ten years had to be hell living with what he did, the pain he caused. Knowing it lost him you. He loved Jimmy and clearly he didn't handle the guilt well. You'll do yourself a solid if you can find a way to forgive him, *and* yourself. You're too young to carry this shit."

Forgive myself for my father dying? How do I begin to do that?

Billy's eyes turn pensive. "Joey was a hothead with a short fuse. I guess I never knew how short."

I nod. There were things I'd pushed to the back of my memory but allowed myself to remember now.

He'd been kicked off the baseball team in his senior year because a teammate flirted with me. Joey followed him after school, pulled a knife and threatened to slice this throat if he came near me again.

"Your mother's right," Billy says. "Back then, I would have killed him. It wouldn't have done anyone any good, just caused more pain." He lets out a long, tired sigh. "Stay at my house until you sort this. Carmine will let you in. Come see me tomorrow and we'll talk more. But now, you gotta let this old broken man cry in private."

"YOU GONNA BE OKAY?" Carmine asks as he unlocks the front door to Billy's third floor apartment above the bakery. I'd felt his eyes on me since I parked my car in the driveway and all the way up the stairs.

"I will be. Thanks for letting me in." Truman trots ahead to explore, toenails clicking on the polished, hardwood floor. I make a mental note to have them clipped. He stops to sniff a shaggy rug, then lets out a sneeze of approval.

"Let me know if you need anything." Carmine points downstairs with a half-smile. "Office is in the basement, under the bakery. Just tell the kid behind the counter who you are, he'll show you where to go."

He really is beautiful with all that gorgeous dark hair, but I'm in no mood to appreciate his looks. All I want is some food and a bed. And to shut out today. But first I need to use my manners.

"I have a lot to thank you for. When I'm not so out of it, I'd love to buy you lunch or something. Oh, and offer you free haircuts for life."

His face splits in a sexy grin. The kind that even on a bad day would make your insides quiver. Unfortunately, I'm not feeling it.

"When you're feeling better, I'll take you up on that. My uncle loves you like a daughter. That makes us cousins, so we *should* get to know each other."

I let out a small cry-laugh and run my hands through my hair, pulling it back into a ponytail. "Well, *cousin*, do you think it's possible to remove the cameras from my apartment?"

His light green eyes twinkle and crease in the corners. "I can do that."

I wrestle my apartment key off the ring, hand it over and watch as he jogs down the stairs lobbing a peace sign. Then I lock the door.

Billy's apartment is a surprise. I'd expected a bachelor pad, messy and uncoordinated, but it's furnished in a rustic industrial style. Lots of brushed steel, polished concrete and exposed brick. A long, brown, distressed leather couch dominates the living area and I know that's where I'll crash tonight. In front of the television after we eat.

Speaking of food, Billy's cabinets are filled to the hinges with human food, but nothing good for a dog other than a pack of hotdogs which I cut into pieces and place on a plate. Truman sniffs them, then gobbles down the lot in about ten seconds flat before I can even open a can of chicken noodle soup for myself.

Probably going to regret it, given his penchant to fart, but I have no choice other than letting him starve. Nary a can of dog food anywhere.

Of course, feeding Truman reminds me of Gianni and how he treats the dogs, which in turn makes my breath catch in my throat.

Fucking lying asshole. My insides ache in a sort of dull, hollow way, but really it's my own stupid fault for letting him get so close. Should have known better than to trust a Cadora.

Don't think, don't think, don't think.

Shut it down.

As I need to text Cass, I turn on my phone. Several messages wait, and I want to ignore them all, because I feel like being a bitch like that.

Gianni: *Where are you?*

Mom: *Let me know you're okay.*

Mom: *Please.*

Gianni: *De Luca, call me or get your ass home.*

Gianni: *Really?*

The last one, even though it's only one word, seems angrier. What the hell has he got to be angry about? He wasn't the one being lied to.

My chest feels as if it's in a vice and with each breath, that vice tightens, but I type, *Yes, really.* As an afterthought, I add. *Truman's with me.* He at least needs to know his dog is safe and not missing or, dare I say it, *kidnapped*.

Before he can respond, I power off my phone. I'll talk to Cass tomorrow when my brain will cooperate and she's done with her date. At least one of us should be having a good time.

Truman does his polka dance thing at the door cluing me it's time to take care of business. And once said business has been dealt with, I fill a bowl with water for him, a glass for me, drink it down, then crash like a zombie on the couch. Cocooned in a comforter I found in Billy's linen closet.

The last thing I think when I close my eyes is of Gianni's warm arms and his lips on my neck begging me not to leave.

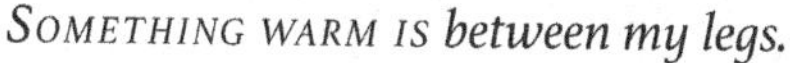

SOMETHING WARM IS between my legs.

Mmm.

Gianni.

He smells like cake and my stomach grumbles. I lick my lips and take a bite, but he evaporates before I can taste him.

Why won't my legs move?

I open one bleary eye and stare down an unfamiliar comforter straight into Truman's. That broad, flat head rests on my crotch, tongue hanging out one side.

And it all comes crashing back.

"God...Dog," I groan and rub the sleep from my eyes. "You had me going there for a minute."

Then it occurs to me the smells are from the bakery downstairs. My appetite wakens along with myself and I wiggle my legs, trying to dislodge Truman. Because he's a manipulative little butthead, he refuses to move.

It's still dark out and the clock on the DVR underneath the TV says it's not even six a.m. yet.

"Off, you big lug." I bounce my hips and he responds with a whine and long, put-put fart.

Gak.

I knew those damn sausages where going to come back and assault me.

"That's very unattractive," I croak at him from underneath the comforter. "How are you ever going to find a Mrs. Truman if you keep farting like that?" He snorts and burrows deeper between my legs.

At last, I get a leg under him and he shifts enough for me to roll off the couch. *Then* the little bastard decides to move and nose-dives off the couch. I let him out onto the large balcony as it's too early for me to take him for a walk. While he sniffs and lifts his leg, marking every corner and Billy's flowerpots, I check the cabinets again, hoping some food-fairy filled them up overnight with anything edible for Truman.

Still nothing.

I have no money and I can't give him doughnuts.

Crap.

I'm going to have to take him back to the house. Maybe if I leave soon I can pack my things and disappear before anyone wakes up.

After a quick shower, I release my hair from the bun on top of my head, then rumble through Billy's drawers with a towel the size of a blanket wrapped around me, looking for something to wear.

"Which do you think, Tru? The Sharks hoodie or the Giants sweatshirt?"

Truman sneezes, circles the floor three times and lies down, head between his paws.

"You're no help," I say and choose the hoodie. Who'd have thunk Billy was a hockey fan. Note to self to hit him up for a game next time the Kings are in town.

Half an hour later, the light is just beginning to turn pink and I yawn as I punch in the code on the keypad outside the gate at the Sea Cliff house.

I crawl up the driveway in my Mini in order to keep the engine noise to a minimum, then park at the side of the house and let Truman out. We walk around through the terraced vegetable garden loaded with lettuce and potatoes to the kitchen door, where Dean's goon, Boris, caught me off guard.

My heart lurches and I let out a puff of air as I remember. The dog bowls are empty, so either they've already eaten or are about to. It's now or I run away like a frightened little girl and come back later.

Well...since I'm here.

I take a deep breath and try the door knob. To both my surprise and relief, it's unlocked. I didn't want to use the front door key Gianni had given me because that would set the dogs off and since I know the house is wired, probably some silent alarm too.

I stick my head in, but see no one in the kitchen. The other three dogs stare at the pantry and besides a quick, cursory glance and a whine from the Doberman, pay no attention to us. Truman lumbers over and takes his place with them. Poor thing must be starving. I catch a glimpse of Connie's dark head and breathe a sigh.

Thank God it's not Gianni.

I sneak through and make it up the stairs and into my room without anyone seeing me. When I step inside, that vice around my chest tightens a notch.

The curtains are still open and it's light enough I can see the ocean and marine birds circling in the distance, searching for their morning meals.

My suitcases are in the walk-in closet and I pluck my clothes off the hangers and toss them in without folding. I'm halfway done when my bedroom door opens and every cell in my body ceases and locks. Maybe if I'm really quiet, he won't know I'm here and go away.

A shuddery sigh escapes me as I feel his energy before I see him and wonder if he senses the change in air pressure too.

Determining it's a lost cause, I carry on and drop my shoes on top of my clothes, pretending I couldn't give a crap.

"Morning," he says.

The pulse in my neck pounds like a tiny trapped animal trying to force its way through my skin.

"Morning," I respond, keeping my back to him. Somehow, I manage to project indifference in my tone, even though what I'm feeling is far from.

"Turn around, please?" When those words come at me, they're loaded with gravel and less than friendly.

I make a show of pulling in a deep breath and letting it out before I turn.

He leans against the closet door, arms folded across that broad naked chest. Despite the lack of caffeine in my system and my funky mood, those ridges and valleys of his six-pack, and the way those sweats hang low on his hips make desire curl in my belly. But it's his eyes, bloodshot and bluer due to the dark circles beneath them, that capture me.

I swallow. "How did you know I was here?"

"Heard your car," he says rubbing his stubble. "Where were you last night?"

When I don't reply, he straightens and tips his head sideways, examining me. That harsh gaze burning over my body like a wildfire. The quarter-sized scar on his shoulder moves as his muscles tense. It's so close to his heart. Just a few inches and he'd be dead. My chest squeezes and my voice gets stuck in my throat. Nothing comes out, except a little croak.

"Answer me, Shelley. Who were you with?" He takes a couple steps forward and I take one back, heels bumping up against my suitcase.

That hard jaw, set in an even harder line, clenches and the air between us electrifies and arcs inside the closet. Despite my instincts kicking in making me want to run, my nipples pebble and rub against the soft fabric of Billy's hoodie.

"Stop crowding me," I snap, because really, if I don't fight I'll be lost. "I'm not your property, Gianni."

"Didn't fucking sleep, woman, because I was worried about you."

"I told you I was fine. You have no right to be worried."

"You didn't go home."

"Yeah because my apartment is *wired*, asshole, remember? You think I'm going to give you a show?"

"Who were you with?"

"Why do you keep asking me that?"

"Just answer the damn question."

Fine. I figure there's no point in laboring the point, since I mostly want to just pack and run. "No one," I finally concede. "Except Truman." I continue gathering my clothes, dropping them into my case, but it seems he's not done.

"That sweatshirt doesn't belong to you. Where did you get it?"

He's joking, right?

"Are *you* accusing *me* of lying?" I stop what I'm doing and turn back to face him. "Holy cow, Gianni. Not that it's any of your damn business but I commandeered it from Billy."

Something flickers across his face, but it disappears before I can figure it out. "What you need to get, De Luca, is you *are* my business." He takes another step closer towering over me, eyes hard and glittery.

This time, I don't budge. "You don't intimidate me and you have no right to question me. You *lied* to me. My whole world's been rocked. You saved my life, and I'll always be grateful, but you lied about something really fucking big."

He stares at me for a long time, his jaw muscles rippling. "You're not the only one whose world's been rocked," he says softly.

I glance at his scar, the ever-present reminder of what happened, and swallow. What must it be like for him to see that scar every day? I want so much to touch it, run my palms down his stomach to his happy trail and ease some of the pain and guilt I know he has to have suffered. But I can't allow myself to.

"You've had ten years to deal with it. I've had one day. Let me finish here so I can get out of your hair," I whisper past the lump in my throat. "You won't have to worry about me anymore."

I will not cry.

I will *not* cry.

"That's not what I mean, Shelley." His hand encircles my upper arm. I freeze as he dips his face so it's inches from mine.

"Honestly, I don't want to know what you mean. But I don't trust you anymore and probably never will again so it doesn't really matter now, does it?"

He flinches like I gut-punched him. "Give me a chance to explain."

"What's to explain?" I throw a hand in the air. "You knew Joey killed my dad and didn't come clean when you could've. Looked me right in the eye when I asked you if there was something else I needed to know and you lied. *You lied* and then you fucked me. End. Of. Story."

"It's not *end of story*. Not for me."

Oh God. How much more does he expect me to take?

"But it is for me."

"No...don't say that."

"Please...Gianni." I blink back the tears. "I can't do this now. It's too much."

I will not cry.

"Shelley..."

"I need space to sort this out in my head."

He lets out a long breath and shuts his eyes. When they reopen, his expression is full of something I've never seen in him before. Anguish.

"I'll give you a little space only because you're asking for it. When you're ready to hear me out, call me. But first, you need to understand something."

Before I can take a breath or process what he's said, he pushes me against the shelves lining the wall of the closet. Boxing me in with those solid hips pressed to mine. Then my hands are caught high above my head in one of his. The other twists in my hair, tilting my head back and to the side. When his mouth comes down, it's hard and fast and greedy, sucking on my lip. There's no coaxing my mouth open, only demanding. At first, I try to fight. I try to push him away but with each passing moment I weaken and then I respond. Because I can't resist him. Our tongues do battle as he invades and plunders my mouth while my heart thunders in my chest.

Though it's wet and deep and hot, it's punishing and layered with anger and something else. Sensations only he is able to invoke flood through my body, through my veins, pooling between my legs. He takes from me, and then he takes even more and like the fool I know I am, I allow it because this is my last kiss.

At some point, he releases my arms and slides his behind me, pulling me closer, grinding himself against me. My hands slide up his chest, along the planes of his pecs, memorizing his skin and the fine dusting of hair, making him groan deep in his throat.

He's hard. So hard it almost hurts as the pressure digs into my belly, but my body remembers him. I whimper, wanting him. *Needing* him.

Then it all goes to hell.

Gianni rips his mouth from mine, stares down into my eyes and holds me like that for a long time. His are clouded with longing and hunger, but also with pain before he grits out in a voice that's a little thick and a lot husky. "That's no fucking lie. Trust in *that* when you have your space."

He releases his grip on my hair and backs out of the closet. As he turns and leaves my room, the last glimpse I have is him scraping his palms over his eyes.

I wait until I hear the door click before I slide down the wall. The empty space he leaves behind is just that, vast and empty.

Like me.

I can't say how long I sit like that as the tears free fall silently down my cheeks before I find the strength to get up and finish packing. But it's a while.

My mind is in a daze when I write a short note to my mother and slip it under her bedroom door. In time, I'll get past my anger, but for now this is all I can manage.

Connie is brewing coffee with Rambo peeking over the pocket of her apron when I drag the first of my suitcases down the stairs.

"Miss Shelley, you want I make you something to eat?"

"No, thank you, Connie. I don't think I can eat."

"I make you toast. You want jam?"

"I'm good, seriously."

"Bagel? I put cream cheese and strawberries on it?"

"Okay," I relent with a sigh. This is an argument I'm not going to win, but I don't have to eat it here. Or eat it at all. "Thank you. To go, if you wouldn't mind."

It's ready, with a napkin on a white paper plate by the time I'm done loading. Along with a coffee in a tall San Francisco Giants travel cup. I wonder if it's Gianni's. If he'll miss it. Or if he'll miss me. After adding milk and sugar, I tighten the lid, then sip, hardly tasting it.

"Is he still around?"

One last glimpse.

She shakes her head and eyes me. "He went for his run with Tinkerbell. He no look so happy."

Yeah. There's a lot of that going around lately.

"Thank you, Connie, for everything. You've been very kind. Can you tell him I say goodbye?"

"*Si.*" She takes my face in her palms and examines my face.

"But you should tell him yourself. You no look so happy either. Ai!" She looks at the ceiling. "Young people...so stubborn."

I give Rambo a kiss on the head and her a quick hug, because anything more will snap the fragile hold I have on my emotions. Then step outside, hating what I have to do next.

Truman and the Doberman are playing tug-of-war with a mangled, soggy piece of rope. Seeing me, he abandons the game and runs over, pink tongue swinging out the side of his mouth. I massage his wrinkles and rub his ears for a minute before I kiss him goodbye, but when I walk back to my car, he follows. I open the door and he jumps in.

Oh jeez.

"No, buddy, not this time." The confusion in his eyes is too much. I pick him up and remove him from the seat. Then plant my butt on the driveway, pulling him into my lap, cradling him while my heart shreds a little more.

"My apartment's too small for you," I sob. "It wouldn't be fair." At this rate, I'll have no tears left. They soak into his coat while I hold him close. "Anyway, I don't think Marshall allows dogs."

Truman nudges me and whines. I kiss him on the flat part of his head and scratch his back.

"I love you, you smelly little butthead," I say when I finally let him go and climb into my car. "I'll come back and see you. I promise."

When I know Gianni's not here.

This time as I drive away, I dare not look in the rear-view mirror. I can't stand to see his mopey little face, and the further I get, the bigger the empty ache in my chest grows.

16

WE CAN BRING THE DOG

~

Two days later

Gianni: *Are you ready to talk?*

Me: *No.*

Four days later

Gianni: *De Luca, this is ridiculous.*

Me: *Stop texting me.*

Five days later

Gianni: *Someone's missing you.*

The bastard sends a photo of Truman. And fucking hell, he does look like he's missing me. His droopy eyes are droopier and those lovable jowls, longer. He even looks thinner. Fuck.

Me: *That's emotional blackmail...and cruel. Like you. Don't do that it's not fair.*

Gianni: *I'm the one being cruel? Perhaps we should let the dog decide.*

Me: *His name's Truman, asshole.*

Gianni: *Like I said, Truman's missing you.*

I turn my phone off, reach for the box of Kleenex next to my bed and burrow my head into my pillow.

Seven Days later

Gianni: *De Luca???*

Gianni: *Right. I'm done with this shit.*

And that's when the knife in my heart twists. Although it's what I want—him leaving me alone—having it in my face, *knowing* he's finally done, is disappointing.

Strike that. It's *crushing.*

I miss him, my body misses him, even my mind misses him but a clean break is the only way I know how to deal. That and a couple pounds of See's butterscotch squares and copious amounts of wine. I'll get over him eventually, just not yet, but hopefully before I gain two hundred pounds. Probably wouldn't matter as I'm swearing off all men forever but I would like to still fit in my Mini.

Eight days later

"Why am I doing this again?" I ask Cass, running my hands over my waist, smoothing the silk chiffon dress she chose.

"Because you're my best friend," Cass answers and tweaks the last bit of hem, letting it out a little. She takes a step back and tilts her head, admiring her work. "And you're doing me and Marco a favor by going in my place so we can have this date."

"Well, I definitely owe Marco. I suppose filling in for you at a charity ball is the least I can do."

"Selfish, I know, but I need you out of this funk. I hate seeing you like this."

I need me out of this funk. And if tonight's charity thing doesn't do it, perhaps my shoes will. All four inches of impending strappy, stiletto hell.

"Hair up," Cass commands and points with her rat-tail comb for me to sit.

"I'm not so sure about this dress." I twist in my seat in front of her mirror to check the plunging back that ends just above the dip in my lower spine, flaring slightly below my hips.

"Shush. The color's fabulous, matches your eyes perfectly."

"Good thing my boobs are small 'cause there is no way I could wear a bra. That makes it about an inch away from indecent exposure."

"Shut up and be still," she says, twisting segments of my hair into what will be a bohemian up-do. "You look hot."

Honestly, I couldn't care less if I wore a burka. Balls are so not my thing but embarrassing Cass isn't an option. Without her and Mrs. See's sugar-inducing comas this past week, I may have considered jumping from the bridge or perhaps using Ziggy on myself.

"Necklace, yes or no?" I ask, fingering the amber heart, digging deep down inside me to find some long-lost enthusiasm. Because it's time to move the fuck on.

"Yes," she answers, "and seriously it's a family tradition. My parents can't go this year and I can't let my brother misbehave alone."

"I heard that." Rory, my *other* boss, says as he enters her bedroom. "Car is here, so whenever you're ready." He's tall and elegant in his tux, with longish, blonde hair, kind of like Keith Urban's. And the polar opposite to Gianni's sexy dark waves.

Cut it the fuck out. I'm not thinking about him tonight.

Noop.

"Wow." Rory touches his finger to his tongue making a hissing noise.

"You like it? Not too much?" I stand when Cass finishes my hair and do a somewhat graceful three-sixty for him. It's the first time I'm bruise-free and look decently pretty since Dean hit then strangled me a lifetime ago.

"Your eyes look super sexy. I'm going to have to bring my bat to keep them away." Rory holds out his arm for me to take. "Ready?"

"Yep." I sigh. "Let's do it."

In the limo, he pops the cork on a bottle of champagne and pours two glasses. "Here's to hot-looking women and may they not all be taken." We clink and soon his quick humor has me, if not exactly laughing, at least smiling as we ride up the steep hills of California Street.

The driver pulls under the awning of the Fairmont Hotel and opens the door for us to exit. Inside, the main lobby is unlike any other. Lavishly dominated by the huge marble pillars and floors, reminiscent of a palace from the Italian Renaissance.

I hope a little of its flair will rub off on me. We take the elevator to the top of the tower and I hold on to Rory's arm when we enter the Crown Room.

Instantly I'm in awe of the view and city lights. And more than a little intimidated by the display of opulence. These people are the elite of San Francisco and the newly rich of Silicon Valley. The women look spectacular in their gowns and jewels, and the men crisp and handsome. I'm about to hyperventilate, grateful Cass convinced me to wear one of her dresses as nothing in my closet would be suitable. I don't even own an evening gown.

Rory senses my distress and reassures me with a wink. "They're just people. Try to picture them without their Spanx and toupees."

With his hand on the small of my back, he escorts me into the room, straight towards the bar.

Good man.

After Rory gives him our order, the dude, who looks like a surfer doubling as a barman, hands me a glass of champagne and Rory a Scotch with ice. We click glasses again and I sip as my gaze sweeps around, hoping to spot someone else I know. So far, not a single one.

"How come you couldn't find another date for tonight?" I ask.

He chuckles. "If I had, how am I supposed to meet anyone? I've dated every available female in San Francisco. My family's bleating like sheep it's time I settled down and made babies."

"How do you feel about that?"

"I'm all for making them. It's the *baby* part that scares me. Did I tell you how sexy you look? These old farts can't take their eyes off you."

My face gets hot and I bite my lip. "You're exaggerating, but you're sweet."

A broad grin spreads across his face. "Nothing sweet about me. If I left you alone for a second they'd descend on you like hungry piranhas on a juicy lamb chop."

A giggle escapes me. "I'm a lamb chop now?"

"Finally," he says on a snort. "I got you to laugh. C'mon, let's find a table and make nice." He holds out his arm, and I hook mine through his as we meander through the crowd, stopping to say hello to important-looking people, most of whose names I can't remember. They all seem very friendly and pleasant and extremely rich.

One particularly over-imbibed gentleman with a comb-over is a little *too* pleasant, and swoops in close. Focusing on avoiding bourbon breath, I miss the sudden change in air pressure and misread the crackling vibe that raises goosebumps on my skin. I sidestep out of his way, and onto someone's foot.

Crud.

I turn to apologize, happy for a reason to avoid more bourbon breath, except my knees lock as I stare straight at a very attractive Adams apple situated in a handsome neck that looks way to familiar.

Holy fizz pops.

It can't be.

My eyes follow that neck to a hard jaw darkened by five o'clock shadow and then up that beautiful, straight nose and into those icy blue eyes.

Even if I had it in me to smile, I couldn't. The shock to my system's frozen the muscles in my face and my poor abused heart stills.

"Shelley." Gianni's stare impales me, and regardless of the champagne I've consumed, my mouth goes paper-dry at his voice.

But that's not all.

Because in my peripheral vision a hand reaches out and attaches itself to his arm. A *female* hand and I instinctively know it's her. I know it without even looking, but when my eyes do slide over and take in the body-hugging, black-beaded dress and the bulging cleavage, I want to die.

I want to scratch out her eyes and yank on that pretty black hair until she's bald, then shove every last strand down that elegant throat hoping she chokes. If that doesn't kill her, I want to take that gorgeous pearl necklace and twist it until it does.

But of course, I do none of this.

Instead, I cling a little harder to Rory, suck it up like a good mafia daughter, and thank my lucky stars I didn't bring Ziggy. I have no desire to spend the rest of the night, or my life, in jail.

Then, by some massive force of will, I ignore the slicing thing in my gut and meet his gaze.

He looks leaner but nonetheless gorgeous. The dark circles beneath his eyes add a touch of danger, making him look more sinister, yet somehow hotter.

How *fucked* am I?

No trace of a smile touches that clenched jaw as his gaze roves over my face then down my body, setting it on fire. My nipples harden and, curse Cass's damn dress, they poke through the thin fabric.

"Gianni." My voice cracks when our eyes meet again. For a moment time slows and everything seems unfocused. Except for him. Over the noise of the party, I hear the whoosh, whoosh of my heart wildly pumping blood to my brain.

I'm fortunate that Rory, God bless him, still has his wits and assesses the situation. He rescues me by stepping in and extending his hand to Gina. "Rory Jones," he says, throwing her a bright, irresistible smile.

Gianni breaks eye contact, although before he does, I read something in them. I swear it's relief as his jaw clenches, then relaxes as he takes Rory's hand and introduces himself and Gina in a clipped voice.

Good God.

The man is relieved.

That I'm here with Rory.

So he can be free to be with *her*? Probably thinks I'm going to go all stalker on his ass.

Well, fuck him.

He's wrong.

Noop, noop, *noop.*

Absolutely fucking NOPE!

In spite of the hollow pit in my stomach and tightening band around my chest, I ignore it and plant a fake smile on my face.

Albeit a small one. I steal a glance at Gina and by the look on her face, she's feeling the same. Her black gaze darts between the men before meeting my own. Only difference is no smile on hers, fake or otherwise.

Okay.

I'm done.

I can't be near them. I clear my throat. Even so, my voice comes out a little scratchy. "Excuse us. Good to see you, Gianni."

Rory takes his cue and curls his fingers on the round of my shoulder, guiding me through the throng of people. Neither of us speak until we're some distance away.

"Dude," he drags out. "That was intense."

I gulp a mouthful of champagne, then another and nod.

"Are you okay?" he asks.

I take another gulp and shake in the negative.

"Easy, lamb chop, you're gonna give yourself the burps."

I ignore his warning and down the last bit then, as predicted, issue a silent burp behind my hand. "That was uncomfortable."

"Uncomfortable?" He snorts and shakes his head. "Uncomfortable doesn't begin to describe it. Who is he, your ex?" he asks, looking over his shoulder, his brow furrowing.

"Hardly an ex. More like an old family friend."

He shoots me a glance full of skepticism. "Calling bullshit on that."

"Okay." I yield and roll my eyes. "I slept with him once."

"Once?" Those eyebrows shoot up. "You mean that dude almost eviscerated me because you slept with him *once*?"

I shrug.

"Hmm. Okay, well whatever," he says folding his arms across his chest, straining that tailored tux. Fortunately for me, he lets it go because at that moment he spots someone a few tables away. "C'mon, I want you to meet someone. Get your mind off... well, you know."

With both hands on the back of my shoulders, he spins and pushes me toward them. I manage to snag another glass of champagne from a passing waiter.

"Rory," the man says, patting him on the upper arm. "How are you and who is this lovely lady?"

I'm introduced to some Silicon Valley something or other, and manage a fake grin, not really paying attention. While they chit-chat about the latest software update of some new gizmo I've yet to acquaint myself with, my eyes rove the room. Like a magnet, they're drawn to the far side, to a certain Sicilian badass.

He's facing my direction, with his head cocked slightly, listening to Gina talking in his ear. As if sensing my look, he lifts his gaze and locks on me like a guided missile, hot and ready to fire. Even at this distance, and with dozens of people between us, I feel the electricity. When after what seems a long time, Rory touches my shoulder, I realize I've been gawking and break eye contact.

Why did the jerk have to be here and why do my eyes keep finding him? This is *not* helping.

"I'm sorry, what did you say?" I ask.

"I said, I hope you're not too bored?"

Bored?

Ha! Highly unlikely; tormented and crushed, perhaps.

"Shelley, it's obvious you two have unresolved issues. You want me to play interference with the black-eyed vixen?"

"Umm..."

"I wouldn't mind, she's kinda hot."

Fuck.

"Thanks for pointing that out." I know he means well, but really?

"Ah shit." He closes his eyes. "Shelley, that was...stupid. Sorry."

"It's okay, because it won't come to that so no worries. I'm gonna spritz up and get a refill." I say, tapping a nail against my empty flute. "Want one?"

"Scotch please." He lays a peck on my cheek and winks at me. "It's gonna be fine. You'll see."

Pff.

Doubt it.

Without further ado, I find the ladies' room, keeping the fake smile on my face in case anyone should be watching. I pull in a deep breath before pushing a stall door open. Blinking hard, fighting tears, I dab the corners of my eyes with toilet paper. Won't do to have mascara smudged and all over my face.

When I exit the stall I say a prayer, but God's not listening.

Again.

If he was, Gina wouldn't be standing in front of the mirror, refreshing her makeup.

"Hello," I say, even though my inner mafia bitch wants to follow through on my earlier fantasy and rip all that pretty, shiny black hair out.

She gives a little huff and a tiny shake of her head, then continues to focus on outlining her perfect lips.

Yep. God hates me.

So.

I ignore her while I wash my hands, touch up my lipstick, and check my rear for any unwanted stragglers. As I turn to leave, I catch her watching my reflection.

It's not like I'm looking for it, and lord knows I wasn't expecting it, but when I see it, it shifts everything. The pain in her expression—quick and sharp like moonlight glinting off a knife's blade before it's gone—is a reality that floors me. She's in love with him too!

As soon as the door closes behind me, my breath catches in my throat.

Shit.

How many women are in love with the asshole? She must know, or at least suspect in that way that women intuit, that we slept together. Except, she's the one with him tonight and it didn't take him long to go back to her either.

I guess that means you win, Gina.

"What can I get you?" the barman-slash-surfer-dude asks, flirting with his eyes. I hardly notice, due to the broken glass swirling in my stomach and laser beams burning holes in my back. Somehow, I refrain from looking over my shoulder. Don't particularly care whose laser beams they are. Gianni can go fuck himself and Gina…well Gina can help for all I care.

Except I do.

I really, *really* do.

Dammit.

Drinks in hand, I weave my way back through the ever-growing crowd to Rory, who's still in conversation with the Silicon Valley whatever, just as the band strikes up.

When he sees me, he stops, slides his arm around my shoulders and whispers in my ear.

"That didn't go well."

"Noop."

"You ready for some dancing?"

"Not really."

"Oh, come on. Let's get some payback, make that fucker jealous. Besides, it's hard to cry when you're focusing on keeping up."

"I'm being a bad date, aren't I?"

"Not if you dance with me."

"Okay," I whisper. What harm can it do. Better than moping around. Only hope my shoes don't let me down.

Rory places our drinks on a table and guides me to the dance floor along with several other couples already moving to an uptempo instrumental number. He's playful and a strong lead, making up funny lyrics to the melody as we go. He has a good voice (because in his other life he sings in a band) and within moments we're swirling around and I'm no longer fake smiling. Gianni and his collection of broken hearts *almost* gone from my mind. As the number reaches its climax, he pulls me close, then with a flourish, twirls me under and we end on a dip. The couples around us smile and clap. Why can't I be attracted to someone normal like him? He's not only funny but a fun date too.

We're still laughing as we're about to leave the dance floor, when a dark, brooding shadow in the form Gianni steps in front of me, looking indeed like he wants to eviscerate Rory.

"Do you mind." It's not a question.

"Yes, he does, go away," I quip.

"It's fine, Shelley," Rory answers. "Go ahead."

I turn to stare. "What? No..."

Before Rory can respond, Gianni's arm slips around my waist and steals me away. I struggle, but not too hard I must admit, since my shoes are not of the kind made to struggle in.

So I relent, weak-ass that I am.

Immediately his presence envelops me and that glass in my gut turns to butterfly swarms. As the music starts, he laces our fingers together, his free hand moves over my lower back caressing my skin.

"You look lovely," he says, breath warm against my ear, sending shivers through me. Then the asshole runs his nose slowly up my neck, scenting me and pulling me closer until I'm against his hard thighs and hips. It's possessive, primal and, dammit...hot.

"And you smell even lovelier."

I so want to lose myself in him and it takes everything to pull my head back to meet his gaze. He doesn't get this from me when he's with another woman.

But, fucking hell, why is he so damn beautiful in that lazy-ass-without-even-trying way he is, making it impossible to resist.

"Why are you avoiding me?"

"You forced me to dance with you, but that doesn't mean I have to talk to you."

"Suppose not, but that just means I'll keep you on the dance floor and I'll keep asking until you tell me."

Well, that's not going to work.

So, I relent again.

"I want a clean break."

His arm around my waist tightens, making me miss my step. "A clean break?" He steadies me, but his brow creases until his Y appears. "From me?"

"Who else, Gianni?"

"Why?"

"You know my reasons. I don't need to repeat myself."

You couldn't call it silence, because of the music, but it may as well have been and it goes on for a while as his eyes burn into mine.

Finally, he speaks. "You're being an idiot, De Luca. You can't see what's in front of your face."

He's got me there. When it comes to men, him in particular, I am an idiot. And I don't trust myself.

I attempt to pull away, move back to Rory where it's safe, but he shakes his head. "You're not going anywhere and this will go much better if you relax."

"I don't want to relax."

"You owe me this dance. You know...for saving your life."

Fine.

I roll my eyes and give in because I can't seem to help myself.

Much easier than fighting, and if truth be known, I don't want to go.

His fingers move across my skin, tantalizing warmth penetrating as the champagne kicks in, or maybe it's him that's so intoxicating. I become boneless and melt against him as we sway to the music and finally I sigh and rest my head against his shoulder, inhaling his smell.

The steel band across my back tightens, pressing me even closer. "You're killing me, Shelley." The husky way he says my name sends thrills through my body. The last time he said that to me...well, was in his kitchen after he gave me an orgasm. "Don't you know what you do to me?" It's then I notice the hard column in his pants pressing against my lower belly.

Everything inside me spasms and a tiny whimper escapes my lips.

I need to see his face, look into his eyes, but as I lift my head, something beyond his shoulder catches my attention.

Gina.

Alone and standing off to the side of the dance floor watching us. How could I forget? The set of her mouth and the shimmer in her eyes says everything.

I may hate her, but hurting people isn't my thing and I definitely don't poach other people's dates. I stiffen and shove against his chest.

"Stop," he commands.

"Shut up."

"Shelley, stop..."

"Gina, remember?"

"What about her?"

"God, you're an asshole."

"Listen to me. I told you there's nothing between us."

"Like I'm going to believe anything you say. You've already admitted you've slept with her. Don't deny it now."

"I'm not denying it. I did, once. A long time ago and not since you've been around. She finds buildings I might be interested in buying, Shelley. That's all."

I roll my eyes and shake my head. "Now who's the idiot? Or maybe you're just that callous."

"Callous? The fuck you talking about?"

I study him and see no deception there. Could it be he doesn't know Gina's in love with him? Well, I'm not gonna be the one to put any thoughts in that handsome head. "You know what, Gianni…never mind. You've had your dance and now I'm done."

His eyes flare. "We're not done because I'm not done. Not even close."

"That's not what your text said," I point out.

"My text said I was done with this *shit*. I'm not done with you."

He's not done with *me*?

Oh boy.

"Why are you making this so hard for me?"

"Hard for *you*? Jesus, woman, you're clueless."

The music ends. We stop moving and I untangle my fingers from his, but he keeps his arm around me. The other couples separate and leave the dance floor and we're left standing alone.

"Let me go."

"No."

"Go to your *date*, Gianni. She's waiting."

The look he gives is so intense, it burns through my skin, through my bones all the way to my soul. His free hand slides up the side of my neck until his thumb finds a place under my chin.

"You've got it wrong," he says. "I'm gonna make you listen to me until you get it and we're gonna do it private." With that, he whirls me around, gripping my upper arm and walks us off the floor. A path between the crowd magically clears, because that's what people do around Gianni. They move out of his way.

"What are you doing?" I try to yank my arm from his grip, but his fingers tighten even more. I look back at Rory, who's grinning like he just won the lottery, making away-with-you gestures with his hands.

What the hell?

Traitor.

Next, we're out of the Crown Room, marching towards an elevator, passing elegant couples sipping on their drinks. He stabs the button with his thumb.

"You can let me go now."

"Are you gonna run?"

"Depends on where you're taking me."

"Somewhere private." My mouth opens to protest, but he steps into my space and cuts me off. "Shut it, De Luca," he says quietly. "Not gonna do you any good."

So, I shut it. Instead, I watch him watching me, fascinated by the muscles working in his jaw as his eyes move over my body, lingering on my breasts. I'd be lying if I said it doesn't turn me on because my nipples prove otherwise. What is it about him that, even pissed off, he does this to me?

By the time the elevator doors open and he directs me inside I know exactly how weak I am. The air is thick, laced with sexual tension and I avoid his gaze, afraid to show how much I want him.

At his floor, he walks me down a long, plush, carpeted hallway. When we stop, he pulls a key-card from his pocket and slips it into a lock.

"You have a room here?" My voice reflects my panic.

Good God. Was he planning on bringing Gina here?

"In."

"No!" I back away. "Why are you doing this?"

"I want to talk where we won't be interrupted."

"Do you have to be so fucking cruel?"

"Cruel?"

"You bring me here?" I'm yelling now. "To your little fuck-nest? So you can rub it in my face while you're here with someone else? What is wrong with you?"

I turn to run back to the elevator, tears prickling the corners of my eyes. "Don't do this, Gianni. Just leave me alone."

His fingers lock around my wrist pulling me back. "I can't, dammit. God knows I've tried."

"Try harder, asshole. You're here with another woman."

"No." He shakes his head. "I'm not with her. I came *alone*, Shelley. Gina just happened to be here. I'm here for *you*. Cass set this up and the only woman I'm planning on taking into that room is *you*."

"Why? For another installment on your damn marker?"

"Fuck the fucking marker." Now he's the one yelling. Both hands scrape through his hair in frustration. "Was stupid for letting you think that."

"What?"

"I wanted you...thought it was the only way I could get you past fighting this thing between us. Once the words were out, I couldn't take them back."

Is he for real? I search his eyes. They're dark, filled with an urgency that makes me want to believe. To trust...because I want it so badly.

"Was gonna tell you that night of the fire...before he took you."

I'm too confused to speak and a million thoughts jumbled into one race through my head.

Cass set this up?

"Will you come inside with me?"

I nod and his grip on my upper arm becomes a caress as he

swipes the key card again. My heart hammers as we enter a suite.

With a huge balcony.

Figures.

He follows me in, past the lavish couch and chairs to the double glass doors leading outside. I push one open, step outside, grateful for the air and wander to the wrought-iron railing. It's a gorgeous evening. Cool, but with no fog. Only a slight breeze and the view's monopolized by the twinkling lights of the Transamerica Pyramid, that new monstrosity they're building in SoMa and the Bay Bridge. Marine craft and party boats dot the smooth water but none of this does anything to calm my nerves.

"Wow," I whisper. He sure knows how to charm.

"Something, isn't it?" he says coming up behind me, so close his breath is hot on my ear. A shiver slams through me and I bite my lip to stop a hiss escaping when his lips touch the curve in my shoulder.

"You're trembling. Are you cold?" Arms come around me, grasp the railing. Caging me with his warmth, yet barely touching. All I have to do is lean back but his particular mix of heat and sex is too dangerous.

"Gianni..."

"That space you asked for? Eight days is enough time away from you. That stops now. How I see it, we have two options."

"Gianni..."

"Shh," he says in my neck. "First, either you and I are a thing or..." He lets out a breath and I hear him swallow. "Or...and I really hate this option. One I'm not willing to accept without a hell of a fight. And only if you convince me you don't want me. We stay away from each other because I can't be around you and not have you."

My brain must have seized because I got stuck on two words.

"A thing?" It comes out hoarse as my throat's suddenly dry. "What exactly do you mean by *thing?*"

Big hands clasp my hips, slowly swinging me around. Staring into his eyes, which are still dark, but now determined, makes my heart pound harder than is healthy. Makes me hope things I shouldn't dare to hope because I'm so afraid I'm misreading what I'm seeing and hearing.

"You asked me," he replies, "if I'd ever had a long-term relationship and I told you I never wanted one."

I capture my lip between my teeth, not sure I want to know.

"That was mostly true."

Oh shit...I'm not prepared for this—to hear about some woman he loved. My eyes drop to focus on his Adam's apple bobbing and I lean back slightly.

"You see, the only woman I've ever wanted a relationship with...is you."

That takes a while to penetrate. To sink into my cells and then into my psyche.

"What are you saying?" I finally whisper.

Those big hands come to my face, one thumb strokes my bottom lip. Goosebumps pop up all over my skin.

"God help me, I'm saying I'm obsessed with you, De Luca. I can't ever get you out of my head. You're in my dreams every damn night. Mornings," he pauses and takes a deep breath, "I wake up wanting you so much I could drill through concrete."

God, his words—ones I've wanted since I was sixteen—have me buzzing to my toes, but scaring me all at once. They're hot and wild and crazy.

"Um...the obsession part kinda freaks me out a little."

"It should. Freaks the hell out of me. Always has. As much as I hate Melnikov, I can't deny I understand him." His lips move to the corner of mine, his breath teasing, yet hesitating. "What scares me more than anything, is never being able to do this.

Never touch you, never hear you make those sexy little noises when you come, because fuck, Shelley, I wanna make love to you more than I want my next breath. And probably will for the rest of my life." He rests his forehead on mine and stares into my eyes. "And that was why I lied. Because I was so afraid of losing the chance to be with you."

The way he's focused on me, so honest and exposed, fills me with want and heat so intense I think I might die if I don't have him.

"Gianni..." I don't have time to say more as he takes my mouth, not gently or sweetly, but raw and desperate. A groan, low and primal in his throat, rumbles through his chest. He crushes me against him like he can't get close enough. Our tongues meet in a frantic, frenzied dance. All my hunger, all my longing in each stroke manifests in the hot, empty ache between my thighs.

Somehow, we've moved inside. His jacket comes off while I tug on his shirt, pulling it free of his pants. I want, no...I'm *compelled* to touch his skin, the firm muscles and the silky hair. Every inch of his body's hard and heated, causing that ember, smoldering all evening, to burst into flames.

Gianni's mouth, the scrape of his stubble as he tastes me, nipping and sucking, takes me closer and closer to what I need.

He slips my dress strap off one shoulder, following with little bites and kisses, then the other shoulder, allowing it to drop to the floor and steps back. A shaky breath escapes him as he examines every curve of my naked, aching body.

"Most beautiful thing I've ever seen, De Luca. You slay me." His voice is rough, and his eyes, heated and glazed with lust, land on my pebbled nipples.

This time the kiss is slow and deep and unbelievable. I might explode before I unbuckle his belt, undo his zipper and push his pants down over lean, hard hips, freeing him. It's intoxicating and dizzying and overwhelming. Everything about him—his smell, his taste, like wickedness and whisky—undoes me. He cups my breast, taking one nipple, rolling it between his fingers, the other in his mouth, sucking. Exquisite sensations pulsate from my breasts, and my hips arch. Then, supporting me with those strong, steely arms, he lowers me gently onto the bed like I'm something precious and prowls between my legs, teasing my knees wider. Slowly he moves those rough palms up the insides of my thighs, followed by his mouth and tongue.

I want more. His mouth in one place and everywhere. As his face inches an agonizingly slow path, my fingers wind themselves into his hair, guiding his mouth to my greedy, pulsing little place, and he complies, laughing a little while my hips rock to meet him.

It doesn't take long for my orgasm to slam through me, or for him to roll on a condom and push inside and take us both on a ride so hot, so crazy and so beautiful I never want it to end.

"I'm a little confused," I say. "You said *always has*?"

We're on our sides, under the sheet of the king-sized bed, facing each other. I twirl that lock of his hair around my fingers, marveling at how dark and shiny it is.

His lips curl into his lazy-ass smile, deepening the grooves in his cheeks.

"For as long as I can remember, I always wanted you, but you were underage and so damn tempting. Felt like a dirty old fuck obsessing over you. That's why I went to Boston instead of Stanford. Too hard to be near you. When I graduated and came back, you were so beautiful, you stole my breath."

Happy sensations fill my chest, making it expand to the point I think it might burst.

"Couldn't stop thinking about you, even when I was gone." His thumb traces little circles around my belly button. "And you and Joey were a thing. I wanted to kill him, but he was my little brother. Knew him and knew he'd fuck up at some point. Figured I'd wait it out. I couldn't touch you anyway, but that didn't mean I enjoyed watching you together."

"Is that why you were always an asshole to me?"

He chuckles. "Like the kid who's mean to the girl he likes? Yep. I kept waiting for you to figure it out. Didn't know who I was madder at, you for being so young and untouchable or him for having you. I couldn't stand it. I never told him, but he knew I wanted you. He always knew. Called me on it after we pounded on that asshole Darren McGee for abandoning you at that freshman party."

"What did you do?"

"Didn't deny it, and told him if he didn't treat you right, I'd beat *his* ass and take you from him first chance I got. Then tried to avoid being around you. You've no idea how hard that was with all the family shit that went on, yet if I knew there was a shot at seeing you I couldn't stay away."

Suddenly it occurs. "Oh my God. You knew he was messing around on me, didn't you? Is that why you kissed me at the marina?"

His brows shoot up. "You knew about that?"

"Gloria's boobs weren't the only big thing about her. That girl couldn't keep her mouth shut."

"I didn't want him to hurt you. He didn't deserve you if he was gonna treat you that way."

I let out a smirk. "Funny. Dean said the same thing. And you"—I tug on that little lock—"you drove me crazy. There were so many women. They were gorgeous and I hated them. I knew I couldn't compete."

He shakes his head and sighs. "You didn't have to. That necklace you're wearing...the tiny letters in the silver?"

Huh? How would he know about those?

"G and L?" I never thought much about them, just always assumed they were the jeweler's marks.

A smile lifts the corner of his mouth, doing ridiculously delicious thing to my insides. "Take a look at the bottom point."

I turn the heart and after a moment of examination, I find it hidden in the intricate filigree.

A tiny C.

Holy fizz pops. My eyes widen and slide to his when it hits me. "What's your middle name?"

"Luigi."

GLC.

"Wait...why are *your* initials on here?"

"Had it made for you in Boston, babe. Your eyes always reminded me of amber. I wanted to give you something when you turned eighteen that showed you how I felt."

I take a moment to let that settle, then blink away tears as the reality washes over me, warm and sweet and so glorious it makes my body tingle.

God!

God!

That means *everything.*

"But I couldn't hold off. What I knew about Gloria. I'd warned Joey, the little fucker, and figured it wasn't my fault he didn't take me seriously. You weren't to be played with. So, I pulled an asshole move and used his phone to text you, then erased it. Was gonna give the necklace to you that day, to let you know you had...*options*. Plant a seed in that stubborn head of yours."

His thumb moves to my breast, tracing little patterns and raising goosebumps.

"But I couldn't find it. Searched everywhere and thought I'd misplaced it. That was why I was late meeting you." He stops and swallows. "Ironically, I wasn't planning on kissing you. But you stood there with the wind blowing in your hair, looking so pretty and so hurt. When I got closer and you realized it was me, you got that look you get in your eyes and I lost my fucking mind." He sighs. "Then everything went to hell...with all the drama I forgot about it, and you left, so it didn't matter anymore." He scrapes his hands over his face. "I didn't know Joey took it until I saw you wear it at his funeral."

Oh...wow.

"Now it's starting to make sense. I didn't understand why you were so angry with me."

He snorts. "I was angry for so many reasons. I didn't know you didn't know Joey killed your dad. Thought you were there to fuck with us. When it became clear that wasn't the case, I was angry because I took one look at you and all those feelings were back. Feelings I'd never had for any other woman. Ever. You have no idea how long it took for me to stop thinking about you and you just walked back in like nothing happened. And later... knowing you'd been with both Melnikov *and* my brother..." He grimaces.

"Gianni?" I wait till he meets my eyes. "You should know I never slept with either of them."

Every muscle in his body seems to lock up as he searches mine. "You serious?" He whispers.

"As a heart attack. I wasn't ready for Joey. Probably the reason he slept with Gloria. And with Dean, it was too soon. It just never went there."

"Aah...Christ." He falls on his back covering his eyes with his forearm. "You don't know what that means," he says after a minute. "Fucking hell."

"And the necklace? I forgot I had it too," I say. "Hadn't worn it since the day he gave it me."

"When was that?" he asks, raising himself back up to rest on his elbow and traces my hip with his finger.

"The day before you kissed me...the day before my dad died. Joey told me it was an early birthday present and then later that same day I found out about Gloria. I assumed that was why he wanted to meet me at the marina. But of course, I never saw him and right after that, everything went down and he sent me that note, dumping me."

"He didn't dump you. My parents doped him up and put him on a private plane to Italy the next day to keep him from you. But it does explain why he followed me to the marina. He knew *I* knew he was fucking around on you and I was going to make a move." He takes a deep breath and lets it out. "Fuck, if I'd known, I'd have done things differently." Agony and guilt flicker through his eyes, making the blue smoky gray, like the rolling fog beneath the bridge. "All the pain I've caused."

I lean over and touch my lips to his scar, tracing around it with my tongue.

He hisses, those hard torso muscles go taut and he grabs a handful of my hair.

"I kissed you back, remember?" I murmur against his skin, loving the feel of its texture and the way he reacts to my touch. "I wanted you too. I've been in love with you since I was sixteen."

Those fingers in my hair tighten, then a moment later he pulls my head back so he can look into my eyes.

"I'm as much to blame for my dad's death as anyone. But in some strange way, I can't help feeling Joey intended us to come together now. When I put the necklace on that first time, I felt his presence. Because of him, Dean hit me. And if Dean hadn't hit me, I would never have been in that drugstore at that exact moment when Cherry Meloni told me he'd been murdered."

"Say it again," he says softly still staring into my eyes.

"What?"

He moves a hand over my thigh, down behind my knee, then hitches my leg over his hip.

"Say it again."

My brows come together because I don't understand. Then as it registers, a blush moves up my neck and a slow smile spreads my lips.

"I love you, Gianni Cadora," I whisper.

The next instant his lips crash onto mine. They're a little bit ferocious, full of hunger and need as we inhale and devour each other. Those strong arms pull me closer, then he rolls me onto my back and positions himself between my thighs. When he finally pulls away he touches his forehead to mine and cups my face in those big, warm hands.

"I love you more than my life, De Luca. There's nothing on this planet I want more than you." He touches his lips again to mine and I'm still reeling from his words when he says, "I wanna ask you something."

"Mm?"

"Take a deep breath."

"Okay?"

"I don't wanna waste any more time. How do you feel about moving in with me? We can bring the dog."

Oh.

My.

God.

Then I show him *exactly* how I feel about that.

THE END.

You stuck with me!
I hope you enjoyed reading this story as much as I enjoyed writing it and creating these characters. I can't tell you how honored or grateful I am you read to the end and would be even more so if you tell your friends about it and leave a review on Amazon (even a short one) telling me what you thought.

This is my first novel but definitely not the last. I hope to release the second of this series (known as the Bridge series) in the summer of 2018 so stay tuned.

You can stalk and join Truman's Tribe at
https://www.facebook.com/AuthorAnnHowes/
or sign up for updates on new releases on my website at
https://authorannhowes.wordpress.com/

I hope to hear from you soon.

And now, for your further reading pleasure, I have included the first chapter of the next book in the series, The Debt.

The Debt

Chapter One

You got some splaining to do

PAPOW!

Zander Milan ducked when he heard the gunshot. His heart skyrocketed into his throat and he credited his survival instincts, still sharp from years growing up in the surly Tenderloin district of San Francisco. Probably saved his life.

Figures.

His end came not when he deserved it in his hellish youth, trolling the streets and surviving shit he had no business surviving. But at thirty-two, after he'd made something of himself. Into the owner of one of the busiest bars in the city.

He used the dumpster for cover when brake lights glowed red as a vehicle at the entrance to his ally reversed. Then white headlights traced an arc and pointed at him.

PAPOW.

Fuck.

He chuckled, feeling like a chump. Not a gunshot after all. An ancient Volkswagen bus backfired as it hitched over a waterlogged pot hole. Only then did the muscle behind his ribcage start back up into a rhythm that couldn't be defined as normal or even healthy.

Apparently, he wasn't going to die today.

Zander shook his head in amazement at the dinosaur heading towards him in a slow crawl and wondered if it was roadworthy. Did they even still make the parts that kept them running? Surely no one in their right mind would willingly drive such a hideous piece of shit.

The van veered left then pulled up directly outside the back doors of his club before spluttering to a silent death.

"The fuck?" Zander muttered as the head lamps dimmed, leaving his pupils dilated and him temporarily night blind.

Before confronting whoever was illegally parked in front of his back-alley doors, he had to get rid of his load.

He lifted the black plastic lid of the dumpster and tossed the two garbage bags with a single swing. They landed with a heavy thunk on the metal bottom.

He sighed and dusted his hands off on his jeans before turning back to face what was obviously some loser, overzealous fan trying to skirt the cover charge at the main door.

Except what he saw when he got closer, made his chest squeeze tight, leaving him breathless. Like all the air had been sucked out of the unusually balmy fall night.

It had to be a delayed reaction to the backfire. At least that was what he told himself. Nothing at all to do with the woman climbing out of the bus, one long-ass leg tipped in a motorcycle boot at a time. Flipping shiny, reddish blonde hair over an exposed shoulder decorated with a skinny bra strap.

She stared at the open metal club doors, with her hands planted on her hips as if contemplating entering.

An electric buzz vibrated though his body like he'd stuck his finger into a socket. He put it down to the adrenaline coursing through his veins.

The first attempt at addressing her failed. His mouth formed the word, yet nothing but a croak emitted.

"Babe," he tried again. This too came out scratchy, forcing him to clear his throat. Then with a little more vigor he said, "You need to move your van. You can't park there."

"I know." The woman responded without turning around. She sounded distracted or…indifferent.

Huh.

"I need to unload my stuff, then I'll move it."

Zander examined her profile under the weak alley lights, trying to figure out what about her left him so rattled. Pretty for sure with curves and bumps in the right proportions and places. He had to admit he liked what he saw a lot. But still.

"Stuff for what?" He asked.

"I'm with the band."

His jaw tightened. "No, you're not. The main entrance is around the corner. You have to pay the cover charge, just like everyone else."

"Look buddy," she cocked her head then turned to face him for the first time. "I'm not a groupie trying to sneak in for free."

He was not a vain man and he would have to be blind not to notice that when it came to women, he got a certain reaction. Especially when they met him for the first time. Most notable; the widening of their eyes. The shyer ones blushed. Some even stuttered.

But none came from this woman.

He did a little head cock of his own, uncertain what to make of her lack of reaction. Had he grown warts since he last shaved?

"Do I have to go up those to get to the stage?" she asked, using her chin to point at the flight of concrete stairs that led up to his office.

"Stage is to the left of the stairs, but that's not where you're going."

She arched a brow, smirked, then pulled the lever on the dented van door. When it slid opened she reached in bending at the waist. All that filled his vision were two rounded butt cheeks molded by a pair of tight skinny jeans. They were perfect and he wasn't sure he didn't lose a small piece of his mind. The corresponding jerk in his groin confirmed his suspicion.

He positioned himself at a respectable distance to her side, trying to keep his eyes on what she was doing inside the car and not completely succeeding.

"Maybe instead of staring at my ass," she shot a look over her shoulder as she pulled on something black, square and heavy, "you can help me with my monitor? The damn thing doesn't have any wheels. It's gotta weigh about fifty pounds."

Zander heard her voice but was having trouble focusing on the words. He was beginning to sincerely hope she was a horny groupie, set out to bang her way into his club. He'd be happy to oblige before he sent her back to the main entrance.

"Who are you?" he managed at last, his voice still not sounding like his own.

"I'm Terra," she answered slowly, like she was talking to someone whose IQ was well below the triple digit mark. "I'm with the band."

Zander straightened at her tone. Finding his balls at last, he parted his legs and folded his arms across his chest in his best *don't fuck with me* stance.

"You must have the wrong night, babe. Because I know the members of the band and you're not one of them."

She stared at him for a moment. "Fine!" She made a hand movement that could only be construed as dismissive. "Don't help. It'll just take me longer to unload."

"Nope." Who the hell did this woman think she was and when was the last time a hot one dismissed him?

"You need to stop what you're doing, babe. Get back in your van and move this piece of shit." It always amazed him the tricks people went to get in for free. He was sick of it, no matter how hot they were. And this one was off the charts spicy.

But rules were rules.

He couldn't expect his bouncers to follow them if he broke them himself.

Terra tensed, then moved that delectable ass, careful to avoid bumping her head on the bus ceiling. She angled and straightened herself into her full height, which was average and a whole lot less than his. Then eyed him like he was a hunk of brainless muscle or a bug worthy only of meeting the sole of her boot. He couldn't decide which.

"First," she swept a graceful hand indicating the van, which he now noticed was painted purple and sported a line of ugly ass orange poppies, "*this* is not a piece of shit. *This* is Iris. Second, and pay attention because I'm only going to say this once more. I'm with the band."

"Bullshit."

"Bullshit?"

"Yeah. Bullshit."

"Oh, for fuck's sake!" She rolled her long-lashed eyes and dug into her bra. Zander's widened, and for a second he thought she was going to pull out her tits and flash him. Given he was a man who got laid more often than he ate breakfast, he was far more disappointed than he ought to be when she produced a phone instead. Fascinated, he watched her jab a few buttons then while it was ringing, put it on speakerphone.

"Yo."

"Dannie," she said. Those clear blue eyes locked with his golden-brown ones. He had the strange sensation he was being pulled through a tunnel into a vortex and there wasn't a damn thing he could do about it.

"Where the hell are you?" Dannie's voice smacking of panic was higher pitched than normal. "You're late."

"Calm down. I'm at the back door. The bouncer's being an asshole and won't let me in. He thinks I'm a groupie."

Asshole?

That shouldn't be funny, but Zander's mouth crooked into almost undetectable smile as he held out his hand, still holding her gaze. "Let me talk to him."

Terra took it off speaker, then slapped the phone into his palm, a satisfied smirk spreading across her face. It was warm from her body heat and made his fingers tingle.

"Dannie, this is Zander."

"Oh, shit." Dannie responded with a groan. "Damn! Sorry, man. Terra's a little mouthy but she really is with us. She's covering for Rube."

"What do you mean *covering for Rube*? Where's Ruby?"

"She bailed on me. On us."

Typical.

He knew he shouldn't have trusted her and now was going to have to have words with her. "You should have told me. I could've replaced you."

"I know that, but we didn't want to get replaced. That's why Terra's here."

"If you fuck this up, you're not coming back."

"Trust me, dude, we won't fuck this up."

"Hmm," Zander grunted, narrowing his eyes as Terra had resumed her earlier position with her tempting ass back on display. She fiddled with the zip on a leather kitbag in the van.

"Can you tell Dannie I need some help since you're not willing?" She tossed at him with a bucket full of attitude. Then hooked both hands into the handle of her monitor and hefted it to the edge of the van floor.

Clearly, she was completely unaware she'd called him, the owner of this establishment, an asshole. The man who would pay her for her performance tonight.

Normally he wouldn't stand for that kind of shit. He hadn't earned his chops by sitting back and allowing anyone to disrespect him. Even if he was hoping to get his hands on the little spitfire doing the disrespecting. Somehow it amused him more than it disturbed him.

Probably because he was fixated on the way her top slipped further off her shoulder, exposing a red and black lacy bra covering mouthwatering tits. The same tits that cradled the phone he still had in his hand. He was reluctant to give it back.

"Give me that," he said, shoving her phone in his back pocket to free up his hand. "I'll carry it to the stage. You can park in the lot behind the bar with the rest of the band."

Zander would be the first to admit he was mostly a detached prick when it came to woman. He loved fucking them but never got involved. Which is why he was unprepared for the jolt in his chest when she smiled. A slow, lazy parting of those juicy lips flashing a hint of even, white teeth.

Shit.

He looped his hand around the handle of the monitor and carried it to the new stage he'd built, ignoring the looks he got from the rest of the band.

They'd stopped unrolling guitar cords and arranging mic stands to stare. Jeff, the scrawny runt of a bass player did a double take, like he was seeing things.

Zander empathized.

"Where do I put this?" he asked. The man's mouth hung open a little and Zander was tempted to snap it shut. With his fist. Probably ruin years worth of Invisalign. Orthodontic bills were not something he needed to add as a line item in his budget.

"Uhh..." Jeff pointed at a gap between a mic stand and an amp.

Zander placed the monitor in the designated spot and without looking back, vaulted off the four-foot-high stage. He sauntered across the scuffed up wooden floors towards the bar.

Because it wasn't like he had anything else to do other than help a woman who'd mind fucked him into helping her.

He suspected all she had to do was crook a pretty little index finger at the nearest man, who'd gladly drop what he was doing in the hopes of a reward. Even if it was just a smile. In his case, she hadn't even crooked a finger.

He'd *volunteered.*

Several of his regulars were already seated at the bar even though it was still early in the evening, nursing half full beers. Friday nights were usually packed and the last two times this band had played, they'd killed it. Hopefully they would tonight as well.

When he'd bought the bar two years ago from Chuck, a grizzled hard-ass biker and longtime lover of his grandmother, it was a dive. Trolled by hookers, die-hards and ill-informed tourists looking for the real San Francisco experience. They usually got more than they bargained for.

Chuck owned it outright and gave him a deal. He financed the mortgage and two weeks before he died of pancreatic cancer, forgave the loan and signed over the deed. There was one condition. In tribute to his grandmother he had to restore it and turn the bar into a haven for musicians. Ginny Milan in her day had killer keyboard skills and toured the music circuit with reasonably well-known bands. Then cervical cancer, that nasty, spiteful bitch, took her too.

God, he missed her.

She was the only real parent he'd known. And along with his mother the only woman he'd had any kind of love for. But he didn't want to plunder that particular compartment of his mind right now.

What he wanted was to observe.

He needed to know more about this woman whose ass he

couldn't seem to exorcise from his imagination. And what better place to do it from than behind the bar.

He greeted the silver-haired bartender he inherited from Chuck with a chin nod. Barney carried a tray of clean glasses that needed putting away and Zander sidestepped to allow him to pass.

Not that he enjoyed dabbling in band politics, but there was something he wasn't getting. When it came to his bar and his bottom line, band politics became his business.

When they played here, they'd always been fronted by the missing Ruby. A skinny waif with short platinum hair and scars on her forearms he knew came from a needle. Zander had seen them up close and doubted she'd suddenly become diabetic. Their history went way back. He wasn't overly fond of her and certainly didn't trust her, but he knew she sang. The only reason he booked them in the first place was because she asked. Offered to sweeten the deal by blowing him which he declined.

Ruby promised she was clean but junkies were notorious liars. There were other places to stick a needle. That he knew from personal experience. The thought uncurled a memory from long ago and sent a tremor through his psyche.

Christ, he hated needles.

Figured what people did with their bodies was none of his concern, unless it directly affected him. Up until now it hadn't. Which begged the questions, where the fuck was Ruby, who was Terra, and why was she filling in?

While he unloaded a case of German beer into the fridge, he caught a glimpse of her. Everything in him locked up tight. Not one damn muscle in his body moved except the ones in his eye sockets as they followed her movements.

The woman claimed the stage like her mother popped her out on one, swinging her ass just enough to make him wonder what else she could with it. Or rather, what he wanted her to do with it and no doubt would fantasize about later.

Fuck, he was fantasizing now.

Zander blew out a puff of air and shook his head. She was just another woman. So why was he so fascinated?

It was clear the band knew her well. Each member greeted her with big-ass goofy smiles splitting their faces while they hugged her. Lucas, the drummer put his shoulder to her stomach and lifted her in a fireman hold. She squealed and laughed like a little girl on Christmas morning, no trace of that earlier sass.

Dannie stood off to the side.

Once back on her feet Terra turned, focusing her attention on him. That distracting smile slipped off her face as the two of them faced off. The happy vibe faded and got replaced with something angrier.

She folded one arm over the other and pulled those pretty lips in. The longer the silence went on, the more tense her stance became, while Dannie looked increasingly sheepish. Like a man who'd been caught cheating.

"You can kiss my ass now, Dannie," she said. Apparently, the sass was back.

"Fuck, Terra." Dannie scrubbed a hand through his shaggy blonde hair. "What do you want me to say?"

"You can say you're sorry."

Zander's head jerked. Shit. This was not a good sign.

He watched Dannie sigh and look over to the rest of the band, like he was expecting them to take his back. They didn't.

"Or," she held up an index finger, "how about this? You can thank me. Either one will go a long way."

"Which one would you prefer?"

"Both"

"Shit." Dannie looked at his boots.

"You hurt me, Dannie. What you did was beyond a dick move."

Hurt her? What the hell did he do?

"It wasn't intentional."

"Yes, it was, you moron," Jeff said while tightening the string he just changed on his bass guitar. "You always know better and never listen to any of us. Cause what the fuck do we know, right?"

What the hell are they talking about?

"That's not fair, Jeff," Dannie said.

"The fuck it is, and you know it," Jeff shot back.

"Just do it, Dannie," Lucas said, attaching a cymbal to its stand. "You screwed up. Say you're sorry, man. We don't have time for this crap."

"Listen to him, Dannie." Terra took a step closer to him. "Or I'm leaving." She jammed a finger in his chest. He took a step back.

Leaving? What?

"Terra..."

"And FYI, I didn't come here for you. I came for them, because I didn't want to them to lose out on this gig."

"I'm not the one who called you." Dannie straightened and cocked his head.

"That's because you didn't have the balls," Jeff yelled.

"Ruby sucks, man." Jake, the rhythm guitar dude and the quiet one finally chimed in. "And not only your dick." He was the only one who didn't sing but could play like a motherfucker. Zander realized that until this moment, he'd never even heard him speak.

"She bailed on us with no notice," Jake continued. "Who the hell does that? Never mind that she can't sing or keep time for shit. Kept coming in wrong. Annoyed the hell out of me."

Zander didn't think Ruby was a bad singer, but what the hell did he know? He couldn't tell the difference between a flat note and post-it note. What he *did* know was how his patrons reacted to a band and if they came back to see them again. Made him wonder just how good Terra must be if the rest of them trusted her this much to fill in.

"Ah, fuck it," Dannie said and hooked an arm around Terra's neck, pulling her into him. "I'm sorry, Tee." He planted a kiss on the top of her head. "You're right, I'm an asshole. Thanks for bailing us out last minute like this."

"Finally." Lucas said as he tested a *ting-ticka-tsshhh* on his cymbals. "Now we can all move the fuck on."

There was something in the way Dannie pulled her into his arms and held her, the way she melted into him that ate at Zander. He didn't like the dangerous, swirling thing in his gut or how his fingers, seemingly on their own accord curled into fists. And he was damned if he was going to admit he was a punk-ass bitch, getting jealous because a woman he met five minutes ago was hugging a man she had history with.

Yet there it was.

He ripped his eyes off the drama on stage and finished loading up the fridge a little harder and louder than necessary.

Barney eyed him but wisely kept his distance and his mouth shut. By the time he finished, so was the soap opera and everyone resumed setting up.

He gathered the empty cartons of beer and tossed them in the store room behind the bar as it was Barney's job to dispose of them. Then headed to his office. He had a phone call to make.

Once he'd shut the door he reached into his pocket for his phone and walked to the one-way mirror looking down over the bar. But the iPhone he held wasn't his. Took a second for him to realize it was Terra's.

He'd forgotten he had it. Zander placed it on his desk and found his own lying on a pile of invoices he still had to pay. He scrolled through his contacts and pushed Ruby's number, letting it ring until it went to voicemail. Figures she'd avoid him.

After the beep he said, "Rube, you've got some *splaining* to do. Where the fuck are you?"

He stood in front of the one-way mirror in his office and watched them, or rather watched *her*. Weirdly, her eyes kept glancing upward. It was disconcerting even though he knew she couldn't see him.

They completed their sound check, then one by one headed to the bar. It was almost starting time and people filtered in, claiming tables. Looked like it was going to be a good night indeed. Especially as some of the crowd were greeting Terra like they knew her. Some gave her hugs, which made him feel a whole lot more comfortable. By the time the band took their places on stage, the bar was two deep.

When Dannie played the opening riff of Guns 'n Roses "Sweet Child of Mine," Zander stilled.

This was new.

There was something different in the way they came together, seemed to gel into a more cohesive unit. People stood and moved to the dance floor.

Terra tossed her hair back and he swallowed. She grabbed the mic, opened that delicious mouth and belted out the words. Goosebumps erupted all over his body.

He got it.

Terra wasn't filling in for Ruby. It was Ruby, the lying junkie bitch who'd been filling in for her. And he needed to know why.

About the Author

I'm a romance nut. What's better than a hot hero who's willing to get dirty to protect and cherish his woman? Well, in my opinion, not a whole lot. A native of Cape Town, South Africa, I currently live in California with my two teenagers and two furry felines, and when I'm not working or writing I like to grow things. Especially avocados of which I eat a lot. Good for your hearts and brains, or so I'm told.

Find me on social media

https://www.facebook.com/AuthorAnnHowes/
https://authorannhowes.wordpress.com/

humphreysmomma@gmail.com

ABOUT THE AUTHOR

I'm a romance nut. What's better than a hot hero who's willing to get dirty to protect and cherish his woman? Well, in my opinion, not a whole lot. A native of Cape Town, South Africa, I currently live in California with my two teenagers and two furry felines, and when I'm not working or writing I like to grow things. Especially avocados of which I eat a lot. Good for your hearts and brains, or so I'm told.

Find me on social media

https://www.facebook.com/AuthorAnnHowes/
https://authorannhowes.wordpress.com/

humphreysmomma@gmail.com

Made in the USA
Coppell, TX
07 November 2020